THE UNDEAD: HEADSHOT QUARTET

"It's with unabashed fanboy glee that I recommend *Headshot Quartet...* Like four horsemen of a literary apocalypse, Snell, Thomas, Sunseri, and Dunwoody lay waste to the old zombie traditions and throw one hell of a party at the end of the world!"
—Christopher Webster, *QuietEarth.us*

THE UNDEAD:
HEADSHOT QUARTET

EDITED BY
CHRISTINA BIVINS
& LANE ADAMSON
WITH ASSISTANCE FROM THOM BRANNAN

Permuted Press
The formula has been changed...
Shifted... Altered... Twisted.
www.permutedpress.com

A Permuted Press book
published by arrangement with the authors

ISBN-10: 1-934861-00-6
ISBN-13: 978-1-934861-00-4
Library of Congress Control Number: 2008921201

MILLION-DOLLAR MONEY SHOT
JOHN SUNSERI

I WOKE UP SWEATING.

The air conditioning had gone to hell along with everything electrical, and it was another hot freaking morning. My balls were stuck to my thigh, I could smell the reek of my pits, my pillow was wet with sweat, and somehow I'd knocked the shotgun off the bed in the middle of the night so it was out of reach.

Good thing nothing dead had found me while I slept.

I'd come to Aruba for the weather. Well, all right—I'd come to Aruba because men were trying to kill me and I needed to not only blow town but get the hell out of the country. The Organization's various factions may squabble a bit amongst themselves, but when it comes to catching and making an example of a thief they tend to get unified real quick. There was nowhere in America or Canada I could go to be safe for even a little while, so I'd used one of my fake ID's to book a quick flight to Philly, then on down to the Caribbean. I figured I had a week or two to figure out a better plan before the wiseguys caught up with Polish Rob and started pulling fingernails to figure out what name I was traveling under, and I might as well get a little sun while I was at it. When I'd left Cleveland a few days earlier it had been snowing, windy and the skies had settled into a constant slate-gray. Getting off the plane at the Aeropuerto Intenacional Reina Beatrix, I'd wished I'd worn shorts instead of my wool suit.

Sunny skies and hot tropical breezes are great when you can go back to your hotel room, mix yourself a Cuba Libre with ice and crank up the AC. They're not so great when you don't have power. The hot days keep coming—the nights never get below seventy degrees, and when you want to chug a gallon of ice water there's only a pool of tepid, smelly liquid in the ice machine's bin.

I rolled out of bed, un-sticking my testicles from my skin, wincing as I reached down for the Remington. I hadn't been able to drink Cuba Libres with ice for several days, but damned if they didn't have a lot of rum in this city, and only me to drink it. I'd polished off a bottle last night while I looked out the window at the flashing lights on Renaissance Island, wondering what the hell was going on out there. By the time the lights had faded and the low foghorn noises had begun to subside, I was half-crocked and seriously thinking of driving one of the hotel's boats out there, taking my shotgun and doing a little damage to some monsters.

Lucky I'm smarter than that. The zombies are bad enough, but those *other* things—the things that come out of the ocean at night…well, let's say that I would've probably been sliced into cutlets the second I left the hotel.

"Yeah," I said to myself, trying not to move my head too much. "You're real smart, Vince. Only smart guys rip off the Mob."

There was a sudden noise from the door and I instantly forgot my hangover. I whipped up the barrel of the shotgun and waited, listening hard.

That's what talking to yourself gets you—you're doing fine, everything's okay, you made it through another night, and then you let down your guard for a second and the zombies find you.

I breathed heavily as I waited for the next sounds; the moaning, the clawing, the thump as a dozen bodies threw themselves against the door. I kept the shotgun perfectly level as I slowly reached down and grabbed my bag. But instead of corpse noises, I heard an actual human voice.

"Hello?" she said, whoever she was. "Is anyone in there?"

The first thing that occurred to me was *trap*. It's an occupational hazard—never knowing if it was a real broad on the other side of the door or a policewoman with a sexy voice and a gang of organized crime detectives waiting behind her with guns drawn and mouths drooling.

The doors at the hotel had—just a few days ago, before the zombies came—locked magnetically, and you could only open them with little credit cards, and *that* whole system had gone FUBAR along with the lights and running water, so I'd found a room whose door had already been open. The maid's cart had been propping it ajar, and the maid was probably out trying to eat brains in the courtyard along with the rest of the dead ones. You could still open the doors from the inside, and I'd rolled the cart into the room and shut the door before bed last night.

It probably wasn't a policewoman, and the zombies probably hadn't learned to talk, but I was careful nonetheless as I slowly approached the door, keeping the gun aimed and my other hand on my bag.

"Hello?" came the voice again, and I winced. Whoever it was, she wasn't keeping her voice down and I knew that the zombies could hear just fine.

"Who is it?" I said.

"Oh, Jesus! Open the door!" she said, sounding excited, terrified and frantic at the same time. "Jesus Christ! Someone alive!"

I reached forward, bag thumping against the door, and turned the knob. A woman spilled into the room, hair flying and limbs flailing as she shoved her way in. I wrapped my arm around her neck and rode her down, causing a *whoof* as she hit, I held her down with one knee on her back and I stabbed the barrels of the shotgun into the nape of her neck. I kicked the door shut behind me.

"Quiet," I said, shoving down with the gun. "They'll hear you."

"Jesus," she said again, but this time at least she whispered. "What the fuck are you doing?"

"Thinking about killing you," I said, and I felt her stiffen underneath me. "What kind of idiot shouts 'hello' in a hotel filled with zombies?"

"You were talking in here—I heard *you*!" she whispered.

Well, she was right. I checked for lividity, for gaping wounds, for patches of hairless scalp, but she looked okay, so I got up.

She felt the pressure disappear from the back of her neck and whipped her head up, the anger in her face melted into amusement as I stepped away and she realized I was naked.

"I'm bigger when it's not so cold," I said, walking over to the bed to get my clothes.

"It's eighty degrees already," she said, raising herself to her knees.

"All right, then," I said. "I got a small dick."

"Who are you?" she asked as I sat on the bed and grabbed my boxers.

"It doesn't work that way," I said, pulling up my shorts, wriggling into them. "I'm the one with the gun. Who are *you*?"

"Tabitha," she said. She stood up, watching my gun. My firearm, that is. "I work here."

"Not any more," I said.

"No shit," she said. "You got something I can call you, or is 'Stubby' okay?"

"I'm Vince," I said. "Pleased to meetcha. Now, how the hell does it happen that you were wandering around up here today?"

"Where else am I supposed to go?" she asked, raising her eyes to meet mine. She was kind of pretty, in a worn-out sort of way. Thirty or so, her hair straggly from lack of washing, her skin an interesting shade of mocha—her tongue sharp as hell. "Those fuckers are wandering around down there on every street, in every building, and I don't have a gun!"

"I didn't either," I said. "But I got one. There's a police station just a mile or two from here, and they got plenty of guns. And there's a Dutch army headquarters I'm going to hit pretty soon, and I'll bet *they've* got some guns…"

"You from here?" she asked, moving closer. She wasn't trying to frighten me or seduce me. It was just that she hadn't seen a conscious, talking human in so long that the contact was exhilarating, and she wanted to feel like she was part of the species again, rather than prey. I was feeling a bit of that impulse myself—and I was glad I had my shorts on, because it had been a while since I'd been with a woman—but I'm a survivor first and foremost, so I raised the shotgun and stopped her in her tracks.

"No," I said.

"Then how do you know all that shit?" she asked.

In response I reached over and picked up a stack of hotel literature, held it up in a fan, and then let it flutter, brochure by brochure, to the floor.

"I never read that stuff," she said.

"Why would you?" I asked. "The only good things about them are the maps. And the addresses of the strip clubs."

I had my pants on by this point, but I hadn't stopped aiming the Remington at her. "Vince," she said, "I'm not gonna rob you or anything. You can put down the gun."

"Lady," I said, "I don't know you. I don't know what's going on out there, or why dead people are crawling out of the ocean and killing people, and then making more dead people. For all I know, you're the one that started it all, and so until I figure out what's going on, you're gonna have a gun pointed at you. *Capisce?*"

"You a wop?" she asked.

The door thumped, and we both froze.

I gave her a look. *You led them up here.*

She glared back. *Fuck you.*

It thumped again, and then there was another thump, as though something had hit the wall beside the door. And then the door again.

And then the moaning.

"Shit," I said.

The moaning trebled in response to my voice, and suddenly there was a chorus of howls, wheezes and low, throaty rasps. The door started to buckle as it was hit twice, thrice, a half-dozen times by dead hands and heads, the walls shaking along with it.

I left my shirt on the floor, stood up and grabbed my bag again. "I'm leaving."

"What?" said Tabitha, looking at me, then the shaking door, then back at me. "How?"

I threw open the window shades, wincing as the sun hit me full in the face, and looked out. The sea was blue and beautiful, as it had been since I'd landed on this godforsaken hunk of island, and the sand sparkled in the distance. There were three cruise ships parked in their berths looking stately and tremendous. On the ground below there were maybe two dozen dead people wandering around in Bermuda shorts and tank tops, bumping into each other and snarling half-heartedly every time they did.

Behind me the thumping grew frenetic and demanding. I wrenched the window to the side, exposing the screen. I stabbed it with my gun, in the upper corner, and the whole thing crumpled outward, bending along the cheap metal. I felt the woman closing in on me, and gripped my bag in one hand, my Remington in the other, and forced out the bottom corner of the screen. It squeaked and swung outward, hanging from the other two corners.

"We're two stories up!" she said.

"Yep," I responded, and lifted one leg up to the window. No time for socks or shoes—I felt the little metal slats biting into my soles as I tested the sill with my weight. "You're welcome to stay here. You brought those fuckers up here, you can slow them down while I get away…"

"Hurry up and jump," she urged, pushing at me. "They're almost in!"

I looked down at the pool. I'd planned this out when I'd picked the room, this emergency escape route. It had seemed easy last night, as I'd judged the distance. Now, with the arrhythmic thumping of zombies roaring from the door and a frantic woman practically shoving me out the window, it seemed farther. The distance to the ground seemed longer.

"And the water's probably disgusting," I said, but I swung the bag out the window and let it fly, aiming for a deck chair near a couple of potted palms. It hit the chair, rattling the metal legs on the concrete deck, and a couple of zombies paused their brainless shuffling to look at it, but it wasn't made of meat so they went back to their routine. The shotgun was next, and I couldn't bring myself to toss it onto the hard ground, so I kind of dropped it to the side, aiming for some kind of flowering tropical shrub that looked bushy enough to break its fall. I winced as my poor Remington tore through the foliage and clattered on the pool deck, and then it was my turn.

The door crashed open behind me and I tensed and shot a glance back at the gibbering Tabitha, who was now trying to shove her way past me.

The first one through the door was a black man with gaping holes where his cheeks had been. His scalp flapped wildly on his gleaming skull as he burst through the door, but he lost his balance and fell hard to the ground. He didn't even throw up his arms to break his fall, landing face-first on the carpet with a moist splat . The next two zombies walked right over him, their feet sinking into his rotten flesh as though it was sodden turf, squirting fetid blood all over the floor. One of the two was a woman who had been big in life, but who was rapidly losing weight as pieces of flesh gobbed off her in putrid chunks. I could see her ribs through the hole where her right breast had been, and her jowls stretched down past her neck in fatty, glistening strands. Her eyes were swollen with putrefaction, but I could see the desperate, glittering hunger in them as she fixed on us and moaned in wheezing anticipation. Next to her was another man, one I recognized—he'd checked me in when I'd gotten here. He'd been supercilious and rude, I was kinda glad he was dead, and even gladder when I saw that someone had pulled one of his arms off. His whole right side was covered in dried blood and black mucus, a knob of bone waving around in its socket as though he was trying to grab for us with his non-existent arm.

It was time to go.

I turned and jumped, striving for as much distance as I could. The metal of the window frame dug into the balls of my feet, and then I was falling through the humid, warm air. The water rushed up to meet me, and I managed a quick breath before I slammed into the pool.

I'd been right. The water was disgusting. I swallowed some as I fought my way up from the bottom, and gagged as I broke the surface of the pool. I opened my eyes and framed in the morning air above me was the beautifully composed form of Tabitha as she executed a perfect dive. I frantically paddled backwards as she hit the pool, but I needn't have worried—she'd aimed a few feet away from me, and she impacted the water like an Olympic diver, barely raising a splash or making a sound.

I trod water for a moment, making sure she hadn't clonged her head on the bottom, but when I saw her swooping around underwater and circling back toward me I turned toward the edge of the pool and clumsily stroked my way there.

Several zombies were looking our way, and I could hear the frustrated howls of the dead people in the room we'd just left. I clambered out of the stagnant, stinking water and looked up. The desk clerk was coming out after us. He didn't even try to jump for the pool—he just flipped over the sill into empty air and cartwheeled the fifteen feet to the ground, his arm was snapped in three places and his skull was caved in. His feet twitched spastically, his torso jerked—but that head injury, pink brain tissue oozing out the cracks in his skull—was gonna finish him.

Two or three of the other zombies were leaving their spots by the poolside bar and shuffling toward us with eagerness in their eyes, their arms stretched forward, their fleshless fingers clawed and their rotting teeth bared.

"What now, genius?" said Tabitha, pulling herself easily from the pool. She looked better now, her wet hair gleaming against her mocha skin, her clothes plastered to her body. I could have looked at her for a while, but I had other concerns, so I made a note to look at her later.

I ignored her question and got to my feet, quick-jogged around the nearest zombie, who lurched as he changed direction, and jumped over the quivering corpse of the desk clerk. I picked up the Remington and checked the receiver for dents, trying not to drip water on the firearm. I didn't see any, but that didn't mean anything—they're tough guns, but they break just like anything else.

Tabitha had followed me closely. I could tell she was scared, but she was handling herself well. I spun around and gestured her to the side. "Move," I said, and though she opened her mouth as though to argue, she quickly ducked and darted back.

I aimed at the nearest zombie, the one I'd avoided on my dash to the shotgun. He'd been blonde and tan and muscular, but the damp, warm air had done bad things to him over the last few days. He looked like he'd accidentally gotten a toxic waste soak instead of a mud bath during his last visit to the spa. His flesh was curdling like month-old buttermilk, his lips had shrunk and hardened into dim red chalk sticks, and the teeth were falling from his desiccated gums— but he still gnashed those that remained hungrily as he groaned and reached for me.

I pulled the trigger and his head exploded in a cloud of black smoke and pink blood.

"Gun still works," I said.

"Look," she responded, pointing.

The pool was one of those fancy infinity things, the ones with edges below the surface. There should have been water flowing constantly over the edges, but the pumps weren't working any more and the water had shrunk down from evaporation and was beginning to grow a thin layer of algae on its surface. The whole deck area was a floor above street level, a narrow fence hidden by frangipani and tropical ferns. There were stairs going down to L.G. Smith Boulevard, and I'd been hoping to get down there and find a car, or at least more space to maneuver—but as the Dutch deader I'd blasted crumpled headless onto the deck and my eyes followed Tabitha's outstretched arm toward the beach and the ships beyond, I realized I'd have to change my plans.

The hotel was directly across the boulevard from the cruise boat moorage, and I'd been mildly impressed by how huge the three ships parked there were when I'd seen them the night of the zombie uprising—cities shoved into hulls and looming over the sea.

From the size of the horde of zombies swarming up the stairs, it looked as though at least one of those ships' dead passengers had finally figured out how to get off the boat and into Oranjestad. Old men and women wearing long Bermuda shorts and gaudy floral-print shirts, some with fancy digital cameras still swinging on cords around their necks—swarthy Hispanic tourists, the men with beards going gray and dead from rot, the women with breasts once full and plump drooping in decay—a complement of black crew members in formerly blinding whites, their flesh decomposing and graying as their clothes got filthy—some without a limb or two, crawling like snakes up the stairs toward us, some blind as their eyes rotted in the salt and sun, homing in on us by sound and scent only, all of them groaning and wheezing and keening…

"You said you worked here," I said. "What's the best way out?"

"Behind you!" she yelled. Two of the pool deck zombies had closed in on us while I was gaping at the Hell Boat's disgorged masses. I spun around, pumped and shot. The bartender who had given me my first Aruban rum-and-Coke when I'd arrived took a direct blast in the face. His head didn't explode like Golden Boy's had, but the shot flayed his face and turned his brain into hash. Beside him, a woman took a fair amount of the shot. Skin ripped from her face and scalp, and her arm, outstretched toward me, whipped back toward her, fingers flying off. But I hadn't gotten to her brain, so she kept coming even as her clothes started to smolder.

I backed up a step, cocked again, and fired.

This time she took the full blast, and her chest opened up under the storm of lead, meat torn from her ribcage, her neck snapping, her head falling back.

"Where?" I asked again, looking back at Tabitha.

"Through the lobby," she said, starting to move. "We can go through the casino and out…"

"Hold on," I said, and looked around. I found the deck chair I'd aimed at earlier. "Gotta get my bag."

"Fuck your bag!" she said, incredulous.

I ignored her and sprinted toward the advancing throng of dead tourists. For a second it looked as though it was going to be a tight race. Luckily the zombies were not only slow but were fighting among themselves to get to me. In their eagerness to feed, they were mostly succeeding only in tangling each other up. I snared the handles of the gym bag, flipped it up onto my shoulder, spun and ran as the first talon-like fingers reached toward me. The stink was incredible—only the fact that I hadn't eaten anything for a day kept me from heaving as I sprinted back toward Tabitha and her escape plan.

She'd reached the bar while I'd made my dash for the gym bag and was breaking bottles on the ground, pouring booze everywhere.

"Jesus, woman!" I yelled. "What are you doing?"

"Fire!" she said, stopping her work for a second, glaring at me.

"Use the 151!" I said, closing with her. "You're not going to get vodka to burn!"

She nodded and reached for the rum shelf, and I turned to watch my pursuers. The cruise ship zombies weren't going to catch me, but there were more dead people coming out of the doors from the spa next to the pool. These were dressed in shorts and tank tops or spandex, some of them were nude, and for whatever reason— maybe because these folks had been in better shape when they were alive—they were moving a little quicker than the ship zombies.

I finally hit the bar, barely ahead of the fitness zombies. I swung the Remington into one arm, reached into my pocket with my free hand, pulling out my Zippo and praying it would still work after my dip in the pool. "Get going," I said. "I'll be with you in a second."

Tabitha gave me a tight nod and began to run into the hotel proper while I flicked a flame to life. I hesitated a second, smelling the wonderful odor of liquor drowning out the rot of the dead—then lowered the lighter to the pool of Bacardi on the bar.

It went up with a *whoomp* and a curtain of bright flame.

I hauled ass.

"Nice idea," I said as we jogged through the lobby. The fire roared behind us, and the stink of burning meat began to hit our nostrils as the zombies tried to fight their way through the infernal curtain.

"And you said vodka wouldn't burn," she panted.

"Where to?" I asked.

She didn't answer, but swerved toward the escalators. I followed, worried. True, the now-unmoving stairs were open, theoretically allowing us to bail over the sides to the floor below if we had to, but they were a bottleneck and I didn't like the idea of getting halfway down and finding ourselves stuck between zombies at the bottom and the top. We ran down them in tandem, one of us on each escalator, in seconds we were on the ground floor, near the taxi turn-around and the fountain—and near the tail end of the horde of cruise ship deaders that were still struggling up the pool deck stairs.

"This way," she said as some of the zombies noticed us. They began their frantic moans and awkwardly changed directions, Tabitha led me down a service hall and in seconds we'd turned a couple of corners and were out of sight.

"This'll take us out the back of the hotel," she said. "What's in the bag?"

"My retirement," I said. "What's at the back of the hotel?"

"The mall," she replied, and I shook my head as I followed her.

"The mall?" I said. "Dammit, woman—I've *seen* that movie! You don't run to the mall when the zombies take over…"

"The mall, then the casino," she said. "We go through there, and we're out onto the main street. It's open, you've got a gun, we can avoid most of the dead fuckers and find someplace safe to hole up."

"I *found* someplace safe to hole up," I complained. "Then some stupid bimbo came shouting at my door…"

"Fuck you," she said. "What do you mean, 'my retirement'."

"I'll show you sometime," I said. "I've also got about two pounds of beef jerky in there, and three cartons of cigarettes."

"Party's on you tonight, then," she said. "We can smoke and eat jerky…"

She threw open a set of swinging doors, and we were in the mall. I hadn't been here in the couple days I'd been in Oranjestad, and I hadn't missed much—stores selling fancy clothes, stores selling that strange mopa mopa sculpture, stores selling ten-dollar pairs of sunglasses and tank tops with 'One Happy Island' scrawled across them in cheap iron-on that would come off in the third wash.

And zombies, of course.

One of them was only six, seven feet away, he was facing in the wrong direction when we entered the mall, I was able to shove past Tabitha and aim the Remington before he got himself turned around. He moaned, which was easy for him because his lower jaw had disappeared in some brawl or accident. Beneath his upper lip was a long flap of bloody gum with a couple of gray teeth stuck in it like walnuts in a brownie. I fired and those teeth, along with a quart of blood thick with pink, quivering hunks of blasted brain and sharp shards of shattered skull splattered on the wall. His body slammed backward, bounced, and fell to the floor.

"This way," said Tabitha, pointedly not looking at the corpse as it crumpled. She turned left and moved down the hall. I followed, scanning the area for targets.

There were maybe a half-dozen zombies in the area. They perked up at the sound of the shotgun blast and started ambling toward us in their various slow-motion gaits, but they were all too far away to cause any problems. We hustled along the hall, passing a liquor store and a yogurt shop. When we passed a store that advertised emeralds, diamonds and rubies, I slowed, peering through the windows as we jogged, making a mental note of the location. I sped up when a couple of women emerged from the darkness at the back of the shop and came toward me, teeth gleaming in the dusky dim.

Luckily there were skylights in the mall ceiling, but it was still hard for us to see. Corpses dotted the floor, but were all of them dead, truly dead? Or would one of them reach out and snag us as we skirted them, sink its teeth into our ankles, turn us into two more of the walking dead? It made for a harrowing trip through the sun-and shadows, but we finally made it to the casino entrance.

The big glass doors were closed.

"This is not a good idea," I said.

"We could go back," Tabitha said, and she wasn't being a smart-ass about it. She understood the significance of those closed doors as well as I did.

Every time I'd gone by on the street side, the Royal Casino had been packed. Whenever a cruise ship unloaded, the bluehairs came straight to the Royal to attack the slot machines. The guests from three ritzy hotels spent a lot of time here doubling down on pairs of nines or putting a hundred bucks a pop on black. The fact that the mall doors were closed probably meant that a lot of those folks were still in there, wandering around through the banks of one-armed bandits and green-felted Pai Gow tables, their brains too fried to figure out how to open the doors and escape.

"That's not a good idea either," I said, looking behind us as the mall zombies began to fill the hallway we'd just come through. Behind *them* was the vanguard of the cruise ship contingent, having finally figured out where we had gone. If we'd both had automatic weapons, we might have been able to fight our way back through them. But we had only my Remington and some beef jerky. We'd last maybe five seconds if we tried it, and then we'd be wandering around with the rest of them until we decomposed to skeletons and dropped.

Not how I wanted to spend my vacation.

"Come on," I said, reaching forward, grabbing the door handle. "We're going to make this very quick and very quiet. Tell me which way to go."

"Stay left past the blackjack tables," she said, closing her eyes for a second so that she could visualize the layout of the place. "There'll be a cashier window, and once we're past that we have to turn left and haul ass through about fifteen banks of slot machines. Turn right at the end of them, and there's a long hallway leading up to the street. Then we're home free."

"Right," I said, stifling a nastier retort in response to her optimism.

The first three zombies had caught up to us, I wanted to aim and blast, but I didn't have an endless supply of ammunition for the shotgun and I thought I might need some in the casino. I didn't waste any more time and yanked open the door, grabbed Tabitha with my free hand and ran into the darkness.

Casinos don't have windows. They don't like people being able to look outside at the nice weather and the normal citizens passing by—they much prefer all attention to be funneled onto the sights of the bright, pretty lights of the machines, the sounds of coins falling into metal trays in a clinking cacophony and the smell of excitement and Cuban cigar smoke. It keeps the customers inside and their minds focused on the important things—like whether the dealer's got that hole ace and whether that fat sonofabitch is going to make his point before he craps out and how good your fifth free Scotch and soda tastes when that pretty waitress brings it out to you.

Me, I could have used a window or two.

We closed the doors behind us and stood there for a second, hoping that our eyes would adjust, but there was nothing for them to adjust to. The only light in the place came from behind us, and that was rapidly dimming as bodies started slamming against the doors and blocking it out.

The room stank like a million pounds of rotten meat. The air was dead still, making the stench an almost-tangible haze that we had to physically fight through, and I felt my gorge come up my throat. Beside me, Tabitha was fighting not to retch as well, making quiet *hurk, hurk* noises.

I took a step forward into the pitch, and the woman stepped with me, but I instantly stopped. There could be a dozen deaders waiting for me three feet away, and I wouldn't see them until I ran into them.

"Shit," I said softly, and let Tabitha go. I reached into my pocket, took my lighter out. Flicked it.

A Bosch nightmare come to life.

The flicker of flame in my hand revealed the aftermath of some unimaginable chaos. As Tabitha had said, there were gaming tables ahead of us to the right—I could see the edges of two of them—but they'd been overturned and broken. Chairs lay in a jumble all around them, their leather ripped, their upholstery strewn like confetti all over the floor. On our left, flanking the aisle, was a bank of maybe a dozen slot machines. Half of them had been pulled down and shattered while the others leaned at crazy angles against the wall, ready to fall. Chips, broken glass and shining steel shards littered our path.

And bodies.

I held up the flame, and in the small radius of its light I saw a corpse raise its shaggy head and see us, limp dreadlocks hanging thick and black around its glowing red eyes. Another zombie was slumped against the wall next to one of the fallen slots, it looked up while halfheartedly chewing on its own hand.

In the jet black distance, others began to moan.

I tore my gaze from the enemy and looked around, I saw a dead man on the ground nearby. I knelt down, brought the flame to his hair and it went up instantly, adding its reek to the miasma already pressing against us, but providing a bit more light.

"Come on!" I yelled, leaping up and moving toward the slots.

Tabitha followed, panting and trying to suppress her screams, and I used the fleeting light of the corpse's fiery head to dart between two machines and leap over a fallen chair. The wall was covered with thick curtains, and I held my lighter to them.

The two closest zombies had struggled to their feet. They groaned in unison as they shuffled toward us, and the goddamned curtains wouldn't light—wouldn't light—wouldn't light—

Finally the flames took hold and started climbing the rich fabric, throwing red radiance into the black gloom. I let the Zippo die, feeling it hot as a coal in my hand. I dodged as the first zombie grabbed for me, but it was too close and I felt the thing's fingers slide down my bare shoulder, its claws opened three parallel scratches in my flesh.

I yelled and dove under the other one's attack. My mind was gibbering in panic. I knew that if the things bit you, you were a goner, but could they transmit their disease through their claws? Was I a dead man walking?

No time to worry about it.

I rolled beneath the swinging arms of the dreadlock zombie and leapt back to my feet, swinging the shotgun and screaming as I blasted away.

My first shot wasn't dead-on, but it was enough to tear off the deader's face and take off a chunk of his skull. He staggered backwards, fought for balance, then finally fell onto his side as his brain splurted out of the hole in his head and clumped onto the carpet. He'd taken the brunt of the pellets, so the other one, the one who'd clawed me, still came forward. I cocked and pulled the trigger again, and he flew backwards into the curtains, the flames licking at him, igniting his clothes. I spat at him as I whipped around, sensing movement behind me.

"How bad is it?" Tabitha demanded.

"He didn't bite me," I said grimly. "Let's get the fuck out of here."

She looked at me uncertainly, as though she wanted to back away from me, and I understood the impulse. *Infection.*

But she also knew she didn't stand a chance getting through the casino without me and my Remington, so she gave me a quick nod and started to move down the corridor.

The next few minutes were the most nightmarish I'd ever gone through, and I'd been picked up by Sammy Colosuano's men once and shoved into the black-windowed back of a Cadillac for a discussion about my boss. They'd let me go after telling me what Big Tony needed to hear, but for a few minutes I'd been sure that they were taking me for a ride, and I'd almost pissed my pants in fear.

This was a lot worse.

I vaulted a Betty Boop slot machine that some crazed patron had torn from its pedestal and smashed to the floor, Tabitha leaped behind me. I almost lost my balance as my bare feet skittered on broken glass, blood immediately oozing from a half-dozen cuts. Another zombie loomed ahead, moving through the machines with half its skeleton exposed to the firelight, looking like a creature straight out of Hell. I didn't have time to aim the gun, so I used it as a club, swinging with all my strength and clocking it on the side of the head so that its skull slammed into its bony shoulder, snapping at the top of the spinal cord. The head fell from its body, but its jaws clacked and slavered all the way down, and then it bounced and rolled as the rest of the body collapsed. Tabitha shrieked and kicked it hard, sending it flying against a roulette table ten feet away with power that Adam Vinatieri would've been proud of.

"Jesus!" she said.

"Keep going," I replied, feeling sharp agony in my shoulder and my feet. "We're almost to the turn..."

We ran another fifteen feet and I skidded to a stop, the cuts on the bottoms of my feet screaming in protest against the thick carpet. Two more zombies came around the corner, entering the light. The wall behind us was now burning fully and the fire reflected off of all the stainless steel, the mirrored ceilings, the metal cages of the cashiers' windows, making the whole casino seem almost alive again. The moanings, rustlings and jerky stumblings of the zombies around us just added to the illusion.

I jacked in another shell and fired, blowing apart the two newcomers' heads. Tabitha darted past me and around the corner. I jumped over the bodies as they fell and followed her. Ahead of us, I saw ten, fifteen, a score of the walking dead coming from the ranks of slot machines to cut us off. Tabitha saw them too, and dodged down one of the aisles.

Something grazed my back and I instinctively flinched and spun around, whipping the butt of my rifle up into a face. Bone shattered and black ooze spurted over my hands and face as the zombie's skull crumpled and I spat in panic and disgust, and turned to follow Tabitha as the thing staggered back from the blow. it enough to stop it.

Tabitha had disappeared. I was able to track her by the loud, excited moans that erupted whenever she changed direction, so I followed the chorus.

She appeared suddenly *above* me, having climbed up onto one of the machines. "Get up here!" she said.

I clambered up, and saw that from this perspective I could track all the zombies as they blundered around, trying to find us, which was great from a reconnaissance standpoint, but not so wonderful when you considered we were basically treed.

Tabitha tensed, shoved-off from the slot she was straddling, and leaped over the aisle to the next rank of machines, landing on a pedestal where a fallen Gold Rush game had been. "I'll draw 'em off," she yelled, tensing for another leap. "Meet you at the door!"

"You crazy bitch," I muttered, but I saw the wisdom of her plan. She wasn't encumbered by gun or bag. With the variety of wounds I'd suffered I couldn't make the jumps she was making. She was pulling the zombies toward her with every motion she made.

I had my share of zombies to deal with, of course. I used the brief respite to get into my bag and grab another double handful of shells, shove them into my belt. When I finished there was a woman below me reaching up, her face a mask of desperation and black slime, her outfit and jewelry worth probably five thousand dollars a few days ago, when fashion meant something.

I blew her away and jumped down, almost atop her. I spent a second yanking the diamond necklace from her smoking neck stump, shoved it into my pocket and started running again.

"Fuck," said Tabitha.

We'd made it to the street doors, one of which was wide open, the other shut but with all its glass shattered and bits hanging toothily from its frame. Sunlight poured in, and I felt I could breathe again, the horrible meat smell finally lessening in intensity. My muscles groaned in protest as I took a couple cautious steps out the door.

There were zombies everywhere giving the impression that Smith Boulevard was still open for business on this balmy day. The dead people seemed like tourists as they ambled along the sidewalks and through the spaces between the crashed cars on the street itself—tourists with fatal, gaping wounds in their bellies, entrails dragging behind them in the sand and dust, tourists with missing arms or vicious slashes in the meat of their legs or toes that had gone black and necrotic with rot.

"Nice acrobatics back there," I said. "You an athlete?"

"I used to be," she said. "Back in high school, in Florida, I was on the gymnastics team and the swim team."

I remembered her beautiful dive into the pool, and nodded. "And now you work at a hotel in Aruba."

"I'm a hooker," she said tiredly. "I don't work *at* the hotels. I *work* the hotels."

I nodded again. "I'm a hit man for the Mob."

"I knew you were a wop," she said, confirming something to herself.

"Racism's an ugly thing," I said, looking around, trying to figure out which direction we should take.

"Shit, right now I'd marry you, man," she said.

"I don't marry whores," I said, and she whipped her head up, anger in her eyes—which quickly disappeared when she saw I was playing her. "Where do we go?"

"Listen!" she said suddenly, and I piped down. Beyond the ever-present chorus of moans from the dead people, there was a noise I hadn't heard in days.

The noise of an automobile.

"Where?" I asked, frantically turning my head from side to side. "Where is it?"

"That way," she said, pointing down the street. I looked and saw wrecked cars, all of their license plates with the 'One Happy Island' slogan prominently displayed. Past the storefronts and a sandwich board advertising The Gecko Lounge and Windmill Collectibles I saw a dozen zombies coming toward us. I couldn't be sure that Tabitha was right, but she *seemed* certain. I began to jog again, my bag's strap slippery on my bloody shoulder, the Remington poised and ready, She joined me as we ran down the street, dodging zombies whenever one got too close.

We turned off the boulevard at the first cross street and ran down the cobbled avenue. Flies drifted in clouds over unmoving bodies, and I fleetingly wondered if they were subject to the same infection we were, if all of those flies were dead but still moving, hunting each other down to eat their microscopic brains. All philosophical ponderings were driven from my mind as we burst into the next street and saw a car cautiously driving through the debris of the holocaust.

You couldn't have done it in New York or Chicago or Cleveland, but here in Aruba it seemed like every car was tiny—Jeeps, Peugeots and other little things, unidentifiable to a Cleveland boy more familiar with Fords and Chevrolets—and when the zombie attacks had happened, the pile-ups had been pretty manageable. The driver still had some problems, of course. As we ran into the street frantically waving our arms and shouting, he was in the process of backing away from a slot he'd thought would take him past a three-car wreck but was a dead end. He whipped his head up, in shock and fear at the sight of us.

"I'm talking!" I shouted. "Using language, here! Got a firearm!"

"There are two of 'em," said Tabitha. "There's a kid in the passenger seat."

"Just so long as there's room for us in back," I said, watching as the driver stopped the car and opened the door, stepping out to look at us, a pistol in his hand. "Hell, I'll ride on the roof."

"Don't shoot!" shouted the driver as we neared, and I saw that he wore a black shirt with one of those backwards white collars. A priest. "I'm warning you…"

"Don't fucking worry, Padre," I gasped as we ran the last few yards toward him, letting the Remington twirl on my finger from its trigger guard. "I've never shot a priest, and I ain't gonna start now."

"Who are you?" asked Tabitha, finally letting herself relax a little as she slowed, then stopped ten feet from the car. "Can you help us?"

The passenger door opened and a black kid got out and stood up, watching us over the roof of the Jeep. A teenager, maybe sixteen or seventeen, his eyes were filled with a mixture of distrust, cocky bravado and maybe—just maybe—a little bit of lust as he looked at Tabitha.

Probably *was* lust. I remembered being that age, and it would have taken something a damned sight more dramatic than a zombie apocalypse to keep my trouser snake quiet.

"Who are *you?*" demanded the priest, and I stopped, making sure the shotgun wasn't pointed anywhere near him. The gun he carried was a Colt Single Action Army, and I didn't want panicking and shooting one of those giant .45 bullets at me.

"The name's Vince, padre," I said, "and I go to Mass faithfully every Sunday at Holy Family in Parma. I give twenty bucks every time the basket goes round, and I've got a cousin thinks the Virgin comes and talks to her while she's asleep."

"I'm Tabitha," said the woman beside me. "And we could really use a ride out of here."

"They're not dead," said the kid, and his voice had that sing-song accent I'd gotten used to from the people here. He was a native. "We have to help them."

Now, if it had been just *me* coming screaming out of the street to accost them, with my multiple bleeding wounds, shotgun and tough-guy frame, I bet I wouldn't have gotten the same kind of welcome from the boy. But Tabitha was sweaty and wet with her clothes stuck to her body in an interesting fashion. She was beaming, pleading and grateful, and our boy obviously saw himself as some kind of white knight come to rescue the fair maiden—so I shut up, grinned and hefted the bag back up onto my shoulder, watching the priest.

We stood in front of the King Hong grocery store and there were zombies inside fighting to get out and meet us. He looked at us for a couple more seconds, and now the zombies we'd dodged when we'd made the last turn were getting closer. He made a quick decision

"Get in," he said. "We'll talk on the road. But give me your gun first."

"The gun stays with me," I said, shaking my head. "Didn't I tell you about going to Mass and shit? I'm a good Catholic, Father—I was even an altar boy for a couple of weeks…"

"Give me the gun or I'll shoot you," said the priest, and he leveled the Colt at me.

"Father," I said, slowly moving towards him, "you don't want to do this. You're not a shooter and I am. You'll miss me. And then I'll take that pistol away from you and shove it up your ass. You understand? I *do this for a living*, my friend, and you really want me on your side right now."

The priest looked at me for a long time—long enough for the first wave of zombies to get within ten yards of us.

"He's a good guy, Father," said Tabitha, and that broke the dam.

"All right, get in," he said, lowering the monster gun. "But if you betray us…"

"I know, I know," I said, smiling, moving toward the car. "My momma told me all the time about Hell."

"We're in Hell," said the kid grimly, but he got back in and slammed his door, then reached behind him to unlock the back seat.

"The church is outside of town a little bit," said Father Willem. "But we're running low on batteries for the flashlights and the radio."

"How about food?" I asked, looking out the window and wincing as Tabitha wiped the blood from the claw marks on my shoulder. "Water?"

"We've got plenty," said Oscar, turning around in the passenger seat so he could see us—and to make sure that Tabitha's touching me was purely Hippocratic, not erotic, in nature. "Father Mike always had enough stores for the whole congregation for a week in the basement."

"But we never thought to replace our stores of batteries," said the priest, cautiously steering the Jeep around a corner and speeding up as the road cleared. He even dodged a zombie that was standing in the middle of the street staring at us, we were past it before it could turn and start moaning in earnest. Me, I would've run the fucker over, but I'm not a man of God or anything. "They're most of them either low on juice or entirely dead."

"You said you had a radio," I said. "Are you picking up anything?"

"There are some broadcasts coming out of Caracas," he said, "but they're spotty and low-powered. The zombies are there, too…"

"What about America?" I asked, jerking as Tabitha swabbed out one particularly deep gouge with her damp cloth. "What about the rest of the world?"

"It's happening everywhere," said Oscar, still watching me. "The dead are rising from their graves…"

"Are they?" I asked. "I just saw the ones coming out of the ocean. Are they digging themselves out of the ground, too?"

"No," said Father Willem shortly. "We checked that. First of all, we don't bury our dead on Aruba—we inter them in above-ground tombs—but none of the graves I checked had any signs that the corpses were breaking out. It's only the dead in the ocean that have risen to attack the world. It seems to be enough, though, don't you think?"

"Underwater nuclear tests or something?" I wondered. "Or is it Armageddon?"

"It could be both," said the priest grimly. "But I have other suspicions."

"You care to share them?" I asked. "Seeing as how we're up against thousands of zombies, any thoughts you might have on the subject would be welcome…"

"We'll talk tonight," he said. "I'm still doing some research back at the church, but we wanted to get our errand run before sunset."

"Yeah, sunset," said Tabitha, who stopped swabbing and looked up at them. "Sunset creeps the shit out of me. What's going on at the beaches? What are those things that come out of the ocean…"

"We'll talk tonight," said the priest again. "Vince, you've had some experience with these zombies. Would you be willing to collect the batteries?"

"Where are you going to get them?" I asked. "Some kind of grocery store?"

"The airport," said Oscar, turning back to look out the window as we finally got out of Oranjestad and onto the little freeway that led to Reina Beatrix. "There's an electronics store nearby, and we figure the zombies won't be as heavy there."

"The zombies are heavy everywhere near the coast," said Willem, smoothly driving around another wreck. "But we're on an island, after all…"

"Fine," I said. "I've been doing smash-and-grabs since the deaders started taking over. I can pick you up some double-A's no problem."

And it wasn't. I only had to shoot two dead people in the head, and I spilled every battery I could find into the bag Willem gave me. It was actually kind of peaceful in the abandoned store, and I didn't even run when I was leaving.

As I exited the Radio Shack authorized dealer, the other three were standing outside the car.

The priest was going through *my* bag.

"Fucking…" I started, and instinctively raised my shotgun, but even as I was about to get *really* mad, he zipped it back up and threw it into the backseat again.

"How about a little personal privacy, Padre?" I asked, steaming, as I stalked toward him.

"Diamonds, Vince?" he asked sadly. "The world's coming to an end, and you're collecting diamonds?"

"The world ain't gonna end," I said, shoving past him. "Eventually, things are gonna get back to normal. And when they do, I'm gonna be sitting pretty."

"What the hell did you do?" asked Tabitha, awe in her voice. "Clean out every jeweler's shop in Oranjestad?"

"Seven of them," I said gruffly, tossing the batteries into the front seat and getting back into the car. "It's easy when there's no electricity. And there are a lot of fucking diamonds on this island."

"You must have a million dollars worth in that bag," she said, climbing in next to me. "Big ones, little ones, uncut ones…"

"My retirement," I said. "Get in the goddamned car. If we're staying the night in some church, we'd better get there pretty soon. You know what happens when the sun goes down."

"You know what the Bible says, Vince," said the priest. "The love of money…"

"Yeah, yeah," I responded. "I also know they hung a thief next to Jesus, and that he went straight to Heaven. What's your point?"

"My point?" laughed the priest, his voice hollow with stress and exhaustion. "I don't have a point. Just make sure you don't die because you're protecting your precious treasure."

"I ain't gonna die," I said grimly. "There's a luxurious mountain cabin somewhere in the Rocky Mountains with my name on it, and a shitload of ski bunnies waiting to help me spend my money. I've had enough of this sun and surf crap."

It was a close thing, getting back to St. Anna, and the sun was low on the horizon as the Padre finally pulled into the little parking lot. He and Oscar had moved all the derelict cars out of the lot and given themselves a clear line of fire from the front doors, and they'd barricaded the other doors with stout hunks of wood stolen from the buildings nearby. The heavy church doors were chained and padlocked, and I approved of the security smarts they'd shown thus far.

"Home sweet home," said the priest, opening his door and stepping out into the lot.

"It's about time," I groused. We'd had a hell of a time getting back—the car had run out of gas, but fortunately, they'd had plastic jugs of fuel in the trunk. While we'd been nozzle-ing the gas into the tank, zombies appeared seemingly out of nowhere on the road and attacked us. Oscar and the priest had blazed away with their pistols, but they'd managed to put down exactly one of the dead men—the rest I'd had to blast with the shotgun, and we'd barely gotten away with zombies hanging off the side of the car. Blood and viscera covered the hood of the jeep, and Willem had had to use the wipers to smear black bile and red gristle to either side of the windshield, lending a grotesque, funereal air to the ride back to the church. "Where the hell did you get those guns, anyway? You'd be better off with clubs…"

"A policeman came to St. Anna's seeking sanctuary when the outbreak happened," said the priest wearily as he got out of the car. "He'd been bitten. An hour later, we had to shoot him in the head with his own gun. He had another one in his car."

"Jesus," said Tabitha. "You shot a guy in the head?"

"I did it," said Oscar, getting out of the car. "It's not right that a priest should kill."

"He was dead already," said Father Willem, looking around for ambushes. He spun the keys around on his ring, searching for the one that would open the padlock. "It wouldn't have been murder."

"It still wouldn't have been right," said Oscar with his lilting island voice.

"And who are you?" I asked. "Altar boy?"

"I'm a waiter," he said, giving me a smile. "I just happened to be at church when everything went down, and I stuck around to make sure the Father would be okay."

"You're a waiter?" I said. "Let me ask you something—I had about six meals in restaurants here before the zombies came, and you people are without a doubt the slowest goddamned workers I've ever seen. One time I had to wait a half hour before the guy even took my order, and I spent an hour waiting for a hamburger. What is it, some kind of union thing?"

"We're on island time, man," he said, still smiling. "You get used to it."

"You really do," said Tabitha. "It took me about six months once I moved here, but…"

"Behind you!" I screamed, and shoved Oscar out of the way, bringing my shotgun up and aiming it over the top of the car. Willem, still fiddling with his keys, looked at me with wide white eyes, then dropped just as I pulled the trigger, which was a good thing for him, because the blast would have taken off his head rather than the head of the zombie right behind him. Smoke from the blast rose in the sunset air, and the deader's blood and bone misted in a red cloud as his body fell. Where the hell had he come from?

"Back in the car!" I said.

"We need to get into the church!" protested Oscar. "It's almost night…"

I realized he was right when another zombie popped up. I saw the open sewer grate at the edge of the parking lot, half-hidden by one of the moved cars, and another rotten head appeared from its depths. I fired again and moved around the back of the jeep, jacking a new shell into the chamber. "Padre, get that lock open."

"Right," he said, and jogged over to the building, still looking for the right key. I felt like going over there and blasting the padlock right off the doors, but then we wouldn't have a padlock anymore. So instead I blew away the new zombie—an Aruban women with fungal growths all over her from the sewer she'd crawled out of. I ran over to the storm drain in time to blast away at the male zombie who'd almost made it out. The shot cut him in half, and most of his torso kept coming, pulled by skeletal arms dotted with rotten meat, while his pelvis and legs fell back into the sewer. He kept coming for me, snarling and moaning, inching forward with his finger bones scraping the asphalt, and from his ruined waist trailed ropes of viscera. If I'd had boots on, I might have stomped on his head. Instead, I ignored him—he wasn't moving very fast and there was something else going on.

"You hear that?" I asked Tabitha, who had come up beside me.

"All I hear is that thing," she said, pointing a shaky hand at the half-zombie.

I jacked in another shell, aimed down and fired, making a Pollock of the parking lot. The thing stopped moaning.

With the echoes of the blast fading in our ears, we could both hear it.

Splashing water. The sound of bodies moving, not at a slow, stumbling shuffle, but with strength and purpose.

The guttural sounds of language.

"They only come out at night," Tabitha said, her hands flying up to her mouth, her body shaking as she took a quick step backward, then another one.

"Maybe they're getting braver," I said, also walking backwards, wincing as my lacerated feet hit pebbles on the blacktop. "How you doing over there, Padre?" I yelled.

At the sound of my voice, the things talking in the sewer went silent. Seconds later, howls of anticipation arose, doubled and redoubled by the acoustics of the pipe. I turned and started to run.

Tabitha paced me, and I spared a backwards glance at the sewer opening as the first of the fish-men started to emerge. I shoved shells into the shotgun as I ran, some of them spilling from my belt, but I didn't slow down. In the five seconds it took for me to get to the church door, Father Willem had unlocked the padlock and clicked it open.

"Get in!" I yelled, spun and fired off a blast at the first of our pursuers.

They were creatures meant to swim the world's oceans, and they looked odd on land, what with their gigantic webbed feet, their big, blank, milk-white eyes bulging out of their leathery faces, their earless skulls lumpy and dripping calciferous, stringy strands—but they were moving pretty goddamned good in spite of it, their backward-bending legs powering them forward in a series of prodigious hops, their harsh words sounding like a hideous mixture of coyote and whalesong. The first one had closed to within fifteen feet when the shotgun blast hit it.

The thing paused as the pellets whanged into it, but screeched in anger rather than pain, and in a heartbeat it resumed its galumphing run with a dozen little black dimples on its leathery hide.

None of the shot had penetrated.

Peripherally, I saw that Oscar and the priest had gotten inside, but I didn't see the woman.

"Where's Tabitha?" I said, yelling to make myself heard over the growling and keening of the frog creatures.

"She's gone!" yelled Willem. "Get inside!"

I couldn't wait any longer, though I'll admit I felt like a bit of a heel leaving the whore to the creatures—but I've felt like a heel before, and I've always gotten over it. I fired one more blast, with approximately the same effect, and then darted through the door as the priest started to slam it shut.

He almost got it closed—but just before he could push it home, a thundering blow rocked it from the other side as the enraged fishman slammed into it, and the priest was thrown back against the wall of the narthex. He hit hard, crumpling to the floor. Instantly, Oscar was there with his Colt, and as the abomination regrouped for one last leap that would send it among us, the waiter pulled the trigger.

I'd been hearing so many shotgun blasts over the last day or so that I thought my ears were armored against the noise, but that Peacemaker roared in the vestibule like the artillery of God Himself. Black blood skidded from the monster's sloping, scaled forehead as the bullet tore through its flesh. It was rocked back by the velocity and size of the slug and staggered a half foot back into the parking lot. I leaped for the door to swing it shut, I saw the monster shaking its head like a dog killing a groundhog. It raised its baleful pearl-colored eyes to meet mine and then its maw opened and a roar vented from its sea-cave mouth, just as I finally closed the door.

"Jesus!" I said. "Goddamn! The bullet bounced right off its skull! From fucking three feet away!"

"Language," said Father Willem waveringly as he fought to his feet.

"Fuck language!" I said. "Where's the damned lock!"

"Here," said Oscar, darting forward and clipping the padlock to the push bar of the door—and just in time, for another titanic blow hit just at that moment, bending back the door and its frame. The steel of the Master held, and the kid slammed the lock home.

Another blow, and another, and then the howls erupted from what must have been a dozen deep-sea voices.

"Where's the back door?" I demanded, frantically waving my shotgun from side to side. It wouldn't take the things long to realize that the door could be broken, sure—but that a better bet would be to come through one of the stained-glass windows to either side of it.

"Come on," said the priest, grabbing my arm and Oscar's, and leading us into the nave. I'd been lying when I'd told Willem that I was a churchgoer, and the last time I'd been in one was when one of the Capo's grandnieces had gotten hitched a few years ago. But for whatever reason, as I ran after the preacher I reached over, splashed my hand in the holy water font and did a spastic sign-of-the-cross as I sprinted down the aisle toward the apse, my Remington wildly waving. Behind us, glass shattered.

We took a quick left before we hit the altar, and Willem shoved us ahead. "There's a door just past the next right. I'll meet you in a second."

"No, Father!" said Oscar, but I was already running in the direction the priest had indicated, and I wondered if the padre was going to provide some distraction for the fish people—like, say, sacrificing himself to save us. I could have used a distraction—the monsters were already pouring into the nave like it was a whorehouse and they randy sailors off a six-month mission.

The priest had darted into one of the alcoves off the apse, and had collected a big, leather-bound book. He made it into the side passage with Oscar and I before the creatures got there.

"You risked your life to save a *Bible*?" I gasped as I sprinted the last few feet. There were two pews holding the door shut, so I shoved them aside with a wooden clatter and whipped it open.

"There are a billion Bibles in the world," said Willem, wheezing with exertion. "But only five of these…" He held it up as he ran, and I could see even from a brief glance that the thing was *old*—bound in ancient leather, with words I didn't understand scrolling across the cover. It gave me a momentary chill, as though it was alive and sentient—but it was just a damned book, Bible or not.

"And you were breaking my balls about the fucking diamonds," I said, running out into the dusk. The ground behind the church was a low slope heading up, ringed by thin frondy trees and stubby cactuses, and there was an access road with a couple of abandoned jeeps on it. I wondered if I'd remember all the hot-wiring techniques I learned as a kid off Mayfield Road. Not that it would matter—the frog monsters would rip our guts out before I even got the casing off the steering column.

The first of our pursuers burst out the door behind us—and was slammed at thirty miles an hour by the priest's Jeep careening around the corner.

The beast flew into the dim air like a cannonball, howling in rage and pain, smashing into some kind of palm ten feet away, cracking the tree in half, the bladed leaves whipping to the ground as the frog-thing spun and followed it down.

"Get in!" screamed Tabitha, her voice frantic, as she leaned over and threw open the passenger-side door.

The fallen tree shook, its trunk quivering and its foliage rustling wildly, as the beast got back to its spatulate feet, roaring in a volume and intensity that didn't speak well for our chances should it get its claws into us. I would've stood dumbfounded at the thing's strength and power if I'd had time—but as it was, I dove for the back door of the Jeep and threw myself in, the priest with his book right behind me. We got a bit tangled up in each other, my bag and shotgun and his concrete brick of a book all jostling for space in the small interior, but we got in and Oscar jumped into the passenger seat, his eyes wild with panic.

Tabitha's window shattered as the next of the amphibious atrocities threw a punch that would have knocked the head off the strongest heavyweight fighter in the world, if he were stupid enough to stand there and take it. Pebbles of safety glass rocketed around the inside of the car, stinging us with their velocity. One of them stabbed the corner of my eye, causing novas of pain and temporary blindness.

I felt the motor roar and the vehicle lurch forward. From the screams of the driver and the priest (who was frantically trying to untangle himself from me), I was willing to bet, that the monster was coming along for the ride. As my vision focused from red-and-blue exploding universes to bright blur to, finally, halfway normal, I saw that I was right.

The creature was trying to latch onto Tabitha's neck with its claws, and Oscar was trying to get a shot at it with his pistol, but the woman was swerving and accelerating and screaming so much that the monster had to constantly grab for leverage on the car's frame, the windshield, the steering wheel. Tabitha was weaving and dodging her upper body frantically, trying to avoid the thing's attacks. I flew straight up, banging against the roof, as we plowed over a trio of cacti. I heard a sudden bang as we landed, knowing that one of the tires had blown.

We went into a sudden spin, and as I tried to angle the Remington for any kind of shot at the monster, it suddenly disappeared. There was a screaming, screeching wail of violated metal, and I realized that the blowout had sent the vehicle sliding against a building up the road, scraping the frog monster right off. Tabitha wailed again, but kept her foot on the gas and the steering wheel pulled hard right, the muscles bulging on her forearms as she fought the skid. Finally, we were limping uphill, the blown tire throwing strips of black rubber up into the air, the rims sparking on the pavement. Tabitha caught her breath and began to slow.

Which was a mistake. We'd been so focused on the threat behind us that we hadn't seen the horde of zombies waiting for us up the hill.

My mind had been circling the subject since I'd seen the fish people clambering out of the sewer after the zombies, but now I really couldn't put it off any longer.

The monsters were at the very least, herding the zombies, and quite possible *controlling* them, and that couldn't be a good thing...

Quickly we were among them, slamming them around like tenpins, blasting rotting bodies apart in grunting, groaning explosions. A head flew off a body and bounced off the already bloody windshield, sending a spiderweb crack across the glass. Tabitha had nothing protecting her because her window had been shattered by the sea creature—and one of the zombies managed to stick itself through the window as we raced by on three wheels and a rim. It had only one arm and its legs flopped against *my* window as we tore through the thickening night, it had a single-minded intensity, a laser focus to bite and bite and bite. I saw the flesh and skin peeling from its skull, one of its eyes was gone and the socket crawling with black maggots, with pink pulsating brain matter behind it. The deader lunged forward as Tabitha screamed and threw her hands up, and there was nothing I could do to stop what was going to happen.

But Oscar could—and did.

He threw himself left, forcing Tabitha back and interposing himself between her and the zombie, his right hand whipping the Colt around, ready for the shot that would blow the deader back out the window, but he wasn't quick enough and the thing sank its teeth into his left arm, in the thick meat right below the elbow.

Oscar roared in defiance and pulled his arm—zombie still attached—up to make the monster face him, and the two of them stared at each other for one lingering moment, the anger, pain and horrible knowledge of his fate in one pair of eyes, and nothing but blank starvation and lust in the glazed single eye of the other. Then Oscar put the .45 to the thing's ear and blasted its skull into oblivion.

Though Tabitha screamed as the shower of fetid, rotten meat, bone, skin and hair showered her, she kept her foot on the gas pedal, and we were through.

"Where are you taking us?" asked Willem quietly, Oscar's head in his lap. We'd rearranged our positions at the first opportunity, and now I drove while Tabitha leaned my Remington out the passenger side window. The priest and the dying boy were in back.

"The navy base," said Tabitha quietly. It was full dark, now, but the stars were bright enough to drive by.

I wanted to make some smart-ass comment about how a hooker would, of course, know all about the navy and its sailors, but instead I said "Aruba has a navy?"

"The Netherlands has a navy," said Willem. "And sometimes the Americans use the base as well. With that lunatic Chavez a few miles away, we're seeing a lot more of you Yankees."

"Oh yeah?" I asked, not caring. I'd never heard of Chavez, whoever he might be, and I didn't care. By now, he was probably roaming around eating brains. "They'll have guns there, right?"

"Probably," said the priest. "I was a pilot before I got my calling, and I was stationed there for a year—and though we're not going to find a huge armory, we may be able to find *something* that will damage those creatures…"

I slammed the car to a stop, looking around at the scenery trying to detect any motion, whether zombic or amphibious, the darkness remained still. I let go of the steering wheel, turned, grabbing the top of Tabitha's seat and stared at the two of them in back. "Did you just say that you used to be a *pilot?*"

"I flew Westland Lynxes," said Willem. "Mostly on antisubmarine missions…"

"Jesus fucking Christ, Father," I said. "Why aren't we going to the airport right now, hotwiring an airplane, and getting the hell out of Dodge?"

"The Lynx is a *helicopter*," said the priest. "Chances are, there isn't anything I can fly at Reina Beatrix…"

"What are those things?" gasped Oscar, sweat beading on his face as he lay in Willem's lap, and everyone grew silent. Tabitha twisted herself around and the expression on her face as she watched Oscar, the man who'd saved her life, talk was heartbreaking.

"You know, Father," he wheezed, his eyes closed. "I don't have much time. Tell me."

"You've got a few hours," said the priest. "We'll get to the base, I'll give you extreme unction…"

"Tell me about the monsters, Father," he said.

"I second that," said Tabitha, her voice cracking. "We need to know."

"Agreed," I said. "What's in that book, Father?"

Willem sat quietly for a long moment, stroking Oscar's kinky hair, looking down at him with a terrible, knowing fondness. The night was silent outside the car, and we idled atop a small hill. On a normal night, a pre-invasion night, there would have been lights twinkling around the curve of the coast in both directions, lights from the low hilltops, perhaps distant lights from cruise ships as they chugged through the waters toward Bermuda or Bonaire. Now it was just the stars and the dashboard, and it was dark enough that I could barely see the priest's lips move when he finally spoke.

"We're supposed to say that they're demons," he said. "That's what they teach us in seminary. But they're not."

"Wait a minute," said Tabitha, anger in her voice. "You mean someone *knew* about these things before?"

"We were also taught about demonic possession, witchcraft and flying devils from distant stars," said Willem tiredly. "We all nodded and took notes, and then went back to figuring out how to deal with crack babies and cheating wives and men who hit their children. Real life stuff. But they're real…"

"What's the book?" I asked.

"I'll tell you about it," he said. "But keep driving. It's a nice night for campfire stories, but if we can get to someplace reasonably secure, I'll feel a lot better about our chances for surviving the rest of the night."

I put it back into drive, slowly rolling down the hill. We'd left the road a long time ago, figuring there would be fewer zombies in the low hills than on the streets, and the bare ground was better on our tortured tire rim than the pavement. I drove about five, six miles per hour, and we were making progress.

"There are other gods," said Willem quietly, but I could easily hear him, even over the thrum of our motor and the occasional *clank* as the exposed rim clattered over a rock in the ground. "Not in the sense that *God* is a god, of course—they're not omnipotent, nor omniscient, and they're more like alien beings than real divinities—but they're powerful. And ancient. And they exist."

"Like that Kali broad, with the four arms?" I asked.

"Like the god of those fish creatures that are waging war on humans all around the globe right now," he responded. "They have a whole pantheon—from their high priest, Cthulhu, who sleeps dead but dreaming beneath the waves of the south Atlantic, to their patri-arch Dagon, who is the eldest and most puissant of their species, to their great overlord Azathoth, who pulses idiotically at the center of the universe, swaying to the strains of a trillion insane pipers..."

"Is that the god we're worried about, here?" I asked. "The idiot god?"

"No," said Willem. "It's Cthulhu, the one at the undersea island. When 'the stars are right', he's supposed to come up and lay waste to the world. And these fish creatures, these Deep Ones, are the ad-vance forces in his army."

"So, what, they hook up all the dead humans in the ocean, send 'em up the beaches to make more converts, then once most of the coastal communities are zombies, they follow with the shock troops?" I said, concentrating on the hillside ahead. We were getting close to the ocean, the smell of salt was wafting on the warm night-time breeze through the gaping window frame next to me. "And they're hoping that the zombie infection spreads fast and far enough that when their god wakes up and starts roaming around, he won't have to hike over the Rockies or the Alps to get to the rest of us? Is that the deal?"

It was silent for long moments, and I risked a look in the rear-view, only to see the priest's eyes staring right back. We locked glances.

"You should've been a tactician; you've completely nailed what's happening" he said, and then, with regret, "I didn't take this stuff seriously enough."

"I'm a gunner," I said. "I shoot people for a living. If I'm not good at tactics, I'll end up with a buncha holes in my body. What else do you know about these things?"

"The Deep Ones are very tough," he said, "but you saw that. Their skin is so armored that they can soak up incredible amounts of damage."

"Yeah," I said. "I had one point blank with the Remington and the shot just bounced off. Hell, even Oscar's hogleg only blasted a little hide off the thing's skull, and he was three feet away. You think a submachine gun would do anything?"

"I think that if you managed to penetrate their skin and hit their vital organs, they'd die just like we do. We'll see if we can find some M16s at the base…"

"And how come all the zombies they raised from the ocean still looked so good?" I asked. "Christ, some of them have been down there since World War II—hell, since *pirate* days—but they still looked pretty much intact when they crawled up onto the beach the other day."

"The Deep Ones have been planning this for a long time," said Willem. "Call it magic or call it advanced technology, but they have ways to preserve their weapons."

"Great," I said. "They're built like tanks, they're practically bulletproof, they hate us, and they can use magic. You gotta love our odds…"

Oscar groaned loudly in Willem's lap, and Tabitha spun back around, panic in her face. I kept driving, though I was ready to stop the car and blow the kid's head off if I had to…but it was just a groan of pain and hopelessness, and it finished with a couple of wet, weak coughs as he sought to catch his breath.

"We're almost there," said Tabitha. "And it takes a few hours for…"

"Yeah," I said. "We'll get him somewhere warm and cozy."

"What else…" wheezed Oscar. "What else do you know about them, Father?"

"They're hierarchical," he said. "According to the stories, the older ones are the more powerful ones, leading all the way up to Father Dagon, who's the biggest, strongest Deep One in history. The ones we've seen are the young ones, and they'll be led by a priest."

"A priest," I said, thinking back. "There was something happening on Renaissance Island last night, with a lot of lights and chanting."

"A ceremony," said the priest. "Their time is coming, and they're performing magical rituals to ease Cthulhu's rebirth into the world."

"Be good if we could take out this priest," I said, slowing down. "Is this where I turn?"

"Yes," said Willem, peering into the darkness. "There'll be a fence around the compound, but I don't imagine you'll have to worry about it being electrified now."

"What else?" I asked, shifting down to help the Jeep climb a slow incline. I didn't want to plow into the fence, further crippling our transport.

"They rule the oceans," he said. "If we were to get into a boat and make a run for Venezuela, they'd have us in minutes. And I'd be willing to bet that there's not a working battleship, nuclear submarine or aircraft carrier in the world right now—they'd have taken care of them first. I'd also be willing to bet that any world capital on the ocean or on a major river…"

"Which is most of them," I said.

"…is suffering zombie outbreaks just like we are," he finished. "Imagine the corpses climbing out of the Potomac or the Seine or Sydney Harbor—and their infection spreading amongst the millions of souls there…"

"Sydney's not the capital," said Tabitha. "Canberra is."

The priest looked at her, and I grinned as I drove, but the grin died instantly as I caught a glimpse of something and slammed on the brakes.

The car lurched as we hit the body lying on the ground, jostling us and causing a pained groan from Oscar. Then we were stopped and I killed the engine.

"Dead person," I said, and threw open the door. I grabbed the Remington and got out, looked down.

The tire rims hadn't cut the corpse in half, but they'd done a damned good job of mushing its midsection, and it stunk like swamp gas from the guy's guts slopped onto the black ground. He'd been blond and young and someone or something had torn his throat out, killing him instantly. And then we'd run over him.

"How come he didn't turn zombie?" asked Tabitha, getting out of the car.

"He died too quickly," said Willem from the backseat. "The infection needs time in a living body. Only the Deep Ones can raise the dead."

"And God," I said sarcastically.

"And God," agreed Willem.

Ahead of us were other low mounds on the ground, all dead bodies. Some were soldiers, dressed in their casual fatigues, but most were Aruban natives or American tourists. I carefully stepped forward and saw that we'd parked in the middle of a battlefield.

"They made a stand here," said Tabitha.

"And lost," I said.

Twenty feet through the gloom, barely visible in the starlight, was a gaping tear in the fence. Piles of burnt corpses huddled near the torn edges of the chain link, but the zombies had finally thrown enough bodies to rip a hole in it, heedless of the electric current that roasted them, lusting for the humans cowering in their compound. The Dutch naval men had been forced to come out of their buildings and engage them—and each side had dealt great carnage in the struggle.

"Can we pass?" asked Father Willem, leaning out the window.

"I doubt it," I said. "Not unless we want to spend a half hour dragging bodies out of the way."

"Help me," he said simply. "We have to get Oscar inside, to those buildings."

"We could leave him here," I said quietly, knowing that the priest wouldn't hear me and knowing that Tabitha would. "He's gonna get back up in just a couple hours. Why waste our strength on..."

"Because he saved my life, man," she said, just as quietly. "He took that bite for me. If you don't want to carry him, I will."

I looked at her and sighed. I turned back to the car and helped Willem drag the moaning, wriggling form of the teenager out of the backseat, and we shrugged him up onto our shoulders and began navigating the body-strewn stretch of bloody land that led to the Dutch military base.

"Holy shit," I whispered reverently. "Is this what I think it is?"

We'd come across more bodies, many of them ripped to shreds, some of them partially eaten, all of them bloated and stinking from their two-day marination in the Caribbean sun. Nothing had moved as we'd dragged Oscar across the formation ground and through the doors to the barracks. So we'd taken the chance and entered the dark building. And now, by the light of my flickering Zippo, I'd come across a miracle.

"It is," said Willem. "See if there's any gas in it."

I spun open the plastic cover and smiled as the smell of gasoline wafted into the dark room.

"If I turn this thing on," I said, "you'd all better be ready to run around and shut off lights…"

"Lights," moaned Oscar, lying on the rough pallet we'd thrown together for him. We'd dragged three dead Dutch swabbies out of the room and piled blankets in a corner for our wounded companion, but he was restless and kept trying to get up. Tabitha had managed to keep him horizontal so far, but I was starting to get nervous. He'd be dying soon, and shortly thereafter he'd be trying to rip off our faces to get to our brains. If it had been up to me, he'd be dead already and his body far away from us. But Willem and Tabitha wanted to keep him alive as long as possible, and I didn't want to piss off the guy who could fly a helicopter, so I just kept fiddling with the wondrous, miraculous generator, hoping it worked.

"Get ready," I said as I primed the thing. "You have your guns?"

We'd managed to scavenge quite a bit of ordnance since we'd come to the base, but Willem had proven himself to be a shit shot for an ex-soldier and Tabitha had never fired a gun in her life. I'd given them both M16s that looked to be in fairly good condition, shown them the safeties and silently reminded myself to be well out of the way if they ever had to open fire.

"Why are you starting that thing, Vince?" asked Willem quietly.

I opened my mouth—and then shut it.

Why *was* I starting the generator?

It's not like we needed the lights—darkness was the Deep Ones' ally, but it also hid us from their search. Though it would have been wonderful to have a cold beer or two—I'd found a six-pack of Balashi sitting on some squid's bunk like it was a present just for me—it would take hours for the refrigerators to cool down enough to chill the brew. It would be much easier—and less conspicuous—to simply cower in the darkness until the sun came up, then slink out to our next destination, whatever that might be.

"Fuck that," I said to myself.

"Fuck," echoed Oscar, his voice thin and feeble.

"I'm going to need lights, Padre," I said. "I've got a project to do tonight, if I can find the right equipment around here, and I'll need to be able to see."

"What project?" he asked.

"You watch football, Father?" I asked, fiddling with the knobs on the gennie.

"American football?" he said. "I've seen some games."

"I'm getting ready to throw a Hail Mary," I said, smiling. "They never fucking work—except when they do."

Willem looked at me and sighed. "Go ahead," he said.

I nodded and cranked the generator.

We managed to turn off most everything before the zombies or the Deep Ones figured out where we were, and while Father Willem gave Oscar the last rites and Tabitha cooked up some MREs on a Flameless Ration Heater, I went exploring. I should have taken one of the M16s, but the Remington had served me well since I'd found it beneath the bar in a beachfront tavern, and I was loath to leave it behind.

I took a military-issue hooded flashlight and cautiously explored the building we were in and the next one over. I found plenty of stuff that might come in handy, including some socks and boots for my scarred, blood-covered feet, but I didn't hit pay dirt until I finally found the armory.

The place had been pretty much cleaned out by the soldiers during the last, desperate battle. Luckily, it wasn't guns or bullets that I needed (though I happily filled my pockets and a small backpack with more shells for the shotgun), but equipment—and the Dutch had a great little state-of-the-art machine shop.

I went back to the barracks, weaving around the dead as I picked my way through the darkness, and when I got there Father Willem was sitting alone on a bunk, his eyes closed in exhaustion.

"Where's Oscar?" I asked, looking at the pallet he'd been lying on. "And Tabitha?"

"In the Officers' Quarters," he said, tossing his head to indicate a closed door ten feet away. "Did you find whatever it was that you were looking for?"

"I did," I said, staring at the door. "What the hell are they doing in there?"

He opened his eyes and I was struck by the complexity of the feelings they showed. There was weariness, pain and desperation—but there was also a kind of peace floating around in his blue eyes, a calm knowledge that, no matter how bad it got, everything would end well. If not in this world, then in the next.

"Oscar seemed to get a bit better, more clear. He stopped raving. I gave him Extreme Unction," he said quietly. "And now the woman is giving him her own blessing."

I stared at him. "You mean she's…"

"Yes," he said. "There's still time."

"There's not *much* time," I protested. "He could turn zombie any minute now…"

"She decided to take the chance," said the priest somberly. And then, unexpectedly, he gave me a crooked smile. "And besides," he said, "Oscar is a teenager. It probably won't take that long."

I looked at him for a moment, not knowing what to say, but then I smiled as well.

"Lucky kid," I said. "My first time, neither of us knew what we were doing, and halfway through it the girl's mother walked in on us, and there I was, with the rubber shoved onto my…"

"Vince," he said tiredly, "I'm still a priest, remember?"

"Yeah, yeah," I said, but I was still smiling. "But you used to be a soldier. You telling me you didn't get a little little while you were in port? Hell, man—you're a *flyboy*, and those mothers get some *serious* poon…"

Before Willem could open his mouth to say shut me up, the door to the Officers' Quarters opened and Tabitha came out, crying silently. Her hair had been ratty all day, but she looked even more disheveled now. The Father shot me a look, and I thought for a fleeting moment what a strange world it had turned into—a priest tacitly okaying some premarital sex and warning a mobster with his eyes not to say anything about it.

"You okay?" I asked.

She looked at me, tear tracks lined down her face in glistening drifts, and nodded. Then she shook her head. She sat down on a bunk and leaned forward, brought her hands up to her face, and began to shake in suppressed sobs.

"You have to go in there," she managed, through wheezing breaths, and for a second I didn't know what she was talking about—and then I did.

"It's time, then?" I asked.

She didn't respond, and after another couple of seconds I nodded to myself, and looked at the priest.

"May God have mercy on his soul," he said quietly. Then he crossed himself, closed his eyes again and clasped his hands together in prayer.

I picked up the Remington—thought about it—put it down. Instead, I reached down to the table and grabbed Oscar's Colt, the one he'd shot the fish monster with back at St. Anna's. I looked at Tabitha and Willem, both of them with their eyes shut, both of them wrapped in heavy emotion and anguish. I didn't say anything.

After all, it's what I did for a living.

I slowly walked over to the door and went inside. Someone had put the blackout blinds on the window, and there was a lamp on beside the bed. Oscar lay there, naked, and I could see the bite wound on his arm festering and turning an ugly gray-green, and though he seemed asleep—spent—he still twitched and spasmed as his body changed, as the life began to drain from him and some new, dark, energy started to fill him.

I moved to the side of the bed and looked down. In that moment his eyes opened and the two of us looked at each other.

I didn't say anything. Neither did he. He fought through his delirium, glanced at the sidearm I held, He closed his eyes and put his head back onto the pillow. Sweat poured from his forehead, his chest heaved, struggling for breath, his muscles contracted into rock-hard bulges. He sighed once and for a second or two, the last second or two of his life, he relaxed into something like peace.

I put the barrel of the gun to his ear and pulled the trigger.

The rest of the night I spent in the armorer's shop, my gym bag next to me and the six-pack of Balashi. It was a nice little brew when it was cold—I'd downed probably a case of the stuff the first couple days I'd spent in Aruba—but it was fairly foul at seventy-degree room temperature. We had rum, but rum would've messed with my precision I needed some kind of booze, though, to take the foul taste of death from my mouth.

I'd killed maybe a dozen people in my life, and scores of the undead, but shooting Oscar had done strange things to my normally-impervious psyche. I swigged the beer and fired up the soldering iron. Working kept me from thinking too much—but I couldn't stop remembering how the kid had accepted his fate with such equanimity, with wisdom far beyond his years. I hoped that when my time came, I'd face it with the peace and nobility Oscar had shown. It probably wouldn't be much longer, either; with those frog things running around this might be the last night I'd spend on earth.

I finished the soldering around three in the morning, yawned, and looked around for a hammer. As I did, I saw Tabitha leaning in the doorway and gave a start—I hadn't heard her coming.

"What are you doing?" she asked quietly. "Willem said something about a Hail Mary, but I didn't understand him."

"It's a prayer," I said. "You ask the Virgin to intercede on your behalf…and if you're down five at the end of a football game with sixty yards to go and two seconds on the clock, you heave up the ball and hope it takes a good bounce or two and ends up in your wideout's hands. You're telling me you've never heard of a Hail Mary pass?"

"I never liked football," she said, looking around the room tiredly. She'd probably gotten a few hours sleep, but it wasn't enough—she looked wrung-out and dissipated, as though some important part of her had started to sputter and die.

At least she got laid, I thought, but didn't say.

"It rarely works, the Hail Mary," I said. "Just about as often as actual prayers get answered, actually. But it's something to do tonight before the sun comes up."

"We're going to try for the airport, then?" she asked.

"Might as well," I said. "Maybe we can fight off a few thousand zombies and dozens of Deep Ones, get to the Aeropuerto and find a helicopter that Willem can pilot. After that, all we have to do is fly to Venezuela and figure out our next step."

"Did he say anything?" she asked suddenly. "Before you…you…"

I looked at her.

She swayed a little on her feet, shaking her head.

"He didn't say he loved you, if that's what you're asking," I said, feeling the bitterness in my mouth again, remembering the recoil from the .45. "He knew what was coming, though—and he accepted it."

"Good," she whispered. "Good."

"Go get some more sleep," I said, standing up and moving over to the tool bench, finding myself a big, heavy-headed hammer. "I've got another couple hours work to do, then we can get the Jeep packed up and start rolling."

"You need sleep too," she said.

"I'll sleep on the chopper," I said.

She nodded at me sadly. "When I was a little girl, my mother used to talk about moving back to Texas. That's where she was from—a little place called Vidor—and she'd tuck me in to bed at night and tell me how great it was gonna be when we got out of Miami, out of the slums, and back to the ranch she'd grown up on. There were rabbits and rattlesnakes and skies a million miles wide, and you could breathe the air and soak in the sun and I could ride horses all I wanted."

I hefted the hammer and smiled at her.

"Yeah," I said. "I don't think we're gonna make it to the airport, either. But you just keep thinking about the wide-open skies and the horses…"

"I've never stopped thinking about them," she said. "Good luck with your prayer."

"Get some sleep," I said, and sat back down. I waited a couple of seconds until I heard her walking away, and then I grabbed a nail, put it on the anvil, and started pounding. It took me three more beers, but I finally finished. I started packing up my bag and thought about the morning to come—now only about an hour away.

"Texas," I said to myself, shaking my head. "Willem's dreaming of Heaven, and Tabitha's dreaming of Texas."

I stood up and hefted the bag. I clicked off the work light and went outside, looking up at the stars for maybe the last time. The sun wasn't up yet, but you could tell it was coming—to the east, the horizon was lined with a low red strip of light, and from our low hill it seemed like I could see forever across the distant oceans.

I knew those waters teemed with monsters wanting nothing more than to exterminate us and with a submerged island on which a sleeping god lay poised to rise and blot out all light, all hope, all life. But the ocean was still gorgeous, and I spent another two or three minutes just staring out at the world and wondering why I'd never dreamed of a better place, a place with horses and rattlesnakes.

I trudged back to the barracks.

The morning dawned hot and sticky. I'd wrapped blankets around Oscar in a makeshift shroud and we'd left him in his bunk. They didn't bury their dead in Aruba, and we didn't bury ours. I'd put the Colt on his chest afterwards, for some reason obscure even to me, but gestures were all we had left at this point.

And we were going to make one last grand gesture, weren't we?

Say what you want about humans, but we tend to fight to the end. The guys I'd killed in my life, some of them had known what was coming and simply quit—but most of them had snarled and lunged and screamed in anger and hatred, and that's what we were doing right now.

The Deep Ones with their zombie legions might manage to wipe out our whole species, but we wouldn't go down without a fight.

"It's light enough now," I said. "Let's see if we can find some kind of armored truck or something—I really don't want to limp on down to the airport on three tires and a rim, a shattered driver's side window and a canvas roof."

"The motor pool's a few hundred meters away," said Willem as he hefted his rifle, peeking through the window at the compound. "I don't see anything out there."

"You hungry?" I asked Tabitha.

"No," she said, her coffee skin pale and wan. "That macaroni we had last night filled me up."

"Jesus," I said, remembering the watery slop we'd eaten. "We get to South America, I'll buy you a burrito."

"Let's go," said Willem, and he opened the door.

I blinked as we walked out into the sunlight. Sensing motion, I whipped my shotgun down and left—but it was only an iguana, spooked by our sudden appearance, and it scurried around the edge of the building before I could get a shot off.

"God, those things are creepy," I said. "And you let them run around all over the fucking island."

"I read something once, a book, that said our instinctive fear and hatred of lizards and snakes stems from some racial memory mammals share," said the priest, "some recollection of a time in which we were locked into a struggle for dominance with the dinosaurs."

"I've got a better idea than that," I said, taking point and starting to walk through the training grounds toward the motor pool.

"Yeah," agreed Willem. "Now that I know the Deep Ones exist, I could come up with a hypothesis that makes a lot more sense…"

"Why'd you become a priest, Father?" asked Tabitha. I'd been wondering the same thing myself.

"What can I say?" he asked, smiling. "The hours suck, the pay's horrible, but the job security is fantastic."

"You really, truly believe in God, man?" I asked. "Even now, with all this shit happening, with the dead coming back to life and monsters crawling out of the ocean to rip us apart? You think God's up there somewhere?"

"God was there during the Holocaust," said Willem quietly as we walked. "He was there despite millions of dying Jews. He was there during the Black Death, when half the world died in agony. He was there when the bombs fell on Japan, and when the World Trade Center collapsed in smoke and flames. And he was there when a young Dutch pilot killed six of his mates in a friendly fire incident in the North Sea."

"Ah," I said, nodding. "Gotcha."

"Father," said Tabitha, stopping. I paused too, turning to look at them. "Will you baptize me?"

He looked at her and smiled. "I will," he said. "But we're in kind of a hurry right now."

"Later, then," she said, I started walking again, turned a corner. Stopped.

"Willem," I said, my voice catching in my throat. "Get the hell up here."

The priest heard the tension in my voice and ran the five paces to my position. He caught up to me, turned—and skidded to a stop as well.

"Tell me," I said. "Tell me you can…"

"I think so," he whispered.

Tabitha had broken into a run as well. When she reached us and looked around the corner she paused in confusion. Slowly, though, she realized what she was looking at.

"It's a Black Hawk," said the priest, stepping forward, his eyes narrowing in concentration. "It looks okay."

"It's probably broken," I said, believing my words even as I felt hope surge up into my heart. "Otherwise, someone would have gotten out on it."

"Unless it's here because someone came *in* on it," argued Willem. "Like I said—Americans use our bases, and that's a Yankee chopper. Maybe when the onslaught happened, some of your boys were closer to us than to whatever carrier they came from—or maybe the carrier was overrun before they could land."

"And maybe this is all a bad dream and I'll wake up back in Cleveland with a hot chick next to me in bed," I said. "But we have to look."

"It's going to work!" said Tabitha. I looked at her and saw her eyes shining. "Maybe there is a God after all..."

"Start thinking that way," I warned her, "and you'll end up eaten."

Maybe it was my gloom-and-doom pronouncement, maybe it was God showing me who was boss, or maybe it was just plain bad luck—but right as I finished speaking a booming howl echoed across the airfield.

And another, from some other direction.

And a chorus of zombie moans.

"Run!" I said, raising my Remington and spinning around wildly, trying to figure out where the sounds were coming from.

Tabitha and Willem didn't waste any time. They flew across the dirt onto the tarmac toward the sleek black helicopter with me following. For a few moments I let myself be deluded into thinking the screams, moans and calls of the Deep Ones were some acoustic anomaly and that we'd have at least a few minutes to check out the chopper before the bad guys showed up...but the first of the dead people appeared from behind the next building over and I knew we were doomed.

Every day the zombies looked worse and worse. I'd seen some stunning decomposition yesterday and had attributed it to Aruba's warmth and the salt air—but these folks were breaking down faster than even heat and abrasion could cause. Maybe it was the sheer impossibility of their undead state that wore them out so fast, or maybe it was a by-product of the magic the Deep Ones and their priests used to reanimate them, but they were getting damned close to being walking skeletons, their flesh dripping gristly from their bones, their hair crisp and brittle in the sun, their clothes flagging in the thin breeze. One zombie neared us, three followed close behind it, a half-dozen shambled around the corner of the next building, and there were nine or ten coming up behind them.

I saw Willem reach the chopper and yank at the big door in back, and Tabitha closed with him and reached up to help—and then a zombie crawling under the carriage popped up like a hideous jack-in-the-box and reached for her.

"Tabitha!" I yelled, swiveling the shotgun toward them, knowing that I couldn't take the shot.

Luckily, she heard me over the cacophony of moans and screams that surrounded her. She whipped down the M16, letting off a burst that whined, screamed and rattled off the tarmac, sending ricochets flying everywhere and sending Willem into apoplectic fits. The zombie exploded as the blast spattered its skull and brainpan. The priest leaped back from the door and shoved the whore's rifle down by its butt. As I closed, I could hear his panicked voice…

"…fuel lines!" he yelled. "If you have to shoot, use controlled bursts!"

"We have to shoot," I panted. "Father, get your ass into this bird and start her up!"

He instantly let go of Tabitha's rifle, returned to the door, flipping up a latch and swinging the panel open. He clambered in, and I turned to the woman as the next batch of deaders closed in.

"Get in there," I said. "We don't have much time."

"I'm out here with you," she said, her breath short and sharp, her cheeks rosy with exertion and terror. "He'll need time to start this thing up."

"Then go around to the other side," I said instantly. "We can hold them off for a while, and hopefully…" but she was already sliding around the tail of the thing, and I let off the first Remington blast of the day, both disturbed at how good the shotgun felt in my hands and dismayed at how many of the zombies were pouring from the compound after us.

I hoped Tabitha had fewer to deal with on her side, or I'd soon feel rotten sharp teeth digging into my Achilles' tendon.

The first attacker's head burst like a piñata, showering brain matter and skull fragments on his comrades, but the other zombies didn't seem to be dismayed, and the rain of slurry just added to their frighteningly disgusting appearances as I jacked in another shell. I moved a little around the front of the chopper, hoping Willem was hauling ass flicking switches and turning knobs. I fired again, taking out two of the nearest deaders in one blast. Maybe their decrepitude was making it easier for me to destroy them, or maybe I'd just gotten lucky, but the pair collapsed ten feet away. A couple of the others stumbled over their fallen comrades and fell to the concrete, temporarily hors de combat—but there were plenty more coming. I kept moving, trying to increase the distance between me and the tide of zombies heading my direction.

From the other side of the Black Hawk I heard the chatter of automatic fire as Tabitha blasted away with the M16, and I hoped her aim was good—the rifle didn't have an unlimited supply of bullets, and she'd have to conserve ammo for a little while or she'd have to reload, and I wasn't a hundred percent certain she'd learned how to do that last night, even though I'd shown her the technique a dozen times.

I fired again, cocking and reloading, another group of zombies staggering under the mist of pellets, two of them falling, another collapsing on a ruined leg, but now another group had caught up to the vanguard. I ducked under the nose of the chopper and swung quickly to my right to blast another deader who'd gotten fairly close. Tabitha was a few feet to my flank, blasting away with the rifle, and in the distance the ocean sparkled with white stars on its deep blue surface.

And then I heard a sweet sound the sound of engines starting up, a whine of turbines turning, and my throat leaped into my mouth with excitement.

"Come back to my side!" I screamed, reversing direction and hoping Tabitha had heard me over the raucous chatter of spitting bullets and the chorus of moans from the dead all around us. "He's doing it…"

I came back out on the door side.

Three of the Deep Ones ambled toward us, only ten feet away, a line of zombies marching before them like the Praetorian Guard.

I howled and blasted, cocking shells up into the chamber as fast as my muscles would work, blowing heads from necks like a kid snapping dandelions. Sooty pellet marks appeared on the fishmen doing no discernible damage, and the bastards threw back their lumpish heads and howled in triumph.

Two zombies marched around the front of the helicopter, propping Tabitha up between them.

The hooker was frantic with fear, but the deaders weren't biting her, weren't trying to tear her limb from limb, and indeed appeared as docile as security guards at a Yanni concert—they simply held her in their arms and looked at me with milky, deflated eyes while the rest of the zombies closed in and…and stopped.

I reached into my bag and grabbed another shell, jacked it into the Remington.

"Yuuu…" came a voice, and I whipped my head around.

The Black Hawk was whining now as its engines engaged further, and its rotors were starting to spin. The door to safety and escape lay six, seven feet from me, but I didn't make a move. Just because the zombies had stopped and were staring at me in serrated ranks as more of their brethren closed in from the surrounding buildings didn't mean that they had to remain that way. I would be grabbed before I made it to the hatch, should they decide to continue their shuffle.

"You…" came the voice again, and it was a deep voice, a stentorian rumble that was never meant to produce English sounds. The ranks of zombies split, the three frog-fish creatures stepped deferentially aside, and a hulking abomination came out of the dawn and strode toward me, its looming bulk monstrous and bowel-loosening.

It stood maybe nine feet tall, and I remembered Willem telling me that the old Deep Ones got big—big and powerful.

This one had to be pretty fucking old.

It wore something on its misshapen, massive head—a tiara of hammered silver with etched patterns on it that made my brain hurt as I looked at them, sketches of strange symbols and stylized figures that danced surreally in my eyes, as though their straight lines were curved and their curved ones straight. The High Priest wore nothing on its body but a belt from which dangled a wicked-looking two-tined blade and a string of dirty gray pearls around its muscular, rippling neck, and it must have massed half a ton easily, all of it slick and scaled and slimy and rock-hard. The sharp teeth in its mouth clashed against each other with gritty, gravelly force as it shoved the unnatural noises of human language from its gullet.

"You fought..." it said. It took another hopping step toward me, the ground shaking as its bulk hit the tarmac, causing small cracks in the black rock.

"You defy..." it said.

"You survived..."

"I'll kill your ugly ass," I said, raising the Remington and aiming it directly at the thing's head, the crown it wore glinting a sick, diseased red as the sun bounced off it.

The Priest stared at me with eyes as big as softballs and just as pale, it took one more crushing step and stopped, threw back its tumorous head and roared with laughter.

Tabitha cringed and wriggled in her captors' grasps. One of the zombies holding her lost a couple of fingers as she writhed, but simply readjusted his grasp and grinned at me with half a face, teeth glinting from beneath ragged, stringy lips.

"The woooman's weapon...might have damaged...me..." it said, wheezing in great, gasping breaths. "Yours can...can...cannot..."

"Let her go," I said.

"You have lost," it said. It was getting better at talking. For a monster that'd lived underwater for God knows how many centuries, it was doing a pretty good job at adjusting to our atmosphere and our lingo. "You have lost, and we will rise."

"Fuck you," I said, knowing that better words have been said in the face of certain death, but satisfied with the emotion behind mine. "You'll get driven back into the sea, you fucking ugly cocksuckers."

"Shoot," urged the behemoth, moving another step toward me, towering over me to the point where the Black Hawk's rotors could almost hit it in the forehead. "If you kill me, the woman will go free and the man in the airship can fly away."

I kept the Remington aimed at the thing's face, and wondered at this showdown. Tabitha and I could have been dead a thousand times over in the last five minutes—the zombies would love to have a quick snack of the hooker's brain, the Deep Ones would probably be very happy about tearing apart the folks who had smashed one of their brothers into a tree with a Jeep, and they would have no problem knocking out the helicopter before Willem managed to get everything in line for takeoff.

But, hell—I'm an Organization guy.

I know all about pride.

When one of the Don's operations goes balls-up, he doesn't shrug and throw another Dean Martin CD into the deck. No, he finds out what went wrong and he spends as much money, manpower and energy as is needed to fix the problem so that it never happens again. If that means that a dozen people have to die, a building or two gets torched and half the police force gets a thousand-dollar bonus in their pay envelopes, so be it.

It's all about saving face.

And we'd done a little damage, our little Aruban gang, since we'd gotten together. We'd cost the priest of the Deep Ones some serious face.

You could think of him as a capo, a godfather. And I knew these guys, knew how important it was to get back any lost respect.

He wanted me to shoot him in the face. I imagined it would be a spectacular sight, that shot ricocheting off the thing's hide, its skull, its eyeballs. And when no damage was done, when the priest smiled that toothy smile again, shaking off the black bits of soot, we would be completely demoralized.

So I nodded, lowered the Remington, and fired a blast into the thing's stomach.

I'd spent hours last night putting together that special shell. A million dollars worth of diamonds, at the very least, had gone onto the heads of the heavy nails I'd found in the armory, connected with steaming silver solder. Each of them was rough, priceless, and harder than any pellet ever fired from a shotgun.

I'd flattened out the points of the nails to make vanes. I'd carefully loaded them into the empty shell, my little ten-thousand dollar flechettes, and packed them perfectly. I'd saved that shell for the one-in-a-million chance that I'd have a shot at the big boss before I died.

The Hail Mary pass landed in my receiver's hands.

The million-to-one-chance turned into my million-dollar money shot.

The Deep One's eyes, round, moonlike and sickeningly pale, bulged out from their sockets as the diamonds smacked into its torso, and maybe half the flechettes bounced off its rhinoceros hide to scream harmlessly, expensively, into the morning air—but maybe half of them burst through the monster's skin.

When they got inside, with the velocity the Remington had given them and the hard work of piercing done, they did a bit of damage...

I couldn't see what was happening inside the monstrosity's body, but I could imagine it. The diamond-tipped darts, once through the formerly-impervious dermis of the demi-god, sought escape and straight lines. But they'd lost a lot of speed and couldn't burst *out* of the creature, so they bounced. And each time they bounced, my little diamond-tipped daggers, they fought paths through soft tissue and vital organs. They slammed against each other as they pinballed around in the High Priest's body, causing more trauma to whatever the creature used for a liver, lungs, kidneys, a heart...but they eventually stopped ricocheting.

By that time, the monster was dead.

I dropped the shotgun and dove for Tabitha, knowing that I was dead, but at least wanting to match Oscar for bravery and manliness in the face of certain destruction, hoping to tear off a head or two before they bit me.

The colossus began to fall as I leaped, and the howls of the other Deep Ones echoed over the macadam. Though the creatures were alien, I still sensed rage and loss in the horrible sounds, but that didn't matter. It wouldn't be the fish monsters that killed me, but the deaders, and though it sounds like a foolish distinction, I was glad to die at the hands of humans, even dead humans, rather than at the fins and claws of hideous freaks from the darkest depths of the cold sea...

I caught Tabitha as the zombies released her, and because I wasn't expecting her to come to me I stumbled and almost fell onto the pavement. But she, bless her athletic little body, managed to compensate for my forward progress and keep us both upright.

"Go!" she said, grabbing my arm and dragging me back to the Black Hawk. "Willem's got it going, now..."

"What?" I stammered, allowing myself to be led, looking around wildly as pandemonium erupted on the Dutch naval base.

"You killed him!" she screamed, exultation and desperation in her voice. "He promised you he'd set me free..."

"Christ!" I screamed back. "He had to have been lying..."

But the zombies were ignoring us now. They were still hungry, still driven by some desperation beyond pure want or need—but the High Priest had been cocky enough, apparently, to give us his solemn word. He'd said that if I killed him he'd let us go.

He just hadn't really expected to be killed.

Or maybe the Hail Mary I'd thrown, that million-dollar money shot, had carried a little of Father Willem's blessing with it.

In any case, the dead humans, those pitiful, skeletal things with nothing left but bones, diseased brains and insatiable appetites, were turning on the Deep Ones.

The fish monsters were too strong to go down immediately, their skin too tough to be broken by zombie bites, but they had to fight to rid themselves of the deaders, and every time they threw one of the corpses off another four jumped on—and eventually, I knew, one of the zombies would hit one of the fish creatures in the eye, or the ear, or some other vulnerable spot in their hides.

I wondered what would happen then?

I shoved Tabitha through the door of the helicopter, feeling the strong wash of the rotors trying to smack me to the ground, but also feeling more powerful than I'd felt in years. I clambered up after her and slammed the door shut.

"Hold on!" yelled Willem from the front of the chopper, and though I knew he meant for me to grab onto one of the straps dangling from the sides of the craft, I chose to grab the woman instead.

And we lifted off.

The sky was blue and beautiful, the sea a gorgeous sparkling amethyst below us. We flew south, and Tabitha kept holding my hand, even after we went up to the cockpit to talk to Willem.

"All your diamonds?" he asked, keeping his attention on the controls and the sea whipping by outside. He was flying the thing, but he wasn't very good at it yet, and he was half-frantic with fear.

"I've got one or two left," I said, not panicked at all. If we crashed, we crashed. It would be a clean way to go, and my conscience was as pure and serene as the sky that surrounded us.

"Enough for a ring?" asked Tabitha.

"Maybe," I said, and then I threw my head back and laughed.

Cthulhu may have been rising in another ocean on the other side of the continent rushing toward us, the Deep Ones and zombies may have been finishing off the remainders of the human race as we made our last, desperate dash for freedom—but for now I was alive and with comrades.

"Too bad you don't marry whores," she said.

"Things change," I said. I kept laughing as the sea shot by beneath us, and pretty soon the other two were laughing with me. The sun kept shining over us and the world spun beneath us, if there were any horses left in the world I was going to fucking find one of them and put my new girlfriend up on his back, and I was going to hop up alongside her and we'd ride to our wedding.

And I knew a guy who'd perform the ceremony.

ONE

RHONDA WHITE HAD NOT been on the third floor of CIA headquarters in well over a year. The last time was when the faxes went down and she had to hand-deliver a document on black market goods. She remembered the offices, with people inside she didn't know. They wore expensive suits and spent a lot of time on the phone, and they all had a particular glare that made her feel she was under suspicion for being alive. Mostly what she remembered, though, was hallway after hallway lined with closed doors, and on each one, a gold placard that may as well have read SOMEONE MORE IMPORTANT THAN YOU WORKS HERE. Even now, as she slid her ID card through the reader next to the elevator, she couldn't begin to guess why she was being asked to come up. Some directors didn't like to discuss secrets over the phones, even within the building. All she knew was that her services were required—which could be bad or good.

Chances were it was either something that needed interpreting, or another rumor about the Castro brothers working with the Iraqis, a rumor that needed to be dispelled. Or maybe some dumb American got himself arrested trying to buy drugs in Havana and needed Uncle Sam to rescue his ass. When were people going to learn that Havana was as deadly as it was exotic, and any sign of disrespect would come back to haunt you? Cuban police got off on messing with Americans—as did many law enforcement agencies around the world these days.

The elevator doors opened and two suited men exited, giving her a nod as they passed by. One of them had a bulge under his jacket where his gun holster was. In the year she'd been working here, she still hadn't gotten used to the sight of so many firearms. Usually, they were carried by men who looked liked they'd just graduated high school; most of the field officers came fresh from the military, which meant they'd had their share of training, she knew, but that didn't make her feel any better about it. She herself did not carry a gun. Never would; it wasn't required for her contribution to the agency. She barely knew how to hold one. There had been no special weapons training classes for her Poli Sci major at Yale… at least not that her advisors had told her about.

She entered the elevator and pressed the button for the third floor, rubbing her hands together as the doors closed. The elevator rose silently, the tiny camera in the upper corner recording her movements. The camera was one of many things she'd had to get used to here. It had been a little weird at first, her every action filed away on a hard drive somewhere, but she understood the necessity of it. There'd been too many leaks over the years not to keep every movement on file. Information was easily bought and sold; everyone had a price, even the men behind the doors with gold placards. Secrets were weapons during times of war, and with the way the world was now, terrorism front page news every night, it seemed America would never know domestic peace and trust like it had before 9-11. As a result, selling classified intel was as much a money maker as selling weapons, drugs or pirated software. Free enterprise, right?

She smoothed her suit jacket, straightened the ID badge pinned to it, pushed her hair out of her eyes and took a breath. Her anxiety rose with the lift. Why? She wasn't sure. But the man who'd rung her desk a minute ago sounded authoritative, his request urgent. For a change, it hadn't been her division director, Dan. No, it was a voice she'd not heard before. Military, she suspected, judging by the formal command—he'd called her Miss; normal bosses didn't say Miss, they said "Hey, you." Or perhaps someone from DOD? Rumor was DOD was hanging around so much these days they were moving into the building. Hell, could just be a new departmental liaison who wanted to say hi— with so many departments here it was hard to keep track of who was who.

Her stomach rumbled. She checked her watch and realized it was getting close to lunchtime. Hopefully this mystery meeting wouldn't last too long. Lunch breaks were becoming a luxury as it was, and she had two reports due by the day's end. Castro's recent sickness had damn near tripled her workload. Sure, the Cuban doctors were still lying at the dictator's request, telling the press that Fidel was going to be in charge for several more years, but Rhonda knew different. Fidel was lying mute in a bed while his brother, Raul, slowly transitioned the country to his own control. His own, ruthless, manipulative control. Things were going to get worse before they got better.

And that meant more long nights ahead.

The elevator doors opened and she stepped out into the hallway. On both sides, closed doors with name placards greeted her. She'd been told to come up to briefing room 323, but she had no clue where it was. She knew she must look out of place standing in the middle of the hall, craning her neck to see which way the numbers went. The hallways here were also lined with cameras, even if you couldn't see them. How long before someone came out and asked her if she was lost? Or demanded to see her ID?

A young page, already going a bit gray with stress, came out of a nearby office. "Excuse me," she said as he drew close. "I'm looking for 323."

The young man didn't miss a beat as he passed by, pointing down toward the far end of the hall without looking her in the eye. More pages came around the corners, each carrying dossiers, manila files, coffee deliveries or some other kind of menial offering to the men and women who sat secretly behind all these closed doors. All of the pages were young, probably still in college. Rhonda had only graduated college two years ago, groomed by a professor who had friends in high places. The pages didn't seem to notice her, as they made their way to the offices around her, closing the doors behind them. The pages served as the delivery system for the exchange of information beyond emails and telephones. Security wasn't even guaranteed in the offices of the nation's secret agent headquarters. Write it on paper, pass it off, shred the paper. Official files? They existed, but whether or not the information they contained was true was anyone's guess.

She found 323 at the end of the hall and rapped on the heavy wood door. The sound of several locks being undone (one or two with whirring servos) only served to heighten her anxiety. Closed doors were one thing, but several locks were another entirely; the directors didn't want these doors opened accidentally. The increased secrecy in a building of secrets again begged the question: why did they need her rudimentary skills? The door opened to reveal a room bathed in shadow—the blinds drawn—and an older man with white hair and black-rimmed glasses looking her over. There was no badge fixed to his dark, pinstriped suit. "Rhonda White?" he asked.

Nothing like being expected, she thought. "That's me."

"Jim Wilkins. Come in. Over here." He closed the door, pressed the keypad (tumblers slid home, locking her in), and directed her to a long dark table. She saw now that the lights in the room were lowered to better illuminate the monitors on the walls. "Have a seat," Wilkins commanded.

She pulled out a chair and sat between two men that she'd never seen before. The younger wore a black suit, though not as nicely tailored as Wilkins', and an ID badge. The elder wore an officer's uniform, no ID badge and a bad toupee. He looked like some kind of higher-level military bigwig. Across from her, her director, Dan Yauch was playing with his pen. The sight of him made her feel a little better and she felt her muscles loosen a bit. Familiar faces tended to do that in these types of situations. He liked her, and she him. He must have recommended her to the men in the room.

Wilkins picked up a remote control from the table and walked over to one of the monitors, which currently was just a blank, blue screen. "Miss White, Mr. Yauch here was telling us you're brighter than a sunspot when it comes to Cuban Intel. Spend a lot of time there, do you?"

The question felt like an accusation and she recognized his voice as the one on the phone. She quickly put together the information coming at her, based on the way Wilkins was running the show and the fact that he hadn't bothered to introduce the other men. He had to be upper level CIA. A commanding presence and a disregard for social protocol always gave away the CIA brass.

"Yes," she answered. "I just got back about two months ago. Is this about Raul's takeover? I'm actually working on a report right now."

"Nah, Raul won't be a problem much longer," the military man said, waving the thought off. Yauch and the other men said nothing.

What did that mean? Was the US going to assassinate Raul? She knew there'd been attempts in the past, but such black ops were rarely discussed openly in front of a lowly analyst. Curiosity tugged at her, but she was fairly confident they would only tell her what they wanted her to know, questions would be futile.

"Let me pull this up," Wilkins said, turning to the monitor. He pressed a button on the remote and a picture appeared on the screen, an angled top-down view of three men in a field. It could be Cuba or anywhere south of the equator. "How many times have you been, all told?"

"I go about every four months," she replied. Across from her, Dan merely nodded, as if to tell her she was doing well so far.

"Then you're aware that Raul is not the only threat to the Cubans right now. Military generals are moving their pawns and rooks up the chess board, so to speak. We're trying our best to keep note of them all. Like fucking cockroaches, these men. Seem to spawn their own little armies overnight."

"I've counted seven noteworthy factions so far," she said.

"You keep good tabs, I see. Just as Director Yauch tells me. Right now though, we're interested in these men here." He pointed to the image.

"I don't recognize this part of Cuba," she said. "Cartel land?"

"No. You don't recognize it because it isn't Cuba. It's Panama."

"Panama? But that's not my area—"

"I know, I know. Let me explain. One of our Recon Sats shot this last week. This man here is Abhur Quayarah. He's Iranian military. Also an arms dealer, a real piece of shit. Had both his wife and daughter killed in an honor killing last year. This other guy here is Manuel Fereza. Chilean. Military as well. He ordered the killings of nearly two thousand refugees a few Christmases ago. Also deals in illegal arms. Both bow to the presidents of their homelands. And both have tried to buy plutonium on the black market in the past year. Thank Christ the Russians have been going nuke crazy over this Chechnya bullshit and buying it all themselves. The goddamn Chechnyans had better back down soon or they're gonna find their asses glowing green with dirty radiation. Then we'll all have a real shitstorm of a conflict to solve. But for now that's none of your business."

"Jim, the point," the military man said.

Wilkins didn't look happy to be reprimanded in front of the others, but he let it go. "You're here because we want to know who this third guy is." He clicked the remote and the picture changed to a close up of a black man in a sun hat. He held a cane topped with what looked like some kind of animal skull, a cat or something. Various feathers and bones dangled from the handle. Around his neck he wore tiny bones, shells, and what were arguably the teeth of a shark. The picture was remarkably clear, but his face was obscured by the hat.

"No idea," she said. "You have a name?"

"We have nothing, Rhonda," said Dan. It was the first time he'd spoken since she arrived. "I went through all of our files and can't find him anywhere. I thought maybe you'd know. I mean, the skull-cap cane and all. Kind of hard to miss."

She shook her head. "Sorry. I haven't seen him before. Are you telling me he's Cuban? How do you know?"

"We don't for sure," Wilkins said. "But we have this." He clicked the remote again and the picture changed to a color shot of a dirty urban alleyway. The black man with the cane was talking to two other men. Behind them an open door revealed what looked like the storeroom of a small arts and crafts shop. There was nothing nefarious about the picture per se, though the men did radiate the type of seediness associated with drug pushers: the slicked back hair, the gold chains, the pinky rings. They were Latino, one about 30 years of age, the other a little younger. They looked familiar, but she couldn't place them. "DEA agents took this in Brooklyn two days ago."

She got the point right away. "So this mystery man, he's in the States."

"Right. Now, these two guys here—" he clicked the remote and the screen closed in on the men's faces—"as I'm sure you know, are Estabán and José Uriquez."

"Of course." Rhonda sat up a bit straighter. She knew of the Uriquez brothers, notorious drug smugglers who had ties to several Cuban drug lords, and to Raul Castro himself. Rumor had it that their father was funding much of Raul's takeover. She relayed this to the Wilkins, who seemed to know it already.

"This alleyway," the man continued, "is behind a store called Regalo del Sol. Sells chotchke swag from Latin America, the Caribbean and Cuba. It's run by a man named Louis Garcia. Also Cuban. In fact, the whole neighborhood is Cuban. Are you putting this together?"

Rhonda nodded. "Our mystery man is meeting with Cuban drug dealers in the States, after meeting with plutonium-hungry terrorist commandos. You want me to do some research, find out who he is?"

Wilkins said nothing, turned his attention to Dan, evidently waiting for him to take over.

Seeing it was his turn to speak, Dan took his glasses off and pinched the bridge of his nose. He looked stressed about what he was going to say. "Rhonda, we need you to do a bit more than that. DEA says this guy is still lurking around Brooklyn. They don't know where he's staying, keep losing him in the maze of low income apartments in the area, but they're confident he's still there. What we need is someone to go in and find out who he is. Someone familiar with Cuban culture. Someone who can pretend to be right off the boat, immerse herself in the neighborhood, get close to this guy and find out why he's meeting with both arms and drug dealers."

"Hold up," she said, putting her hands out in an effort to stop the conversation. "You want me to go undercover? I'm an analyst, not a field agent. No way, send someone else. I'll help whoever you send, but I'm not going anywhere."

"We would if we could," Wilkins said. "But our other Latin-trained field agents are spread thin checking out possible terror camps near Ibagué. Right now, there's no one around who knows the ins and outs of these people like you do. You're the top Cuban analyst at our disposal. All we're asking is a couple of days. Bump around, see what you can find out, then we get you out and get someone else to replace you. But if we don't move now this guy may disappear back into the shadows. You won't be in any danger. Promise. We'll have an agent keeping watch over you, and DEA will be informed of who you are as well. All we want is a name for this guy."

Dan leaned across the table. "Rhonda, it'll be safer than going to Cuba itself."

"Bullshit, Dan. When I go to Cuba I sip Mojitos and buy fabric, read the paper and talk to a poor reporter or two. I don't fraternize with drug lords. Do you have any idea what these guys do to people who cross them. You'll never even find my body it'll be in so many pieces."

"I won't let that happen." This came from the man in the black suit seated next to her. It was the first time he'd spoken.

She turned to him. "And you are?"

"Special Agent Steven Plante."

"No offense, Agent Plante, but you won't need to protect me because I'm not going."

"We need you," Dan said. The look in his eyes made it clear he felt bad asking this of her, was maybe even under pressure to do so. But she didn't care how bad he felt, she wasn't going.

"I'm not trained for this, Dan. You know that."

With a sigh, Wilkins turned off the monitor and sat down at the table. "Listen, Rhonda, Cuba is more volatile now than ever. If this guy is selling arms to the Iranians and Chileans, we need to know about it. But I can't pull my other people out of Columbia just yet, not for a couple more days, and we sure as hell can't send a white person in—they'd stick out like a sore thumb. If this cane-wielding bushman is a Cuban arms dealer, we need someone who will fit in and knows how Cubans operate. Cuba is your specialty, so that means you. All we want is a name. That's it. Agent Plante here will be nearby at all times."

"You think that makes me feel better, that you need a man with a gun to shadow me so I don't end up as pigeon food?"

"You won't get hurt, Rhonda," agent Plante said. "These guys won't suspect a woman to be infiltrating them."

"Infiltrating? Sounds like I should have night vision goggles and an Uzi."

"Look at it this way, Rhonda," Dan said. "You know how this place works. You know how people get ahead, and it's not by riding a desk, no matter what your position. It's by proving yourself. You want to move up, you want a big desk of your own? This type of thing, it'll look real good someday. Trust me."

"It's just a couple of days," said Wilkins. "We've got a room already set up for you. Everything's taken care of. Just give us the word."

Rhonda looked around the room, saw all eyes boring into her. They had each flaunted positions of power and were placing a huge weight on her shoulders. She wondered if she even had the option of saying "no." Her ego allowed her to be a tad flattered that they were asking her to undertake a job this important, but intellectually she knew it was lunacy to even consider it. What if she got in trouble? What if she was found out? She was a thin woman, barely five-foot-seven. All the self-defense classes in the world wouldn't save her from a pissed off drug dealer with a gun.

Still, what Dan had said was basically true: if she ever wanted her name on one of the gold placards that adorned those closed office doors, she had to prove she was worth more than the occasional report on an ailing dictator. She sized up Agent Plante beside her. He was fit, looked like he could handle himself. He was making no effort to conceal the gun under his shoulder.

"Just a couple of days?" she asked tentatively.

"Three… four… at the most," Dan said. "Promise."

With a sigh, she nodded.

TWO

The Leer Jet left Ronald Reagan at six o'clock. Rhonda had been given just enough time to drive home, pack a bag, and return to headquarters where a black sedan whisked her and agent Plante to the airport. Now, twenty-six thousand feet above the earth, she sat in one of two comfortable leather seats that surrounded a small table. Her laptop was sitting on the table, its screen showing an aerial photograph of Cuba. She put her briefcase on the small table next to it and opened it. She felt self-conscious; she'd been on private jets before, but never without a superior sitting next to her. It felt weird to have the whole work area to herself. A flat screen TV on the nearby wall was tuned to CNN, and a wireless modem enabled her to check her emails and surf the web. A small bar at the back offered a number of spirits, from which she'd already prepared herself a rum and Coke. She'd asked Plante if he wanted anything, but he'd respectfully declined.

He sat across the table from her in the other leather seat, reading the day's newspaper. He was pretty quiet, all things considered. Not too hard on the eyes either, even if the "All American" haircut was a little vanilla for her taste. The movies dictated that this was the type of situation where they got into trouble, had an adventure and fell in love, but the wedding ring on his finger said differently. So much for capricious trysts.

From her briefcase, she took out the dossier Dan had given her before leaving. Inside were printouts of the images she'd seen in the briefing room, along with other, similar ones taken from the same satellite but at different angles. Files on two of the men accompanied the photos, each containing additional photos collected over time. All of the materials made her feel like some kind of spy. *Your mission, should you choose to accept it...*

The black man with the cane did not have a file, just the current photos. Her first order of business would be to run through her computer files and see if she could find a photo of him anywhere. Maybe he would pop up next to another known criminal, despite what Dan had said about him not being in the system. She'd been keeping meticulous records of all things related to Cuban politics since college, and her photo archive was extensive. Thankfully, the agency had beefed up the memory on her computer so she could store just about everything she ever deemed useful. All of it was backed up on a hard-drive and several DVDs in Dan's office—and more than likely a bunch of other places she wasn't privy to.

"Sonofa..." Plante said, shuffling the paper.

"What?"

"Hmm? Oh, sorry, nothing. The Red Sox lost."

"You're a Boston fan?"

"Born and raised. You?"

"Pittsburg by way of Miami."

"Miami? That why you got into Cuban studies, Poli Sci, all that?"

She chuckled. Everybody always thought that. She should know better than to bring it up at this point. "No, actually, my interest in Poli Sci stemmed from my fascination with the civil war. Dad was a Lee fan. I had a boyfriend in high school who was Cuban though, and I spent a lot of time at his house, learning a lot about his culture, listening to his grandmother talk about her life in a small village. When I got to Yale, some students were organizing a photo trip to Las Turas. I overheard them in the dining hall one day, and my big mouth interjected to correct them on something or other. After that, they started probing me. I realized I knew more than I thought I did, and pretty soon I found myself going with them, all expenses paid, as some kind of guide."

"All expenses paid?"

"Some rich kids go to Yale."

"Spoiled brats, you mean."

"So I'm a brat?"

"Dunno, are you rich?"

"Hardly."

"Then there you go." He smiled.

From the pile of photos, she plucked one of the Mystery Man and placed it on top. "Anyway, I found myself with a renewed interest in the culture. Fascinating people. Like this guy," she held up the photo. "The skull on the cane, the feathers and shells and shark teeth. You know what Santería is?"

"Some crackpot religion."

It was a typical response from someone raised under a mainstream religion. "It's not as crackpot as you think. The American press harps on the weird parts of it, like animal sacrifice, but it's really a beautifully spiritual way of life, full of angels and spirit guides and a very rich folklore. Some of its roots are based in Catholicism, you know?"

"Not real Catholicism."

"Yes, real Catholicism. The West African slaves who were taken from their homes and shipped into areas of the Caribbean were forced to convert to Catholicism. But they retained much of their original beliefs in deities and spirit guides, and so over time the two religions mixed."

"It's for weirdos."

"It's not any weirder than Christianity. You ever think about some of the stories the Bible tries to pass off as real? Walking on water, turning water into wine, rising from the dead."

"You an atheist?"

His tone didn't sound negative, but she remained quiet nonetheless. People tended to get heated up over religion.

"I don't care," he said, sensing her hesitation. "Just curious."

Against her better judgment, she decided to risk it. "I would say I'm an agnostic. My parents spent their Sundays watching football, not praying to God. Which is probably why I find religion fascinating. I'm not swayed by any one practice. I just like the folklore, the characters. So many stories and theories and unexplained mysteries. Who knows, maybe the things in the Bible really did happen. Maybe spirit guides do protect us if we wear shells around our necks. It's only crackpot if you don't open yourself to possibilities."

"Still sounds atheist to me."

"Atheistic."

"Correcting my English now?"

"Sorry. Habit. I write all day long." Nice move, she thought. A tryst was out of the question but you could have at least been friendly. Now he thinks you're an arrogant bitch. "What were we saying?"

"Religion. I'm Episcopalian, and crackpot or not, no matter how much I pray to God the Red Sox are not going to make the playoffs with this kind of record."

At this point the pilot came on the PA and announced they'd be landing at JFK in a half hour. In a normal plane that would mean putting the laptop away, but here the announcement was just a matter of policy.

With their talk interrupted, Agent Plante went back to reading the scores. Rhonda returned to flipping through her computer's photo archive. Any person or persons she knew had already been flagged and labeled. Her file on Castro and his aides was enough to take up most people's hard-drives. Each photo contained a caption with names, dates, and locations. Sometimes an explanation of the circumstance was included, which was the case with the one she had just opened up. The photo showed one of the Uriquez brothers having a beer with a Slavic man wearing an eyepatch. The caption read: "ESTABAN AND NICO KITOWICZ, PLANNING POSSIBLE HEROIN RUN TO CANADA."

For the next fifteen minutes she flipped through photos of the Uriquezes, but the mystery man was never with them. If he was selling arms to the Iranians or Chileans—or anyone for that matter—she should know who he was. Hell, she had pictures of the guy who cleaned Raul Castro's bathroom for Heaven's sake.

Vexed, she stared at the close-ups of the mystery man. He was very dark skinned, the kind of deep African skin that seemed to contain shades of blue. The sun hat protected his face in many of the photos, so she was forced to piece his features together from different angles. All she could make out were sunglasses and teeth that could stand the attention of a dentist. There was a mark on his right cheek, a scar of some sort, perhaps a run in with a knife. Many black market dealers boasted of wounds, badges of honor derived from confrontation with enemy factions. Having the scar meant you lived… and frequently meant the other guy did not.

The necklace he wore was surely something related to Cuban Santería practices. She'd seen feathers on believers before, as well as the shells, but never the shark teeth. That alone did not indicate something unusual. It was hard to keep track of all the movements within the religion. More distracting was the cane. Bone white, it looked made of ivory, with subtle carvings running up and down the shaft. The skull on top was small enough for the man's hand to almost cover it completely. The bottom jaw was still attached, and the fangs from both the upper and lower jaws were long and sharp. Something about the sloped forehead looked familiar to her, but she could not place the animal.

Dan should have sent the photo to someone who could identify the species. He probably didn't think it would matter, that it was just some kind of showy artifact. But depending on the type of skull, it could mean any number of things. There was a good chance this man participated in specific rituals which offered prayers to that animal's god. If they could find out what sect of Santería worshiped that particular animal, they could find out where it was practiced, and maybe find someone who knew this man.

Then again, it could just be a showy cane. Ominous for the sake of being ominous. She'd have to ask around when she got a chance, find out if a skull-topped cane served a purpose beyond ambulatory assistance.

For the remainder of the flight, she made notes of anything and everything that seemed important. When they landed, she had several pages of notes saved to her computer.

A car was waiting outside the airport to take them into Brooklyn. It was an old Buick with dents in the doors, most likely done on purpose to look inconspicuous – the tinted windows, on the other hand, might have the opposite effect. It had been a while since Rhonda had been to New York City. Before long, the towering high-rises of Manhattan loomed majestically through the windshield, and with them, the allure of treasures buried in those criss-crossed streets. How she wanted to spend a day shopping in SoHo, and supping at a bistro in The Village, taking in art at the MOMA. Maybe, if she could find the time, she would.

"Back in D.C., who was the man in the army uniform?" she asked. She'd been wondering about this since leaving headquarters.

Plante, who was seated in the front seat with the driver, made no motion to turn and look at her. "You don't want to know," he said.

"Am I allowed to know?"

"Well, I could tell you but I'd have to kill you."

"Hardy har. I'm CIA, too. Guess that means I get to kill you as well."

"Have you killed a man before?"

"Not exactly."

"Wounded?"

"Does throwing a drink in my ex's face count?"

"I dunno. Sounds a little cliché."

She leaned forward and adopted a serious tone. "It was a pot of hot coffee."

Plante paused. The driver looked at him, looked back at the road. Plante cleared his throat. "Yeah, okay, I'll give you that one."

Rhonda cracked a smile. "Thought you would. That's what he got when he thought he could push me around one morning when he was bored."

"Don't tell me you stayed with him."

"For another year. But not like you think. He groveled and kissed my behind. Did whatever I asked. That coffee let him know who was boss."

"And you're still together?"

Why is he asking about my personal life, she wondered. Was the wedding ring just a front? Or was he one of those married men that had some lame zip code rule that he laughed about with his bar buddies. "No," she answered. "He left seven months ago. Men don't like it when you're in positions of power. Or when you're smarter."

The driver looked at Plante again; he was enjoying this.

"Well, point is," Plante continued, "you've never killed a man, and that guy in the military duds... has. Lots."

"Lots? What, like he's Rambo or something?"

"Just... lots. At least that's what I've heard."

"So they didn't tell you who he is either."

Plante laughed, suddenly exposed. "Not a clue."

"And the other man? Jim. What's his deal? He wasn't so quick to offer his position either. Is he your boss?"

"Nope. My Uncle."

"Uncle Jim?"

"His real name's Sam."

"But I thought..." And then she got it. Uncle Sam. Nice. Plante obviously thought he was a comedian. Just like every other man out there. Maybe he'd ask her to pull his finger next.

Outside, the tiny brick homes with tiny lawns began to give way to inner city dwellings. Eventually, the roads wound between car service centers, laundries and bodegas, the signs out front changing from English to any number of foreign languages. The further in they went, the more the people changed as well. Simple white and black gave way to Hispanic, Slavic, African, Asian, and more. A true melting pot.

The car turned off the main road, wove its way deeper into a maze of low income apartment buildings. A grayness bled from their facades, spreading depression through the city like carbon monoxide through a house: odorless, tasteless, invisible but deadly. Whatever dreams the tenants of these buildings had, they were being choked to death. A few more streets and the area grew noticeably less safe, now with gangbangers playing dominos on the apartment stoops and pit bulls tied up to fire hydrants. Trash seemed to accumulate the further they drove into the neighborhoods. Rhonda marveled at the driver's ability to navigate these streets; it was no wonder crime was rampant—there were so many alleys and side streets for bad guys to duck into. It was probably a good thing the windows were tinted, she thought. As it was, the car probably looked like it belonged to a drug dealer and not several upper middle class people in the wrong area. And Hell, might as well just come out and say it—Jim Wilkins had been right, a white person here would attract serious attention.

Despite being black herself, Rhonda definitely felt unsafe in this area. It was the kind of neighborhood people called "hard." To live here gave one "street cred," a way to get something from nothing, pride from prejudice. The odds of it ever getting better were slim. It was too hard to get a good paying job, too hard to get ahead in life, but it was easy to get respect. The only problem was respect didn't pay the bills, and too many of these people would gladly trade respect for a livable income, freedom from violence and a playground without used syringes.

The car finally moved through the bad area and into a little nicer part of town. The trash was gone, and the people a little less sketchy. It was still inner city, and the intrusive stares of some of the shadier characters sitting on the stoops told her it was not one hundred percent safe, but it was certainly better. At least here, she felt she could walk down the street during the day and not have to look over her shoulder. Night might be a different story. The car pulled over to the side of the road and parked.

Plante turned around and handed a card to her. "This is a subway pass." He pointed out the window to the stairs leading underground, showing her where to catch a train. "For later. First, get out and go to building 145. Right there." He pointed to the building across the street. "Your apartment is number 14. Here's the key." He handed her a brass key. "And here's the key to get in the front door." He handed her another one.

Stunned, she took them both and held them up. "Wait. You mean I'm staying here? Why not in Manhattan?"

"Don't worry. It's safe. The idea is for you to be close to the area the Uriquez brothers were last seen. That way you can keep tabs on them from home if you need to."

"And what about you?"

"I'm a couple of stops down."

"Why not here?"

"The agency has special safe rooms all over the city, but unfortunately only one here. They do it that way sometimes to make sure vested parties are not clumped together. The next closest room is where I'm staying. It's either that or I sleep on your couch."

"The agency has never heard of a hotel?"

"This is safer."

"Not from where I'm standing."

"Relax. You'll be fine."

Rhonda could feel herself about to lose it. "You keep saying that but what if something goes wrong here? You're not going to be able to protect me."

"Rhonda, seriously, you're just here to gather some info for us. This place is designed to keep you safe. But, if you miraculously get in trouble in the next hour, there's a coffee pot in your apartment."

She sat still for a minute, her insides fuming. Did Dan really think she was going to be okay living on her own in what had to be one of the worst neighborhoods in America? And what was with this Plante guy? He'd reassured her back in D.C. Now, he was coming off as unreliable as she'd first feared.

With a huff, she unlocked the door, told the driver to pop the trunk so she could get her bag. The car waited until she went up the steps to her building and disappeared inside, and then drove off. As the car disappeared into the maze of surrounding streets, she kicked the door. "Assholes."

She took the stairs to number 14, slipped the key in the lock and opened the heavy door (a little too heavy, she thought, like it had a lead core). The apartment was fully furnished; in fact it looked as if someone was already living in it. A good-sized TV in the living room, a comfortable looking recliner and couch nearby, a dinette set with place settings already prepared, a bookshelf on the far wall, stocked with a number of different novels and biographies. She set her bag down and flicked the light on in the kitchen. No cockroaches scurried off, which was a good sign. Out of curiosity she opened the fridge, found it fully stocked with all sorts of foodstuffs. And hey, look at that, peaches. She loved peaches. Which sent a little shiver down her spine—what else did the agency know about her?

She stood still for a few seconds, waiting to hear loud music coming through the walls, screaming from upstairs, gunshots from outside. But there were none. Maybe she could survive here for a few days after all.

THREE

The night passed uneventfully, with the exception of a brief car horn singing the praises of someone who couldn't find their key fast enough. When she got out of bed in the morning, she found a text message waiting for her from Agent Plante. It gave directions to Regalo del Sol (a couple stops back into hell), and Plante's cell phone number. Who knew if it was really his; she was pretty sure she'd entered the level of secret agentness that bore the warning Don't Trust Anyone. The rest of the message suggested she head out there and see what she could discover.

She made herself a cup of coffee and some toast, ate a sliced peach, showered, dressed, and walked to the subway across the street. She took the train out to the dirty neighborhood they'd driven through last night, trying to figure out just what was expected of her. Gather information? Get Mystery Man's name? How was she supposed to do that? The only instruction Plante had given her was not to flash any photos of the men around.

When the train got to her stop, she got off and made her way up the steps into the sunlight. Hordes of people were out on the street now. A few of them leered at her, and she wondered if the knee-high skirt she'd thrown on was too short. A pair of police officers, both Caucasian, were standing on the corner playing with their night sticks. They didn't really seem to notice anyone. They looked bored; they ignored the illegal businesses operating on the block. Clearly their post was designed to "protect" this neighborhood from terrorists, not each other. The irony was staggering.

She made her way past them and followed Plante's directions, turning down two small streets lined with various shops, most of them selling worthless knick knacks, fake designer clothing, and God knew what else in the back rooms. Children, blissfully ignorant, played along the sidewalks while their parents worked inside. A street vendor bared his snaggletooth grin at her, waved her over to purchase some kind of alien meat sandwich that smelled like dog food. The occasional nut-job brushed by her talking to invisible men, or God, or aliens, or the clouds.

With the sun out, she felt a little safer, but the area still had a palpable sense of danger. There were no cops standing near the stores she was passing now, and in the doorways of surrounding buildings the shadows of men reminded her of how easy it would be to disappear before anyone knew she was gone.

Plante's directions had her zigzagging around alleys and tiny concrete parks where bottomless milk crates served as basketball hoops. The buildings grew worse, windows broken, doors off the hinges, paint peeling, bricks missing. While not nearly as bad as the poverty-ridden areas she'd witnessed in Cuba, it was still very disconcerting. That people actually lived in such squalor here in the United States was beyond her. Where was all the tax money going?

A little girl of about ten sat on the curb, her feet in a puddle of car oil, (Where was the car now? Had it been stolen or was she just being paranoid?) looking at pictures in a *Vanity Fair* magazine. It was faded and wrinkled from being wet. Doubtless the girl had plucked it from the trash. No wonder crime was rampant in low-income communities; if you wanted something you had little choice but to just take it.

Regalo del Sol was located on a street that was lined with trash bags, and full of potholes. Murky green water, shimmering with oily rainbows, filled the holes from a recent rain. Men in heavy jackets with football team logos stood about smoking cigarettes, watching her pass. The language they spoke was consistent with inner city slang, so thick she wasn't sure what anyone was talking about.

To her surprise, several of them spoke to her in Spanish. "Hey, baby, you look lost. Want us to take you home?" The accent had hints of Cuban in it. Did they know Mystery Man?

She also wondered how the hell Plante was supposed to help her if they came after her. Even if he had eyes on her somehow, these creeps were only a few feet away, too close to outrun. She decided to play it tough instead, something she'd learned during her trips to Cuba. Without looking, she flipped them the bird, said "Pendejos," and kept moving. Their laughter followed her as she stopped at the next corner and found the shop she was looking for. Steeling herself, she entered it. The small bell wired to the inside of the door announced her arrival.

Regalo de Sol was dark inside, the front drapes closed to lessen the effect of the sunlight on all the dust. Incense burned somewhere behind the counter, suffocating the room with a mixture of spices and woods, strong enough to make an allergy-prone person pass out. The items on the shelves were not unlike the ones sold in the market squares of Havana. Wood carvings, books, some t-shirts, the occasional hand-made toy, figurines of the Virgin Mary and Jesus, paperweights, belts, belt buckles, pens, hats, cigar cutters, lighters, candles, oils, incense, cigarettes, pots, coasters, jewelry made from smooth stones. A sign on the front counter announced that the store did not sell Cuban Cigars. Rhonda was pretty sure that was a lie. Researching how smugglers snuck illegal goods into the country was one of her areas of expertise. They got the stuff in on a daily basis come hell or high water.

Behind the counter, a small, chubby man with coke bottle glasses watched her intently. She smiled at him, gave a little wave, but he did not smile back. The glistening sheen of sweat on his bald pate reflected the dim halogen bulb from above, turning his head five shades of puke yellow. Years of bad acne had left deep pits on his cheeks. Gourds would mistake him for a family member.

Beyond the man, Rhonda could see a small access hallway lined with junk, and at the far end of it a door. Most likely the door to the back alley where the photo of the Uriquezes and Mystery Man had been taken; it was hard to tell because the pane of glass set in the door frame was cracked and frosted. Still, if this was the shop, then it had to be the alley in question; the thought made her heart beat a bit faster. Here was a known hangout of the Uriquez brothers, a hot zone that the DEA deemed significant enough to stakeout. Were they watching now? Had they planted microphones inside somewhere? Where were José and Estabán?

"I help you?" the man asked. His glasses slid down his nose so he pushed them back up again. The sweat on his face seemed to be dripping down his neck now. If Rhonda didn't know better, she'd say he looked real nervous about something.

"Yes," Rhonda replied, sucking in a deep breath. Here we go, she thought, be strong, think about that closed door in D.C. with your name on the gold placard. "I'm looking for some artifacts. Sharks teeth, some shells, for a prayer."

"Prayer? What prayer?"

She quickly wracked her memory for what she knew about Santería and its practices. "To show allegiance to the Orishas."

The man switched to Spanish. "Where are you from that you need such items?"

"Macabi."

"Strange accent for Macabi.

"I moved when I was young."

He looked her up and down, lingered on her bare calves for a minute. "And these items... sounds like Santería."

"Yes, exactly. For prosperity and good fortune. Do you practice it?"

"No Santería here, miss. This is a strict Catholic establishment."

"But you have these vials of ground hog's tooth." From the shelf nearby, she picked up one of the vials, put it back. "You must have something I can use."

"The tooth powder is for headaches. There is nothing else here that can help you. I'm closing early today. Good day."

She was taken aback, but she wasn't about to be bullied. "But, I could have sworn I saw a man here the other day buying these things. Are you sure?"

"Look around you. Do you see this kind of shit in my store. No Santería here. No."

"But the man…"

The shopkeeper ran his arm across his head and wiped the sweat away. His eyes grew larger, and he looked behind him at the door to the alley, then back again. "I don't know who you're talking about. There was no man here. Must be another store. I think you should go."

"No, it was here. He had a cane—"

Before she could finish, the front door swung open, the bell ringing frantically, and Rhonda's jaw dropped. Estabán Uriquez, wearing his dark sunglasses and smoking a thin cheroot, made his way up to the store counter. As he passed, he gave her a look up and down, the kind that said if he had the time he'd show her a thing or two about inhibitions. "Let's talk," he said to the shop owner.

The sweat on the shopkeeper's head became thick enough to swim through. Estabán made his way around the counter, took the man by the shoulder, and led him down the access hallway toward the rear door. He opened it and ushered the shopkeeper out into the alley.

Feigning interest in a hollowed out coconut shell that had been painted to represent a cereal bowl, Rhonda waited until the door was fully closed before inching her way behind the counter. Through the milky pane of glass in the door, she could see their silhouettes, could see Estabán pitch his cheroot to the ground, but she could not make out what they were saying. She needed to get closer.

"I get shot for this I'm gonna kill you, Dan," she said to herself, a joking way of controlling her fear. It didn't help.

The closer she got, the clearer the sounds of an argument became. Bits and pieces in Spanish which she tried to piece together: "Listen , cousin, this asshole has messed with the wrong… has lied to us... sold us powder... haven't seen José in days... using us to hide..."

She was right against the door now, hoping against hope they couldn't see her peering out. The crack in the window pane had split the protective white coating just enough that she was able to peer out and see Estabán and the shopkeeper (his cousin?) talking heatedly and gesticulating wildly. It was hard to tell if they were angry, or frightened, or both. Anxious was the best way to describe their attitudes, she finally decided.

And then the small shopkeeper gasped and pointed down the alley. Estabán turned (she lost sight of his face for a minute as the crack only allowed so much of a view) and they both looked down the alley together. The Shopkeeper made the sign of the cross over his chest, said, "A dios mio!" Estabán nodded a bit as if to acknowledge some moment of truth he was about to face.

"Hola, amigo," Estabán said. "I was not expecting you yet."

From somewhere close by came shuffling footsteps and a new voice, low and gravely, the kind of voice that came with health warnings. "And yet you speak of me so freely, Mr. Uriquez. Do you not think I can hear it when my name is spoken?"

Was a name spoken, Rhonda wondered. Had she missed it? Whoever was speaking was standing just far enough back that he couldn't be seen through the crack.

"Fine. Let's talk. Your sample," said Estabán, "was not in good faith. It did not work. I think it was fake. Can you explain this?"

"Nothing is fake if you know how to sway the loa," the new voice rumbled. "You have met my friends, yes?"

And then there were more footsteps, pairs of them, accompanied by low moans. The shopkeeper yelped, turned and ran, much faster than a man of his girth should be able to. Rhonda plastered herself against the wall next to the door, assuming the little bald man would run indoors, but he did not. He simply tore off down the alley somewhere. Poof. Gone.

The footsteps grew closer, moving a bit slower, scraping the ground as they came. The moaning stopped, became more of a heavy breathing. Relying on auditory senses was not painting a clear enough picture for Rhonda— she needed to see what was going on. Was this the man with the cane? Was he with the other two men from the photo? She was clearly witnessing a criminal liaison of some sort. Her first thought was that they were using drugs to fund weapons buys, but her second thought was more along the lines of: you need to get the hell out of here right now before you become tomorrow's trash.

She chanced another peek out of the door window's crack and froze at what she saw. Estabán's hard face went slack, he took a step back. A pair of arms, black but yet not black, more of a dark gray, reached out and yanked Estabán out of Rhonda's field of view. The gravelly voice spoke with pleasure, a hint of chuckle following the words. "I will show you how the powder works, mon frer. I will show you the loa you scoff at. Bondye at his fiercest." Then, clearly a command to whatever men were with him: "Hold him still."

Estabán struggled, the gray arms gripping his shirt tightly. He flailed with all of his might, and briefly, his face came into view through the crack. His eyes were slick with terror, and spittle dribbled down his chin as he fought with those who held him. Grunts and heaving breaths escaped him as he fought to break free. "May God curse you!" he shouted, the voice of a man thinking, knowing, he is about to meet his end.

Finally, with a triumphant pull, Estabán freed himself from the iron grip and raced off down the alley.

"Get him!" the gravelly voice shouted. The sound of footsteps followed, moving fast. Not far away, Rhonda heard bodies collide and a struggle ensue.

A shadow framed itself in the door, as though it were looking through the frosted glass at her. Could it see her through the crack? Ice formed in her veins, her stomach pulled tight, realizing the shadow belonged to the gravelly-voiced man. Instead of entering, he turned and made his way toward the struggle. "Bring him in here." He had moved from the door to the other side of the alley, out of her field of vision. There was the sound of a door opening, and then silence.

Taking out her cellphone, Rhonda dialed Plante. The phone rang but there was no answer. "Shit! C'mon, pick up already." She dialed again and got the same response. Furious, she left a message telling him to get him or his men or whoever over to the alley behind the shop, that she was pretty sure Estabán Uriquez was about to be hurt.

With that done, she leaned against the wall for a moment, wondering what the hell she should do, wondering how much those gold door placards were really worth. And where the hell had the shop-keeper taken off to? Was he getting help? Was he hiding under a dumpster somewhere?

Okay, one quick look, she told herself. Just to see who the men were. If it was them, she'd tell Dan and get the hell back to DC, let someone else come in and deal with it. After all, for as hard as it was supposed to be to find this guy, he'd shown up pretty quickly. There was hardly a need for her to be here.

Slowly, she opened the door, just a crack, just enough to peek out and see that the alley was empty. Trash littered the ground, some cardboard boxes stacked here and there, a broken palette leaning against the building's side. Scuff marks in the debris were evidence of the struggle, but she could see no men. Across the way and a little to her right a door was standing slightly ajar. The window next to it had been boarded up, and someone had spray painted on it. It must be a back entrance to the building next door, she thought. They had to be in there.

Stepping cautiously, she made her way across the dirty alley, slinked up next to the boarded-up window. From inside she could here muffled voices; one sounded like a man trying to scream with something over his mouth. The gravelly voice was speaking, but she could not make out the words. The voice grew angrier, transitioned into a strange mixture of singing and talking, chanting, like a priest at church. Somewhere beneath it, moaning and grunting.

There was a short squeal, followed by a gurgle. The door flew open and rebounded against the building's back wall with a clang. Estabán Uriquez stumbled out, his hands wrapped around his own neck. Blood pumped out between his fingers with the force of a geyser, cascading down his arms and collecting on the floor of the alley.

Rhonda stifled a scream, palming her hand over her mouth. It was impossible to look away.

"Go out and get him," came the gravelly voice. Shuffling footsteps grew louder as they got closer to the back door.

They'll see me, Rhonda thought. They'll kill me, too. There was no time to curse Dan or agent Plante or reflect on her life or any such thought processes. There was only time to think that maybe she could get back across the alley and in through the back door of Regalo del Sol before the men came out. The footsteps were frighteningly loud, so close to the door, bringing the moaning toward her.

Knowing she was dead if she didn't try, Rhonda pushed off the wall and bolted across the alley. Estabán saw her, surprised at the sudden sight of a woman, and reached out to her. She skirted him like a wide receiver heading for the inzone, saw the deep gash running across his neck, and knew that he was only moments from death. She reached the door of the Cuban goods store and tore it open, threw herself inside, and shut it tight. She barely paused to slide the deadbolt before she turned make her way to the front door. But she stopped. She had to know. Had to see whose voice she heard. Just a quick peek. Sweating, she turned and looked through the small crack once again.

Bang! Estabán's body fell into the door's window pane. As he slid to the ground, he left a dark wetness on the glass. A light moan escaped with his last breath, and then he was silent.

As the fog of shock left her, she noticed the shuffling hadn't stopped and was coming from down the alley toward Estabán and toward her on the other side of the door.

"Pick him up, quickly," said the gravelly voice once again, from just outside the door. Through the crack, she saw a torso in a dirty blue button down shirt, a pair of gray arms, rife with welts and sores, reach down and grab hold of Estabán's body. "Take him back and wait for me."

In response, someone groaned, started to drag the corpse through the trash to the far end of the alley.

A shadow grew larger at the door, reached out and grabbed the handle. Through the crack, she caught a glimpse of something horrific, something that caused her breath to catch in her throat.

An ivory cane, topped with a skull.

It was him! Mystery Man. Here, outside the door, playing with the knob. He turned it, but the deadbolt held. "Interesting," he said. "To be suddenly locked from de inside. Les Invisibles at work, no?"

Shit, Rhonda thought, they saw me. They're coming in.

The door knob jiggled again, loose in its housing. A shoulder pushed into the door frame, rattling the wall. Whoever was on the other side really wanted to get in. Would they break the glass, she wondered. Would they come around from the front?

Fuck this, she thought, and raced to the front door, her legs shaking uncontrollably. The jingling bell may as well have been a spotlight and siren it made so much noise. As soon as she hit the sidewalk she pressed the talk button on her cell phone to redial Plante. This time, he answered. "Agent Plante."

"Get down here right now! Right fucking now!"

"Rhonda?"

"Now!" With that, she ran back through the maze of streets toward the cops at the subway entrance, stopping only when they made her sit down and explain what was going on. Through her tears and heaving breaths, she hoped to God they understood what she was saying.

Estabán Uriquez had just been murdered before her eyes.

FOUR

Plante arrived about twenty minutes later and accompanied a local squad car to the scene. Rhonda rode silently beside him in the back seat, doing her best not to tear him a new asshole. He kept repeating that he was sorry. Like it would matter now if she'd had her neck slashed. Sorry could not raise the dead, all sorry could do was sweep dirt under a rug for a little while. Apparently he'd been in the bathroom when she'd called and had left his cell phone in his blazer, in another room. Apologize all you want, she thought, you almost let me get killed.

She took out her phone once again and called Dan, told him she was done with this assignment, and his response was typical, having already been briefed by Agent Plante. "We had no idea something like that would happen. You've got to believe me. Were you at least able to get a name or see which way this guy went? Did they say anything important?"

"I don't know. All sound was drowned out by the beating of my own fucking heart as it tried to leap out of my fucking chest. Did you hear what I said? I'm done."

"Now, Rhonda, let's hang on a sec. You weren't hurt, and I doubt these guys even knew you were there. Checking the door doesn't mean anything. Guys like that just like to be thorough. I'm not making excuses for Agent Plante, I'll give him a piece of my mind later, but all told you did a good job. Showed real initiative, the kind of thing that I was telling you this agency takes into consideration."

If that's what they considered initiative, then what did people have to do to become directors, she wondered, cover themselves in honey and fight hungry bears?

"So we know that he's selling them some powder," Dan continued. "Probably cocaine, and it's probably being used to fund weapons deals."

Way to repeat my own intel back to me, she thought.

"What about this backstabbing part?" he asked.

"Don't know," she replied. "Estabán seemed to think this guy screwed him over. And there was some mention about his brother José having gone missing. Like I already said, I couldn't hear all of it. And like I also said, I don't care. I'm coming back to D.C."

"Listen, Rhonda, just—"

"Just what, Dan? I'm an analyst, not James Bond. You want to know who's running pot into Miami, I can tell you. You want me to sneak around in the dark playing with a gun, you can think again."

There was a pause, followed by a long sigh. "Ok, you're right. I'm sorry. We'll get someone else on the case. But I may need you to bring them up to speed with all you know, maybe act as a consultant. Can you do that?"

"No problem."

"Good. Just hang out for a little bit until I can get a jet out to pick you up. Maybe help Plante out. He's a good guy, really. I'm sure he'll apologize profusely. And Rhonda?"

"What?"

"Seriously. Good job."

She hung up, turned away from Plante, who was, Dan would be pleased to know, still apologizing.

The car made it's way into the alley, driving slow to avoid trash-cans and discarded pallets, and stopped near the rear door of Regalo del Sol. Plante told the officers and Rhonda to sit tight, and then exited.

Through the windshield she watched him spin in a circle and then throw his hands in the air as if to ask what he was supposed to be looking for.

"You've got to be kidding me," she said to the officers, knowing they could care less about anything she said. Why wasn't Plante making notes? "What's he doing?" She mumbled and reluctantly exited the car and sidled up to the agent.

"I told you to stay put," he said.

"What's wrong? Why aren't you…"

What she saw made her jaw drop. There was no blood. No sign of a struggle. Nothing. A complete absence of anything that corroborated her story. It made no sense.

"Thought you said he was bleeding all over?" Plante asked.

"He was. Gushing everywhere. I saw the blood hit the ground."

"Nothing here."

She pointed to the ground. "But it was right here. He fell down and they took him away."

"Where's this door they went into?"

"Over here." She led him to the door that Estabán had been dragged through. Together, they went inside, Plante drawing his gun as they stepped past the threshold. Inside was a series of abandoned rooms, metal struts and dry wall revealing the skeleton of the building. It had either been a very cheap apartment or very out-of-the-way office at one point, but now the walls were faded gray, the windows boarded up, dust covered everything like a blanket, and water stains coated the dirty yellow rug under their feet. There was no blood in here either.

"I'm telling you his throat was slashed," Rhonda said. "They must have cleaned it up."

"No way you can clean something like that that quick."

"Maybe there was a tarp."

"Doubt it. Looks like none of the dust has even been disturbed. Look, we're leaving footprints in the rug. Where are theirs?"

I wish I knew, thought Rhonda. How the hell did they get rid of the blood? What kind of professionals are we dealing with here?

Plante walked into the room and made his way to the other side of the building. There was a front door but it was boarded up. He gave it a tug just to make sure it hadn't been disturbed. He came back and walked past her out to the alley again. She followed him, found him looking up and down the alley. As if trying to deduce something, he opened the back door of the Cuban store, went inside the tiny access hallway, and then closed the door.

"I locked that when I left," she said to herself. Had the Mystery Man gone around front and checked the interior of the store after she'd run out, gone out the back door again?

She heard Plante inside shouting hello, looking for the owner, but there was no answer. Evidently the bald shop owner was still running for his life. Through the door she heard his voice. "Rhonda, I can't see you. Move to your left."

She took a couple steps toward the back wall of the alley, realizing that she could not make out his form behind the frosted glass. Thank God, she thought. Maybe they really hadn't seen her. Yet, if Mystery Man had gone inside the shop, what reason could there be other than to come after her? Unless he wanted to find the shop owner, whose whereabouts were evidently still unknown. She heard Plante's voice again. "Hold it! Okay, I can see you. Walk closer."

She followed his command until she was past the door, almost to the police cruiser. The door opened and he came back out. "So line of sight through that crack is mostly in the line you just walked."

"I already know that. Remember, I was there."

"Can't see that other door from inside the shop. The front door in there…" he said, indicating the empty building they'd just come from, "… is boarded up. And the alley dead ends over there. So where'd he come from?"

"What do you mean?"

"Well, if you were there…" he explained, while pointing to the back door of Regalo del Sol "… and you said he came from this direction, a dead end, except for the front door in that abandoned unit, which is boarded up, then how'd he get into the alley?"

The question was logical, but Rhonda suddenly realized she had no logical answer. If he hadn't come from the other door, which was the only other one back here that wasn't boarded up or chained shut, then that meant he'd have had to scale down the far wall of the alley. Which seemed ridiculous when she thought about it.

"I don't know," she finally answered, feeling stupid, which in turn made her feel angry. Who was this prick to question any of her story when he couldn't even stay off the shitter long enough to protect her like he said he would.

"C'mon," he said. "Let's go."

"What do you mean 'let's go'? What about Estabán?"

"He ain't here, Rhonda. There's no sign that anyone was ever here except you."

"Are you saying I'm lying?"

Plante held up his hands to stop her from continuing. "No no no. I'm just saying there's no evidence of anything happening here. There's nothing we can do. I'll have NYPD come in and check it out, dust the doorknobs, and if they find anything, then we'll go from there. For now, let's wait to hear what they say."

Reluctantly, Rhonda nodded. Without some traces of the murder, or the missing shopkeeper's testimony, there was little they could do.

As she made her way back to the police car, it was all she could do not to check herself into the local funny farm. How could there be no signs of what she'd seen? It didn't make sense. She knew what she'd seen. Estabán had been murdered, and her mystery man had done it. Him and his moaning, shuffling henchmen.

FIVE

Dan called as she was watching a show about Bigfoot on the Discovery Channel and said he wasn't going to be able to get a jet to her until four o'clock tomorrow. Something about a crisis at the Canadian border that needed attention. She thanked him, apologized for snapping at him earlier, and went back to the show.

"How do people believe this shit?" she asked. But for some reason, she found herself enamored by it, watching it until the end when she finally shook her head and reprimanded herself for watching such dreck.

Opening her laptop, she browsed through the photos of Mystery Man that Dan had given her earlier. In none of the photos could she see anyone with the man, other than Fereza and Quayarah, of course. No henchmen, though. Yet *someone* had been helping him in the alley, possibly two men by the sound of it. The gray skin of the arm that had dragged Estabán away flashed through her mind again, the fingers spindly and crooked, the flesh bubbling with sores. The way they'd moaned, as if someone had cut their tongues out.

Eventually she slept.

In the morning, she moved through her usual breakfast ritual and found herself sitting in front of the television again, waiting for Dan to call. The phone didn't ring until after the morning talk shows were over, only it wasn't Dan, it was Plante.

"Sleep well?" he asked.

"Yes. Fine."

"Good. I always toss and turn after a day like you had."

So, he believes me, she thought. At least that's something.

"Local PD finally got back to me about an hour ago. They didn't find anything at the scene."

"And Estabán? Have they seen him?"

"No. Same with the guy who runs the store, man named Louis Garcia. They put an APB out for him. You were right, he's related to the Uriquezes. Distant cousin."

"And DEA, did they see anything, get any pictures?"

"Sorry. Turns out they aren't even in the area any more. Nobody told us till now. They've got their hands full with something else."

"What something else?"

"It's classified."

"Don't hold out on me, Plante. You owe me."

"Owe you? I was taking a dump. I said I was sorry."

"Sorry doesn't work with ladies. We either want flowers or classified information, so spill it."

He sighed. "Fine. They're chasing down a lead on José Uriquez. Info is muddled right now."

"They know where he is?"

"Not exactly. Seems one of José's girlfriends here in the city came home and found him lying dead and bloody on her floor."

"His throat cut?"

"Didn't get that much info. But thing is—you're gonna love this—she ran down the hall to call the police. When they arrived, the body was gone. Nothing there. So she changed her story and said maybe he was just sleeping. Either way she moved out and nobody knows where she is either."

"Sounds familiar."

"I guess. These drug guys… sometimes they sample their own stuff, get a nosebleed, pass out. It's typical. So DEA pulled out of the Regalo del Sol stakeout and are trying to find José and/or his chick."

"Jesus."

"Yeah, well, that's the world these guys live in. So Dan called me and said he's flying you out later."

Dan called Plante, she wondered. Why not her? Was he upset with her? "Four o'clock," she explained.

"Safe trip," he said, his way of saying goodbye without getting invested.

But now, hearing about José, she couldn't deny she was curious as to what was going on.

"Plante, you think Bigfoot exists?"

"Yeah, I married her."

"I'm serious. This is all very Unexplained Mysteries. I mean, Estabán was sliced open, so how could there be no blood. This girl says José is dead, but he's gone when the cops show up."

"So?"

"So, drugged out or not, she would have touched him. Dead people are cold, clammy, their eyes are glazed. Only in movies do people confuse unconscious with dead. Dead is pretty obvious."

"I'm lost, what's this have to do with Bigfoot?"

"Unexplainable," she said. "I don't... it's got me curious. This whole disappearance stuff"

"You mean," he replied, "that you want to make sure you're not crazy. Relax, I believe you. The shopkeeper's gone, and you said Estabán mentioned his missing brother. It checks out. So if you say our friend in the sun hat slit his throat, I'm not denying it. But until we figure out what *did* happen, we'll just chalk it up to the fact you were peeking through that crack. It could have skewed your sight."

"Not likely."

"Anyway, I'm gonna head to DEA offices and talk to some people. You hang tight until the plane comes. Like I said—safe trip, okay?""

"Thanks."

Plante hung up. Rhonda dropped her cell phone in her purse and stood still for a moment, just thinking. So much of this didn't make sense, and like the Discovery Channel dreck, she couldn't look away. There had to be something in that alley that gave a clue to what she'd seen. Something to point them in the direction of the Mystery Man. What was it he'd said to Estabán, something about the *lower*? Something about a *bond eye*? What did that mean?

The clock on the wall read a few minutes past ten. Plenty of time to check things out. Just a quick glimpse into the abandoned rooms of the building behind Regalo del Sol. The room where they had slit Estabán's neck.

"Don't even think it, Rhonda," she said. "It isn't worth some stupid gold placard." But she did think it, and she did want that placard. Who wouldn't? And besides, what were the odds lightning would strike twice in the same place?

SIX

Walking through the turns of the alley was a little creepy. It would have been far easier to cut through the store, but the door was locked by order of the police, the shades drawn. Apparently Mr. Garcia had run to the end of the earth and decided to stay. After skirting a good sized mouse, and holding her sleeve over her nose while passing an overturned trashcan, she found herself at the spot where Estabán had reached out for her. The area was quiet, nothing but a lone pigeon in the far corner pecking at a bug of some sort. It ignored her as she drew closer. "Don't suppose you saw where they went," she asked it. It cooed and looked for more food.

Beyond the now familiar door and boarded-up window, she stepped into the abandoned room and found it had not changed since yesterday. Still dirty, still covered in dust, still insignificant. Aside from the fact that a man had lost his life in it.

The thought sent a chill down her spine. Just what did she think she would find here? His ghost? Some specter that would rattle chains and show her what happened twenty-four hours ago?

"This is nuts. Plante's right, there's nothing here." Her watch said it was noon, time to get lunch and put this all behind her. As she turned to leave, her eyes caught something strange on the boards covering the far window. A powder. A white powder.

Drugs?

She took a tissue out of her purse. She knew from her research that cocaine did not have a discernable smell, which was why cops on TV always tasted it. Supposedly it tasted a bit like uncoated aspirin, and the only way to tell if it was actually cocaine was by its effect. Essentially, if it wasn't flour, or baking soda, or Tylenol, it was coke. Then again, it could be PCP, some kind of hallucinatory narcotic. She was not about to try it. It'd be far too easy to get into her bloodstream, and the agency required drug tests. There'd be no way to explain it to Dan. But some mixtures of drugs could be traced to their origin, right? Drug dealers were known for putting some kind of stamp on the product. It couldn't hurt to try.

She scooped a bit of it into the tissue, sending a little cloud of white into the air, and placed it back in her purse. Any doubt that it wasn't drugs was put aside at that point when she became a little lightheaded. *Oh great, is this a contact high? That's all I need!* Panic overtook her as she tried desperately to remember if PCP could be absorbed through the skin. She'd never experienced a contact high before, wasn't sure you could even get one from cocaine or PCP, and prayed the slight dizziness was just lack of air in the room or something; she was trying to be careful here. For a few seconds, all her appendages felt too heavy to move. Then, slowly, the sensation passed.

She secured the clasp on her purse, and then stopped, frozen. Suddenly there was moaning coming from the other room. "Ooooo."

"Oh no," she whispered, her heart racing. Someone was in here with her!

The moaning came again, louder: "OOOOOO." It was followed by shuffling feet, coming her way. Her mouth dry, her neck glistening with sweat, she backed up against the boarded-up window and fought back tears. Coming here was the stupidest decision she'd ever made. What the hell did she think she was trying to prove coming here alone? It had to be one of Mystery Man's thugs, come back to check the scene of the crime same as she was doing.

A shadow passed across the wall opposite her, lingered for a second, and moved on. That's when she realized the moaning wasn't coming from inside the abandoned rooms, but from outside the window, on the street. She turned around, pulled at the boards over the broken window, creating a wide enough gap to see through.

On the street, his skin gray, his hair disheveled, Estabán Uriquez was ambling away like a drunk.

Moaning.

Rhonda raced to the front door, forgetting that it had been boarded up. "Shit." Estabán's moaning was getting farther away. She raced back to the window, pulled the board out again and watched as the man she'd seen murdered yesterday turned the corner at the end of the block and disappeared.

Knowing she was playing with fire, she wasted no time running back out into the alley and heading toward the street. When she got there, she could just about make out Estabán turning onto another street two blocks up, heading north.

Running after him, she took out her cell phone and dialed Plante's number. He picked up and said, "More Bigfoot questions?"

"I've found Estabán."

"What?"

"I'm following Estabán —"

"I thought you said—"

Beep.

She felt her chin hit the call button on the phone and disconnect the call. "Shit!" she screamed, checking the LED to be sure. "Shit shit shit!" Frantically, she hit redial. This time, Plante's phone was busy. He was probably trying to call her back. "Sonofabitch!"

She reached the end of the block, ignored the curious stares from locals. Some of them were pointing toward the subway entrance at the other end, muttering things like, "Did you see that mothafucking guy?"

Odds were they were talking about Estabán, so she hurried down the stairs into the subway station. Beyond the turnstile, she saw Estabán on the platform, swaying ever so lightly. People were backing away from him, keeping their distance like he was a rabid dog.

The headlight of the oncoming train slashed the darkness of the tunnel as it drew close. Rhonda tossed her cellphone in her purse, knowing it wouldn't work underground, and found her fare card. She passed it through the reader and ran to the train as the people were getting on, making it through the doors as they closed.

Estabán was standing at the end of the car, his head hanging down as if he were trying to memorize his shoes. He was still dressed in the clothes he'd had on yesterday, and the front of his shirt was stained with a deep brown.

Blood.

Briefly, he looked up, and Rhonda gasped. His face was ashen (was that traces of coke smeared around his mouth?) his eyes clouded over, like a man suffering from a life-threatening disease. Pustules dotted his face and neck, giant craters of blood and puss that seemed to pulsate as the subway car shook. An evil gash, flaked with dry blood, ran across his neck. The cut was deep, and for a second Rhonda thought she could see his spine. Then he was looking down again, an almost inaudible moan escaping his lips. "oooo."

A fetid homeless man sitting nearby said, "Somebody die in here?" and moved to the other end of the car, starting a process by which anyone who was not recently murdered or covered in their own feces congregated like packed sardines in the car's middle.

Fortunately, the people crowded close around Rhonda, which blocked her view, but allowed her to spy on Estabán without having to worry about whether or not he noticed her. Evidently everyone else thought he was just another homeless man, and as was the norm, decided to ignore him and avoid eye contact.

As the train swayed, so did Estabán, his hair waving before of his downcast face. There was something different about the man, something beyond the blood, pale skin, gaping sores and gigantic knife wound that should not have allowed him to move among the living. He was emotionless, empty, apathetic. Agnostic or not, Rhonda thought he looked like a man who'd had his soul sucked out of him. Yet there he was, standing, moaning, living… if you could call it living.

The train stopped a few times, letting more people on than got off. Each new set of travelers immediately remarked about the smell. Some even took the initiative to make their way to a new car, braving their way past the homeless man; none of them ventured past Estabán.

The train went under the river, making its way into Manhattan. The lights flickered. Those with earphones on simply closed their eyes and moved to their own soundtracks. Others watched the floor or the ceiling. Some held paperbacks, attempting to read under the strobe effect. Rhonda took her cell phone out of her purse and got ready to call Plante again.

It wasn't until they hit the Union Square station that Estabán shuffled forward to the door. In a very uncustomary move, the crowd parted and let him pass. It must be the smell, thought Rhonda. They were not so nice to her, creating a roadblock she broke with her elbows. "Move!" she said.

"Move, yourself," someone replied.

On the platform, she found Estabán climbing the stairs. People stared at him as he made his way to the street, shuffling like he'd lost control of his legs. Some pointed, some gasped, some stopped and stared after him. A few even looked as if they were debating whether or not they should call a paramedic.

Rhonda weaved her way through the crowd on the stairs until she saw the bright afternoon sky open up before her and smelled the harsh concrete of Manhattan. The square was alive with activity: musicians playing guitar, skateboarders flipping ollies, activists handing out flyers, students reading books, tourists taking photos, and a collection of everyone else just sitting on the curbs enjoying the kinetic energy of the city.

Estabán stopped among them. Surrounded.

Rhonda hung back, hit redial on her phone and placed it to her ear.

Suddenly, Estabán exploded, literally. He disappeared in a roaring wave of heat and fire that engulfed everyone around him, sending a collection of New Yorker body parts into the air that rose quickly, stopped and came raining down onto a thousand screaming people.

SEVEN

There was a ringing in Rhonda's head, a high-pitched whine shrieking in her eardrums. The pounding sensation in her skull wasn't helping matters either. She rubbed her hands through her hair, felt wetness, and knew instantly what she was feeling. Tacky blood, mixed with melted skin, forming a kind of gel that shaped her hair in a number of directions. But she found no bump or cut, which meant none of the blood was hers. Thank God. Like everyone else who'd been right outside the blast radius, she'd been pitched backward onto her ass, instinctively covering her head with her arms as the falling body parts smacked down on her.

Sitting up, she saw a smoking crater where Estabán had been standing. The square held silent for a second, everyone dazed or in shock. A scream found its way to the forefront of the scene; it was possible it had always been there, fighting its way passed ruptured eardrums. Soon, panic took over. People sprinted away, cried, or stood still trying to figure out what the hell had happened. There was so much redness everywhere. A man held a small child's pink backpack and roared, "Ally!? Ally!?" Another young man stumbled toward the subway station holding a woman's head—maybe his girlfriend's—in his hands. He didn't make it, he just fell down unconscious at the first step. Around the square, hordes of people, wailing and shaking, looked for their missing limbs. It seemed that everywhere Rhonda looked, she saw body parts. A foot, a hand, a leg, a chunk of torso, a head. A man holding a hand to his ear while a mixture of blood and burnt skin slid down his cheek, screamed in a panic, "It's a bomb! A suicide bomb!"

This made some of the wounded get up and run. Others stood defiant, and a few tried to help whomever they could. No matter what television would have people believe, the cops were on the scene so fast Rhonda was sure they'd simply popped out of thin air. One of them, an older officer who was sweating, yanked her from the ground, asked if she was hurt, and took off running when she explained she was okay. Within minutes every flashing light in the city converged on Union Square.

Rhonda hobbled away, wincing as a dull pain pulsed down her tailbone, and made her way to the next avenue. Those who saw her coming asked if she was okay. By the time she found the bus stop at the next block, the news was already out. Then the questions changed, people wanting to know if it was a terrorist, if she'd seen him. What could she say? Estabán Uriquez was not a terrorist. He was a drug dealer. He lived for money, buying extravagant things and obtaining power. The Uriquezes could give a flying fuck about the governmental policies of America. Still, she had watched him explode with her own two eyes.

At least, she'd seen his body explode. A body that appeared to be… wrong… somehow. The slashed neck, the gray skin, the pustuled faced. He'd looked like a corpse.

The bus took her to the Flatiron building, where she got off and found a small café. The waiters rushed over with towels and water, told her they'd called an ambulance. No matter, she knew it wouldn't come, not with the bloodshed at Union Square needing real attention. She checked her cell phone, saw that Plante had left her a text message: COMING TO GET U. WHERE?

She hit redial once again. "Plante?"

"Jesus Christ, Rhonda. Where the hell are you? They're saying a suicide bomber detonated himself at Union Square."

"I know," she said. "It was Estabán."

Silence. Then, "What?"

"It was Estabán. I followed him to Union Square. As soon as he got outside he… he exploded."

"Wait a minute. Hold on. Estabán? Are you sure?"

"I'm pulling his stomach lining off my head right now. Yeah, I'm pretty sure."

"Why the hell would he do that? It makes no sense. Cuban drug cartel doesn't use suicide bombers."

"Plante, listen, there was something very wrong with Estabán. I watched him on the train. I think he was…"

"What?"

"You're gonna think I'm nuts."

"Try me."

"His neck was still cut. I mean, really cut, back to the spine. No one lives with a wound like that. And he looked like he'd been buried and dug up a thousand times over."

"What are you saying?"

"I'm saying. I think he was… he just wasn't… human."

"Huh?"

"He was alive, but, I don't know how. I'm sorry. I can't explain it. You just have to trust me. Estabán was not Estabán."

"Okay, stay there. I'm coming to get you. They're closing down mass transit for a little while so this might take a bit. Just hang tight. I'll be there soon."

It took over an hour for Plante to get her. He arrived in the same car they had taken from the airport, with the same driver. While she was waiting for Plante, Dan had called to check on her, and to her disbelief, she told him she was staying.

"Why the change?" he asked.

"I don't know. To make sure I'm not crazy. To find out what's going on."

"Plante called and said you saw the whole thing, that it was our friend Estabán."

"You believe me?"

"Don't know what to believe. But if it was, then we could certainly use you there. But if you are staying, you don't go anywhere without Plante. I asked the guys upstairs to send some more help your way. They're redirecting agents already."

"Thanks." She hung up.

Plante had urged to her to go to the hospital, but she waved it off. It wasn't that she was trying to be tough, and her head and tailbone did hurt a bit, but mostly she just wanted to wash off the blood that belonged to all those dead people. It felt oppressive. Besides, she'd seen the carnage, and there were people who needed doctors more than she did. She wasn't going to tie up valuable resources.

Plante's ID got them through the roadblocks NYPD had set up at the bridges, and got her back to his place in Brooklyn. It was his idea, to stay together, and all things considered, she agreed with it.

The shower was good and hot, and it took a while to scrub the red gore from her hair. Twice Plante knocked on the door and asked if she was okay.

"I'm fine," she lied, and then began to cry, watching as the blood spiraled down the drain, a grim reminder of all the life that had been lost just hours ago.

After she dried off and threw on a bathrobe (there were "his" and "hers" bathrobes in the apartment; was there anything the agency didn't think of), she plopped down on the couch. The arresting scent of chocolate wafted out from the kitchen.

"What're you making?" she asked.

Plante stuck his head out. "Hot chocolate and pancakes. I know it's dinner time but I'm not a great cook and this was easy and—"

"No need to explain. I love pancakes."

For the next thirty minutes they ate and watched the Discovery Channel. The program was on animals who hunted with night vision, and how the military was trying to train them to help in covert operations. Even bats get roped into the government's bullshit, she thought.

Plante was feigning interest in the show, occasionally looking at her with what appeared to be genuine concern. He's still apologizing, Rhonda realized, but it wouldn't hurt to accept his hospitality a little longer.

"You cook for your wife?" she asked.

He nodded. "When I'm home."

"What's she do?"

"She's a graphic designer for an ad firm."

"Been married long?"

"Four years. You know what the four year anniversary gift is?"

"Fruit."

He looked impressed. "You are smart."

"Nah, its all Discovery Channel."

"Yeah, well, she took me apple picking in Virginia for our anniversary. She's that kind of girl. Traditional."

"How's she feel about this?" Rhonda pointed to the gun hanging under Plante's shoulder.

"Oh, she doesn't know. I tell her I work for the CIA but she thinks I'm lying."

It was a joke, Rhonda knew, but she wondered how many women really *did* think that line was just a dumb attempt to pick them up. "Am I getting too personal?" she asked. "I have this thing about knowing a person inside and out. Getting close."

"Don't get too close, I told my wife I'd be good."

Rhonda rolled her eyes. "Not like that. Just knowing people in detail. I guess its part of my job. It carries over."

"Once we start powdering our noses together, then I'll say we're getting too close."

The phrase triggered her memory of the tissue in her pocketbook. She slapped her hand to her forehead. "Shit, I almost forgot." She retrieved her purse from the coffee table, opened it up, and handed Plante the wadded up tissue.

"A booger? For me? You shouldn't have."

"It's not a booger. There was this funny white powder in that abandoned building behind Regalo del Sol. I think it's coke or PCP. Maybe we can trace it."

Plante opened the tissue, stared at the white powder. "Trace drugs? Maybe. I'll put a call in. Chances are we have someone here in the city who can check it out."

"I think Estabán had been using it," she said. "When I saw him on the train he had some powdery substance on his face."

Plante simply nodded, took out his cellphone and disappeared into the kitchen. Rhonda had no idea who he was calling, but she questioned why he had to do it away from her. She was part of the agency, too, wrapped up in this as much as he was. Why the secrecy?

After a minute, he came out, said, "Okay, there's a lab here that will look at it. It's PD, but they've done some work for us before. I'm gonna run this over and see if they can rush it for us."

"Was that Dan?"

"No. Someone else."

She cocked an eyebrow. "Uncle Sam?"

"A gentleman never kisses and tells."

"I'll take that as a yes."

"Take it however you want. I should be back in a couple hours." He was halfway out the door when his phone rang again. "Hello. Yeah. No shit." A long pause. "Garcia is still MIA. I'll tell her."

"What was that?" Rhonda asked.

"That was Jim. He was with your boss, Dan. Word just came down that the explosion was a massive pack of C-4. They're still cleaning up the scene, recovering body parts and what not, but they found a hand. They think it came from the bomber. Trace evidence was scorched into it. They ran the prints already."

"Estabán?"

"Estabán."

"My God."

Plante left.

For the next twenty minutes, Rhonda stared out the window at the sky and made mental notes on what she knew. She already knew Estabán was the bomber, there was nothing new there. But she couldn't get the sight of his slit throat out of her mind. Judging from the reaction of everyone who'd passed by Estabán during his death march, they'd seen it too. How could a man walk around with his head nearly severed from his body?

Eventually she turned from the window and called Dan. He had nothing new to report. Like everyone else, he was waiting for NYPD and the FBI to sift through the enormous crime scene that was once simply, Union Square.

"What about Jose?" she asked. Estaban's brother was still missing, still reportedly wounded despite his girlfriend initially reporting him dead. A familiar story now.

"No idea," Dan replied. "DEA doesn't feel the need to share every detail, but they know we're on this as a matter of national security, so I'm hoping they call us if they find out anything."

"Can't you pull some strings?"

"Rhonda, I'm in the analyst business, too. I don't have the authority to call them and demand answers. As soon as I find something out, I'll let you know." He hung up.

The apartment seemed to close in around her, like a booby trap from *Scooby Doo*, so she grabbed her jacket and purse, deciding to get her laptop from the other apartment. Her travel bag and toiletries were there as well, and if she was going to do anything with her hair, she'd need them. Hell, there was no real reason to stay with Plante, anyway, other than to have someone to talk to. Should she just leave him a note saying she'd gone to stay at "her" place? Then again, it was conceivable that Mystery Man was looking for her, if in fact he'd seen or heard her behind the door, so sticking close to Plante (and his gun) might not be a bad idea. Either way, she needed her laptop. She'd decide on the way.

As she got on the train, the sun was beginning to set. There was still a good hour of daylight left, which should be enough time to get there and back (if that's what she decided to do) without having to worry about the animals of the night. The trains were running again, but only so far as the river where they were stopping and coming back. The only way in or out of Manhattan was by taking a bridge, in a car. The controlled traffic allowed the police to perform security checks and hopefully keep any more bombs from crossing the river. No doubt they were profiling anyone of Middle Eastern descent. Had the news of Estabán even gone out to them yet?

On the train, she found a copy of *The New York Post* and looked it over. The big story was something about the mayor making a racist comment. The train was fairly empty, only Rhonda, an old African American woman sitting across from her, and a Latino teen, listening to his iPod, a few seats back.

They were both commonplace, but something about the old woman grabbed Rhonda's attention. She was wearing a necklace of shells, animal teeth and small feathers, almost a spitting image of the one Mystery Man wore around his neck.

Rhonda got up and moved to the seat next to the woman and made uncomfortable eye contact with her. "Hi," she said. "I like your necklace."

The old woman touched the shells. "Oh, thank you, child."

"It's, um, interesting. Where did you get it?"

"I got this here necklace from Louis. He makes them."

"Why shells?"

"To show the loa I support them."

There it was. That word. "The lower?"

"No, child, the loa. The spirits what guide us through these dark tunnels of life."

Rhonda was silent, trying to make sense of the cryptic words.

"Oh, child, I don't mean to scare you. The loa be our guardian angles. Only sometime they lead you astray you don't show reverence. The teeth keep the bad ones at bay."

"So you practice Santería?"

"Santería? Goodness, no, Vodou. I wear these to honor Bondye."

Another word Rhonda had heard. "What's that?"

"Not what, child. Who? Bondye the creator, our guide, our judge."

"I'm sorry, I'm not following."

The old woman laughed. "No matter. Most people don't follow. Most think it all crazy. Vodou, but ain't like the movies, it like they church. It ain't none different. Go to church, sing, rejoice and love the saints. Same as other religions, child. I's raised on it back in Port Au Prince."

"Haiti?"

"Oui, child. Haiti be where I was born. Come to these here states ten years ago."

Before Rhonda could probe further, the woman rose and grabbed the support poles near the door. "My stop, child."

"This Louis, would he sell me one of these necklaces?"

"Louis will sell you air you want to pay him for it. You want his address?"

Rhonda nodded. The train stopped and the doors opened. The old woman took a cautious step onto the subway station platform, turned and pointed into the dark train tunnel. "Two more stops and get out. There be a blind man at the station sucking on a lonely harmonica. You ask him for Louis's address. Tell him Mother sent you."

"Mother?"

"He'll know." The doors closed, and the train was moving again.

Mother had not been lying. When Rhonda got off the train there was a blind man near the stairs playing the harmonica. Wearing thick sunglasses and a corduroy cap, he was part of a three piece ensemble consisting of himself, a guitarist and a man pounding on a pickle jug; they were turning out some kind of painful hybrid Dixieland-blues.

Rhonda noticed he also wore a shark tooth necklace.

At the mention of Mother, the band stopped playing. The blind man broke into a wide grin of jagged teeth when Louis's name came up next. Air sucked through them with a whistle as he gave Rhonda an address: 1345 Lilton Street. "Ask around. You'll find him," he said. He didn't question what she wanted, he simply returned to playing the discordant music that sounded like knives scratching on metal pipes.

Outside, the sun was much lower, the grayness of night hovering close to the ground. The neighborhood was alive with activity, but not the kind that made her feel safe. People sat on stoops, some dressed in gangbanger gear, others, older, dressed in overalls with sun hats on their heads. Was one of them Mystery Man? Perched on a milk crate, an elderly woman with yellowing eyes gnawed on a chicken leg, a plate of bones near her feet. Children ran in the street, their dark African faces covered in crusted food and dirt. Here again, as was becoming a common occurrence, trash seemed to grow from the sidewalks.

Everyone stared as she walked along, the type of baleful gazes that grew more powerful the harder one tired to avoid them. She'd grown up listening to her mother's stories about growing up in the ghetto and knew it had been like this place. You were either part of it or you were an outsider. If you were an outsider, you'd best show some respect.

No surprise—1345 Lilton Street was a dilapidated apartment complex with a small courtyard. Off to the edge of the courtyard a basketball net was leaning sideways over a tiny patch of concrete. The stoop was crammed with teenagers smoking weed. They made no effort to move as she stepped past them. "Louis live here?" she asked, hoping that this particular Louis was notorious enough to not need a last name. One of the kids hooked a thumb over his shoulder, indicating she should go inside. "Dat way. In da back?"

"Yanking it for Bondye," said another, his Haitian accent thick as mud. They all laughed.

She found the front door unlocked and stepped inside. The smell of rot and decay hit her full on. With the exception of a frosted transom over the front door, sunlight did not penetrate the interior. To her left, a staircase rose up into more darkness. To her right, a gaunt black man stood in a deep shadow, watching her.

She gasped.

His yellow eyes blinked, and for a moment he seemed to disappear completely, but they reopened and she found him again.

Show no fear. He just lives here. That's all.

"Louis?" she asked.

Slowly, he pointed up the stairs, receded into the shadow and was gone.

Rhonda's heart beat faster. Her mouth went dry. There were so many shadows around her. How many people were standing in them, watching her? Where had the man gone? Was he moving around her? There's a good chance she would have run out of the building and called this goose chase quits, but right then her cell phone rang. It was Plante.

"Yeah," she said.

"It's me, I'm at a lab in midtown. The powder you found isn't coke."

"What is it?"

There was a long exhalation. "I'll let Dr. Gorman explain it."

A new voice spoke to her. "Miss White, this is Gerry Gorman. I understand you found this powder in the projects in Brooklyn?"

"Yes. It's not drugs?"

"Actually, it is drugs. Just not coke or PCP. It's a mixture of various neurotoxins. I was able to place some of them, in particular traces of teradotoxin."

"What's that?"

"It's poison, from a puffer fish."

Rhonda thought about kids licking frogs and eating fungi to get high; if they were moving on to poisonous fish, they must be getting desperate.

"Miss White, I also found traces of bone dust. Human bone."

"I don't get it. Like someone crushed up human bone and fish and tried to smoke it?"

"Either that or... Miss White, have you ever heard of coupe poudre?"

"No. Should I have?"

"Probably not. I feel stupid even bringing it up. It's really just a myth. A substance reportedly used in Voodoo rituals. I've never seen it, and I don't think anybody outside of small villages in Haiti have. If it even exists. My guess is someone here tried to fashion some for themselves. Probably found a recipe on the internet or something. Maybe to get high, maybe not."

Remnants of the conversation between Estabán and Mystery Man came back to her, something about the powder being fake. Had Mystery Man sold the Uriquezes this coupe poudre to make them sick? To trick them? Why?

"Hang on," Gorman said, "Agent Plante wants to speak to you."

She waited while they exchanged the phone again. "Hello," Plante said.

"I'm here."

"Okay. So, I don't know what to make of this neurotoxin stuff just yet but I'm coming back. Uncle Sam wants me to sit tight until he figures out the next move. Everybody and their grandma is out looking for José Uriquez and our Mystery Man so right now we're kind of like extra cooks in the kitchen. I can swing by the other safe house and get your stuff for you."

Safe house. It sounded weird to Rhonda. She was staying in a safe house and didn't even know it. She couldn't help thinking about who might have stayed there before and why. "No thanks," she replied, "I'm gonna head there myself when I get out of here."

"Huh? Where are you?"

"Not sure. Lilton Street. More projects. My guess is Regalo del Sol isn't too far from here, a stop or two back. Nice neighborhood, if you're a cockroach."

"Jesus, Rhonda, what are you doing? You're supposed to be sitting at my place, waiting for me. The city is on high fucking alert right now. All the cops are preoccupied. If something happens—"

"Relax, I'm fine." But she knew she wasn't; she had no idea where the man in the shadows had gone and night was falling quickly. "I just need to talk to this Louis guy. I think I may be able to find out where we should be looking for Mystery Man."

"Give me the address. I'm coming to get you."

Wanting to avoid an argument, she gave it to him.

"I'll be there in fifteen minutes. Don't move." With that, he hung up.

Rhonda moved toward the stairs, turning back once to make sure those yellow eyes weren't following her. She steeled herself with a deep breath and made her way up.

As she ascended, the stench of rot grew thicker and the darkness grew blacker. Were the lights merely burnt out, or was this the way it always was? You wouldn't know if anyone shared the staircase with you unless you bumped into them. Along the walls, grime formed blackened Rorschachs. One of them suddenly moved, scurrying away at lightening speed, and she had to hold back a scream at the realization that it was a giant bug. Too big to be a cockroach, she thought. But then again, in this place, maybe not.

The sound of a boy singing meandered down the steps, a lazy tune wrapped in a foreign tongue, laden with hints of Spanish and French. Some of it sounded familiar, but not enough to grasp the full translation. It was beautiful, though, no matter what the origin, and it had a gravitational pull that drew Rhonda forward. It was abruptly cut off by an angry adult voice, and the sound of a hand spanking the boy's bottom ended the concert with a startled cry. And this, dear God, was followed by the bleat of a lamb.

Rhonda stopped short at the top of the stairs, thankful for the bit of waning daylight penetrating the dirty window at the end of the hall. Overhead, a tungsten bulb zapped and flickered, giving its last breath to illuminate the floor. All the doors to the units were closed. "No gold placards here," she said. Good old anxiety bringing the jokes out once more.

She took a step down the hall, noting boxes and bags of trash that had been put outside the units awaiting trips to the dumpster. She passed the first apartment; from deep within it, she heard a record player scratching out a low bluegrass tune, and wondered which apartment was Louis'. She made her way to the next unit and stopped short. A small boy was sitting against the wall, half hidden by a broken rocking chair that was slated for the junk heap.

"Hé!" he said, waving her over.

Swallowing her trepidation, she moved closer, knelt down. In his hand he held a small toad. Where'd he caught it was anyone's guess. It hopped back and forth from palm to palm.

"Hi there," Rhonda said. "That your pet?"

The boy scrunched up his eyes, titled his head. He looked like a dog trying to concentrate on a far off sound. Every time the light flickered on Rhonda could see the necklace of tiny feathers he wore. She could also see his swollen lip, glistening with a fresh bead of blood. He'd been hit recently. Maybe the spank she'd heard was not delivered on his bottom. Had he been banished as a means of punishment? What would happen if she was caught talking to him?

"I'm looking for Louis," she explained, keeping her eyes on the doorknob behind the boy.

He repeated the name. "Louis."

"Do you know which one?" She pointed to the doors around her.

"Lá bas," he said. "Houngan. Pourquoi?"

She recognized his accent now as Haitian, but his fat lip was giving him a temporary speech impediment. Sadly, she was not entirely sure what he was saying. It didn't matter, she decided not to go into details, both for her sake and his. "Merci, petit," she said, trying desperately to remember any French she'd learned, which was little. She gave him a pat on his head, causing his quizzical expression to return. Such a cute fellow, she thought. Just how bad would his life turn out growing up here? It'd be a hell of a struggle to get ahead, that was for sure.

As she stood and walked two units down, to the door the boy had indicated, she heard him begin his strange song again. Please don't bring your father out again, she prayed.

She knocked on the door, and watched flakes of paint shake loose, drifting slowly to the floor the way leaves fall from a dying tree. By the time they gathered on the floor, she heard the gruff moans of someone approaching the door on the other side and her anxiety rose another notch. The door opened but snapped tight on its security chain. An aging black man stuck his eye in the crack and looked her up and down. He looked downright pissed off. "Qu'est-ce qui?"

"Um… Anglais?"

"Oui. Yes. What you want? Busy."

"My name is Rhonda. I'm told you provide charms to appease the… loa."

"He looked her up and down again. "You? Loa? No. You lie."

"No, I don't. I want to buy one of your necklaces. Please? I have money."

At this, he laughed, a witch's cackle. "Oui. Yes. For the loa. Twenty dollars."

Twenty dollars! It seemed kind of steep for a necklace made of shells, teeth, and the occasional feather. Maybe she could charge it to the agency.

The old man undid the chain, stepped back, and motioned her inside. He was dressed only in a pair of dirty khaki pants. His nude chest was covered in dark hair and several scratches that ran like worms. Most of the apartment looked like it had lost a battle with a mudslide. Dark brown stains covered the walls, ratty clothes littered the floor, the furniture was all on its last leg.

She followed him into what was arguably the living room.

"Oh my God!" she screamed.

In the middle of the floor, a young lamb lay with its head in a giant wok, its neck slit back to the spine, its tongue hanging loose. Its eyes still fluttered, staring up at her. Had to be the same lamb she'd heard bleating just minutes ago. A fresh kill. Blood spurted from the wound into the wok, collecting in the basin. The man watched her expression and the way she put a hand up to her mouth, and he laughed his witch cackle.

"For Bondye," he said. "Now you see I know you lie."

She turned away, but the gaze of the creature's eyes still seemed to float before her.

"What you really want?" he asked.

"I want… I want to know what it all means? The loa, Bondye, all of it."

"Pourquoi? Why?"

"Because I'm looking for someone. Someone who wears the necklace I described."

"You mean this." Louis stepped over the dying lamb and took a small box off the shelving unit that ran along the wall. Various jars and wooden containers held collections of small bones, rocks, roots, herbs, animal pelts and more. From the box he pulled out one of the necklaces she'd described.

"It protects from bad spirits, right?"

His eyes rolled toward the ceiling, as though he were trying to remember something. He crossed his arms and extended his right hand out a bit, palm face up.

"Hard to say. Maybe your dollars bring back my memory." He let the silence following his words swell.

It took Rhonda a moment to catch on. Great, she thought, I'm gonna have to pay this guy to talk. She reached into her pocket and pulled out a five dollar bill and slapped it into his hand. "So," she said, "does it protect from bad spirits or not?"

"Oui," he answered, quickly slipping the money into the pocket of his khakis. "But then again no. Depends how you use."

"Can it be used for... evil?"

"Ah. Oui. The bokor use for this."

With a tilt of her head, she motioned to the lamb. "Are you... bokor?"

"Me? No." And again he laughed, rubbing his hands up and down his belly.

"Why are you sacrificing the goat?"

"A manje, to keep balance. Such is demand for loa. Or maybe, it dinner." He held up the necklace again, shook it. "Twenty dollar. For you, it good luck. I bless."

From her pocketbook she took out a twenty and handed it to him. In exchange he gave her the necklace, which she wadded up and placed in her purse. "Thank you. Can I ask you another question?"

"Oui."

On the floor, the lamb kicked out and was still again. Rhonda thought she might lose it any second. "I'm looking for a man who walks with a cane. On the cane is a skull of some sort."

"Monkey skull," the man said, nodding.

"Money skull?"

"Oui. To talk to the devil men."

"You know the man I speak of?"

Louis moved around her, lifted up the lamb's head to open the gash wider, allowing more blood to flow. "This lamb know bad men about. Bondye take care of them. The man you seek."

"Who do I seek?"

"Jean Pierre."

And there it was, she thought. Finally, they had a name. Just to be safe and make sure he was talking of the right man, she asked about the powder. "Do you know what he's doing with a white powder?"

Louis stood up in a flash, grabbed her by her arms, and dragged her to the door. She tore at his fingers, but they were curled around her biceps in a death grip. He opened the door and forced her out. "I no speak to Jean," he said. "Get. Go. Now!"

With that he slammed the door in her face. Tears were running down her cheeks, the shock of his grip kept her frozen in the hallway. What the hell had that been about? One second he'd been humoring her, the next his eyes had gone wide with fear. What had she said to set him off?

After what seemed like minutes, but was probably seconds, her feet began to move. The shock was dissipated by the realization that what had just happened didn't matter. She had a name. That was her whole mission here in Brooklyn and she had done it. Dan would be pleased. Maybe that gold placard would be there when she got home after all...

Outside the dirty window at the end of the hall, a sallow moon was just barely able to cast its glow through the grime; night had fallen. She wanted to get the hell out of this neighborhood and back to the safe-house. She composed herself and headed back toward the stairs, noting that the little boy was no longer in the hallway.

When she reached the stairs, she heard footsteps coming her way, from below. Inky shadows blanketed the stairwell, obscuring everything. There was no telling who was coming. Maybe the little boy, maybe the man she'd seen in the foyer. For the first time in her life she wished she had a gun.

With a *bzzz*, the overhead light flickered out and did not come back on. The darkness was so total she could barely see her hand in front of her face. The footsteps clomped up the stairs slowly, getting closer. Clomp... clomp... clomp. Another pair of feet joined in. Maybe two, three people total, making their way toward her at an unnaturally slow pace. Clomp... clomp... clomp. And... breathing. Familiar heavy breathing.

It couldn't be.

There must be another stairway at the other end of the hall, she thought. Another way out. I'll just take that one and hope to God Plante is here.

When she turned, she realized there was nowhere to go. Framed in blackness by the small amount of moonlight that came through the far window, a large silhouette blocked her way.

"Louis." Even as she said it she knew it was not Louis. The squeak in her voice was filled with fear.

"No, my child," the voice said. The gruff, gravelly voice from the alley. The man who'd murdered Estabán.

Mystery Man.

"So dark in here," he said. "How I would love to behold the features what puts forth dis voice of an angel. Allow me…" The silhouette reached up and tapped the tungsten bulb. It flickered to life with a wan coffee stain glow.

Before her, she saw, up close, what Mystery Man looked like. At least six and a half feet tall. His wicker sun hat fell over his head like a giant saucer, his dark sunglasses hid his eyes and parts of his cheekbones, the lenses reflecting back the ghostly image of a woman with a gaping mouth. On either cheek, those long scars were thick enough to grab onto. His dark yellow button down shirt hung loosely around his lanky frame. Necklaces strung with various bones, feathers, runes, teeth and beads jingled around his neck. A collection of ostentatious rings adorned the fingers of his hands. His right hand wrapped around the monkey skull on the ivory cane, as if he were trying to read its thoughts.

An intense negative energy radiated from him. If death had a personal assistant, it would look like him.

Rhonda took a step back, her heart racing.

Behind her, the footsteps on the stairs continued to get closer. She risked a look back, and thought she might lose the last remnants of her sanity. Five or six steps down, the dim bulb barely illuminating their faces, two men—if you could call them that—stared back at her. Their faces, like Estabán's, were cursed with sores. The skin, even in the darkness, looked gray. Their heads lilted side to side as if their necks were made of Play-doh. She could not see their irises, only a thick milky white where they should have been.

"Stay," Jean Pierre said, holding his hand out to the men. They remained still, low moans drifting from their sagging jaws. There was something decidedly inhuman about them.

"Now," Pierre said, dipping his head down to her again, his voice rasping like screws grinding against concrete, "Did I hear someone mention my name?"

"No," Rhonda replied.

He lifted the cane and shook it. Inside the monkey skull, something rattled. "Untruths. For I was called. My name spoken."

"No. It wasn't me. I was just going—"

"And yet you've come all de way here. Why?"

"No reason. Just… lost." The men on the steps moaned again. Her feet wanted to carry her away from them, but Jean Pierre took another step toward her, forcing her to make herself smaller.

He shook the monkey head again, listened to it rattle. "I smell you before. Yes."

"What? No."

"Mademoiselle, I recognize dis scent of fear."

"No, I…" Hurry up, Plante, she prayed. I don't want to die in this crap hole of a project.

Pierre leaned in close to her, sniffed her neck. "Oh yes, I know dis scent."

A banging from one of the far apartments caused Pierre to look away. Rhonda reached into her purse, felt around for something to use as a weapon. Her hand locked on the necklace Louis had sold her.

Pierre now seemed very interested in the sounds coming from the apartment down the hall. He shook the cane again, the contents of the monkey head rattling down the corridor. "Louis," he said. He spun back to his men on the stairs, shouted, "Come."

They stormed up the steps, on the verge of roaring now. Rhonda moved away from them, noticing their faces as they walked into the sallow light. Aside from their stench, which bordered on fetid cheese, what caused her to gag was the decay of their faces. Far worse than what she'd seen on Estabán, with milky cataract eyes, deep blue lips, flaking epidermis, black fungus and deep gashes across their necks.

She couldn't hold back her fear anymore, screaming with all the air in her lungs. The two creatures brushed past her without a second thought, shuffling toward their master. Rhonda was about to run down the stairs and out into the night when Pierre grabbed her by the shoulder.

"A gift," he said, and blew something in her face. A powder, stinging and dry.

She stumbled backward into the nearest wall, tearing at her eyes with her fingernails as the powder erased her vision and sent waves of intense heat through her sinuses. It seemed only a second before her thoughts were shimmering in and out of focus. This was followed by a numbness spreading through her chest. By the time she lost control of her appendages, she was sliding down the wall with tears streaking from her eyes.

Reality folded in on itself.

EIGHT

The world is covered in saran wrap, blurred and full of lens flares. She is not awake, yet she is not asleep. She is somewhere else. In the distance, the sound of Pierre's weathered voice speaks of betrayal and gifts to the gods. At their mention, her view suddenly changes, and she is now lying naked on a dirt floor, encircled by dancing men and women. A pole rises from the earth next to her, adorned with herbs and bones, ascending into an onyx sky where unhappy shapes swim through the clouds like veins of light under the surface of a lake. Drums beat wildly, a pulsing rhythm that manages to spin the world. Around the pole men and women undulate, their ebony bodies slick with sweat, eyes rolling back in their heads. Mist swirls around them, moving as if it has a life of its own, encircling their torsos like vines. Touching them in a way both tender and sinister. She watches the dancers bend low, placing their hands in the mud beside her, crawling on the ground now, growing horns from their heads. Their skin sprouts hair, their pupils grow ovoid and green, tails flip from their bare behinds. Now they are not human, but a hybrid of man and animal, tongues lolling as they salivate. They crawl over each other sniffing, licking, and with a feral cry, begin to copulate. With each pelvic thrust, the mist grows more solid. Phalluses flash in the strobing lights from the sky, pink and slick with joy. The mist takes shape, becomes the form of men and women. Some of the mist people are still, watching. Others are angry, joining in the orgy, making slaves of their partners, tearing their holes wider. Knives are drawn from somewhere and the hybrids bleat as their throats are slit in time with orgasms.

With a fury, the mist people sup on the blood, coating themselves in the viscera of the dead. These are the loa, she knows, though she does not know how she knows this. And yet, they are not the loa. They are something more, something far deadlier. The feasting goes on for what seems like hours, until all parts of the animals are consumed, everything from eyes and tongues to phalluses and hooves. Now full, the spirits hover toward Rhonda, who is unable to move from the earthen floor. Blood from the slaughter runs over her feet, arms, and face, the stench of copper thick in her nostrils.

There is a hand in front of her, coated in blood, nails curled like scythes. It wants something from her but she cannot speak to ask it. Not that it matters; it traces the lines of her body, between her breasts, over her belly, down to the soft flesh between her legs where it grips hard, squeezing. In her mind she is screaming, begging to wake up from this dream that is not a dream. More hands join in, all made of mist and blood, and squeeze all parts of her body. Their nails tear open her flesh and reach inside, rip the entrails from her cavity, toss them aside. With liquid skill, they move into the newly opened spaces inside her. In here, they skin the inner walls of her flesh, tearing her dermis layer by layer. They do not stop until two small points of light float up from her gouged heart.

The loa then leave her body, reach out and take the lights. One for the angry loa. One for the peaceful loa. Their deed done, they float skyward toward the clouds, trailing the lights behind them. How badly Rhonda wants to reach out to them, to take back what was hers. The gros-bon-ange, the ti-bon-ange. Her big and little souls. Gone now. Wrenched away.

Death is imminent now.

But the loa do not make it to the sky. There is something stopping them, something bringing them back to her, faster and faster, like missiles gunning for the earth. The ground ripples as they slam into her body, her souls stabbing back into her heart.

Sensing that her arms are working now, she reaches into her chest cavity and seizes her beating heart. When she pulls her hand away, however, she is not holding her heart.

She is holding a necklace.

If the Big Bang was real, it was now replicating itself within Rhonda's head; the flashes of light and incessant pounding were enough to make her wish for death. Her tongue was cotton, her eyes were crushed glass, her skin itched with the ferocity of fire ants. Every inch of her face was throbbing.

When she reached up to feel her lips, she felt something in her hand. Opening her eyes created a whole new world of hurt as her vision fought to focus on something, anything, that would confirm she still had normal sight. The tungsten bulb glowed above her once again, throwing the same, steady, sallow hue over the hallway as if the walls had coughed up bile.

With a shudder, she bent over and vomited on the floor. Her muscles locked, tears ran down her cheeks, and she was sure she pulled something in her neck. The action left her gasping for breath and crying. After the pancakes were expelled in a mush puddle around her knees, she leaned back against the wall and noticed, finally, what was in her hand.

"Necklace," she said. Louis said it would protect her. From what, she didn't know. With effort, she pulled herself off the floor, saw remnants of a white powder outlining where she'd been. The scene came back to her now—Pierre, saying something about Louis, blowing the powder in her face, her vision wobbling as shadow demons came and danced throughout her mind. And then the blood orgy.

She wiped her arm across her face, saw the powder on her sleeve as well. Was this the same coupe poudre she'd found in the abandoned building where Estabán had been murdered? Had to be. Some kind of neurotoxin, according to Plante's lab friend. From a puffer fish. Didn't sushi chefs serve pufferfish? Something about it inducing coma? So that was it: Pierre had drugged her. But where was he now?

She stood up, the vertebrae in her back cracking like kindling in a fire. The hallway was not as empty as she'd thought; standing in front of Louis' door was the little boy with the toad. He was watching her, half curious, half afraid. "Louis," he said, pointing through Louis's half open door.

Rhonda held the wall as she moved toward the little boy, listening for Pierre and his two… creature's… whereabouts. "The man in the hat," she said. "Where is he?"

"Louis," the boy repeated.

That's right, she thought, he doesn't speak English. What the hell was French for "where's the maniac with the two drugged-out lepers?" The boy stepped aside as she reached the door, indicating with his stricken visage that she needed to look inside. She did, at first unsure of what she was seeing. Horribly, it sank in, and she could make out the way Louis' body had been gutted and hung from the ceiling by a large chain.

With a scream, Rhonda turned and ran for the stairs, descended into the darkness. The bottom floor was pitch black, the sun having gone down long ago. She ran for the front doors but stopped short, backpedaled a couple of feet. Two glowing eyes hovered in the darkness, blocking her path. She curled her fists around the necklace, prepared for a fight, her muscles pulling taut. Not again, she thought. I will not take any more of this. "If you touch me I'll kill you," she said, never more sure of her words than right now. "I swear to God I will."

The eyes stepped out of the darkness, took shape in front of her. "Rhonda?"

It was Plante.

Together, Plante and Rhonda waited for the police to arrive to deal with Louis' body. Rhonda gave a statement, let an EMT check out the rash on her face (he recommended she buy some aloe), and left.

"What the hell are you doing?" Plante asked when they got back to Rhonda's safe house. "You're like a goddamn murder magnet."

"That's not funny. I was checking some things out."

"And what did you find? I hope it's something good. I hope it's worth all the reports I'm going to have to file on this stuff."

"Please," she said sarcastically, "don't talk to me about reports. I write reports all day long while you're out playing cowboy."

"What's that mean?"

"It means… fuck, I don't know. I just got attacked and you're giving me a hard time! Aren't you concerned?"

"Of course I am. If you die I might get fired."

"Forget this." She picked her purse up off the couch and made for the door. Plante stepped in front of her.

"Ok," he said, "sorry. I'm a little frazzled is all. Every time you go out a new problem arises. It's making things a little tough. This was just supposed to be a recon job. Get in, get some info, go back home. Now we've got murders, a suicide bombing, some guy blowing poison powder in people's faces. What's next, a giant gorilla gonna grab you and climb up the Empire State building?"

"I'm not blonde."

"Well thank God for that." He was worked up, his chest heaving. It took a few seconds before he started to calm down.

"Did you get it all out of your system?" she asked.

"Yeah. I'm good. Okay, spill it. What'd you find out?"

"What I found out is that Mystery Man's real name is…" She hesitated, wondering if saying his name would summon him. Still, she knew she had to tell someone. "Jean Pierre."

Plante was speechless, his mouth open and searching for words. He settled for, "Fantastic. We need to run him through the system."

"Just let me get my laptop."

"No prob. We going back to my place?"

"You make it sound like a cheap date."

"Hey, I'm not cheap, I have Bisquick. C'mon, I'll make you some pancakes, replace the one's you lost."

"No deal. The way they tasted coming up—I'm off pancakes for a long time. But if you stop and get me some White Castle, I'll accept your apology."

"White Castle?"

"Yeah, I know they're shit for the system, but I'm upset. You should let an upset women get what she wants."

"Deal."

Rhonda packed up her belongings, shouldered her laptop case, and followed Plante down to the subway.

When they got back to Plante's safehouse, White Castle now jostling in their bellies, Rhonda lay on the couch and began snoring. As much as Plante wanted to use her database to check up on this Pierre guy, he knew she needed the rest.

He placed a call to Uncle Sam instead. "Hello?"

"Plante? That you?"

"Yeah, it's me, Jim. Ever hear of a Jean Pierre?"

"This our guy?"

"Yeah. Ugly fucker in the sun hat. He drugged Rhonda today, mutilated a Cuban man to boot."

"He follow you?"

"No. Ben's outside in the car anyway, keeping watch. He's got surveillance set up pretty tight."

"So… Pierre. We know anything about him?"

"Not yet. Rhonda's got her notebook with her, but she's out cold. I'll give her an hour to nap and then wake her up."

"Pierre," Jim said again, mulling the name over.

"Figured you'd have heard something about the bombing by now. Pierre's name come up?"

"I haven't heard shit for hours. FBI is afraid to get its hand slapped, so right now they're just piecing things together. Won't release info until they're sure it's a fact. But I'll have my Chilean contacts shake things up, see if they can get intel on this Pierre. If he's dealing with Fereza then chances are other Chileans know him as well. I hear anything, I'll let you know."

"Thanks, Jim."

"And Plante?"

"Yeah?"

"You see him, I want him breathing."

"Gotcha." Plante hung up the phone. He looked at his wedding ring, felt a pang of loneliness flutter through his gut. Two weeks, he thought. It had been two weeks since Vanessa left. Couldn't take it anymore, she'd screamed. Was tired of lying in bed wondering where he was, whether or not he was safe. He couldn't blame her; he'd been told early on that marriages in this business had a poor success rate. Desk jockeys, directors—sure, they managed to get by. Even have kids. But field agents, the strain was too much.

She'll call soon, he thought. She has to. It wasn't like she didn't love him anymore; she just wanted him to put down the gun and go sell life insurance or something. They'd work it out. Somehow.

He hoped they would, anyway. Making her pancakes was the best part of his day. This Rhonda woman didn't seem to care about his epicurean delights. Too bad for her. Not that she was a bad person, and hell, she wasn't hard on the eyes, but she was talking about some weird shit lately. What had she seen in that run down apartment building? She really had looked ready to kill someone.

From the couch, the sound of her snoring cut into his thoughts. Maybe I'll give her more than an hour, he thought as he retired to the bedroom. He lay on the bed and turned on the television, keeping the volume low. The news was replaying the scene of the bombing— the screaming people, the carnage. Then an aerial shot filled with nothing but flashing red and blue lights. Five minutes later he was out like a light.

He slept more than an hour, so Rhonda did as well.

NINE

The morning news was completely focused on the bombing investigation, and Rhonda was willing to wager they'd stick with the story for at least another month. These days it was the news' job to milk a story until it yielded nothing but dust. When they got to dust, they spun the story and started over, from a new angle.

On the plus side, the FBI was reporting that this was not a Muslim Jihad-related attack. After 9/11, the last thing the Muslim-American community needed was more scrutiny based on hearsay.

"Sleep well?" Plante asked when he got out of the shower.

"Oh yeah, very comfortable couch."

"My bad. You looked peaceful. I was gonna wake you but I... I guess I fell asleep."

"Figured you'd be up all night making calls."

"I made one. I read once that narcolepsy is a symptom of extreme stress. Maybe that's it."

"I've heard that too. I'm surprised, you don't seem like a guy who get's that stressed."

"I don't. Just my body does. And speaking of calls..." he disappeared into the bedroom. A few seconds later Rhonda heard him on the phone.

She powered up her laptop, waited until it loaded the startup programs, then ran a search for Jean Pierre in the off chance she already had his name in there. It was still running when Plante came out of the bedroom, now dressed in a suit, his shoulder holster invisible under his jacket. "Uncle Sam checked in with the local PD, says nothing new yet."

"You told him about Pierre?"

"Last night. This Pierre either has no record, or it's a fake name."

"What about Louis?"

"What about him?"

"What was all that stuff in his apartment? The dead lamb, the bottles and boxes of bones on his shelves?"

"Shit," he said, "I don't know. You tell me."

The computer beeped. Her search hadn't come up with anything. "There WiFi in here?"

"Far as I know. I'm not really that computer savvy so I just go with what they tell me."

Rhonda clicked on her wireless card icon, searched the room for the wireless connection. The computer found it but it required a password. "It's encrypted," she said. "I don't suppose they told you the password."

"They probably did. But unless they used my birthday, I'm not going to get far by guessing."

"Who knows it? Uncle Sam? Dan? The creepy military guy who's killed 'lots'?"

"Uncle Sam is in a meeting right now. You can try your boss. You never know who knows what with this agency."

It was worth a shot, she thought, but when she dialed Dan a few seconds later, she got his voicemail. She hung up without leaving a message. "Dammit."

"Not in?"

"No. Maybe he's in that meeting with Uncle Sam."

"I doubt that. Not this meeting."

She cocked her head, noting the twinge of arrogance in his voice. "Oh yeah? Why's that?"

"Because Dan is squeamish around blood, and Uncle Sam is... getting information out of some naughty Chilean boys."

"That mean what I think it means?"

"Depends on what you think it means. Want pancakes?"

"No. Enough with the pancakes. And please, don't make me think the man I'm doing this for is out torturing people."

"Torture? No no no. Torture is illegal. He's merely administering some heavy persuasion. And before you get all high and mighty, know that any protestations would fall on deaf ears right now. I'd rather some religious fanatic with an RPG suffer a few broken fingers than the women I love gets blown to bits while she's out grocery shopping. Shit." Plante turned away, went into the kitchen and started banging pots around.

The way he'd mentioned his wife sounded heated, and yet, it was so completely touching it almost made Rhonda want to go to say something reassuring. Something was up, but it wasn't her place to ask, and besides, what would she tell him even if he did offer insight into his private life. Her list of successful relationships wasn't all that impressive; as a matter of fact, he'd have better luck making his marriage a happy one if he steered clear of her advice. One thing was for sure—Rhonda White, Love Doctor was not a gold door placard she would ever see.

She didn't need to think about the intricacies of love, right now, she needed to concentrate on getting online. The words and phrases Louis had used, the way he'd been bleeding that lamb, all of it pointed toward a possible religion, and she had a hunch which one. All she needed was confirmation, and then they could stop searching for Pierre's origins in Cuba, and start looking somewhere else.

She strode to the kitchen, found Plante eating a bowl of cereal. "Call the driver. We need to go into the city and find an Internet café. I have a hunch."

"Yes, ma'am."

The streets of New York were full of the normal hustle and bustle, people racing this way and that, cabs speeding around one another like life was a video game. The energy was kinetic. Who says perpetual motion is unattainable? Maybe it would stop for a beat, like it did when the towers fell, but there was an undercurrent of pride that pulled New Yorkers forward again. This was their city. Tear down all the buildings and blow up all the streets, they would just climb on the rubble and start building it back up, the way ants did. Never stopping. Always moving. It was admirable.

They were almost into Soho when Plante's cell phone rang. He answered it, muttered a few yups and ahas, but it was the "are you fucking serious?" that caught Rhonda's attention. When he hung up, she didn't even have to ask what the call was about. "That was Uncle Sam. You're not gonna believe this."

"What?"

"They found José Uriquez. He was up in Westchester, breaking in through the window of Senator Mills' house with a gun. He tripped a silent alarm."

"They catch him?"

"Catch? Not really. Get this—when the cops showed up, they told him to get on the ground, which he did. But the bastard never got back up. When they yanked him to his feet, his face was blue, eyes glazed over, stank like hell. His throat was cut. The ME say's he's been dead at least a week."

"What? But how? How was he breaking in if he's…"

"I don't know. But they found traces of something on his face."

She knew exactly what he was going to say. "Powder."

He nodded. "And Bingo was his name-o."

"It's Pierre. He's doing it. Somehow."

"Animating the dead? You realize how that makes you sound."

"You didn't see those guys with Pierre. You didn't see Estabán. I know it makes no sense but I know what I saw. And now this… this thing with José. He's up and walking around and the Doc says he's been dead a week! Admit it, something unexplainable is going on here."

"Seems that way."

"If you can believe Jesus rose from the grave, why not this?"

"Because it's nuts."

"Just try. For one second."

"Shit. I dunno. Nothing makes sense right now. Tell me what's this hunch you have? Because right now all I know is we've got two dead drug-dealing brothers walking around with their necks cut, singing zippety Goddamn do dah, when they should be six feet under! What the fuck is going on!" He punched the back of the front passenger seat. The driver flinched, but kept driving as if he hadn't noticed the outburst.

They drove the next couple of blocks in silence, until finally the driver pulled over at a small café and let them out. "Don't go anywhere," Plante told him. "NYPD comes by, have them come in and talk to me."

The café had a minimalist décor: tiny tables, tiny chairs, art deco on the walls, most of it made of cheap plastic that probably sold for far more than it was worth. The owners thought they were creating a unique sense of space, but Rhonda felt like they had simply fallen victim to a bad interior design firm.

She paid the cashier for an hour of online service, fired up her laptop once again and immediately got a signal.

She brought up the Google browser, typed in the letters "LOA". All sorts of pages came up about religion, most notably that of Vodun, which developed much in the same way as Santería in Cuba but was practiced by the inhabitants of Haiti. This made sense, considering the old woman on the train had said she'd grown up in Port Au Prince. Rhonda scanned through a few of the sites, getting a poor man's education on Haiti's social structure and slavery history. Then she came across a site about zombies, about how evil priests, known as the bokor, had been accused of raising the dead to work in the fields. It was superstition, and no site went so far as to claim there was a truth behind it other than to say there were recorded incidents of dead people showing up in town after their burials. But even these incidents were labeled unexplained rather than definitive proof of zombism. Rhonda showed the pages to Plante.

"You ever hear of Voodoo?"

"Like I said about Santería, it's a crackpot religion."

"Some followers of Voodoo believe you can raise the dead with a certain type of ritual. According to this the dead can then be controlled through the use of this coupe poudre."

"Which Dr. Gorman already told us is a bunch of BS."

"But what if the powder Pierre uses is real? What if he's one of these bokor?"

"I don't buy it. I refuse to believe that the Uriquezes were the walking dead. No way. This is nuts. We're missing something, that's all."

"Then explain how I saw Estabán murdered, how I saw him walk onto the train the next day, get off at Union Square, and blow himself up. Explain how José was seen lying dead in his girlfriend's apartment then breaks into a senator's house a week later. This... powder... whatever it is, Pierre knows how to use it. For real."

"It's bullshit."

"Listen, Plante, I had this stuff in my system. When I was under its influence, I saw things that... that were so real and so frightening. I know it sounds dumb, but I think I saw these loa... these spirits that control our fates."

"Don't tell me you're a dead person now, too."

"You don't believe me?"

"Not really. There has to be an explanation. I mean, if he got this stuff into your system, how come you woke up and were fine?"

Instinctively, Rhonda's hand reached inside her purse, took out the necklace Louis had given her. "I think, because I was holding this."

"I hope you didn't pay for that thing. I've seen better crafts made by grade schoolers."

"Fine, scoff at this. But I think we have to consider it. Louis said he blessed it for me. And he said something about bleeding the lamb to keep bad people away."

"It obviously didn't work. Pierre still showed up. See, it's a bunch of hooey."

"You're being obstinate. You were raised Episcopalian, right? It's typical when one is raised under a certain faith to decry other ways of worship. That's part of the religion's job, to declare their way of worship the best way. Some would even call it brainwashing. Remember the Crusades? But understand for just a second that your religion is not the only religion. Maybe there's truth behind these Voodoo rituals... then what?"

"You want me to believe that dead people, zombies, are walking around New York trying to eat people?"

"Not eat people, no. That's just movies. They're motivated by something else. Estabán blew himself up in a public square, José was climbing into a senator's window with a gun."

From the way Plante squinted his eyes, Rhonda could see his gears were turning again. "What? Assassins?"

"Maybe."

"Okay, okay, supposing this shit is true…" He looked toward the ceiling, said, "bear with me a for a second, big guy," and then looked at her once again. "If it's true, then Pierre isn't trying to pass off this powder as drugs to the cartels for money to buy weapons with…"

She nodded. "The powder *is* the weapon."

He paused, then: "Shit."

"Which explains why Estabán was so angry. Pierre sold him the powder, but according to these Web sites, you have to be ordained as an actual Voodoo priest before you can perform the ritual."

"But why sell it in the first place? And why the Uriquezes? Money has to be involved somehow. But for what?"

"DEA."

"Huh?"

"The DEA… they were keeping tabs on the Uriquezes, right?"

"Supposed to be anyway. They're all over the bombing case now, seeing as how Estabán was involved. Which might explain how they didn't know where José was sooner."

"Can you call them?"

"Why?"

"Ask them if Estabán and José had ties with the Chileans or Iranians."

"I don't get it."

"There's nothing to get. Can you just find out?"

"Yeah, yeah. Hang on." Plante made a few phone calls, motioned with his finger that he was on hold a few times, then spoke some more. When he hung up, he was smiling. "You drive a Ferrari?"

"What? No."

"Then they're not paying you enough. You hit it on the head. The Uriquezes had a couple deals go sour with some unknowns from both Chile and Iran, as well as Russia, Australia and some other places in South America, Peru and whatnot. DEA has photos of them meeting with these people, and I'm willing to bet the guys in those photos have ties to Abhur Quayarah and Manuel Fereza."

"The men in the satellite photo."

"Exactly."

"So there is a connection here. Somehow."

Plante put his hand to the back of his neck and massaged it. "Let me try this: The Uriquezes fuck over these military whack jobs, Quayarah and Fereza, sell them crap product or something. So the military can't sell it or use it or whatever they planned to do with it. So they hire Pierre to come to the states and kill the Uriquezes. Payback."

She held up her hand and stopped him. "Close. But not quite. Guys like that wouldn't use a wild card like Pierre, they'd just send in men with guns. I'm thinking Quayarah and Fereza weren't buying drugs from the Uriquezes, but weapons. Estabán and his brother are into more than drugs, as most cartels are. Trust me, I've done plenty of research on them. They'd have guns for sale. But something goes wrong. Maybe a bad deal like you said. The Uriquezes are on their shit list now, but they're small potatoes. What they need is to find another arms supplier. So Quayarah and Fereza hear about this coupe poudre stuff, turn their sights on Pierre—"

"Or maybe Pierre sends out word through the black market announcing his new business."

"Maybe. Either way, they want to see if this coupe poudre is as powerful as it sounds. Think about it—it's the best weapon you could ever have, because how formidable is an army that can't die."

"Pretty fucking formidable."

"Right. But it's not like cocaine, you can't just taste it for purity—"

"Plus you need to be a priest, right?"

"Right. So instead of selling it to them, he shows them how he can make it work for them. Shows them how it's real."

Plante smiled. "He takes out two birds with one stone. He kills the Uriquezes, which puts him in their good graces, and then uses the corpses to carry out terrorist acts to show how powerful it is. That makes Pierre and his powder one hell of a force to be reckoned with."

It was her turn to smile. "And bingo was his name-o"

"This is nuts, you realize that. There's no way anyone will believe this shit. Hell, I don't even believe it."

"Unless we can bring Pierre in alive, prove what he can do."

"Alive is the goal. I'm not so sure letting anyone get their hands on his powder and his magic is such a wise idea."

From the street outside the café, someone screamed.

Gun drawn, Plante raced out the door, Rhonda on his heels. "Stay back," he warned her. The driver side window of the company car had been shattered. Slumped over in the front seat, the driver was bleeding from a large gash in his neck. Plante reached in and checked the man's pulse. "Sorry, Ben," he whispered.

"Dear God," Rhonda said. "Is he…"

"Yeah." Plante scanned the street, looking for the killer. "Anybody see it happen?" he asked the crowd on the sidewalk. A bike messenger spoke up. "Dude, I don't know what the fuck I just saw. Some black dude all cut up and shit just whipped out a machete and offed that guy like it was nothing. He took off that way." He pointed down the block toward Houston Street.

"What do you mean all cut up?" Rhonda asked.

"I mean the guy looked like a turkey ready to be stuffed. His chest and stomach were wide open. I swear there wasn't shit inside. It was just, you know, like, fucking empty. The man should be dead, not waving a machete around."

Plante grabbed Rhonda, started jogging toward Houston. "You don't think…"

"Louis?"

"Shit." He took out his cell phone, made a call as he ran. Behind him, Rhonda was doing her best to keep up. Thank God she'd worn sneakers and jeans this morning. There was no way she'd be doing this in heels.

Gun still out, Plante reached the main thoroughfare of south Manhattan and tried to pick a murderer out of the hordes of people walking on the sidewalks. The way he turned about it was obvious he'd lost the quarry. He spoke into the phone: "It's me, Plante, put me through to the morgue. Yes, the morgue. Now." He waited a moment, then: "You had a body come in last night, Louis something. Black guy, Haitian, split down the middle. Yeah, that's him. His body still there? Yes I'm serious. Just fucking humor me and go check."

Before the person on the other end could reply, Rhonda stuck an arm in front of his face and pointed across the street. "There. That's him."

Plante saw it too, the creature that was once Louis moving quickly up 2nd Ave. Into the phone he said, "Nevermind. I found him. I was you I'd get better locks for your storage units."

Flipping the phone closed, he stepped out into traffic, almost got squashed by a cube truck. Rhonda yanked him back, said, "New Yorkers aren't gonna stop. Wait for the light. I can still see him."

It took a few seconds for the light to change, during which time Plante threatened to shoot it, then the city worker that installed it, then the mayor, anyone who was responsible for him not being able to cross.

Then, together, they raced across the street, cutting wide of the mass of people who were in the crosswalk with them. On the other side, they tore up the sidewalk, weaving in and out of window shoppers, tourists, and the occasional homeless person. "Where'd he go?" Rhonda asked, swiveling her head this way and that.

A scream from the end of the next block caught their attention. Standing in the middle of the street was Louis, a machete in one had and a gun in the other. He was spinning around, waving them above his head. His skin was gray, hanging open around his rib cage like a loose vest. Where it was split down his belly, you could see naught but a hollowed-out maroon interior, glowing slightly pink as the sunlight showed through the skin of his back. Pustules and blisters of various sizes marked his face like craters. The pupils of his eyes had given way to a chalky film, as if someone had jammed eggshells in his sockets. A thin coating of powder flaked from his cheeks. When he saw them looking his way, he roared, a guttural declaration of war that sent people scattering away from him.

"Get down!" Plante shouted to the crowd. People crouched low, trying to hide behind garbage cans and apartment stoops. Taking aim, he squeezed off a shot, hit Louis in the neck. The wound opened like a flower blooming at high speed, but no blood spit out. A normal person would have pitched backward to the ground and died in minutes, but Louis let loose with another roar and took off running to the next block.

"Where's he going?" Rhonda asked.

"Beats me, but he's gonna kill someone. Bet on it."

They ran after the creature, waving for people to get out of their way. Plante shouted that he was the police, which seemed to work when the people saw him carrying the gun. The creature was fast, much more agile than a man of Louis' age should be. Certainly faster than a corpse should be. It was leaping over hydrants, skirting around cars and knocking people over like they were made of straw. Most people gaped after him, stunned, as if trying to find a hidden camera somewhere. A few teenagers even laughed.

A deep burn began to ignite in Rhonda's lungs; she had not run like this in a long time. Riding a desk all day like she did, it was a wonder she was even in the commendable shape that she was in. But this was seriously starting to hurt. She figured she had four, maybe five more blocks in her before she keeled over.

"Louis! Stop!" Plante yelled, but the dead man kept running, roaring every few steps. Police cruisers passed them, lights on, sirens whooping. Word had gotten out, and it couldn't be long before Louis was captured now.

If that happens, Rhonda thought, at least they'll believe our story, send the marines in to find this Pierre guy.

To Rhonda's amazement, the cruisers kept speeding up the street. There was no way Louis could have run that far. Not that quickly. You idiots, she thought, he's back this way.

Confused, she stopped and looked. Louis was nowhere to be found. He was gone. "Where'd he go?"

Plante stopped, turned, bent at the waist and walked back to her. He was trying to catch his breath, between inhalations and exhalations, he sputtered out, "Don't know. He was here a second ago. Look around, he has to be somewhere."

There was a set of bulkhead doors a few feet away, leading down to the underground storage area of a live/work loft building. She bent down and grabbed the ring used as a handle and pulled it up. Two white eyeballs glared back at her, a gaping mouth hissing like a Tasmanian devil. She screamed and let the door slam shut again.

"He's down there," she said, her heart beating so fast it hurt.

"Look out." Anticipating an attack, Plante pointed his gun toward the bulkhead, reached down and threw open the door. It swung up with a clang and remained upright. For a flash, Louis's ruined face snarled up from the shadows before he roared and took off into the dark recesses of the basement.

Without a word, Plante ran down after him.

A shot rang out. Then another. Then Plante's gun came sliding back from the darkness, into the light at the foot of the stairs.

A loud crash punctuated the beginnings of a struggle. Something large and metal bounced on the ground, followed by glass shattering. Storage shelves, Rhonda surmised. There were grunts and the sounds of fists on flesh. Plante howled and cursed in pain. Louis roared in response.

"Rhonda! My gun! Hurry!"

It was hard to move her feet, but Rhonda forced herself down the stairs, ducking her head into the shadows of the basement. How she wished the police would come back. For a second she even considered phoning 911, but knew Plante could be dead by the time she made a connection. She picked up the gun, hefted it in her hand. It was surprisingly heavy for such a small weapon. Could she really pull the trigger? Even if it meant life or death?

Another cry of pain rushed at her from the far side of the basement. It sounded like Plante. Everything was pitch black beyond the triangle of sunlight that extended from the bottom step and disappeared ten feet from her. Moving slowly, she raised the gun in front of her, walked toward the sound of the fight. The darkness closed over her, reducing everything to shades of gray. Shelves, as she'd thought, lined the walls. They were stacked with boxes, plastic storage bins, paint cans, fabrics, plumbing pipes, and bric-a-brac she couldn't identify. The sounds were coming from another room, a room so black she could barely make it out.

"Rhonda!" The call echoed off the cold, cement walls.

Sweat running into her eyes, she eased into the room. Plante's grunting grew immediately louder. So did Louis's roars. She felt along the wall for a switch, flipped it on.

In horror, she plastered herself against the walls as the scene before her came to life. Louis sat on top of Plante, his teeth buried in the agent's neck. Blood was flowing from Plante's carotid artery, forming a lake of crimson on the dirty, cement floor. The creature looked up at her, snarled with blood-stained teeth and said, "Twenty dollars." The voice was barely human, air being forced through pipes that no longer worked properly.

Oh God, she thought, it knows me.

Beneath the creature, Plante tilted his head back and looked at her, reaching out to her. "Shoot it," he said, his voice now a low wheeze. A large hole the size of a fist had been chewed into his neck.

But before she could squeeze the trigger, the creature leapt up and ran to the far wall. It tossed aside a collection of boxes and snatched the machete that had been flung there during the fight. With another leap, it landed back on Plante and swung the machete into the agent's face. It struck home with a *thonk!* It all happened in the blink of an eye. Too fast to follow.

Plante went still, his outstretched arm lowering itself as his life faded out.

The basement was silent for a heartbeat, then broken by the creature's heavy breathing. It stood up, walked over to where its own gun lay on the ground, picked it up and faced her.

Rhonda was barely aware that she was crying, the gun in her hand shaking so badly she was sure she'd drop it. The creature cocked its head and licked its lips. Was it going to bite her or put a bullet in her, she wondered. The gaping wound in its belly drew her sight, a mockery of biology that dared her to explain it to her superiors. There was nothing there, no stomach, no intestines, no lungs, liver, spleen, pancreas or anything that would classify it as human. Aside from a spine stained off white and red, the creature before her should not be alive.

Yet it blinked. It moved its mouth. It twitched its nose. It raised its gun and pointed it at her.

"No!" She fired. Missed.

It fired back, missed as well, the bullet spitting out a chunk of wall near her head.

Heart pounding, she sprinted back toward the bulkhead. Her foot caught on one of the toppled shelves and pitched her onto her stomach, knocking the air out of her. Her purse came undone and the contents spilled into the sunlight at the foot of the stairs. The necklace, wrapped around her compact, came to rest just out of reach. Behind her, she could hear the moaning of Louis' corpse walking her way. Getting closer. Pulling back the hammer on its gun.

"Please God, please God, please God," she crawled on her hands and knees, a pathetic being looking for a miracle. The type of crawling a cat will do after being hit by a car, making its way to the side of the road to die. Painfully. Slowly. Her hand wrapped around the necklace, and this made it all okay for some reason. Now, it can kill me, she thought. I'm just too tired to keep running. I don't care anymore.

Rolling over, she placed the necklace on her chest. The creature stood above her, looking down with dark red teeth. Had it really been eating Plante, she wondered. Or was it just an easy way to kill an adversary? Most wild animals went for the necks of their prey, drained the blood until the prey died, and then dragged it away for

later feeding. What was this thing before her? The undead. Yet…
aware. And remarkably strong.

Was it overtaken by the loa right now? Was a demon living inside it? Or was it truly just flesh overrun with coupe poudre, rendering it immune to the laws of biology?

Did it even matter?

"Just do it," she said.

The creature roared, raised its arms above its head, shook like a child throwing a tantrum. Rhonda saw that it now carried both guns. Then, with a final hiss, it ran up the stairs and out into the daylight.

Twenty-seven shots followed, complete with the terrifying screams of people caught in a crossfire that held no meaning other than to spread fear.

She closed her eyes and prayed.

Hands were grabbing her, pulling her along the ground, rolling her over. Two faces broke into her line of sight. Young men, one blond, one with spiky black hair, both wearing blue jackets with red crosses on the shoulders. One of them placed an oxygen mask over her face, the other tipped her up to get a hand under her back, feeling for wounds.

"Are you hurt?" Spiky asked.

Rhonda shook her head, wondering how long she'd been lying there talking to God. "I'm okay," she finally said.

"I'm gonna help you up. On the count of three," the blond man said. On three, they lifted her into a sitting position, then up onto her feet. Each taking an arm, they walked her up the basement stairs and into the daylight. The street above was a disaster zone. Bodies lay everywhere, some covered with sheets, others covered with EMT jackets because, as was evident, they'd run out of sheets. How many, she wondered. Too many to count. One for every bullet Louis had fired.

"There was a man with a gun," she said as they led her to the curb. Spiky was holding a small oxygen tank, which he set beside her.

"He's dead."

"But how?" Through the mask, her voice sounded like Charlie Brown's teacher.

"Police got him," the blond man said.

"Where is he?"

"Don't know. Think they took his body away already. Must have been wanted because some guys in suits went with them."

Suits? Hadn't Dan said something about more agents coming down? "Did you see it?" she asked.

"The body? No. We were too busy covering... um..." He broke off, realizing his job-like attitude toward the victims could be misconstrued as insensitive. "You're real lucky you didn't get hit. Smart of you to run down there. What happened? You trip over something?"

"No. I..." and then she remembered Plante was still down there in the back room. "My friend is down there. Agent Plante. In the back."

"You sure?" asked Blond. "I checked it out. No one else down there but you. Maybe another crew took him to the hospital."

"He was in the back. He had..."

"Just you, miss."

Tears filled her eyes as she remembered the sight of Plante with the machete in his face. Oh God, she had failed him. If only she'd not been so afraid and shot Louis when she had the chance. He'd still be here, cracking a joke, offering her pancakes, supporting the insane story she knew as the truth. Is this what he'd signed up for? The job was dangerous, sure, but had he ever suspected it would end with a blade in his skull? It was just supposed to be a simple recon job. Get in, get out, get an office with a gold placard on the door. How would they tell his wife? Did Dan even know about it? What about Uncle Sam? The tears came in rivers now.

"Here," Spiky said, placing something in her hand. It was the necklace she'd been gripping in the basement. The necklace that had enraged Louis (been blessed by him), maybe even saved her life. If you believed that kind of stuff. Which of course, she did now. The EMT also placed her purse in her lap, said, "I put your stuff back in it. It'll be okay. You don't look to be hurt. Just a bit stressed. We'll get you out on the next ambulance."

The hospital was the last place she wanted to go. If Pierre had sent Louis to kill her and Plante, then what she needed was to get out of New York, back to D.C. where she could let the company handle this mess. "No. I'm fine. Really." She took the oxygen mask off and handed it to Spiky. "Thanks for the help."

"Miss, I don't know that we can just let you go. I mean, you might be hurt and not know it—"

"And the cops want to talk to everyone involved," added Blond. "They told us to tell them which witnesses could talk."

"Well I'm not staying," she said.

"But miss—"

They stopped protesting when she took her wallet from her purse and flashed her company card. It wasn't a badge or anything like that, but it did say CENTRAL INTELLIGENCE AGENCY, and that was good enough for the EMTs; they didn't know any better.

"Shit," Spiky said. "Is this related to the bombing yesterday? Is this, like, terrorists?" His face went three shades of pale. Chances were he was thinking about the guys in the suits, wondering what type of intelligence they represented, wondering if his hometown had just become the new Fallujah.

"Something like that," she said. "Maybe stay indoors for a few days. Where do these ambulance go?"

"Depends on what's taking drop offs. Beth Israel, Cabrini, Bellevue. Who knows. Between yesterday and today the rooms are filling up quickly."

"Thanks." As she pushed past the police cars, having to flash her ID once again, she couldn't help but feel she was contributing to the madness. Was it terrorism? Was it something less broad? And more importantly, where the hell was Plante?

Twenty minutes later she was stepping off the subway at the stop near the safe house, shouldering her laptop once again. Thankfully, no one had snatched it from the Internet café when she'd gone back for it (who said all New Yorkers were rude?). The company car, with Ben's body being looked over by the police, had still been parked outside.

When she hit the street, her cell phone beeped; someone had called her while she was underground. The LED showed Dan's name, who was exactly the person she needed to speak to. Still, she feared some kind of outburst. "It's me, Dan."

"Rhonda. What the holy fuck is going on up there? Something about a mass shooting is all over the news. I saw you in the background. You all right? What happened?"

"I wish I could explain it. Plante's dead."

"How?"

What was she supposed to say? A zombie hacked him up? "He was slashed with a machete."

"By who?"

"One of Pierre's men. At least he became one of Pierre's men. It's a bit complicated."

"Tell me it wasn't Plante's gun that killed people. We really don't need our name attached to this shit."

"I didn't see it happen, but I'm not taking odds against it."

"Jesus Christ. This is bad."

"Worse. This Pierre guy is using some kind of…" What?

Magic? Voodoo? It sounded ridiculous. "He's got people carrying out his terrorist plans that wouldn't normally do it. A kind of drug, but not in the traditional sense. God, I really don't even know how to explain it. Look, he knows we're here. Whoever was driving for us—"

"Ben."

"Okay. Ben. He's dead too. His neck was cut. Which leaves me and whoever else you sent. And with what we're dealing with, I'm pretty sure we're sitting ducks."

"I don't know who got sent. It was decided upstairs."

"I was mostly referring to me, anyway. Pierre knows I'm here. Knows what I look like. Knows I was asking about him. I had a run in with him and now I think he's been following us somehow. I need to get out of the city, and you need to send some professionals in to get him."

"Okay, I'll do my best to get some local boys to run protection for you. Can't promise anything. They were already spread thin with the bombing. This new shooting makes it worse. Can you get to the safe house?"

"I'm here now."

"Good. I'm getting a plane up there STAT. Figure it'll take a couple hours. Can you wait that long?"

"Yeah, I think so. I'll compile a file of what I know on the plane. And Dan?"

"What?"

"I'm not crazy, and I want that to go in the file that talks about the work I did here. I didn't almost just get killed too many times to count to not have this work out for me. Hear me? I'm not crazy."

"Why would I think that?"

"Because when you read my report there will be no other explanation. But I'm not crazy."

"I know you're not crazy, Rhonda. Crazy people don't analyze, they send analysts into situations they shouldn't be in because even crazier bastards convince them it's a wise move. Just get to the airport. Be safe."

She closed her phone, put it back in her purse next to the necklace, and entered the apartment building. The interior of the apartment safe house felt wrong somehow, as if a piece of it had been taken away. Plante's jacket was supposed to be hung over the chair at the dining room table. Pancakes were supposed to be cooking in the kitchen. It's funny how you can feel a person is really gone for good when you know they won't ever walk back in the front door. But there was no time to grieve right now. Time was tight, even with a two-hour window. Briefly she debated calling a cab to get her to the airport, but with the way things were going it wouldn't be hard for Pierre to have one of his men pick her up. No, she'd have to take the subway out to the airport, stay around people, which meant at least a forty minute ride, and time getting through security (even federal workers have to pay their dues when it comes to aviation safety). First she collected her bags and piled them on the couch. Then she grabbed a granola bar from the kitchen, stuffed it into her laptop case. After making a final room-to-room search to make sure she had everything, she picked up her bags and opened the door to the hall.

Standing there, smiling down at her, his sun hat blocking out the light from the overhead bulb, was Pierre. "Bon jour, mademoiselle," he said, and struck her across the face with the back of his hand. The force of the blow was like hitting a brick wall in a car doing sixty. It sent her to the ground, and for the second time that day, she had the wind knocked out of her. Fire laced its way from her right cheek down through her neck and into her stomach. The taste of copper tingled on her lips. Get up, she told herself. He's going to kill you!

"Move and I will hit you again," he said, making his way into the apartment. Behind him, two creatures shuffled in after him and stood to the side. They were the same two creatures she'd seen in Louis's building, the same two that had crept up the stairs like puppets. Only now she could see them in the light. Their cheeks were torn into strips of skin with holes large enough to pass fingers through. Their teeth were rotted black. What little hair they had was white and stringy, stuck to their gray pates with shiny oil. Eyes were all white, but seeing her without difficulty. There was no powder on their faces, but the telltale sign of blisters and sores were in abundance, one blister so large it closed the eyelid of the creature on the left. From these sores a yellow slick bubbled out and meandered down to their mouths. They swayed, moaning, their faces focused on her with an intense yearning.

"You anger me, mademoiselle. I leave you to rot inside youself. And yet here you be, running around de city, speaking my name. It come to me on de wind, spoken in awe, tickling me. Reeking of de same scent o' fear I know well. To haste, I fear, is to dishonor Bondye. And so I no more hasten. Dis is de word of our fathers and mothers, who grow angry at such insolence."

Rhonda crab-walked further into the living room, until she came up against the coffee table. She put a hand to her lip and felt the swollen bubble where Pierre had split it. Blood coated her fingers. But her hand was not trembling, a sign of her resignation that there was quite possibly no way out of this. She would die here in this safe house, alone, under the hands of this magician. She bit back a giggle at the irony of dying in a "safe house." And what then? Her corpse used for another bombing? "What are they?" she asked, tossing her eyes to the creatures. Speaking hurt her mouth, but she had to know. "How are they alive? Did you kill them? How does it… work?"

Pierre took a few steps forward, squatted down in front of her. When he reached out and ran a finger across her mouth, she did not flinch. "Le zombi. Yes. Men who owe me for de life I provide them back home. I not a selfish man, you see. But I not a selfless man, either. Dis for dat, as it be said. When you know how to satisfy de gods, you can ask for favors. Mighty powerful de loa be, spinning dis earth on their knees. A tiring job dat require de occasional rebirth. And so I give it to dem. What's left be for me. Again, dis for dat."

A throbbing was beginning in her jaw where a bruise was forming. The smell of his hand was still thick on her skin, a mixture of earth, musk, and body odor. This, of course, was the least of her worries. When Pierre commanded it, his two servants would tear her apart limb by limb and there would be no way to overpower them. The question was, did she even want to try?

Pierre stood back up, said, "Here," and one of the creatures shuffled forward, its tongue now lolling out of its mouth. "De blade."

The zombie removed a large pocket knife from its tattered pants, handed it to Pierre in a gray and decaying fist.

Pierre took the blade, cutting the creature's flesh as he pulled it free. No blood ran from the wound. "For Damnballa, Zakka, Ogou, I give dis gift of flesh." He laid the blade sideways across his palms and brought it to his chest. "It only hurt for a minute," he said, looking at Rhonda the way a doctor might to a child about to undergo a shot. For the next few seconds he spoke in a mixture of Hatian

French and at times what seemed another language entirely. The bass of his voice rumbled through her body. The words became a chant, a steady beat that promised to move the universe.

The zombie on Pierre's left swayed in time with the words, and a long line of drool stretched to the floor like monofilament. It even looked like the creature was smiling, enjoying the entertainment, anticipating something grand. When Pierre was done chanting, his eyes now shockingly stitched with bloodshot veins, he flipped the knife around in his hand, blade pointing down for stabbing. "Mademoiselle, dis be a brief adieu."

He lunged at her.

Instinct took over and Rhonda shoved off her feet, up and over the coffee table and landed on her back in front of the couch. The coffee table tipped over on top of her just in time, Pierre was right behind her and the table met the knife he plunged toward her. The sound of the zombies' loud grunting filled the room, a raucous noise that bordered on laughter, like children watching a cartoon. Pierre's sun hat tipped down over his face for a second and Rhonda kicked out again, sending the table into Pierre's knees and knocking him to the ground. Up and over the couch she went, picking up her pocketbook and swinging it into his weathered face. The purse was full and made of heavy leather—the smack resounded throughout the apartment. Pierre let out a surprised grunt and covered his head with his arms.

Even as Rhonda headed to the door, Pierre was shouting, "Stop her!"

The two zombies moved quickly——one jumping in front of the door, the other blindsiding her with a tackle that sent her sliding into the kitchen. Her purse came to rest beside her and the necklace peeked out from inside. With one hand she snatched it up, with the other she grabbed the counter top and hauled herself up. The two zombies came at her, mouth's snarling, their brows drawn into Vs above their chalky eyes. All signs of the slow shuffling creatures they were seconds ago had vanished. Now they were agile. Were their slow movements just a ruse? Had they simply been waiting for a command to run? "Stop!" Rhonda said, holding up the necklace.

They stopped. They roared. They shook with rage.

A ceramic bowl was in the dish rack next to the sink. She grabbed it and threw it at the zombies, catching one in the head. It shattered and a shard struck home, piercing the creature's cheek. The creature did not make a sound. From the silverware drawer she took a knife, held it in front of her next to the necklace.

"So you believe." It was Pierre, pushing his way between the zombies to stand in front of her. "Dat is good. To believe make it easier for de loa."

"I don't know what you mean. I don't believe shit

except that my superiors know who you are and are gonna kill you."

"I doubt dat, mademoiselle. They do not chase men like me. Maybe some of my acquaintances, but not me."

"They will now."

"Lies. All lies. But no matter, for you believe de real truth. The truth of what awaits you. So hard to make believers see what be there always. Let me take dis." He reached out and snatched the necklace, held it up in front of his eyes and laughed. "Poorly made, but I see Louis' powers be stronger than I'd thought. Had I de tools at my disposal I would reverse the spell. But dis work as well." He dropped it down the garbage disposal in the sink and flipped the switch on the wall. The shells popped and cracked, the sink shook slightly at the effort of breaking it all down. It was the sound of hope dying.

The two zombies came closer, their mouths still gaping, their tongues flicking. What they wanted was a command, but Pierre merely stood in front of Rhonda smiling.

"And now…" he said, reaching into his shirt pocket and removing a small burlap sack held shut with a bit of twine. He untied it, letting the sack fall loose. Inside was a white powder, similar to what had been on the faces of the creatures Rhonda had seen in the city. Just like what had been blown in her face yesterday. She knew it was all the same. "To resume," he said, finishing his thought.

The knife came up quickly, caught her in the belly. Her scream cut the air, but she had no way of knowing if it was heard outside. This being a safe house, the glass was surely bulletproof, the walls reinforced. And besides, the screaming made the pain worse so she stopped.

Pierre stepped aside and let her pass, her face slack with shock and disbelief. It was really happening. She was really going to be murdered. As she pushed past the zombies, she looked into their blank stares, prayed to God it would not end for her this way.

"No no no no," she gurgled, now in the living room, holding the wet hole in her belly. She reached for the front door again. I need to call Dan, she thought. I need a doctor. But she didn't get the door open because the two zombies charged her and tackled her to the floor. "Hold de bitch down!" came Pierre's voice.

A strange sensation bloomed in her stomach, the feel of her life rushing out through the deep stab wound. Blood stained the front of her shirt, running down into her jeans, making everything slick and warm. She was on the ground, the faces of two dead men growling over her. Past their decaying heads she saw Pierre, bobbing his hand up and down. Then he bent down, turned his hand over, and let the powder from the bag sprinkle down into her eyes. The world went white.

TEN

Every television and computer in the agency's offices was tuned to the media coverage of the New York City slayings. First a suicide bombing that killed fourteen and wounded thirty more, then a shooting spree that left over twenty dead. Witnesses were spouting stories of bloodied men walking the streets with guns, some of them with open chest cavities. The media was having a field day with their bullshit speculations: a new kind of enemy agent that engaged in sadistic rituals before unleashing whatever wave of terror it saw fit. Not just Middle Eastern, but from Africa, South America, maybe even Canada. America will never be the same, they said.

"Nice," Dan replied, "spread xenophobia, you idiots. You're gonna get yourselves shot. Morons."

It was only going to get worse from here on out, at least until they figured out who was doing all of this. If it was this Pierre, in league with Iran and Chile and God knew who else, they had to find him quickly.

The phone rang. He turned the volume down on the television. "Yeah."

"It's me. Rhonda."

"Did you land yet?"

"Yeah, we're taxiing now. Dan, I was attacked... again."

"Are you okay?" She sounded weak, her voice gruff and strained.

"I've been stabbed, but I bandaged myself up. I'm okay for now. Did you locate Plante?"

"No, not yet. I left messages at the hospitals and we've got men out searching for him. All those bodies, he may have been mislabeled. Fucking emergency response teams don't have training for this kind of thing, I don't care what FEMA says."

"Dan, I think we may have been compromised."

"How so?"

"I can't explain over the phone. I need to talk to you in private. Can you meet me somewhere?"

"Sure, where?"

"I don't know. Wild guess here, but I'm assuming we have some kind of safe house near the offices?"

They did, but Rhonda wasn't supposed to know where they were. In fact, he didn't even know where they all were. "I'll have to run it by my superiors."

"That's fine. They'll probably want to come see what I have to show them."

"Okay. Hang on." He put her on hold and dialed Jim's office and explained the situation. Jim gave him an address and a time. Dan clicked back over, gave Rhonda the address. She repeated it slowly, writing it down somewhere. Her voice seemed to be getting worse. How badly was she hurt? "Was it Pierre who got you?"

"Yes," she replied.

"We're gonna find him. Don't worry. This is off the record, but we were able to get some information from our friends in Chile. This Pierre is a drug dealer of sorts, has a number of alleged murders under his belt. Quayarah and Fereza swear he's their ticket to tackling Yankee Imperialism... their words. I don't know who they think they're dealing with, but no drug dealer gets away with this kind of shit in America. He'll be strung up by his balls in a day or two. Mark my words."

"I hope so. I'll see you in a few."

"Glad to have you back. You did good. I'll be talking to my superiors about you when this is all done."

"Thanks, Dan." She hung up.

Dan leaned back in his chair, looked at the television again. The scene showed a collection of body bags on the street, blood thick and brown around them. "Where are you Pierre? And where the fuck did you come from?"

The safe house was actually a condo out past American University. Dan parked the car outside and turned to Jim, who was riding shotgun. "Place is a shithole."

"That's the idea. But it's impenetrable."

"I could get inside," said the man in the back seat.

Dan glanced in the rear view mirror, saw the white-haired man staring back at him. The military outfit had been replaced with a simple black sweater and black suit pants, which somehow seemed more impressive; a man who wore all black was a man with secrets. His name was Hugh Brenon, the agency's own magic man. If reports were to be believed, Brenon had overseen some of the more impressive black ops in recent years, a few of which were staged out of Camp Warhorse along the Iranian border. Infiltrating enemy strongholds and gathering information on enemy positions was his forte. The man did not cry over spilled blood, and he'd spilled plenty of it himself. Twenty years of that type of work—Dan knew the blackness in the man's eyes had been hard earned, but what scared him the most was that officially, Brenon did not exist.

"Where's our girl?" Jim asked.

"Don't know," Dan replied. "Let's wait inside before people get nosey and call the cops on us or something."

All three got out of the car and made their way up the steps to the condo. Jim slipped the key into the deadbolt, jiggled it, looked concerned. "It's unlocked."

"How?" Brenon asked. It was more of a command than a question.

"Don't know."

The door was heavy metal, painted to look like your average wooden entryway. Jim pushed it open and all three watched the way it sung wide with a slant. They stepped inside and Brenon ran his hands over the hinged side of the door, humming in contemplation. The hinges were hidden inside the metal, and the metal was warped. "Someone broke it," he said.

Jim and Brenon removed their weapons (Brenon's came out of nowhere). Dan followed a few steps behind as they slowly moved toward the living area. The blinds were down, the lights off, a small clock on an end table clicking solemnly. Daylight might have seeped through and provided enough light to see, but night had already fallen. The room was dark with vague shapes in various shades of black, any of which could be an enemy in waiting. Despite the mild weather outside, the room felt far colder than it should be. There was a definite smell, much like gym socks that hadn't been washed in a few weeks.

"Dan?" It was Rhonda, stepping out from the adjacent bedroom. She stopped in the darkness of the shadows, silhouetted against the wall.

"Rhonda," Dan said. "Shit, you scared us."

"I almost shot you, miss," Jim said.

"I appreciate you not doing it, Uncle Sam."

"Uncle Sam? What's that mean?"

"Nothing," she said, her speech heavy with phlegm. "I see you brought the whole gang."

There's something wrong here, Dan thought as Rhonda moved into of the middle of the room, his eyes beginning to adjust to the gloom. The way she was speaking, she sounded drunk, or sick, or both. He could see her mouth moving, even when she wasn't speaking, as if she couldn't control her jaw. "Rhonda, you don't look good, let me see where you're hurt. If you've lost too much blood—"

"No! Stay there!" she roared.

Spittle hit Dan in the face, stopping him short. Yes, definitely wrong, he thought. This was not the Rhonda he knew. But then, maybe she was just in shock. Being attacked twice in two days could certainly do that to a person, especially if she was dealing with a knife wound. "Fine. Let's turn the lights on, sit down. You can you tell us what you know."

"The lights don't work," she rasped, her body swaying slightly. "And what I know is that the loa are angry."

"Who's that?" asked Jim. "The Iranians? Some new cartel?"

"Not quite," she said.

"I'm opening the blinds," Brenon finally said. Rhonda shouted no again but he ignored her and pulled the drawstring, revealing bulletproof glass and letting in the moonlight. Dan was the first to really see her face, and took a step back. Jim lowered his gun, said, "My God." Brenon turned to see what the matter was, took in Rhonda's appearance, but said nothing. The man was a stone.

"Rhonda," Dan said, "I'm calling an ambulance."

She drew a large steak knife from behind her, held it out straight. "Don't move." With spaghetti legs, she shuffled further into the room, the moonlight now shining heavy on her features. Her eyes were dry and clouded over, a smattering of dirt and blood splotched her face. For a moment, Dan felt like he was standing on a boat in rough seas, nausea fighting to take hold. He tore his eyes from hers and noticed a large bruise, like a slice of eggplant, on her right cheek and numerous sores, like tiny anthills around her nose and mouth. White powder coated all of it.

"What the..." Dan said. "How..."

"Put the knife down, missy," Jim said, raising his gun again. "I can see you're pissed off, but no need to go all PMS on us. We want to help you."

"No," she hissed, "you want what I know. And what I know is that Bondye's time has come. Soon, all the world will walk in his everlasting shadow. And America, the evil snake, will be no more."

"Fuck this shit," Brenon said, and stormed toward her, raising his gun. In a flash, she whipped the knife at him. It flew through the air, too quickly for him to duck; his reflexes were not what they used to be. It slammed into his neck, slicing through the Adam's apple, and stuck out the back. With a gurgle, he fell backwards, his legs kicking, his arms reaching for the blade.

"Rhonda!" Dan yelled. But she wasn't listening anymore, she was charging Jim, who fired a shot that smacked her in the chest. All Dan could think was that this was all wrong. His superiors should not be shooting at Rhonda. Rhonda did not kill people—let alone have the skills to throw a knife like that.

He had to get out, to get help. If Pierre had drugged her, there was no telling what secrets she had revealed. Cuban analyst or not, she had access to sensitive information, may have overheard things in the offices that shouldn't have been said. Loose lips and all that.

She tackled Jim to the ground, apparently unconcerned that she'd been shot. With a snarl she bit down on Jim's neck, tore back and forth like a dog at a chew toy, and then yanked back, taking a chunk of carotid artery with her. Jim fired again, a wild shot that hit the ceiling.

Finding his legs, Dan turned to make for the front door, ran smack into another person, a large man judging by the shadow. He shoved off the man and fell onto the couch, knowing there had to be a gun nearby. On the floor next to him, Jim was screaming bloody murder while Rhonda dug her claws into his chest, burrowing into his flesh, trying to wiggle her fingers past his ribcage.

Brenon's gun was still in his hand. Jim's gun was under his body. There was nothing closer that could be used as a weapon, except for Dan's own fists. He balled them up, knowing that he was a poor fighter. "Stop right there."

The man stepped closer, and Dan could make out who it was. "Plante?"

Plante moaned, a low humming that could be heard over Jim's screams of pain. On rickety legs, the agent moved closer, reached out and grabbed Dan's leg, began to yank him toward the arm of the couch. His face was worse than Rhonda's; the pustules and eyes were the same, but a long gash began at his forehead and ran down the center of his face, splitting his nose clean in half, and ending with a giant open wound near his lips that looked like a severe cleft palette.

As Dan tried to find words for what was happening, a new voice broke into the symphony of moans and wails. Like sandpaper, it rubbed at the walls of the room, with enough dark vibration to strip the paint. "Easy, my friends. Do not ruin dem too much. Perception be de skeleton key dat makes us invisible." From the shadows of the bedroom, a new figure emerged. Tall, gaunt, surrounded by an aura as dark as his ebony skin and black clothing. About the only thing Dan could make out for sure was the shape of a large sun hat.

Mystery Man. Jean Pierre. Holding what looked like a large machete.

"Up," Pierre commanded, and Rhonda stood up from where she'd been tearing a hole into Jim's chest. The man was dead. Blood had pumped vigorously from his exposed carotid artery, coating his face, and his chest was torn in jagged strips from Rhonda's clawing. She shuffled over to Pierre's side and stood next to him. "Leave him," he said to Plante, and the thing with the gash in its face let go and moved away.

On the couch, Dan shivered. He could see the wound in Rhonda's gut now, the hole in her shirt that revealed her insides. It didn't take a doctor to know both she and Plante should be dead. But somehow they weren't. It didn't make sense, just like Rhonda had suggested earlier.

"You can't do this," Dan said, glancing toward Brenon and gauging how quickly he could dive for the gun.

"Oh, but I can, Mr. Yauch," Pierre said. "Yes, I know you name. Mademoiselle tell me. And this…" He waved his arms around the room. "It be written in the heavens, and there be no way to fight it. The trail was done blazed long ago when de spirits ruled supreme."

Can I get to the gun, Dan wondered. And if I can, will they die? Will Pierre die? Could I make it to the door and take off in the car?

As if in answer, Pierre called out, "block de door please," and two more figures moved out of the shadows of the kitchen. Each one wore a pilot's uniform, and each one had a slice across its neck. They stood at the end of the couch, blocking access to the outside world. "My army," Pierre said, introducing the men. "More where dey came from. Once yours, now mine. It be a new world order, yes? You enemies want my aid, and now I show dem how it work." He laughed, a sound so hollow Dan thought he could crawl down it and die.

"They can fly planes?" he asked.

"No. But I do. I do a lot of tings, Mr. Yauch. Master o' trades, as dey say."

"I work for the CIA. Do you have any idea—"

"Of course I do. Dat be de whole point, is it not?" Pierre hefted the machete, handed it to Rhonda. She (it) took the blade and stared at it for a second, mesmerized by the dark stains on it.

"Rhonda, if you can hear me, you gotta wake up," Dan said.

Pierre threw his head back and let out a torrent of laughter. "Mr. Yauch, she no wake up again. There no ti bon ange left, see? Just my voice in her head. Forever and ever. So de loa command. And now, time to go." He nodded to the two dead pilots. "Please, restrain dis man."

With a jolt, Dan leapt up and tried to run through the creatures, but they hooked their arms around him and brought him to his knees. With every thing he had, he let out a screaming plea for help, but it was answered only with urgent moans.

"Dear girl," Pierre said, giving Rhonda a push on her shoulder. "Do show Mr. Yauch why we be here." As Rhonda stepped toward Dan, the recent gunshot in her chest still fresh with the stench of burned flesh, Pierre pulled a small bag from his shirt pocket. He dipped his hand inside and pulled out a tiny mountain of white powder—it looked blue in the moonlight, like crushed sapphires. "So many important men in one room. The places we will go, no?"

"Please, Rhonda," Dan said, struggling against the creatures' strong hands. Their fingers dug into his arms and neck, rendering him immobile.

"For the loa," Rhonda wheezed, her dead eyes staring into his. "For Bondye."

Beyond her, Pierre began sprinkling the powder into Jim and Brenon's faces, chanting as he went, looking heavenward and back to his newest recruits, speaking in tongues.

He stopped, looked at Dan and said, "Such high clearance men. I believe we go see your president now. I have promises to keep, yes? America, a new day for all." He laughed.

It seemed so crazy, Dan thought. Yet, they'd been fooled as easily as the secret service would be. He almost wanted to laugh, but his quivering lips kept him from it. He was pretty sure he could hear Jim moaning now, could see the man's legs twitching. It couldn't be, but it was: he was coming back to life. They'd all be coming back to life, somehow, so they could help end everyone else's. So many days analyzing the globe, fleshing out terrorists, locating enemies, always asking, how do you defeat an enemy that wants to die? Now, he had to ask a different question: how do you defeat an enemy that *can't* die?

You don't.

With a graceful swing, the machete came down across his belly, spilling his insides onto his own lap. They were warm.

1. THE HOUSE BY THE CEMETERY

"THE CEMETERY'S JUST A short walk from the cottage," Dane told the others. His left hand briefly left the steering wheel as he gestured at the tree-lined road. "There are no leaves right now so you can actually see it from the windows."

"'Cottage'." Casey smiled thinly. "Quaint."

"That's what the website said. It's just a little house dropped right smack in the middle of the woods, like someone accidentally put it there and forgot about it."

"A page out of early American history." Kara said, quoting the realtor's description.

Dane pursed his lips and gave her a scolding look out of the corner of his eye. She tilted her head in a way that allowed a couple of raven locks to frame her emerald gaze. He hated the way she made him love her, that infallible look she gave him. He told her, on every possible occasion, that he despised that black magic of hers. In response, she would only smile. Dane stopped drumming his gloved fingers on the steering wheel long enough to gesture past her toward the woods, He pointed to the remains of an old stone wall that was visible between the frost covered birch trees. "It's built from rocks like those, but the whole interior's been redone. I took a virtual tour while I was on the phone with what's-her-name."

"Paula," Kara corrected.

"Right. New wood floors and oak paneling, except for the faux-stone surfacing in the kitchen. Ceiling's still unfinished; you can stare right into the rafters. I coaxed the truth out of her about that. Oh, and there are bird problems. You don't mind if a couple of lovebirds nest over our heads, do you?"

"I was anticipating that." Casey said, his eyes meeting Dane's in the rearview mirror. He was squeezed into the back seat with the luggage that couldn't be fit in the rear. Casey as baggage. They each had thought of the arrangement in those terms, but no one said a word.

"It's got heating and, yes, indoor plumbing. There is a great old fireplace in the living room. Paula had her guys leave a cord of wood at the side of the house."

"That won't be enough."

"I know. I'm going to go out and cut some firewood. We can both go, Casey."

"Hey, I planned to lock myself indoors the entire time. What's this about manual labor? Can't you and Kara collect wood on your walks?"

"It'll be fun." Dane said.

"This quaint little cottage hideaway with birds nesting in the ceiling and an axe by the back door is intended for your inspiration, not mine." Casey tousled his wavy blond hair. He liked playing with his hair and watching himself in the window's reflection. He was bold in his vanity, unashamed.

New-fallen snow crunched beneath the wheels of the hatchback. Though it was late in the afternoon, the sky was bone-white. Dane loved this weather, when in the dead of night the sky had a gray pallor that oddly illuminated the world below. That was his inspiration.

The house itself was more for Kara, due to its proximity to the old graveyard. She would probably trudge out to the graveyard early the next morning to sketch the trees and make rubbings of the headstones. Then she would be prepared to immerse herself in her work, and dedicate the remainder of the season to her painting. Kara was a workhorse, turning out several complete canvases in a day, each a fragment of the tableau that would be her thesis. She was intent on taking this place with her when they left in late January. She would take it on canvas, each memory captured by her brushstrokes.

Dane was a sculptor. He would probably work in their bedroom. They would share the bedroom closest to the living room to benefit from the warmth of the hearth. He preferred his clay to resist him a little, the relative cold of the house would help. It was part of his process to fight the unformed piece of clay and make it malleable, but he didn't need it frozen solid. He too would take away memories from the woods and cottage, perhaps even the graveyard. His would be fused in a surrealist amalgamation built from his subconscious in clay.

Casey was the rogue, as always. He hadn't yet told them what he planned to do with his time. He wouldn't be venturing outside, they knew that much.

Daddy had paid for the cottage rental. Dane's father had always encouraged his son's artistic pursuits. The old man's hands were soft and only moved with flourish when signing checks. Fortunately, he loved lining the walls of his homes and offices with Dane's works. Showing his colleagues how another investment had paid off brilliantly, an investment in blood, semen and dollars. A growing investment in his boy, his masterwork

Dane had modeled briefly to pay a few bills, a vain attempt to get by without Daddy's help. He had his father's pale blue eyes and his mother's freckles. High cheekbones and a sharp chin peppered with stubble. His striking looks gave him the typical look of a model. Kara had begun her artistic work as a photographer. That was how they met: she had done a few sessions with Dane, two of them nudes. She hadn't painted him yet. He thought she might do that after he asked her to marry him.

Casey grunted in the backseat, taking Dane out of his memories. He saw Casey pull a disposable camera from his woolen coat and scan the roadside for shots. He had yet to snap a photo. Maybe he was doing it to express disdain at the blandness of their surroundings. Dane couldn't decide if Casey was really lost and searching for a subject and medium with which to start his project. He had bad feet and sometimes used a cane. Dane had expected him to enjoy posing himself with his walking stick and heavy scarf amongst the barren trees, but it seemed that perhaps Casey was genuinely concerned at his lack of imagination. He'd had a bit of a rough time this semester. Maybe it was the fear that he really couldn't forge a living standing around galleries, fucking anonymous people and making acidic remarks. Where would he be right now if he hadn't taken Dane and Kara up on their offer? Sitting alone in the apartment with a bong between his naked thighs? Dane smirked. No, he'd probably be calling them up to tease them for leaving the city when the holiday parties were getting into full swing. They'd been friends for as long as he could remember, and he continued writing off Casey's attitude as disingenuous. He hoped that things like this little trip might bring back the boy Dane had once known. The mere fact that Casey had accepted the invitation was promising; maybe he was tired of his posturing too.

The cottage was down a side road, thick with trees, but it was the stone walls and earthen hues that concealed the cottage. The road was under a carpet of snow, and had Dane not known the way he might have driven right past the little house. It was unlikely that anyone would even pass by, but because he liked the feeling of isolation, he would park the green hatchback behind the house where no one would notice them from the main road. There were no other homes on it and it ended only few miles away, where it ran into an access road.

The realtor described the cottage as an escape, a still life, and of course a page out of early American history. The foundations of the house and the cemetery were at least a century and a half old. The entire parcel of land, quiet and cold as the grave, played host only to sleeping trees and the skeletons interred deep beneath the frozen soil. Lazy twirling snowflakes landed on the crumbling old property walls dotting the landscape.

Kara clasped her hands and studied the cottage as they pulled around it, Dane carefully navigating a path between the stacks of firewood around the chimney's spine, and the forest. "Perfect. Perfect, perfect, perfect." Kara said.

Casey snapped his first photo. "That'll make a nice postcard. This is all postcard country, you know it? I guess it'd make a few nice paintings too, the sort that line the front hallway when you visit Mom and Dad."

"Is that a shot at me?" Kara asked with a hint of irritation in her voice.

"No, no, you'll make something of this place, using the graveyard and all that. You don't paint backgrounds for use as backdrops. I'm just saying that, as someone coming out here in search of a creative spark, I see bleakness."

"Are you writing a poem?" Dane tightened his hands on the wheel and rounded the corner of the house. "You knew coming out here…"

"I like to think that I can find life in anything. It's a challenge, is all. And I like challenges." Casey leaned so that he could smile at Dane in the mirror. "Tonight I'll pack some herb in my ol' corncob pipe and take a stroll through these woods."

"Corncob pipe." Dane scoffed. He stopped the car and tugged the key from the ignition. Paula had given him only one key, which unlocked the front door. The back door was in the kitchen and Paula had warned him that it had a couple of bolts locking it from the inside. He thought it might be safe just to leave it unlocked, a pleasant departure from life in the city. He squeezed Kara's knee. "It'd be great to have a place like this all the time, you know? You could come out during any season for a week or a weekend and bring along everything you need in a couple of bags."

She gave him a big-eyed look and a peck on his wrist. "Making plans?"

"Just saying."

They lugged their things around the side of the house and piled them in the entryway. Dane stretched his arms and sauntered into the living room. He glanced at the rafters but didn't see any birds. Fortunately, there were no droppings on the floor, either. It seemed the bird problem had been resolved. In the kitchen, pots, pans and utensils hung from racks attached to the rafters above a table. There was a stove set into the wall which would offer some extra heat and the back door was beside the sink. A hallway led to the three bedrooms and one bathroom. Kara had already laid claim to one of the bedrooms for use as a studio. Begrudgingly, she had agreed to share it with Casey if he decided he needed more space. The master bedroom, which would be Dane and Kara's, adjoined the bathroom. Kara's studio and the third bedroom were on the other side of the hall. The third bedroom was in the back corner of the house, and was perfect for Casey.

Casey dropped his things on the floor and immediately sequestered himself in his room. He began bouncing around on the squeaky twin bed. The windows didn't have curtains, so he draped a couple of shirts over the bare rod. As he stripped off his winter padding, he called down the hall. "You two need any help with your shit?"

"We're good," Dane replied.

Kara ran her hands along the thick comforter on their queen-size bed, gazing thoughtfully at the headboard. "I love this frame, it's so ornate. Are these sheets clean?"

"Should be, but… we can run them into town and wash them at the laundromat while I grab some wine or whatever."

"Mmm, 'wine or whatever'. You're making me horny."

Dane burst out laughing and opened the door on the right, "This is the closet," he said, moving onto the next door. "Here is the bathroom and that's the heater room" He turned back to her and sat heavily on the bed.

"Do we call Paula when it breaks?"

"Not if, but 'when'?"

Kara nodded and continued. "I don't mind crashing out by the fireplace if we lose heat, but water is another story. I am not going to play nature girl to the extent of missing my shower and shave. I want to grow my hair out, by the way. I think it'll lighten up a bit. Do you like that?"

Dane hummed in the affirmative and, lying back, patted the pillow beside his head. "Yeah, if it does break we can call Paula and a local guy will stop by. Speaking of which, toggle the thermostat, will you?" He gestured to the instrument above the rickety old bureau.

Casey appeared in the doorway. "Is this house haunted?"

"Why would you ask that?" Dane said. He loved stories of old houses with 1800s-era specters walking the halls. Casey preferred stories of dead scandal-makers dragging their entrails, gossipy rather than mysterious stories. A life-long fascination with the idea of shades and echoes from the past reverberating through a homestead was something they shared. Casey's penchant for gossip and uncovering buried secrets was probably what drew him to American ghost lore. Dane just wanted to touch the past a little. He hoped that someday, God willing, he'd be a part of history, leaving relics in clay and marble. What of all the nameless people who'd led quiet, simple lives and then faded away? He wondered. Maybe there were still tiny ripples of their existence that appeared now and then. It was a romantic thought, maybe not as interesting as Casey's tales of debutantes re-enacting their murders, replete with lesbian overtones and goat heads discovered under the floorboards. Casey was all titillation. He sought reaction; he felt it gave his work meaning. There was no message or statement. He only wanted to see the reaction of his audience in their shocked and adoring faces.

"So," Dane repeated, "why do you ask?"

Casey shrugged. "Well, do you know who built it? Who really lived here before it became some real-estate conglomerate's vacation house?"

"Someone boring, I'm sure." Dane replied.

"Boring to me, you mean. Hey, lots of glamorous madmen came from humble beginnings. If only Ed Gein had graduated from a farm house and grave robbing... if he had come out further east and skinned a few socialites, he'd be the... " Casey was grinning broadly. Bringing up Ed Gein, or any other serial killer usually provoked shock or disgust from his audience, which he loved.

"Is that what you're getting at?" Kara interrupted. "I mean, is that why you're here. Your bent has always been sort of a post-

modern perversion. Are we going back to the roots of American grotesque?"

"Maybe." He raised an eyebrow and his hands in tandem.
"You'll just have to wait and see, won't you?"

"You're not going to dig up anyone, are you? Try to marry Gein
and Madison Avenue in a store window for your exhibit?" She
frowned.

"Too much effort. But if you guys ever have a year-round place,
like Dane said, maybe in the spring… "

Dane hurled a pillow across the room. Casey caught it and bit
down with a playful growl. "I'll let you get settled in. I'm gonna
smoke a bowl and walk around the place. Grab me if I start to look
like Nicholson in *The Shining*."

Casey walked out and padded down the hall in his toe socks. He
thought about their little exchange, and how funny it would be later
when he dug up the corpses. Funny to him, anyway. "How predict-
able am I?" He'd quip as he scattered bones across the floor. Their
reactions would be worth the effort. He fished through his backpack
for some pot.

2. FIRST NIGHT

Casey sat on his bed in the dead of night, a nice marijuana buzz and
his belly warm with wine. He looked out the curtain-less window at
the woods. He could see Dane's car off to the left, and past that, an
endless expanse of trees. The night sky was almost white.

He was wearing a wifebeater and white shorts. This was a pretty
picture, he thought, a quaint picture of faux-poverty, he thought, his
take on the "page out of American history". His bare chicken legs
dangling over the icy floor, his perfectly mussed hair reflected in the
window. "Quaint", "old-fashioned", these terms generally bred con-
tempt in Casey's mind, but the terms described this hovel to a T. It

was *ironically* quaint, he told himself. The irony would drip from every syllable when he described this adventure to his friends in the spring.

As promised, the living room had a clear view of the cemetery. He probably wouldn't be able to make it all the way out there tonight. If he was up to it, when Kara went down the following morning to take pictures or whatever it was she did, he'd go with her. Of course, Dane would come along. Dane was the mutual friend between himself and Kara. Dane couldn't stand being alone, he wouldn't stay cooped up in the cottage without someone to talk to. He was a pleasant guy. He and Dane had moved in different social circles as they grew older, but still had things in common. It was refreshing to spend time with someone who didn't necessarily seek to entertain or be entertained in every waking moment. Casey's party friends were "on" all the time. Dane enjoyed the quiet, dark spaces between the action. Kara was different from Dane, she was wilder. Casey thought he remembered seeing her at some wild parties in his freshman and sophomore years, prancing around in her underwear. There was a little devil in her but she liked Dane's intellectual certainty. Even when he got high he was still that safe little Rockwellian philosopher, cobbling together elements of the quaint and the mundane to produce something he thought sublime. Casey thought the results less sublime than contrived.

He had a sudden craving for a plate of the cold ham, left over from last night's dinner. It would give him something to chew on while contemplating the monochromatic expanse of this winter wonderland. Pulling on a robe, he crept out the door and down the hall in his bare feet.

An ache wormed its way through the flat soles of his feet, up through his ankles. He cursed and doubled back to grab his cane. His progress to the kitchen was silent. He passed the couple's room angling his head toward the door and heard muted talk. There was nothing interesting to hear so he continued on to the kitchen He set his cane on the countertop and pulled open the refrigerator. His hands moved fluidly, grabbing a few slices of ham with one hand, while the other reached into a cabinet and took a plate. His mind was blank until his fingers curled awkwardly around the cane handle. It was an arched handle…

It wasn't his.

He turned to see a man standing there, half in shadow, leaning on what Casey recognized as his cane. The man's gray hand looked like a cluster of petrified roots snarled around the right-angle handle that Casey knew so well, the handle that now rose into the air. He followed its progress; the man's other thin hand emerged from a dirt-caked sleeve and took hold of the cane's shaft. He held it toward Casey like a gun.

"Dane?" Casey called, hopefully.

A sharp crack erupted through his nose causing lights to flash before his eyes. He felt cartilage folding, then snapping, blood began to run freely. He collapsed, falling to the right. The hard floor resisted his weight. He rolled out of his robe, still seeing spirals of light, knowing with dread that it wasn't Dane.

The cane. The cane. *My cane for his. A game.* He thought incoherently.

He was facedown and felt blood collecting around him. *I'm still stoned. It doesn't hurt. Here we go, getting up.*

He didn't feel the second crack on the base of his skull. He simply plummeted into a blinding white hole of unconsciousness.

Dane stirred from sleep, though he wasn't sure why. He listened for a moment and, hearing only silence, nudged Kara beneath the covers. "Want to?"

He found her to be a fascinating lover, her sexuality linked to her art. In periods of creativity she would awaken Dane in the middle of the night, staring through his eyes, looking through him, while riding him in cool silence. He'd hoped the cottage would be such an inspiration, and that she'd fuel her creativity atop him.

"We could." She rolled over, crisp covers rumpling, and patted his head. "Do you really want to?"

"I'm awake is all. Something woke me up." He said. After a moment he reconsidered, "Nah, we don't have to. Just come over here."

She worked her soft shape into his angled limbs, the comforter shifting overhead. Their warm breath mingled, scented with mint and wine. Beneath the covers, she smiled at him. "You feel so nice. I wonder how cold it is out there."

"No way to tell with my skin percolating like it is."

"You smoked with Casey?"

"A little. I shouldn't get into the habit while we're out here. You know how I am, I start swimming in ideas and end up drowning, getting nothing done."

"A little won't hurt. You like going to bed like this."

"I want to build a dream-set out of this place." Dale grinned. His teeth were slightly spaced, a goofy freckled grin. "I want to get out there and get every inch, every fleck of bark and snow and stone into my system, then go into dreams and play with it like a pile of leaves. Does that make sense?"

"You always make sense."

"Haunted, what a trip that would be. I think what I can do is, pull apart this place and get the ghosts out, they're the glue of the whole thing. Talking about sculpture now. I think ghosts are fragments of memory and experience imprinted on everything. If I could document it in the waking hours, then go into dreams and get at those ghosts. It'll be a ghost-themed series, the sculpts I'm doing."

Kara stroked his brown hair while he talked. His face lit up like a child when he was on a tangent about tapping into his dreams, to feed his creativity. It was adorable to see him that way, how he glowed when she was really listening and understanding what he said. He said he had tried talking like this with his dad; pouring out his artistic intention, putting it into words that he knew were lofty and pretentious but were the only ones that worked with the old man. The words didn't really matter though, the real statement would be in the clay. Daddy would smile and write his checks. They'd both smile, Dane would say, but it was like a transaction taking place on two different worlds. Dane deposited the checks with an empty heart.

Maybe later his father would understand. Maybe when his dad saw the finished work, or when he saw other people seeing it.

"Haunted… " Dane's words drifted off, mumbling. He focused his marble-sized pupils on her face. Affecting the *Sling Blade* voice she was all-too familiar with, he whispered, "Wanna glass o' wine, mrhmm?"

"Sure."

"Be right back." He gathered his shirt about himself, stepped into his pajama bottoms and slipped out.

Emerging into the kitchen, the first thing he saw in the moonlight was a dark spot, with slight smudges around it on the linoleum.

Behind him, the front door squeaked. He turned and saw Hell.

The man was down the hallway, standing upright on one leg. He was male, that much could be discerned by his blocky frame and the way his muscled shoulders and arms extended on either side to grip the wall. A colorless scrap of cloth was draped over one shoulder; the rest of him was smeared with ash-like soil.

(*He's only got one leg and he's holding himself up there in the hallway and his FACE*)

His face was gone. Bits of putty-like flesh clung to the skull. What looked like bluish skin was pulled so tight across his body that it appeared it might snap off in one great reveal, exposing nothing but a broad ribcage. The torso tapered to a waist that was concealed mostly in darkness, his sex hidden. Below, one thick leg bore his weight. Where the other leg should have been, there was a stump.

His hands were planted on either wall of the entryway like great dead spiders.

Where his eyes should have been, worms boiled. Despite their frenzied revolutions they stayed inside the head of this wretched…

(*DEAD*)

… guest, showing the length of their fat healthy bodies to Dane in a mad dance.

Dead! It's arms were so strong, they had to be to move this maggoty thing about! The sinewy arms looked like well-fed pythons, supporting his weight and advancing with ringing CLAPS along the walls it's one leg just hop-hop-hopping as it came into the kitchen.

Dane shrieked at the almighty horror and grabbed madly at his sides. His left hand found a cane, that was propped against the counter. The man flew at him, and he swung his entire body with a cry.

Dane struck desperately at the man. He hit nothing.

Nothing, he just took an icy spin through the air of the empty kitchen. His feet tangled in something on the floor and he went down with a raucous crash.

Dane stared into the empty doorway and hollered "OH MY BLEEDING *CHRIST*!!!"

Kara burst from the bedroom. She saw Dane lying on the floor behind the table, and squealed. "Whatwhatwhat?!?"

He rolled over, to prop himself up, fumbling to free his feet from what looked like Casey's robe. He spit unintelligible syllables about the man that had pulled himself down the hall on one leg. He thought he was still somewhere in the room, maybe overhead, maybe on the ceiling—

His fingertips touched the dark spot on the floor and pushed through it like a brush through paint, leaving a messy scribble as he slipped and collapsed. He landed with his face inches from the puddle. Blood. He screamed again.

The back door flew open, and Casey staggered through, his mouth crimson, teeth gnashing in a gibbering howl.

"Let's look at what we *do* know." Kara said for the tenth time that night. They had turned on every light in the house, every corner of the kitchen was brightly lit. The three were gathered around the table under the garish light, cell phones in hand. Casey held a rag over his nose and mouth and answered Kara in muffled shouts.

"Someone was in the house. Someone busted my fucking nose. He had a cane. Now I don't know if what Dane is saying about this one-legged guy is entirely accurate. I mean… "

"Hey," Dane barked, holding out his reddened fingers. "What's this?"

"My blood, from when the guy cold-cocked me!" Casey grunted. "That verifies *my* story, friend, not yours. Look, we're both still floating a little. We're still high. I say a guy with a cane attacked me and dragged me outside. You say a rotting gimp came tearing along the walls at you and then just disappeared? That when you hit him with the cane, poof, he was gone? Can we just put these two things side by side and look at them? Like Kara said."

"I said... " Dane began.

"My story makes sense." Casey muttered, flecks of blood raining down on the cloth as he lowered it from his face. "Dane saw the same guy after I fought with him... " Dane opened his mouth again, but Casey pressed on, "—but in his head he got it all mixed up. It was a guy with a bad leg, not one leg. He didn't have his cane anymore, because he wasn't using it to walk. He used it to smash my face. Dane didn't hit him because he was too fast, not because he just disappeared... "

"Your cane was the one I swung at him. I'm sure of it." Dane murmured. He was turning his hands over and over, still trying to discern what was real.

"I'd like you both to get your stories straight and make them the same damn story before we call the cops." Kara said.

Dane absently shook his head and said "Cops? I don't even know what I saw anymore. Cops walk in here and they're going to see a couple of doped-up morons in their underwear describing the same intruder two different ways."

"Which is why I suggest we go with my description," Casey intoned, "the one that isn't craaaaaazy. I'm fairly lucid, I've got blood on my face and I can tell a convincing story. So let's just drop your thing about the Flying Torso. Kara, call the police."

"Why would someone come in here and drag you out into the snow? And then leave?" Dane placed his hand over Kara's phone, trying to infuse his babbling with some reason. "Maybe some derelict thought the place was empty."

"He switched canes with me, that's what gets me, why would he do that? He switched canes, then when I realized it, when I turned, he just knocked me into next week. I woke up lying out by the car."

"I bet you scared him," Kara said, "as much as he scared you... maybe he was confused, delirious or drunk, and maybe he even thought he'd killed you. Dragged you out there and then took off into the woods."

"Do you think he'll come back?" Dane wondered aloud.

"He didn't take anything. He didn't go into any of the bedrooms, at least I don't think so." Kara pulled her hair around her face and let out a long sigh.

Casey sat back, lost in his thoughts. They wouldn't call the police, or anybody else. They would simply lock all the doors and leave the lights on at night. It was an absurd misadventure that he felt oddly responsible for... as if, had he been sober and asleep, maybe they wouldn't have ever known that the old derelict had wandered through the house and left. As it was...

He saw a flash of the man with the cane, recovering a bit of memory. He recalled that quarter-second glimpse in his mind's eye, the bit of the man's face he'd spied while en route to the kitchen floor. A gray, sallow face, hairless, sunken, with a monocle. A monocle! Skin grew around the edges of it, pressed deep into the papery flesh around the eye socket. Bubbles of pus encrusted the edges of the glass. It looked as though the skin had healed itself by growing around the glass after being broken by it's pressure. He had looked emaciated, a large filthy suit hanging from his gaunt frame. Frail as the man had seemed, he'd sent the cane handle into Casey's face like a corked bat.

"I want to sleep," he told the others. Kara was the first to nod. "Okay, let's secure the place. Dane, will you check on the car. Let's just go to bed and figure this out come morning."

"Yes," Dane said dully, "That'll work. Okay."

They left all the lights on until sunrise.

3. THE GRAVES - SECOND WARNING

By lunch, they had decided that the whole surreal event was something that should remain an uncertain memory. Kara wanted to go see the graveyard. With the evening's events still fresh, the men didn't want to be alone and decided to join her

After bundling up and pulling on thick winter boots, they tramped across the snow to the main road. The air was still, and the earth and sky shared the same pearly tone. Kara quietly studied the way that the trees flanked their progress as she led the group.

"I guess we just chalk that whole business up as one of life's little mysteries." Casey said, patting Dane's shoulder. "Sure, this mystery smashed my nose into my skull, but they can't all be as pleasant as we'd like."

"If anything else happens… "

"Relax, I'm not complaining. I don't want to mess with the police. It's just funny. How fucking random is that? And what we saw."

"You mean what *I* saw." Dane corrected him, watching the cold freezing his breath into clouds. "I saw the ghost of a 'rotting gimp' climbing the walls, you saw a hobo with a cane."

"Right."

The headstones were lightly dusted with snow. Most of them were simple, squat pillars that had fallen into decay long ago. As they reached the first of them, Kara knelt and began gently brushing snow and debris from the stone. She held her breath, her movements were painfully delicate, as if the stone would crumble under the pressure of her work or simply, her breath. The elements had had their way with these relics, they were hard to read. She exhaled deeply and examined the barren stone. Satisfied, she pulled tracing paper from her coat. In her gloved hand, she clenched a thick charcoal crayon and with the other, lovingly laid the paper over the scars in the stone. She vigorously rubbed the charcoal across the paper until a couple of letters came into sharp relief. It appeared to be a name, the only letters visible were a *B* and a *J*. Casey, grinning, opened his mouth, ready to create an obscene phrase out of the letters. Dane drove an elbow into his side before he could spit it out. "Would you just... " Dane pleaded.

"I suppose I'll go dick around over there," Casey said with an aloof shrug, and walked past them, further into the cemetery. For several hundred yards, headstones dotted the earth. There were remnants of an old iron fence that once surrounded the whole place, now just errant rusty spikes, wrapped in frost protruding from random spots on the perimeter. Beyond the fallen iron, the birches, stripped of leaves, were plentiful.

Kara had moved to the stone behind the first. "Look at this." She motioned to a little alcove in the headstone. In it was set a tiny bell, warped by time and vandals, but still fixed in place. Below the bell was a hole. "Do you know what it is?" Kara asked.

"This guy feared being buried alive." Dane explained, suspecting that Kara knew all about it, but still wanting to impress her. He watched his breath leave his mouth as he circled the grave. "The cord would have led right down into his coffin, so that if he awoke to find himself interred after some sort of death-like illness, he could ring that bell and summon the caretaker to his rescue. Before medicine was more exact, people were actually declared dead, but were simply ill. There were people buried alive. It became a cultural phenomenon - the terror of live burial. In a cemetery this old, these people were probably laid to rest in the late nineteenth and early twentieth centuries, I wouldn't be surprised to see a few more of these alarm bells, or at least their housings." He joined Kara in kneeling before the headstone. "I'm surprised this is still here. Do you think we could pry it out?"

"Oh, don't." She said. Her lips were painted bright red and formed a scolding smile. "I'm going to sketch this. Why don't you toddle off and see if you can find any more?"

"'Toddle'?"

"What would our babies look like?"

"Okay, you've got me, I'm on the run."

He shoved his hands in his pockets and backpedaled in mock horror, narrowly missing a half-headstone jutting at an angle from the frozen ground.

Across the graveyard, Casey leaned against a robust tree and tried to piece together names based on the weathered symbols before him. "Bart? Bartholomew? No, shit… Betsy. Dane!" He waved to his friend, who was pacing around a black cross. "Here lies Betsy Timmons and SON."

"Dead baby I guess," Dane said breathlessly, leaning against Casey, "maybe she died in childbirth? The dates are all gone. You know I've heard stories of women taking sick, being buried alive and giving birth in their graves."

"I've heard stories of rich women burying their children born of infidelity in tiny coffins and putting stepping stones over them in their gardens."

"The sick crap I'm talking about is actually documented, not pulp trash thought up just to make someone nauseous."

"Oh, it doesn't make me nauseous." Reclining on a tree, Casey smiled, flashing his perfect teeth. Gripping his cane with both hands he dug into the topsoil. "Honest question, between the two of us: how hard do you think it would be to dig up one of these guys?"

"Oh, for God's sake."

"I'm serious. And don't call for her to bail you out, let her finish rubbing those old fogies off! You know how the Germans and Chinese have done the plastination thing? Replacing cadavers' water and fat with plastic to immaculately preserve the body for artistic manipulation. Now obviously you can't do that with these remains but… "

"You're talking about grave-robbing. We're getting back to Ed Gein territory. What, you want to make furniture out of bones? Not only is it illegal, it's uninteresting. Did you think about that?" Dane knew that if he registered any shock or distaste to Casey, it would only serve to encourage him. Being offensive was quite the motivator for Casey. The only hope Dane had of discouraging his ridiculous idea was to challenge the artistic rather than ethical merits of such a project.

"That isn't what I want to do." Casey pouted and his face darkened. "Never mind. Look, no one gives a shit that these graves are out here, that memorials to peoples' lives are out here in the middle of fucking nowhere. They're forgotten and their children's children's children have been forgotten too. This isn't a holy place, it's a scrap yard, it's no different than the rest of these woods really. What lies beneath our feet, if it hasn't turned to dust, means nothing to no-body."

"I appreciate your heartless sentiment, Casey, but the fact remains that desecrating this place would be against the law. You go back to school with a wagon full of bones and people will want to know where you got them. I know you want to do something extreme and shocking and that you want people to just stand there and gawk instead of asking themselves if it actually *means* anything… "

Dane let his voice die, he had tipped his hand and now Casey understood why Dane really objected to the plan. Both their eyes followed the last statement as it drifted up toward the heavens.

"Well." Casey said, lips disappeared in a satisfied, ugly little smile.

"You know what I mean."

"Yes, I do."

"Casey."

"Do me a favor? Fuck off? I need a smoke."

"Are you serious? I trivialize your work and you're going to give me a fuck-off and have a joint? Ugh." Dane shrugged the chill from his shoulders and considered another attempt at making his point. Before he could speak, Casey pivoted away on his cane, fumbling for his lighter.

Kara had continued her work, finding more graves with bells. Five in fact, in a row. They were right on the north edge of the cemetery facing the house, the old decrepit fence ran between them and the cemetery proper. She had focused on these five; the rubbings were complete and her sketchbook was filling rapidly with disjointed impressions of the markers. She didn't want to get too involved in her sketches, so decided to use her camera to get a clear shot of the stones. The cemetery wasn't going anywhere, she could always come back if she needed to.

The name on the fifth stone was easy to read: MAX. Looking through her viewfinder, she noticed something below the name. She dropped down in front of the stone and began a new rubbing. An image emerged below the name, it looked like it might be a sailing ship. A freighter, maybe. Who were these people? She wondered. Was the fear of misdiagnosis the only reason they had feared being buried alive? Was their culture haunted by a folk legend, or were the concerns specific to their little community? Why these five in a row? She stood and walked back and forth amongst them, trying to find some commonality among the markers.

L.S.

She realized that it was an L.S. etched near the bell's housing. Each of the five headstones had the initials. She jotted them down. Movement at the corner of her eye drew her gaze to Dane, who was sort of following Casey around the cemetery. It looked like Casey was ignoring him. It made her wonder what others found endearing about Casey, particularly Dane. Casey was unremarkable. He wasn't interesting enough to loathe, he wasn't as offensive as he thought (or wished) he was. But Dane, he sometimes trailed after him like a damn puppy. She preferred to think that Dane was trying to be a friend, offering some sound advice rather than seeking acceptance. Dane wasn't the desperate sort. He didn't even seek his father's validation *that* feverently, he just took the checks.

When they were in college, Casey was a bisexual terror, roaming the upper echelons of the school's social empire. He was savvy enough not to play the Hot Topic emo-goth slut. Although to an outsider they all looked the same, these groups did have *some* nuance in their conformist non-conformity. God, he loved to play with them. He was happy to be their golden boy for as long as it took for him to get what he needed. What did he *do*? Kara was stumped. What was he *about*? Casey was a chameleon, a reflection of the people around him. He mirrored their gaping faces and grasping hands, their applause and laughter. After playing the vapid heartbreaker at some pajama party he was off to somebody's something in a crisp suit he'd borrowed/stolen from Dane. In short he was an amalgam of the self-aware counter-culture clichés, mostly harmless but... Kara wondered. It was guys like Casey that eventually realized they were preening ghosts and snapped in an awful way.

I can't wait to get away from school and all this poseur crap, she thought.

The ground seemed to burp beneath her, breaking her reverie.

She was crouching over the resting place of someone named RIPLEY, she peered between her knees at the particles of dead leaves dotting the snow. She tried to figure out what had just happened, had the earth... no. But it did feel like there was some distant tremor, didn't it? She looked around the cemetery, the only things moving for miles around were her violently pounding heart and Dane and Casey trudging around.

Whatever the sensation was, it left her. She returned her focus to her camera.

She could still see Dane and Casey moving in her peripheral vision. One of them moved toward her and stopped a short distance away. She glanced up, over Ripley's headstone, and saw it.

It was a man, a man that looked as though he had been painted in angry black and gray slashes, torn from a canvas and dropped in this cemetery scene. As she straightened up, Kara began to make sense of his sloppy appearance. He was dressed in sopping rags, layer upon layer of wet, material clinging to his tall, skeletal frame. His face was still indistinct at this distance, it was just a mess of black and gray like the rest of him. He was standing stock-still, not more than ten yards from her, and just staring. At least, it felt like he was staring... she couldn't quite make out his eyes. But she felt it and he was staring her down. His blackened hands closed into fists. She saw his raw knuckles exposed. Then his face came into focus.

It was a melting, sloughing ruin of dead flesh.

She threw her arms out, falling back on her ass in the snow before Ripley's gravestone. The man-thing didn't move, but his clothing did. What she thought was liquid was actually some kind of viscous slime oozing down over his shoulders, chest and legs. It caught the light off the snow and looked as though a hundred tiny, winking eyes were descending down the tattered shirt of the man, the dead man. She tried to shriek. It froze in her throat and she sat there, quivering.

The cold stinging her nostrils was likely the only thing preventing the odor of him from knocking her all the way down, but to think that was to acknowledge that he was real. He was a goddamned corpse, covered in foul sludge. With that realization, a scream finally escaped her and shot into the sky.

Dane and Casey spun at the edge of the woods at the sound. They quickly scanned the cemetery, but Kara was nowhere to be seen. They took off across the yard, racing toward the line of headstones where they had last seen her. Listening as they ran for a second scream, there was none. Dane shouted her name. Looking everywhere but right in front of him, he tripped right over her, narrowly avoiding braining himself on a jagged rock.

"Jesus!" He gasped. Kara turned her white face toward him, her lips moving soundlessly. He crawled over to her and grabbed her arms. "What is it? Are you all right? Say something!"

Catching up to the scene, Casey stopped and scanned the trees. Had he seen something moving out there? Impossible, he thought. If he had, he would've spotted it by now for sure. His thoughts immediately returned to the man who had attacked him in the cottage. These trees weren't thick enough to hide an anorectic much less that shambling bum.

(or a ghoul with a monocle cutting through its eyelids)

He peeled off his gloves and let out a groan. "How did you fall, Kara? Dane, you're probably giving her a panic attack for the love of God."

"No, it's not that!" She cried. "I saw someone! I am really really sure that I saw someone. Someone fucking horrible right here! Where is he? He was right here in front of me! Oh *shit!*"

In her mind, she tried to make sense of what had happened, but if they couldn't see anyone in the vicinity, then there wasn't anyone here, period. She was positive someone had stood in front of her, she thought she could still smell him. Defeated, she buried her face in her hands and sobbed. "I saw someone."

"Okay, so do we want to rethink ghosts?" Casey asked.

Dane shot him a cruel glare, warning him "Don't. Just don't."

"Well… ?" Casey gestured about them.

"You don't just say 'okay, so it's ghosts'," Kara snapped. "At least *I* don't. And I'm stone-cold sober, goddammit. I'm still shaking." She looked to Dane for reassurance. "Dane?"

He embraced her, rubbing her arms and shoulders to warm and comfort her, whispering nothings into her hair. When he felt her body begin to soften and relax, he spoke softly encouraging her to take action. "I think that maybe last night's scare has gotten to you. You know what, we should call the police. Let's just file a report and have someone come out here and take our statements. They might not do jack, but we'll feel better and at least there will be a record of our complaint. Okay? Let's do that, for peace of mind."

"The voice of reason." Casey said, mocking Dane. He slipped his gloves back on. "Something interesting could be going on, but I guess we'll do the safe thing and skip back to our house in the wood."

"Shut up Casey." Kara muttered. "I mean it."

Disgusted, he retreated across the cemetery.

4. SAMUEL

Paula Hertzfelder-Green intended to pass off her trip to the cottage as an "are-you-all-settled-in-great-here's-my-card" visit . A quick knock 'n' smile with a sly glance through the front of the place. Though the college boy and his money were reputable, she knew that the crème de la crème of the art-brat scene were as prone to cooking meth as were her trailer park clients further down the coast. Pulling up to the house, she was pleased to see an absence of tire tracks and footprints, only one small car at the back of the cottage. It didn't look like the kids were even home. She got out of her Beemer and took in a sharp whiff of that winter air. All part of the package, she reminded herself. As the website said, it was "a page out of early American history."

She slipped her key into the front door and brushed her red curls behind her scarf. Then, fixing her "realtor smile" on her face, she knocked lightly, calling out "Dane? Anyone here?"

There was no answer, so she opened the door slightly to peek through the entryway. She relaxed a bit as everything seemed to be in order.

A young sparrow peered over one of the living-room rafters at her. Feeling emboldened by the challenge the bird presented, she narrowed her eyes, stepped into the house, and pulled the door shut behind her. "I knew we hadn't seen the last of you."

The bird regarded her with curious black pinpricks of eyes. It appeared alone in a small nest scraped together from bark shavings. They'd been able to clear the old nests out of the ventilation ducts, but it never failed that more would crop up in the rafters... but it was odd that this little bird was here in the dead of winter? Strangest thing she'd ever seen. Thank God it added to the "rustic charm" of the place. Still, if this baby were to fall to the floor and break its tiny neck, it would spoil the bons vivants' entire season when they came home to find it gasping its last breath. They'd harangue her out of money.

Paula reached up tentatively with one hand, holding her breath, telling herself she'd just snatch the bugger and toss him outside. Be done with the whole thing. It stared, motionless, at the approach of her gloved fingers.

She never heard or saw anything coming for her. Suddenly, two curved hooks speared her back, each piercing a kidney, pushing a bubble of mucus from her throat and all the breath from her lungs as she let out a guttural scream. She was lifted off the floor by his hooks. She kicked her feet frantically, her eyes glued to the ceiling as something beyond pain took her over, wrapping her in a seething cocoon of agony.

The sparrow watched the dead man with his shriveled yellow eyes and hook hands. The ghoul carried Paula across the room, turned her around and slammed her into the wall with a roar. The cottage's interior rattled. The sparrow's head trembled, but its beady black eyes never left the dusty, creaking hook-man and the choking woman in his embrace.

She was slammed again, this time against the opposite wall. The glass in the windows jumped. Paula's eyes swam wildly in her head, trying to identify her attacker, to make sense of this nightmare. He took her in his arms and spun her around the room as if in a dance, all the time in her mind thinking *I'M GOING TO BE RAPED, THIS IS A RAPE, HE MEANS TO RAPE ME AND LEAVE ME HERE, IF HE'LL ONLY JUST PUT ME DOWN AND END THIS.*

The man was holding her like a bride, the hooks stabbing into her once again. Her head lolled back and blood bubbled over her lips, it ran over her lightly rouged cheeks, and into her ears. As he brought her across the threshold and out the back door, she lifted her head and was finally able to see his face: a shit-colored, pitted skull. The hooks pushed stubbornly through meat and nerves, skewing her vision as agony tore up and down through her body.

He carried her past Dane's car and on through the trees. As her life ebbed away and she lost all sensation, he finally threw his arms apart and tore her in half.

"It's dead." Kara said, cradling the little bird's head, it's little black eyes staring blankly. When they got home, it was lying on the floor under the rafter. Dane swore, disgusted, and sat down in a recliner by the hearth. Casey had gone back to his room as soon as they reached the house.

"Do you want to leave?" Dane asked. He noticed a few spots of blood on the wall and floor beneath it. Had the bird flown into it? Kara set the creature back on the floor. "No, I don't know. Something is happening here, Dane. I'm just going to say it. I think Casey was right."

"About what?"

"Ghosts. A haunting."

She grabbed some tissues from the shelf and enclosed the sparrow's soft body in the Kleenex and said, "We all believe in ghosts, right? Or want to."

"Yeah, but if that's what's going on - and let's say for a second it is - that means Casey was assaulted by one. Bloodied up and knocked unconscious. And whatever showed up in front of you and me disappeared into thin air. Regardless of how remarkable that may be we're done and we should go. I'm not gonna mess around with that stuff. Now, alternately, we could forget this ghost crap and accept that it was just some guy. We call the cops and let them deal with this nut."

"You thought you saw… "

"Forget it!" Dane pounded his legs. "Maybe I did see a ghost, but whatever it is, it's dangerous and I'm not prepared to take any risks when it comes to you."

"To me? So you only want to call the cops because you think something might happen to me?"

"C'mon, it's not a he-man thing, don't you feel the same way about me?"

"I know you can take care of yourself. As can I."

"I'm so not prepared to get into this." Dane pushed his hands through his hair over and over, kneading his scalp. "Ghosts tearing around the woods? That's crazy. How are we supposed to do any work if we're even thinking about that? We're trying to get our damn theses done… and that's a dead bird you're holding, hon!"

Kara looked up at the rafter and noticed a crack in the underside of the beam.

Dane gave an exasperated moan and rose. Kara continued studying the ceiling. "I'm going to talk to Casey." He stalked past her, hoping the vacuum of his presence would tear her attention away from the ceiling for maybe a second, but she didn't even glance after him. He stomped down the hallway.

The fissure in the beam was old and clotted with bits of dust. The crack yawned slightly beneath where the sparrow's nest had been. Kara reached up and dug around as much as she could. She was surprised when the wood yielded to her finger. The crack widened and something wedged inside caught her eye.

A key!

It was stuck fast in the beam, an old-fashioned key like the one that unlocked the front door. She looked around the room for something with which to pry it loose. She remembered the nail file she kept in her purse and grabbed it. She worked the instrument like a little pry bar into the oak and wriggled the key downward so that she could pinch the head of it between her fingertips. With a small grating noise, the key came free in her hand, she stared at it for a moment and wondered what it opened.

There was a flutter of excitement deep in her chest. All of the strange things that were going on couldn't be explained by mere coincidence. Casey seemed convinced that there was something supernatural going on and was happy to find out what it was, so was she. She paused, wondering why Dane wasn't intrigued by the prospect of a ghost. She pushed the thought away, titillated by having her chance to uncover a mystery, she began her search. She walked around the living room with its skimpy furnishings and ran her hands along the cobbled mantel over the fireplace as she passed.

Her fingers bounced along the rough and cold stone of the mantel. The sensation was broken briefly by the absence of so much texture—she had felt something different. She turned quickly toward the mantel and searched for an anomaly in the pattern of the bluish stones. There was a glint of gold and she realized that there was a little keyhole. Among the rocks that comprised the shelf, there was a lock set in an ornamental fashion.

She gingerly inserted the key into the lock, and rotated her wrist with a barely concealed tremor. There was a click followed by the sound of something dropping. After a moment of pushing and knocking on the stones, she found that she was able to slide out the stone that held the lock. Turning the stone over revealed that it was hollow, and that tucked inside was a tiny leather-bound book. In a block script, someone had gently scratched onto the cover that this was a *Journal* belonging to *Samuel*. A ratty old string was tied around it; she loosed the frayed knot and opened the journal.

1907 – September 14

The congregation is dwindling and I think my days here are coming to an end. I'm happy. There's been a terror creeping over me these past months, when I lie in bed, when I'm out digging, and God help me, even when I sit in worship at the chapel. Pastor Mark's eyes are hollow and without light. He doesn't speak to me anymore, just stays in the rectory all day. I have seen him out in the church-

yard at times, late at night, loitering about, sometimes going into the shed and lighting one of my lanterns. I keep nothing out there anymore except shovels and other tools. God, he scares me.

Based on what she read, Samuel was the graveyard's caretaker, and this his house. The cemetery wasn't a family plot, but was attached to a local church. It must be part of a parish she realized, wondering where the church was or had been. She gently turned the yellowed pages, eager to learn more.

1907 – July 20

I haven't told anybody about this and I don't think I will. My hound died early today and I took him out beside the house to lay him to rest. I dug a shallow grave and set him in it, wrapped in his old blanket. As I was about to cover him up, the sun began to rise, and when the light hit him I thought it was nice that he might be warmed one last time before I buried him. So I was standing there, looking down at the old boy, and I knelt to pat his head... and he moved! I swear it he did, he moved his old head and he was dead as dead can be, no doubt in my mind about that. He'd not been eating all week, just coughing up a bit of blood now and then when he shuffled from one end of the house to the other. He was done for and yet he lifted his head and looked up at me, and he made the most godawful, baleful sound, from deep in his throat!

I brought the shovel down on his head, as many times as I could before my arms refused to go on. I was crying, I admit that freely, I wept for him.

1907 – July 23

I thought about telling Pastor Mark. I'm afraid he might say something mean though. There's been nothing but spite in his wretched bones lately. I feel terrible speaking that way about a man of the cloth, but everyone has noticed and Lord, we've all prayed about it. His sermons have been all fire and brimstone, but he speaks without passion, rather he speaks with a sort of mocking sneer, as if he no longer believes in Heaven or Hell, as if he's enjoying the way the congregation cowers before his pulpit. Yesterday when Mister Walker stayed to talk with the pastor, I heard the pastor tell him that there's no such thing as death, that it's a 'great joke' on us all. To say such a thing to a man who's just lost his precious little girl! He did seem quite cold and out of sorts when he spoke at her burial. He even told me not to waste my time digging six foot deep. 'What difference does it make whether it's two or six', he said to me, 'she'll hear her pitiful mourners wailing and feel them stamping on her face'.

Poor Alice Walker, becoming lost and tangled in the birches in the dead night, she must have died in such fear and the pastor's words could not have given her soul any comfort!

Kara flipped forward, gritting her teeth as bits of paper flaked away beneath her fingers.

1907 — October 13

Mary Powell is in hysterics. They've taken her to the rectory following the disrupted service, and the doctor is looking in on her. She says she saw Alice Walker in the churchyard. Some of the men wanted to exhume her coffin, but I insisted she'd had a peaceful burial, and Pastor Mark actually came to my defense. But he had fire in his eyes when he cast them upon Mary Powell! All this is bringing back talk of the negro girl, Dominique, who went missing last year. People continue to drift away from the parish.

1907 — December 1

Someone stole my hound's remains from his grave last night. I heard a clatter against the side of the house and went out there to find the hole, and the old boy's mangy head lying by the door. God has all but left this place. I'm leaving - I'll tell Pastor Mark tomorrow.

1907 — December 4

I'll put this in the mantelshelf once I've finished this entry, and I'll hide the key, hoping that someone other than the pastor finds it. He's a devil! I saw him with those girls, the dead girls! He had them in the rectory, and by God I won't even think to describe what he was doing with them! I don't know how, but he brought those poor souls back to use for his pleasure. What power does he have? But those girls, the dead girls, I swear they were resisting him, were held against their will, their tiny bodies… I feel faint, I feel sick, damn the man! I want to run into town and tell the others but I must leave this record first in case I don't make it! Scott Mark is a devil and the earth beneath this place must be Hell's gate, for it spits bodies back up!

Perhaps the cursed area must only be between the churchyard and this house, for my hound came back, but not the bodies interred in the yard. Pastor

Mark must have dug little Alice from her resting place and put her in that unhallowed ground as well. I am too frightened to imagine what he did to that poor negro girl to bring her back. Thank the Lord that the consecrated earth in which our parishioners are buried does not allow for their resurrection, else they'd join the pastor as his puppets! I pray he lets them rest!

I must hide this now, I don't know if he saw me. I must do something to prevent this from going on.

Dane had calmed down considerably since his talk with Kara. He was feeling guilty for storming out on her and for being harsh with Casey earlier in the day. Deciding it was time to mend fences, he went down the hall and knocked quietly on Casey's door.

"Come in." Casey called out.

Dane stepped into the room "Casey," he began, "what I said out there, I was frustrated, that's all. I didn't mean it."

"You probably just wanted to get a rise out of me, putting me down like that. Right? No sweat, I can relate." Pulling a baggie from his backpack, Casey slouched on his bed and began shaking the seeds from a dry nug of marijuana.

Dane slumped in the doorway. "We need to talk, Case."

"I want to go into town." Kara said, suddenly appearing behind Dane.

He turned and asked, "To the police?"

"No," she replied, "the library." Ignoring Dane's arched eyebrow, she pushed past him and waved at Casey. "Hey, you want to know what I found? Before you smoke yourself into oblivion again? Do you want to look up for a second?"

"No." Came the sullen response. The boy busied himself with the baggie.

"Dane, c'mon." Kara tugged her boyfriend's arm. "Let him pout."

"It's an hour's drive just to get there. What've you got?"

"I'll tell you on the way. Let's goooo!"

When Casey finally looked up from his baggie and pushed his bangs out of his face he saw that the doorway was empty. He heard the car starting outside and glanced out his window. Well, he thought, they were off to the library. "Pretty pair," he murmured. He pulled his rolling papers from underneath the pillow. He slipped one out of the package and stuck it to the tip of his tongue.

Outside the window, among the bony trees, a gaunt man with hooks for hands stood and watched the boy.

Somewhere else, somewhere very dark, far from the warmth of the cottage, a halved woman was being torn apart by hands stiff from hunger and the cold.

5. L.S.

Kara read passages from the caretaker's journal to Dane on the way to the nearby township. The modest library was situated across from the city hall on a quiet main thoroughfare. The building took up an entire block and was surrounded by a yard, painted white by the snow. As Dane listened to Kara, he tried to organize the bizarre fragments of the journal entries into a mosaic that somehow included the events of the previous afternoon and evening. "What became of this parish?" He asked.

"We'll find out soon enough." Kara anxiously gripped her door handle as they pulled into a parking stall before the library entrance. Once inside, they found a small circulation desk situated amongst racks of new hardcovers and featured children's books. A stout teen trying to look awake by keeping his head propped attentively (he was actually dozing) at the desk glanced up at them through half-slit eyes.

"Hi." The boy said lazily.

"Do you have a section on local history? Folklore, maybe?" Kara asked.

The kid gave her a look of complete incomprehension. "You mean like the census, or what?"

"She means," said Dane, stepping forward, "something like stories about the early settlers of the town, about an old parish up north. Do you have any books about the town founders?"

"Nine-seven-four in nonfiction—that's history of the northeast U.S." The boy recited dully. "Religious stuff's in the two hundreds."

"We'll just browse ourselves," Kara said and tugged Dane along.

In a back corner, Kara found exactly what she was looking for. Thom Yeats' *Early Quinessett and Outlying Townships* looked like it had never been cracked open. It was a surprisingly voluminous tome. She and Dane removed their coats and gloves and sat themselves on either side of a reading table. They were warmed by the sunlight streaming in through the tall narrow windows behind them.

"If the journal had been sitting in that mantel for the last hundred years, what makes you think there's anything about it in this book?" Dane asked.

"I'm looking for information about the decline of the parish and anything about those girls. Dominique, the black girl who went missing in 1906, and Alice Walker who in 1907 was buried somewhere in the cemetery."

She stopped and scanned several pages in silence. "I think I've got it. Regarding the parish, anyway. Parish of St. Andrew. Patron saint of Scotland. Saint Andrew was a disciple, eventually crucified on the Saltire Cross, that x-shaped cross. I guess that's what's represented on the Scottish flag? Anyway, the parish's numbers dropped in the early 1900s, and never recovered following the disappearance of… Pastor Scott Mark."

"Disappeared?"

"In 1907. It says 'Pastor Mark, whose character had fallen into ill repute among the parishioners, was seen by many as a dark cloud that had fallen over the modest church community. In fact—get this, Dane—after he vanished, some whispered that he may have had a hand in the mysterious disappearances and deaths of seven young girls between the turn of the century and the time that he himself went missing.'"

"Is there anything about the caretaker? Samuel?"

Again she searched silently. Dane had finally caught the curiosity bug and leaned forward with interest.

"Nothing." Kara said with a sigh.

Flipping ahead to another chapter, Kara read that "'The churchyard was used by locals for another forty-nine years while the defunct St. Andrews fell into ruin. It would eventually be bought up by city fathers and torn down. The community demanded that the very foundations be covered by earth and stones, in an effort to exorcise the property of its accursed past. The churchyard still stands today as an historic site.

"'The last men interred there were five wealthy locals who were members of the Leichenhaus Society, known as the L.S. *Leichenhaus* meaning a corpse-house, or waiting mortuary, these were a popular fixture in Germany at the height of society's fear of live burials. Bodies would be kept briefly at these 'waiting mortuaries' until it was certain that the person being buried was indeed deceased.'"

"The gravestones with the bells, at the edge of the cemetery." Exclaimed Dane.

"I saw an 'L.S.' on one of them." Kara told him. "The men were Max Underwood, Brion Jensen Frost, Charles Ripley, Edgar Morris and Harold Whitehurst. And, yes," she read further "'each purchased a plot and headstone complete with a bell system in the event that they were not dead, but in a death-like coma.'. There were also 'rumors of tunnels carved deep underground, allowing them to escape from the cheap pine boxes in which they were buried and crawl to safety in the event that no one heard the pealing of the bells attached to their headstones.'"

"Talk about paranoid." Dane shook his head in bemusement. Hearing the journal entries excited him. By the time they arrived at the library, the gravity of their own situation had given way to the depth of this mystery. "Well, get back to Scott Mark and the parish, because if we're being haunted my guess would be that it revolves around the priest."

"We've all seen men, though, wearing suits if they wore anything at all - not little girls or a clergyman."

"What, do you think the L.S. is out to get us? Wait, what about Samuel?"

"Why would he attack Casey, or mess with any of us at all for that matter?" Kara asked. "It doesn't add up… maybe it was just a homeless guy after all."

"I'm sure now that I saw a guy with one leg in the front hall." Dane insisted. "And the man you saw couldn't have been a man at all, if he was, we would have seen him run off? There's nowhere to hide out there. What if what we saw were ghosts and what attacked Casey was… was, something else?"

"Let's keep reading about the L.S." Kara's eyes drifted further down the page. "It says here that each died under unusual circumstances in the 1950s." The Fifties—it occurred to Kara that the deteriorating grave markers seemed much older; it was as if they'd been corrupted by something other than the elements. She continued reading aloud while musing over it. "Max Underwood, a shipping magnate who owned a mill in Quinessett lost his hands in an industrial accident. He caught an infection after having prosthetics fit to his wrists, and died in his bed. Harold Whitehurst's home burned to the ground. Brion Frost contracted an unknown illness that crippled him before he died. Edgar Morris… " She grew silent, and a visible tremor moved through her body. Dane touched her hand and she started. "Sorry. Morris fell into a vat of chemicals at Underwood's mill, which he had taken control of when Underwood passed—they didn't find much of him that was recognizable. Melted his skin off."

"And the last guy?"

"Charles Ripley. Was seen leaping in front of a train, *severing his left leg almost at the waist.*"

"Oh my God."

"We've got to get back to the cottage."

In his box, his tomb, his prison, he called out to them. Scott Mark's piercing, unholy scream could be heard only by the dead. He called out to them.

It was Samuel, stupid grinning Samuel, who'd sealed him into this endless Hell beyond Hells. At least he'd been able to fatally wound the bugger beforehand, but it was no consolation all these countless years later. Even his communion with the dark forces felt empty, as if there was in fact no intelligence behind the energy that sustained him, as if it were merely the foul leavings of an idiot-god long dead.

And the girls, *his* girls, he no longer had their cold comforts, as he had in life. They'd been a welcome distraction for his flesh, for so long he had been denied such distractions while in service to his former God. The girls quieted the naggings of his body while his mind reached out to the unknown and sought the voice of a new god.

With death, the new god gave him many gifts, conjuring mists into any shape - to haunt and terrify the living, and his favorite, most potent power… the control of those foolish men, now dead…

The L.S., he had reached them in their opiate deliriums as they sat in the churchyard. Their minds were so pliant as they sat in that haze, muttering about death and dying, about wanting to *defy* death. In fact they had given themselves to him when they chose grave sites on the border between Christ's worthless churchyard and the seething earth that contained his new Lord's dark energy. At this very moment, lying in their tunnels, chewing a woman's warm red meat, they heard Mark's baleful howling and with their maggot-eaten brains they vaguely heard his beseeching. With the mental voice of a fire-and-brimstone preacher, he called to them.

KILL THEM NOW, KILL THEM AND FEED SO THAT YOUR FEEBLE ARMS AND LEGS AND MINDS WILL HAVE THE STRENGTH NEEDED TO PULL ME OUT OF THIS BOX! NOOOOOOWWWWWW

They had been able to feed on the occasional vagrant during the warmer months, but their strength was waning; they needed to gorge themselves before he could trust them to complete the final task. He felt them moving beneath the earth now. He smiled a lipless, broken smile.

Deep in the woods, a heavy stone slab shifted and was pushed off to one side. Leathery hands stained with blood emerged from a gaping hole.

The L.S. gathered topside and moved towards the cottage.

6. CASEY

Lying on his bed with his hands tucked behind his head, Casey laid plans to head out to the graveyard at twilight and unearth a few head-stones.

He had decided that he didn't need to dig up the bodies to express himself, he could use their meaningless memorials instead. The pieces of rock with the names, once meticulously carved, now nearly obliterated. Stones with great chunks missing from the sides. What would he do with them? He answered himself, deciding that he could take them and wrap shiny Christmas ribbons around the stone, paste on images of emaciated models from fashion magazines—no, even better, he'd carve nudes from the stone itself! Not tasteful nudes. Pornographic statuettes. Taking these forgotten, "revered" symbols and reshaping them into modern obscenities—a commentary on what truly endures in the public consciousness. He mentally patted himself on the back. He'd have to buy some equipment and toil beneath the winter moon all night in order to loose the stones from that frozen soil. He didn't care, it would be worth it.

Sitting upright and waiting for his senses to follow his movements, he threw a hand out in search of his bong and heard it clatter on the floor. The filthy water splashed over his discarded socks. He shrugged and stepped over the mess to fetch a new pair. How long had the lovebirds been gone? Maybe they were back. "Daaaaaaaaane," he hollered, he stumbled as he tried to pull one sock on and then the other, while walking. He leaned out the doorway. No response. The house was his.

He went into the kitchen and saw a bundle of tissues beside the sink. He peeked inside and groaned. A dead bird. "What is this, my dinner? Thanks, Kara!" He called, trudging back to their room to turn up the thermostat.

As he toyed with the knob, there was a clunk from the heater room in the corner. The system didn't begin its telltale hum. He crossed the room and pulled the door open. The heater unit was silent. He smacked it and growled. "C'mon, don't make me call some podunk repairman out here and make small talk alone with him. Piece of crap."

Returning to the kitchen, he grabbed a bag of chips from atop the fridge and tore into it. Dane and Kara, why the hell had he come out here with them? He would've found something to do, back in the city. His thesis would've fallen out of his ass at some point without any effort. Maybe he would just loot the churchyard and leave this dump after that. That was it, he decided. He would go back to the city. He needed to call some people and tell them of his impending holiday comeback. Casey walked back to his room and scattered chips across the floor as he bent to grab his phone.

No signal. Maybe if he went outside. He got his coat.

He walked through the kitchen, heading for the back door when he noticed that the dead bird was gone. He couldn't remember if he had tossed it in the garbage, but couldn't think of anything else he would do with a dead bird, so figured he must have thrown it out.

Despite the cold, he was in no rush. He sauntered along the path left by the departed car, shaking his phone. He circled the cottage and meandered in the direction of the cemetery. Casey noticed sets of shuffling shoe prints in the snow, but figured they were from the trio's earlier excursion. He listened through his pot-induced haze for a dial tone from the cell, but still nothing. Eventually, the snow-capped gravestones loomed ahead. Deciding not to waste the trip, he walked over to them and stooped to test a few, seeing if any could be worked loose.

One stone had a diagonal crack that had become filled with ice; over many winters the freezing water had expanded and exacerbated the fissure. He gave it a kick and felt the top half of the marker yield. Squinting, he sang "Mister Wallace, this is your resurrection day," and forgetting his damaged legs for a moment, swung his boot into the stone.

The top of it sailed off, and pain rang through his leg. "Shit!" He hopped backwards, wishing he'd brought his cane along. "Fuck me." Thank God he was stoned and the ringing pain lessened to a dull ache. Casey grabbed the chunk of rock. The letter W and part of an A were barely visible. Then, a shadow fell across his vision, darkening the letters.

He looked up and saw the man with the cane. Beyond any sliver of doubt, this man was dead. The maggot pressing against the glass of his monocle only confirmed his conclusion.

Casey staggered back, shaking his head. "You're not real—you can't touch me—this isn't—"

On the edge of the cemetery, behind the cane man, Casey saw another figure. The man with the cane appeared to be frozen, with bits of frost on him, but the other... It was hard for him to tell. He looked wet and indistinct, covered in some sort of tarry substance that looked like melted flesh.

He turned to run. His legs complained, ankles threatening to fold beneath him, but he pushed ahead, into the trees. Dane and Kara, he thought to himself, they had the car, the stupid idiots were cruising around town an hour away and his goddamn phone was worthless. He realized he was still holding the chunk of gravestone and clung to it like a security blanket. Where was the fucking house??

He saw a building up ahead—not the house.

A chapel.

An old, weathered white chapel with a tall roof and steeple reaching into the featureless chalk-white sky. He couldn't understand why they hadn't seen it before, he must have run further away from the house. The chapel was just sitting there in the midst of the birches. Casey half-stumbled in disbelief, unease crawling over him the closer he got to the church. He couldn't let it stop him, not with the dead men gaining on him. He had to go inside. It was his only hope.

Before he could even set hands on it, the door opened with a heavy groan. Brittle leaves followed Casey into the aisle between two rows of pews. Dark-colored stained glass windows framed the quiet scene, and clouds of dust moved silently along the backs of the seats.

The door thundered shut behind him. Casey ran to the pulpit.

Casey thought he could hear fists beating on the doors. *Why don't they just throw them open? Can't they come in here?* Casey felt a twinge of hope as he crouched behind the pulpit. *Maybe they can't! It's a church, isn't it?*

These thoughts still rang in his head as the floorboards violently exploded behind him. A creature burst up from under the chapel. It was a broad-shouldered undead man with blackened hunks of flesh clinging to his big bones. Moving quickly, he dug his claws into Casey's shoulders and hurled him into the pews.

The seats crumbled like mirages, Casey slammed into the floor with a choked-off cry. The stone flew from his hands. He rolled into pew after pew and they simply gave way to his rag-doll body. The burnt man stepped down from the pulpit and began to unwind a chain from around his right forearm.

"Oh *God*—"

The chain whipped out, catching Casey's foot. The creature yanked hard on the chain, the force pulling Casey briefly into the air. He fell on his shoulder blades with an impact that sent bursts of light through his brain. Dust rained down from the ceiling. The burnt man gathered the chain and advanced on his prey.

"Why are you doing this? Jesus, stop!" Casey threw his hands out pleadingly. "I don't understand! I didn't do anything! What do you want! Tell me! TALK!!"

The burnt man opened his cracked lips, pus running down his chin, and made a sound.

"*Maaaaaaaaaaaaa.*"

Casey turned to run out the doors, forgetting the chain around his ankle. It pulled taut and sent him crashing facedown to the ground.

The burnt man reached the boy, lifted him and tossed him against one of the windows; it buckled, but didn't shatter completely, instead raining little red and green daggers of glass on Casey's back. The picture of St. Andrew began to disappear as the window caved in. The chain landed beside his head with a jarring clap. He rolled aside and screamed bloody murder.

A charred hand closed around Casey's throat. He had the distant sensation of being lifted off the floor as his windpipe collapsed. He found himself looking into empty black eyes like those of the dead sparrow. With his free hand, the burnt man punched out two adjacent windows, lashing the chain around the beam between them. He wrapped the other end of the chain around Casey's throat, hanging him there.

Bitterly cold air swept into Casey's lungs. "Please," he croaked, "why?" The burnt man said nothing. He just stood there. The doors behind him opened.

The melting man and the cane man entered, shambling across the floor to join their companion. They weren't alone.

One of their two companions was familiar from Dane's description - he had only one leg and pulled himself along by his hands, pushing now and then with his leg. The other man had hooks for hands. Casey watched as the zombies came toward him. Realizing his fate, he emptied his bladder on the chapel floor.

They stood around him in a semi-circle. There wasn't a sound. "Don't eat me." He whispered.

The burnt man reached out and touched two fingers to Casey's face; one on his eyebrow, the other on his cheekbone, and applied pressure to the eye. Casey screamed and squirmed while the others moved in to hold him down.

His view of the dead men blurred suddenly, violently, and he was keenly aware that his eye had been plucked from its socket and was being tugged out. Then his vision blurred again, the entire scene faded; he saw that there was no chapel. He felt bark digging into his back and realized he'd been lashed to a tree. *What? How could that be, a ghost building? And these things, these zombies, they've been more like flickering specters—appearing and disappearing from our view—or maybe they were always there, just as the chapel never was, something is playing with our powers of perception.* Someone.

Their master.

Then the pain hit, real pain, sobering pain that tore Casey from his haze. Every second of the remaining moments of his life were perfectly clear: the sounds, smells and most of all, the pain. He screamed with all his might as the burnt man closed his teeth on the stringy optic nerve.

A hook slammed into Casey's soft belly and pulled upward. Warmth and agony spread across his waist. Hands dug greedily into him, raping him, introducing pain to parts of his body that he never knew existed. His head jerked against the tree, blood rocketed from his eye socket and lips. "STOOOOOOOOOOOP-P-P-P-P-P-P-P!!" He screamed - the forest did not answer.

They were peeling off his clothes, fondling his goose-pimpled flesh, wearing yawning smiles. One of them patted his cheek with a blood-caked hand before going after his other eye. Casey was freed from the horror of seeing his own devouring. He felt that God was mocking him as his other senses sharpened.

Chewing, grunting, shuffling to get a good position at the feeding trough, they pulled out his entrails with relish, blood and shit soiling the snow at the base of the tree and spilling over their shoes. Ripley pushed his head through the mess, eager for Casey's toes.

The boy died in their cold, hungry embrace.

7. BACK TO THE HOUSE

Dane pulled around the cottage. The back door was wide open. "Nice," he muttered, his stress compounded by both anger and concern. Kara jumped out as he shifted into park. "Wait up!" He called.

She ran inside and called Casey's name. His room was empty, as was the rest of the house. His cane was propped against the wall. "Where could he have gone?" She yelled.

"Don't know!" Dane replied, from elsewhere in the house.

Kara glanced in the bathroom, pushing the shower curtain back. She caught a glimpse of herself in the mirror and saw fear draining the color from her flesh. *What am I afraid of? What's going on?* She asked herself silently.

Behind her in the mirror was a window to the garden. She thought she saw something in her peripheral vision, but before she could focus on it, the window exploded with glass flying into the room at her. A hook at the end of an arm swiped at her as a horrible, disfigured man clawed his way into the small bathroom.

She toppled head over heels through the doorway and into the hall. Dane appeared at the other end as she let loose an incoherent wail. He started toward her. She shook her head madly.

The zombie, had hooks for hands—*Max Underwood*, her mind registered, recalling what she had read earlier—tumbled into the bathroom into a heap on the floor. Fortunately, his fall was not graceful and his head hit the door, knocking it shut with a slam. Dane grabbed Kara's shoulder. "What's Casey... "

"Not Casey!" She shrieked.

The doorknob rattled. She imagined the miserable thing on the other side of the door with a hook around the knob, trying to haul itself to its feet. The thought was enough to get her on her feet, she turned and pushed Dane down the hall ordering him "Out! Car!"

They emerged from the hall and tore through the kitchen, crashing out the back door. Horribly, standing between them and the car, was the melting man. *Edgar Morris*, Kara thought, putting the story of a chemical bath to the zombie before her. In his slimy hands he held a piece of a broken headstone.

Dane's jaw dropped. He searched for words, for something to make sense of this, to define it and send it away. "You... get... "

The Morris-thing raised the stone over its head, eyes on Dane. Without thought, Kara ran at it, using her right shoulder and all of her strength to knock it to the ground. The stone flew from its hands and landed on the roof of the car. An oily mess that reeked of rot saturated her jacket, making her stomach lurch. Momentum carried her as she leapt over the fallen zombie. Unable to maintain her balance, she landed roughly on the ground.

Dane circled the undead man. Kara grabbed the rear bumper of the hatchback and pulled herself up, yelling, "Keys!" Dane pulled them from his pocket and shook them at the zombie like a voodoo charm. The sight of Morris getting up, leaving a foul snow-angel of sloughed-off flesh on the ground, mesmerized Dane, he was frozen where he stood.

"C'MON!!" Kara screamed.

Kara's cry shocked Dane into motion and he ran around the car to the driver's side door, he fumbled to get the car key out of the shaking pile in his hand.

"FuckFuckFuckFuckFuckFuckFuck." He chanted, each "fuck" louder than the last.

Strong hands closed over his shoulders. A second monster, the burnt man threw him into the side of the house like a ragdoll. His fist opened as he flew, the keys falling in the snow.

Harold Whitehurst. They were all coming, she thought realizing that more would be on their way. Whitehurst advanced on Dane's crumpled form with deliberate slowness. Kara watched Whitehurst as he moved toward Dane. Behind her, Edgar Morris had gotten to his feet.

She frantically looked around for something to defend herself with and help Dane. Her eyes fell on a little branch on the ground. She grabbed it and ran at the Whitehurst-thing, smashing it over the back of its head seconds before it reached Dane.

The zombie turned, half of its face nothing but smooth bone, the other half a charred mess with flakes of blackened skin on the edges. He looked at her with eyes that surely couldn't see and there was blood between its teeth. Fresh blood. Instantly she understood. Casey. Casey was dead.

Luck was with Dane once again as he scrambled to get up - his hand landed on the fallen keys, he snatched them. Kara was facing Whitehurst, wielding the branch. "GET TO THE GODDAMN CAR!!" He hollered. She dropped the branch and ran before Whitehurst could grab at her. Dane charged. Whitehurst was still looking in the girl's direction, so Dane was able to knock him clean off his feet. Hoping he could get in the car before the creature could stand, Dane made for the driver's door of the car. He wrenched the door open with a triumphant howl, launched himself inside and reached over to unlock Kara's door.

The car started. The zombies beat on the windows. Dane laughed hysterically, dropped the car into gear and stomped on the gas.

The cane man, Brion Jensen Frost, stepped into their path.

Without thinking, or maybe *only* thinking *KILL HIM*, Kara reached over and grabbed the steering wheel. She jerked it hard to the left and the car shot toward the Frost zombie.

They plowed him into a tree. The impact sent snow flying from the branches overhead and from the car. The broken headstone; that had landed on the roof of the car after Kara attacked the melted thing flew like a missile into Frost's head. The monocle was blown to bits and there was an explosion of maggots, bone and rotting gray matter. The slush that splashed on the hood of the car, thick with maggots, looked as though it was alive. The impact of the car sent the rotter's arms flying, its cane spiraling off into the air. The body slumped over, twitching helplessly between the vehicle and the tree.

Dane shifted into reverse. A dry sounding sputter came from under the hood, but the car did not move.

"No no noooooooooooo," Dane shouted, "Please God!"

Kara turned in her seat to look out the rear window, Whitehurst and Morris were still coming. "What do we do?!" she cried, searching Dane's face for a sign of hope.

"Back inside!"

"There's one in there, in the bath… " Remembering Underwood. Her next thought was of his hooks, she quickly processed the possibilities… he wouldn't be able to open the door with the hooks. But could he break down the door? If he could, he would be out here by now, wouldn't he? They could still hole up in one of the other rooms—her studio. Satisfied that he was trapped, she nodded and told Dane "No, we're good! C'mon!"

They threw open the car doors together, climbed out of the car and made wide circles around the zombies.

Kara's mind buzzed with questions as they moved. Maybe they should just make a run for it into the woods, but who knew how far they'd get in the middle of nowhere? The sun was dropping along with the temperature and they were running from the fucking undead for Christ's sake.

They managed to get to the house without the zombies gaining enough ground to catch them. They ran through the kitchen and into the studio. Kara threw the lock while Dane dragged the bureau in front of the door. Together, they upended the entire bed and leaned it against the bureau.

Dane eyed the curtain-less window. "What do we do about that?" He turned with fire in his eyes, seizing the bed from the bureau, he hefted it across the room, snugging the mattress between the frame and his chest. It covered the window perfectly. He tried to think of a way to secure it. "Kara, tell me you've got fucking nails in your supplies."

The art supplies were stacked against the wall, folded easels and canvases piled atop each other. She did have nails, and a hammer too, she used them for securing stretched canvas onto frames. Dropping to her knees before her backpack, she rummaged frantically through it. She and Dane grabbed handfuls of nails and took turns beating them through the edges of the thin mattress into the old wooden bedframe, securing it over the window.

The door began to shake. Dane turned the hammer over in his hands, wielding the claw as a weapon. He and Kara stood together in the middle of the room.

"Oh shit... " She said, an idea dawning on her in a moment of elation. She pulled her cell phone from her coat.

No signal.

A hand burst through a panel in the door, scrabbling at the top of the bureau. Dane ran forward and buried the hammerclaw in the hand. The hand retreated, taking the tool with it. "No!" Dane snarled.

He heard the dead men moving away from the door. Silence crept in.

"Dane… "

He raised a finger to silence Kara and edged toward the hole in the door. He couldn't see any of them. Was that it? They gave up, just like that?

Kara looked questioningly at him. "I don't know," he whispered, "I just don't know."

The zombies moved into the living room and stood stock-still, listening to the soundless screams of their benefactor, Scott Mark. His commands rang in their minds as he called to them from his tomb. *THE FLOOR, IN THE FLOOR! TEAR IT UP! TEAR IT ALL UP!*

Whitehurst pried the hammer from his hand. He knelt and began striking the boards beneath his feet.

Dane and Kara listened to the hammering. It was coming from inside the house. "I think we can get out of here." Dane said.

"How?"

"Window. Break it and climb out. We'll just run. Run to the access road, to the highway."

"We'll never make it that far! We'll freeze to death if they don't catch us!"

"How could they?"

"They got Casey!"

Dane stood back with a solemn pallor. "He must have done something. He messed up. *We* can make it."

"I won't go. I'm scared. Fuck, Dane, aren't you scared?"

"Of course, but what else do we do, sit here and wait until they get bored with whatever they're doing and come back for us? You think they'll leave at sunrise? You think they have any intention of letting us leave here alive? They want us!"

"I don't think they do."

"Then what, pray tell, do they want, Kara!" He was grabbing her arms in a vise-like grip. She tried to pull away, but he was too strong. He stared point-blank into her eyes. "What?"

"Something to do with the parish… " Kara said quietly.

"What?!" Dane didn't wait for an answer. Instead, he tore at the bed, pulling the nails free with his bare hands as he wrenched the entire frame away from the window. "We *run*." He hissed.

Ripley, the zombie with one leg, flew at the glass. A thousand blinding particles of glass grazed Dane's face, he shut his eyes tightly, just in time - and Ripley drove him to the floor. Kara grabbed at the zombie's back. He backhanded her with a sharp CRACK, sending her reeling. Ripley pawed at Dane's open screaming mouth.

Ripley managed to get a firm hold on Dane's tongue and wrenched it free with a wet snap. An arc of blood spattered Kara's face.

Dane let out a wretched moan, pushing Ripley's gruesome face away, and spit a mouthful of blood into the air. It only seemed to entice the zombie, who forced Dane's hands to the floor and lowered his broken teeth toward his throat.

"Gaaaaaah!!" Dane blubbered. He was trying to say Kara's name. Hot tears knifed through the blood splashed on her cheeks. She reached out a trembling hand, nowhere near close enough to save him, nowhere near strong enough. Her terror and shock kept her from taking action.

Ripley closed his jaws over Dane's mouth in a cruel kiss and ripped a flap from his cheek.

Kara bolted to the window. Her boyfriend's dying cries filling her head, she closed her eyes, pulled herself over the sill and out into the twilight.

Max Underwood punched his hooks through a rotted floorboard and tore it to shreds. Edgar Morris reached past him with oily hands to take hold of a small steel box with rust flowering across its surface. The zombie brought the box out of the hole and set it on the floor.

Harold Whitehurst lifted the lid with a creak, and all three of the ghouls recoiled. There was no sound, but a ghastly scream heard only in their brains.

The severed head of Scott Mark, sustained by the same dark energy that gave them all unlife, gnashed its black teeth inside the box.

8. BELOW

It was night. The sky was a dull gray, and a fog had settled on the birches like a blanket. It coiled around Kara's stiff limbs, kissed her face and stirred across her eyelids.

She huddled on the ground, concealed behind a clutch of trees that stood between her and the cottage. She awoke from a fitful sleep and propped herself up on one elbow. She studied the house, one thought in her head.

I left him.

The back door opened and a slow procession emerged, one of the zombies was carrying a box. They didn't head toward the cemetery but in her direction. She stilled every trembling nerve in her body. Her mind screamed *no, no, no.*

How long had she slept? How many hours had they been in there, sitting on the floor around Dane, feasting on his flesh, painting her canvases red with his blood? She thought of a hundred inconsequential things that had meant everything between the two of them. *We last made love three nights ago. His favorite color was orange. He hated that car but he wouldn't let his dad front the cash for another one. I wanted to paint him someday. I wanted his children.*

They weren't headed directly for her, and she relaxed slightly. When they stopped, the first one knelt and did something with his hands on the ground. He stood and began to disappear into the ground. A hole? She immediately thought of the tunnels that the L.S.

were rumored to have dug underground, allowing them escape from their graves. The others followed the first, climbing down into the earth, she was alone again.

Maybe the car still worked. This was her chance. She struggled to her feet, mist swirling around her. She was terrified, so she tried to distract herself with memories. *His favorite song was "Walking After You" by the Foo Fighters. He always wore his socks to bed, even if he was otherwise naked. His kisses tasted like honey, most of the time.*

She found herself walking toward the hole, her guilt driving her on. She had to know.

We met in the diner across the street from campus, found ourselves packed into the same booth along with some other random people. That place was always crowded at all hours of the night. He was sketching a statue. I told him the proportions were off and he said that was the idea. I asked him how his proportions were.

The hole yawned beside a big stone slab. There were spots of blood in the snow. Her breath mixed with the fog, clouding her vision; she leaned over the hole and peered in.

He never cried. Didn't smile often. He really loved me. I left him back there.

I only saw three zombies leave the house. The realization came too late.

Max's hook pierced her a millimeter from her jugular, pushing ever so gently into her throat. She held her breath and waited, his weight pressing against her back, his teeth brushing her earlobe.

He nudged her onto the lip of the hole. Then he pushed her in.

She landed with a thud and crumpled to the earth. The tunnel wasn't a little crawlspace; it was big enough for her to stand in. The fog was washing down into it, strangely luminescent. She found that, defying reason, she was able to see the details of the place.

Max's legs fell over the edge of the hole. She backed away, wondering in which direction the others had gone. It probably didn't matter. There was probably only one way in and out. Blood trickled down her neck and over her breast. He'd kill her as soon as he got to her and take her to the others so they could feed again.

Kara ran.

She followed the curve in the tunnel and found herself in a wider section with two paths ahead of her to choose from. Without hesitation she took the one to the right, not bothering to look for foot impressions in the soil.

The dark energy seeping from the ground was a warm light to Scott Mark and his minions. He looked up at them from the box and told them:

FLESH! BRING ME FLESH. I NEED EVERY LAST POUND OF FLESH YOU CAN FIND, ALL FOR ME, BRING IT NOW!

Rebuilding himself seemed an impossible task. But he'd endured this long, had assembled and controlled this pack. What feat, if any, was beyond his grasp? From the first moment that he realized the true power lying outside the parish, from the first time that he knelt naked on a slab of rock and communed with it, he had known his own potential for godhood. No more worship for Pastor Mark, only the glorification of the self. It had started with the girls. The pleasures that his previous god withheld from him had been taken with relish. Each child was much more compliant after they'd been strangled and their souls replaced with the dark and mysterious power that came from the earth. Even then, yes, there was still some fight left—they became little more than animals, after all—but he liked a bit of a rough struggle. He longed to have that again.

The rotters were still hunched over him, staring blankly. He screamed: *FLESSSSSSSSSSH!!!*

Then he felt the girl's presence nearby. She was in the catacombs. He wanted her for his first meal, oh yes, her soft, plump insides. *SHE'S HERE, DOWN HERE. FIND HER AND BRING HER TO ME! ALIVE! I WANT HER BLOOD SPILLED IN MY MOUTH!*

The three of them turned and wandered out of sight. He gave an audible croak, tittering in his mind.

He watched carefully waiting to see his meal, but something else came into view. His laughter stopped.

Before he could emit a mental cry of terror, a boot came down and crushed his brain inside his skull.

As she passed the mouth of another passage, Kara pulled off her coat and threw it into the tunnel, hoping to throw Max off her scent. The undead must have spent decades down here expanding this network, biding their time until... until what? What had been in the box they took from the cottage?

Her legs gave out. Exhausted and in pain, she fell to the ground with a wail of despair.

Max rounded the corner behind her. He readied both of his appendages to plunge into her back.

She heard shuffling behind her and knew it was one of them. *I'm going to die, and I'll never know why.*

Kneeling, Max slammed one hook into each buttock. Pain shot up her spine. She allowed herself to scream, knowing that it was now over.

A piece of timber appeared from the shadows, being swung by someone unseen, and struck Max's head, throwing him off Kara and violently tearing the hooks from her flesh. She saw a form fall atop the hook man, and they struggled. Forcing her legs to work, she wormed her body away from the fight. Max's head was dashed against the tunnel floor with amazing force, bits of bone flying in every direction with each wet impact.

The back of the zombie's skull opened and a foul gray mass exploded onto the dirt. Max stopped resisting his attacker. The other moved away from him. Kara stared upward but couldn't make out the person who'd saved her. There was little chance of being able to get to her feet either. She could only watch as the Samaritan walked off down the passage.

Samuel had been a clockmaker at one point, apprenticed to a Quinessett merchant, before his hands began to fail him, forcing him into the caretaker job. Though his fingers were too shaky for the artful touch required of a clockmaker, he'd kept up some tinkering as a way to pass the time on long nights. With his old hound asleep at his feet, a lantern glowing in the window that looked out on the grounds between the cottage and the churchyard, it was a pleasant time. He had made the shelf in the mantel and a lockbox for his few valuable possessions.

The night that he finished the journal—the night that he'd seen Pastor Mark with the girls—Samuel prepared to flee the cottage and seek help in town. He pulled the lockbox from one of his many hiding places, this one beneath the floor and emptied its contents onto his worktable to make sure everything was in order. He had a few gold watches that the Quinessett clockmaker had bequeathed to him, and a small amount of money. It would be enough to get him far away from this place, once he was certain that Mark's evil had been put to an end. How he would accomplish that was still a question that haunted him.

He was staring at the watches, considering his plans for Mark when there was a furious pounding on the front door. Samuel, turned with a start and grabbed one of the pokers from the cool ash of the fireplace. "W-Who goes there?" He called cautiously.

In reply, Scott Mark threw the door open and came at him with a monstrous cleaver. In his shock, Samuel froze until Mark was almost upon him. The glint of the cleaver sparked his action. He dodged the cleaver but was slow to raise the poker; the men crashed together, toppling over the worktable and crashing against the wall. The lantern in the windowsill fell with a crash. The poker clattered across the floor. Mark gained control and straddled Samuel. He brought the cleaver down.

The cleaver bit into Samuel's shoulder, blood spurting wildly, both men letting out hideous cries. The caretaker threw a fist at Mark but only succeeded in getting his fingers caught between the pastor's teeth. Samuel wrenched downward with all his might, snapping his jawbone.

The pastor fell away, the cleaver remained in Samuel's shoulder. The caretaker pried it free.

Mark regained his footing and held his jaw, he reached for the poker with his free hand. He screamed as he stabbed the poker through Samuel's gut and into the floor.

With his last burst of strength fueled by terrible agony, Samuel hurled the cleaver.

The cleaver sheared Mark's head off, both objects spiraling across the room. Jets of blood rose and fell, hissing, into the flames of the broken lantern. The clergyman's body crumpled.

Samuel felt his life ebbing from him. He knew he would never make it into town. He looked across the room, trying to judge the distance to the door. Facing him, was Mark's severed head. He shut his eyes tightly, praying that when he opened them again, the hallucination would be gone.

The eyes were darting about, frantically!

Samuel lurched upward, pulling the poker from the floor and out of Mark's body. He snatched the lockbox off the floor and rolled the head into it. He slammed the lid down and pushed the box into its hole. He grabbed the boards and scrambled to get them in place. Two spring-loaded locks set into the boards clicked, securing the pastor's tomb.

Samuel, dying, knew that he had to get out of the house, away from the accursed earth that bestowed a terrible new life on all which lay in it.

But Mark's head was still here, and its eyes had been alive. Samuel moaned in horror. Mark had already been reborn in the few seconds since his death.

Samuel remembered the promise he made in his journal. He swore to end the clergyman's evil. If he could not stop him in life, he had to stay on in death to honor his oath. This evil could not continue.

He lay there, on the floor, and bravely waited for death. He bled out quietly and died with a prayer on his lips.

Whitehurst, Ripley and Morris searched the catacombs for the girl. They instinctively headed for the tunnel entrance. On the way there, they found the crushed remains of Max Underwood.

Hands shot out from the darkness. One hand grabbed Whitehurst's head, the other Morris' and smashed them together. A geyser of rotten materials was loosed. Ripley, the one-legged zombie, scrabbled away with a confused grunt.

From around the corner, at the end of a bloody trail, Kara watched.

Her savior, emerged from shadow. Dressed in brown tatters, it too was a zombie, its face dry and decayed, eyes all but gone. And its mouth… the mouth had been fixed with metal appliances that fit over the jaws like prosthetic teeth.

The hands were also machines. Intricate mechanisms with tiny gears spinning within, like clocks.

This clockwork ghoul, as she thought of him, caught Ripley's only leg and swung him into the earthen wall. He lifted him and gouged Ripley's eyes out. He slipped his fingers into the holes in Ripley's skull and dug deeper, in search of the jellied remnant of his brain. His fingers found their prize and it spilled from the ocular cavities, ending the rotter's unlife.

A century of abstaining from flesh, being kept alive only by the earth's dark energy, had turned Samuel into a dusty skeletal thing, necessitating the prosthetics. His experience in life as a clockmaker had served him well, he needn't depend on eating flesh to hold his form. He was able to augment his frame with small mechanical devices.

Surely he couldn't see Kara lying there, but he seemed to sense her presence all the same. Her vision faded. The wound in her throat had opened, she was almost finished. The fog settled over her again.

Samuel stood alone in the darkness for some time. He knew that the girl was his for the taking, it was clear she had no strength to fight. But he had resisted the urge to eat flesh for nearly a century, and would not succumb in victory. With no regard for Kara's body, he turned and shuffled off into the catacombs.

It wouldn't be long before her body, lying dead on this unholy earth, began to move.

9. SUNRISE

Dane wasn't dead.

He lay on the floor of the studio feeling the sun wash over him. He had lain in the same spot, in shock until a few minutes earlier, when his mind began to replay the night's events. They had eaten most of his face, along with his fingers and toes, but then had suddenly risen. They had left, looking as if they were hypnotized. They had walked away like zombies, he thought to himself, giggling madly.

His laughter died out when he thought about Kara. He decided he wasn't angry with her. If he'd still had his tongue at the time he would have told her to run. What he really didn't want to think about was what he might have done were the tables turned. He didn't want to think about much at all, actually, but for some reason his death was taking so damn long and he had nothing but his miserable thoughts. Inanely, he heard the words of his favorite song.

They should have called the cops after the first night, but they all really wanted a haunting, didn't they? And they'd gotten one. A perfect haunting, everything in its place, like clockwork. Someday people would talk about it. Their bodies would be found, a story would be pieced together. One of them would be called insane and accused of the massacre. Or maybe they would think some Manson type showed up and killed them. Regardless of the story people told themselves, they would never know the truth. Who could imagine the horrors they had seen and felt. Maybe his dad would be pleased.

His art would skyrocket in value after his shocking death. Would he tell his friends about the gruesome discovery of Dane's body as they perused a gallery of Dane's early works?

In time he left this life and began another. He got up, walked out of the house, and found Kara. And they were together forever.

PROLOGUE

GREGORY CLOSED HIS EYES and dreamt of a blue ball—which materialized in his hand.

He sat alone in his sandbox in the backyard, enclosed by a solid wood panel fence and Japanese maples, red as flames. A breeze swept through, carrying the chirrup of birds, stirring his soft golden hair. In the house, his parents were arguing. That's all they ever did.

The ball wasn't perfect, wasn't exactly what he'd imagined. The blue had faded. And the rubber bore teeth marks, as if something had chewed on it.

He threw the ball into the grass. It bounced, landed, and rolled to a stop against a pile of other faded blue balls bearing teeth marks.

Gregory held out his hand, closed his eyes, and tried again.

"Daddy!" he cried, waking from a dream where something was crawling, panting, reaching—"Daddy!"

His father opened the bedroom door, flipping on the light. Gregory cringed under his covers, weeping, shaking. "In the closet," he said.

From down the hall, Mom asked, "What's wrong?"

"Nothing, *dear*," Dad called back. "Just a bad—"

Something thumped inside the closet.

Dad snatched up the baseball bat that Gregory never used. He clutched the doorknob, puffed himself up with air, and yanked open the door.

The thing inside was just a lump of black tissue, rasping and gasping, its three deformed arms groping at nothing. Its lip twitched, its one eye lazy. The thing had pissed itself.

Dad yelped and beat the mutant to death.

"Just a rat," he told himself, and that's what he told his wife, refusing to let her in. "Just a rat." He even tried to convince Gregory of it.

Dad trash-bagged the corpse and made it disappear. He never talked about it again. He just set rattraps and laid out poison. "For the rats," he said.

"Pee pants, pee pants!"

The kids encircled him on the playground, pointing, laughing, and throwing pea gravel, shouting their idiotic cliché. Lucas Lacoe was at the head of the pack. He had pushed Gregory down and was yelling louder than all the rest.

"Pee pants, pee pants!"

Gregory couldn't remember why he'd peed his pants. He had been focusing, trying to dream up a spaceship that could fly him far, far away. The shuttle had been on the verge of appearing, pressing against the membrane of reality. But Gregory's psychic muscles had flagged under the object's weight. And it didn't help that a little pang in his bladder distracted him.

Then, just as the spaceship began to form out of the ether, Lucas Lacoe shouted, "Look! Wittle Gwegowy pissed his pants!" and Gregory found himself on the ground.

Now all the kids were jeering down at him.

Crying, he squeezed his eyes shut.

The spaceship landed on Lucas Lacoe.

It crushed him.

The school was shut down and there was an investigation. The final reports said they had no clue where the shuttle had come from, that it wasn't even a real shuttle. Sure, it had electronics, but none of it was wired correctly—the craft was incapable of flight.

It was more like something a child would draw.

New mutants showed up in Gregory's closet and under his bed. Some of them vaguely resembled the monsters from the movies his dad watched: zombies, vampires, werewolves. Some of them were far worse.

The basement filled with creatures too. When you opened the door, something would slither behind a stack of boxes or scamper under the stairs; eyes stared at you from every crack and crevice.

His dad couldn't kill them all. And the rattraps and poison were useless: the monsters ate all the rats.

Gregory eventually filled four toy boxes with faded blue balls. After that his dad started throwing them away. Toy boxes were expensive. And a boy only needed so many balls.

His dad took up smoking.

His mom smiled brightly all the time.

Her face looked like it might shatter.

Gregory woke to the gunshot.

He crawled out of bed, carrying his stuffed bear with him, wiping sleep out of his eyes. He found his dad in the master bedroom, kneeling on the floor, weeping silently as he stared at the revolver in his hand. The zombie he'd shot still had a piece of his mother's throat between its teeth. She lay on the bed, covered in red spatters, sleeping with her eyes open.

His dad didn't even look around. "Go back to sleep," he said.

So Gregory did.

Hours later, his dad came in. He stood in the doorway, just a silhouette. Then he approached Gregory's bed. He still held the gun.

ONE

He woke in an alley in a halo of blood. His head hurt. It was nighttime, and on one of the buildings a dim bulb flickered. Beyond the ringing in his ears, he could hear cars. A coppery smell filled his nose and tainted the back of his throat.

"Uh?" he said, sitting up too fast. His stomach rolled and he almost puked.

On the back of his head, a lump throbbed, tender and swollen. Touching it made him dizzier, sicker, and his fingers came away bloody. His hair was drenched and dripping red.

He prepared to stand, but the world rocked. So he closed his eyes and waited for it to stop. It didn't. He pushed himself up and leaned against the brick building.

"What the fuh?" he muttered, holding the side of his head.

He remembered nothing: how he got there, how he got the wound—nothing. Where there should have been memories there was only a blue fog. He couldn't even remember his name.

The man looked down at his hand and didn't recognize it. The fingers were long, the nails trimmed and clean. No wedding ring. Fingerprints meant nothing to him.

The man with no name wiped blood out of his eye and stumbled toward the end of the alley, passing a Dumpster along the brick building.

A woman screamed.

He froze, swayed, blinking to clear his double vision.

Two bums dragged the woman into the alleyway, clutching at her purse and blouse. They made strange moaning sounds. He couldn't make out much—the light didn't reach that far—but he could see the victim's blond hair.

"Help!" she cried. "Help me!"

He took a step back, ready to run. But the muggers didn't look around, didn't acknowledge him at all. They staggered as if drunk. Even in the dark, he could see they were skinny, starved—mongrels. And the stench wafting off them… they smelled rotten.

A footstep—someone behind him.

He whirled, reeled, almost fell.

His ambusher shouldn't have been standing, shouldn't have been alive. Not with his guts hanging out and his throat torn open. Not with those milky dead eyes.

The stalker lunged, knocked him to the concrete, tried to bite off his nose. The man brought up his forearm, catching the attacker at the throat. The gaping trachea suckled at his arm like a mouth. It was cold. So were the guts that had slumped into the lap of his blue jeans.

The vagrant groaned, and the reek of a decaying belly wafted out.

The man with no name swallowed vomit. He flexed, preparing to throw off the attacker—and something like electricity built in the air. The vagrant flew sideways. He smacked into the brick building and crumpled to the ground, broken into odd angles and jags of bone. He twitched, gurgled, and clutched at nothing with his one good hand. Then, as if driven by an invisible force, his head slammed against the brick until the skull caved in on the brain.

Dead.

The woman's screams grew harsh. The two muggers had dragged her to the ground and were gnawing on her shoulder and arm, sucking, slurping, tearing.

The anonymous man clambered to his feet and retreated toward the other end of the alley, toward the sound of cars, the noise of civilization. His legs wobbled. His chest shook. The electricity, or force, or whatever it was, chased him like lightning.

"Please!" the blonde sobbed in the darkness behind him. *"Plee-hee-ease."* At this point, she wasn't even talking to him, too deep in shock. Still he stopped. Something about her voice, something about its desperate quality compelled him to turn around. Something about it gave his legs the strength to march forward, as if he were a bullet with no other choice.

The sky split open and bled rain. It pinged on fire escapes and crackled on the ground. Electricity arced between raindrops.

"Get off her!" the man shouted, and the Dumpster began to shudder, as if afraid of his voice. The cannibals didn't even look back.

"I said *get off!*"

On his last word, the Dumpster jolted forward. He flinched, shied back, once again ready to run. The trash bin plowed into the brute kneeling beside the woman. She cried out as the bin rolled over her arm, cracking the bone. The mugger was crushed as the Dumpster veered and crashed into the building. The bin tipped over, clattered on the ground, and vomited trash. The rain used it as a steel drum.

The second cannibal never paused in his feast, working quicker now the woman had passed out.

The man without a name faltered as the whole alley trembled around him. A lid rattled on its trashcan; litter rustled on the ground. Even the rain quivered. The man expected the trashcan lid to fly like a discus and behead him, expected the mortar in the building to disintegrate and the bricks to come tumbling down. They didn't. On a subconscious level, he knew the alley was vibrating because of him.

He was causing it. But he didn't know how to control it, and that was bad.

He wished he had something he *could* wield. Like a gun.

Suddenly he did.

A .45 materialized in his hand. He flinched and almost dropped it. But the woman's unconscious whimpers superseded his surprise.

He stalked forward, kicked the mugger off the woman, and shot three rounds into his face. He suspected that if he kept shooting, he would never run out of bullets; more would simply appear in the magazine. But three rounds were enough. They reduced the vagrant's head to a flap of skin and a crescent of lower teeth. Everything else was splatters, chunks, and fragments of bone, all rinsed in the rain.

The woman's eyes fluttered. They roved around, focused on him a second, and then closed again. The cannibals had torn up her shoulder and bicep, and her forearm swelled where the Dumpster had broken it. She needed a hospital. Apparently so did he. The dizziness hadn't left, the fog hadn't lifted. And he hadn't noticed until now, but he had been mumbling something under his breath for who knows how long. He had been saying, "It's blue."

Something whooshed through the darkness above him. A figure wearing a cape or a trench coat, silhouetted against the rainy sky.

The air in the alley shifted, thinned, and the rain became muted. It felt as if the world was phasing into two dimensions. And whatever was up there—it was causing it.

"Stay away!" the man roared, but his voice had no power; his energy had fizzled out.

He bent to grab the blonde's wrists—he couldn't leave her, not now, not with something prowling the dark.

A vagrant jumped him from out of nowhere.

She stank like the others, and her face was runny with putrefaction. Her rags were dry despite the rain. And there were more cannibals, emerging from the night. They forced the man to the ground and piled on top of him, raking at his clothes. Teeth pinched skin through his t-shirt. The flesh slipped out from between them, and the jaws snapped shut on a bite of fabric. More teeth started gnawing on his jeans. Hands groped for his eyes, but he buried his face in the concrete and tried not to drown in the runoff, unable to breathe anyway beneath all that weight.

His vision grew dark.

And then someone started pulling the attackers off him. He heard meat splitting, bone cracking. He could breathe again. He could see.

A black man the size of a small boulder was ripping the mongrels apart with his bare hands and tossing the bits aside. Ugly scars webbed his throat. He popped one vagrant's skull like a zit, closing his eyes as brains exploded all over his face and shaved head, as the rain quickly washed them away, down his gray shirt and his camouflage cargo pants.

The man with no name wriggled out from beneath the last two vagabonds, and the black boulder stomped their heads. He wore huge black combat boots. On his last stomp, the rain stopped—just like that.

Silence.

The tick-tock of water drops.

The man with no name swayed, feeling see-through and two-dimensional. He had expended all of his energy.

"Get him out of here," a woman behind him said. She wore a black trench coat and was kneeling beside the blonde. She held her hand over one of the victim's wounds, and white light emanated from her palm; underneath it, the torn muscle and skin began to scab, scar, and heal. The healer's whole body glowed. He couldn't look away. She was an angel. He had died, and she had come to deliver him unto God.

"It's blue," the man with no name said, his eyelids heavy, his head light. He fainted as the black boulder stepped toward him.

TWO

Something panted in the darkness. Something like a huge, slavering dog. Something with teeth.

He woke in the back of a minivan, slumped against the cold window. He groaned and held his head. It hurt, but not like before. Not like a concussion. The wound on the back of his skull had disappeared. Rain had washed out all the blood.

The black boulder was driving, speeding past pastures and corn, and the angel with the healing palm sat shotgun.

Dangling from the rearview, an air freshener masked stale cigarette smoke with the scent of evergreens. The radio was on. It was tuned to static.

"Where is she?" the man with no name asked, sitting forward. "The woman I saved. What'd you do with her?"

The boulder shot him a glare in the rearview. His eyebrows formed a crag above his gray, deep-set eyes, and his hands—big as river rocks—tightened on the wheel.

"She's safe," the healer said, staring out the windshield.

"I'm supposed to trust you? Who the hell are you?"

She turned her head to reveal her profile. She could've been sculpted from ivory, her features were so delicate, and her blond hair looked nothing like matter, everything like light. "The question is, who are you?"

He glimpsed himself in the rearview: blond hair, blue eyes—a stranger. He picked at a rip in the seat, then opened his mouth to say something—he didn't know what—but before he could spit anything out, the healer craned around and planted her palms on his temples. His vision flashed, and then the blue fog rolled in, blinding him. He called out, but didn't make a sound. Something echoed in the distance, something like a million voices, sounds that had carried even though their sources were dead, the way light will carry long after its star has expired. The sounds, he guessed, were channeling through her. He could discern nothing intelligible.

The healer let go of his head and the fog steamed off, the noises faded away. He almost got sick again.

"Blue," the healer said absently, frowning.

"What did you just do to me?"

She studied his face for a long time, as if trying to figure him out; the boulder was staring at him too, in the rearview mirror.

Finally, the healer turned to watch the road unwind. "I read you," she said, pulling on black leather gloves. "Your consciousness, I mean. Your memories. I saw blue."

"I don't believe in psychics," he said, although he couldn't remember whether or not he did.

"You don't know your own name, do you?"

He paused longer than he would have liked. "Of course. My name's Blue. That's probably what you saw."

"Hmm."

They drove for a while, listening to the radio, listening to the static.

"So," the man named Blue said, "are you going to tell me—"

"His name is Brimstone, Stone for short. And my name is Halo."

Blue smirked. "They sound made-up."

She turned her head to reveal her profile again. "So does Blue."

He started to say something but couldn't think of a retort. So he widened the rip in his seat and tried to conjure up a gun like he had in the alley; the concentration just worsened his headache. He wondered if it had really happened in the first place. Maybe he'd had a gun to begin with. If so, did *they* have it now?

"It was real," Halo said. "The gun. You *made* it real. You have powers. You've just exhausted them and need to recharge, kind of like a battery."

"I told you," Blue said quickly, "I don't believe in that crap."

Halo changed the subject. "We're not going to hurt you," she said, even though Brimstone was stoning Blue with his eyes. "Relax."

"What *are* you going to do?"

"Shhh!" She leaned forward and turned up the static. Blue heard only fluctuations in the hiss, something like rain, but Halo cocked her ear and listened hard, as if something resonated beyond that.

A minute passed, and Halo turned down the radio. "It's safe," she told Brimstone.

The big black man nodded. He made a U-turn, drove back a few yards, and pulled onto a dirt road obscured by the corn. He turned off the lights. The road was bumpy, and he took it fast. Stalks and leaves whipped the van. From the arm of a scarecrow, a black bird took flight, blacker than the sky.

"I want out," Blue said, holding the handle above him, his heart claustrophobic in his chest.

"We're almost there," Halo said.

"Almost where? What the hell's going on?"

"We're taking you to see him. We're taking you to see the Crow."

As she said it, he realized the black bird was following them, flying alongside through the night.

Blue stood up, bracing himself against the seat as the van jostled and jumped. He tried the sliding door. Locked. Yet he couldn't unlock it. The latch had been removed.

"Hey!" he said, reaching between the two front seats. He was going to clamp a hand on Halo's shoulder. "I want—"

Brimstone caught him by the wrist. Without even looking up from the road. Blue's bones grated together—*strained.* And he knew the black man wasn't even trying; he possessed enough power to rip off the entire limb if he wanted to.

"Stop the van," Halo said.

Brimstone frowned at her.

"Do it."

He slammed the brakes and skidded to a stop, billowing dust around them. The motor idled as he put it in neutral.

Halo turned to face Blue, her eyes bright and wild, as if some star had kindled inside them. She placed her gloved hand on his chest. She smelled vaguely of cigarettes and breath mints. "Do you want to know who you are?"

"I—"

"Do you want to know who you are and where you came from and why you're here?"

"I—what're you... I *do* know—"

"No you don't know—no you *don't*. Back there in the alley, you did things, things we've never seen before, but we've seen stuff like it, and if you sit down, if you trust us, we can help you find out who you are and just what you're capable of. If you come with us, if you have faith, we can show you things you never thought possible. So we're giving you a choice. Either you come, or there's the door." She pointed at the one he'd tried to open. "Don't waste our time."

The light in her face—it almost made him weep to look at it, almost made him smile. It almost made him growl too, because if you let something that bright get close to you it might reveal just how dark you are; it might reveal all your shadows.

"Let go of me," Blue said, staring at Halo but speaking to Brimstone.

The black man looked at her. Keeping her eyes fixed on Blue, she nodded.

Brimstone let go.

"I don't know who you people think you are," Blue said, rubbing his wrist, "but I already told you: I don't believe in special powers."

He turned around, tried the door—the lock mechanism clicked as Brimstone punched a button—and Blue stepped into the dark. He almost expected Halo to coax him back inside, almost wanted her to, but the van left him alone in the corn with a cloud of exhaust, motoring away toward some distant house lights.

He shivered as a wind whispered in the corn. The van had been warm with body heat, with people. The big empty was cold.

He looked toward the main road, the road that led to the city. It was all dark back that way, an impenetrable midnight blue. At least the other way had lights, a kind of guidance.

Blue sighed. He felt a terrible emptiness—and he wanted to know why. So he crossed his arms against the chill, and he walked toward the house lights.

From somewhere in the corn, the black bird squawked and flew on ahead of him.

THREE

The house was a two-story Greek Revival, a white block with a pedimented gable and an entry porch with towering Doric columns. It looked like the Parthenon, as if it didn't belong in this era but in ancient Greece, back when Hercules fought hydras and Odysseus obliterated Troy.

Blue stopped to stare up at it. A row of windows spanned each story, with sashes and six-pane glazing. Lights blazed behind each one, but he could see nothing past the lace curtains.

The van was nowhere to be seen.

Blue put one foot on the stairs leading up between the columns. Straight ahead of him, narrow skylights surrounded the front door, and a rectangle of transom lights crowned it. Through the skylights he could see a staircase and a grandfather clock. That was it.

Cigarette smoke lingered in the air.

He was overwhelmed with the feeling that someone was watching him, with the undeniable urge to run, to get as far away as he possibly could. But the house was a magnet and much stronger. He climbed the stairs and walked across the porch to knock on the door.

"You've come," Halo said on the stairs behind him. A statement, not a question. As if she'd known. She outshined the porch light, making it seem dreary and depressing.

Blue made fists so his hands wouldn't tremble. He took a few steps toward her across the porch. "I want to know my name," he said. "My real name. I want to know who I am."

Halo nodded, her golden eyebrows arched with empathy. "And we'll get to that. We will. But first we need to get your strength up. First we'll feed you dinner."

"And then?"

"And then you'll meet the Crow."

She stopped there, and he almost asked her about the Crow—who the hell was he? why'd they speak of him as if he were a god? that kind of thing—but Brimstone opened the door behind him and laid a heavy hand on his shoulder.

The giant had changed out of his wet clothes but basically wore the same outfit: camouflage pants and a T-shirt, only this one white. He wore an apron over it, pink and three sizes too small. It read, "Queen of the kitchen."

"Dinner served?" Halo asked.

Brimstone nodded.

The dining room featured a long table surrounded by black Hitchcock chairs with gold highlighting. Seating for ten, place settings for three. The floor was hardwood, oak tongue-and-groove, and the table sat on a Savonnerie rug with a burgundy border, a cream center, and flowers growing in ornate designs all around. Candles fluttered in candlesticks along the tabletop, and the food sat steaming on platters in the center. The steaks had been grilled, the mashed potatoes whipped to buttery fluff. The corn looked like rods of miniature light bulbs glowing yellow.

Brimstone pulled out a chair for Halo. She thanked him and a smile warmed his face, the rock softening to flesh. Not for long though. It went cold and stony as Brimstone performed the favor for Blue. For some reason Blue expected him to pull the chair out from beneath him as he went to sit down. It had happened to him before, he thought, when he was a child and the bullies seemed just as big as Brimstone. Was that a memory—was it coming back?

Brimstone let him sit and then poured wine for everyone, a pinot noir. He shucked his apron and sat beside Halo. The head of the table remained empty. Reserved for the Crow?

The two strangers dug in, piling their plates. Blue's stomach had never stopped growling since he'd caught a whiff of seasoned meat out on the porch. His throat felt parched. But he was still shaky too, and that killed his appetite.

"How'd you know?" he asked, wringing his napkin under the table. "How'd you know I was in that alley?"

Halo paused with a mouthful of steak. Brimstone glowered. Nothing new there. The big guy would probably regard him with disdain if someone sneezed and Blue said gesundheit.

Halo chewed thoughtfully and swallowed. "I'm psychic," she said. It sounded sarcastic, but he could tell she meant it.

"And how does one become a psychic?" he asked. "Take a class at the community college?"

Halo dabbed her mouth with her napkin and then folded it in her lap. "Some people are special, they have special powers. Psychic abilities, telekinesis, levitation. Science can explain some of it—like Brimstone, here: he's got two mutated myostatin genes that give him his muscles, and his bones are like concrete because they're denser than yours or mine—but the unexplained parts? Some people call them miracles, and I think they're close. Man's said to be made in God's image, that all of us have the spark of the divine. I think people like us, people with special powers? I think we've just harnessed that spark. Or maybe we've been blessed with more of it. Maybe we're like Hercules. Maybe we're mortal gods."

"So that's why you're psychic?" Blue asked. "Because Zeus knocked up your mom?"

Brimstone slammed his fist on the table, making plates jump and forks clatter, nearly toppling the candles. The scars on his throat were a livid red. He went to stand up, but Halo took his arm.

"No," she said. "We owe him an explanation. We owe him at least that much."

The giant took his seat and crossed his arms; they looked like anacondas that had swallowed small dogs.

"No," Halo finally answered, shaking her head. "My ESP, that's something science can explain. It's sort of *loose* science, but…" She sighed and stared down at her hands. "I was six when it happened. Mom was taking me to gymnastics. I'd seen the Olympics and had always wanted to be an Olympic athlete, so… A SUV ran a red light and slammed into us. Mom, she…" Halo pursed her lips. Brimstone took her hand, and she gave him a brief, grateful smile.

"The SUV hit the driver's side," she continued. "I lived. But my skull was crushed. My brain—it rewired around the damage… into parts of the brain we don't normally use. The doctors said it was a miracle, but I've always healed quickly. And I've always been able to heal others—I've *always* had that ability. Mom wanted me to be a doctor, said God had given me His healing touch, that I could *save* people, but—the paramedics wouldn't let me touch her, and she…" Halo cleared her throat. "Anyway…

"Ever since the crash, I've been able to hear things other people can't, kind of a river of voices; the collective consciousness, I think. My brain is different—it *works* differently now. I can hear when someone needs help. It's always loud with special people, but you… you were like a bomb going off. I knew you were in trouble, so we came. And then we brought you here. The end."

She met his eyes, hers blue and sunlit summers with a breeze and a welling of rain; he felt a pang behind his breast. "I'm sorry," he said. "I didn't—"

"It's all right. You deserved to know." She polished off her wine with a few gulps.

He sipped at his. It burned. He wanted it to.

They sat quietly for some time, no one eating, staring down at the table except for Brimstone, who stared at Blue. The food grew cold.

He felt selfish and sacrilegious for disturbing the silence, but he had something else gnawing at him. "So," he said in a low, dark tone, "why am I really here? Truthfully."

Halo shook her head. "The Crow will have to tell you that." Then she laid her napkin on her place mat and excused herself from the room.

Brimstone picked up his steak knife. He took one last hard look at Blue—and then picked up his plate. And then Halo's plate. And then all the serving plates. A *mountain* of plates. And then he stooped through the door.

Blue cursed under his breath. He grabbed his glass and downed the rest of his wine.

In the kitchen, plates clinked and silverware tinkled as Brimstone loaded the dishwasher. He slammed it shut, slammed a few cupboards, and then came back to clear the table right down to the wood. Once he had finished, he sat in his chair and glowered.

"Don't talk much, do you?" Blue asked.

Brimstone ran a finger across his Adam's apple, simultaneously indicating the scars there and threatening to cut someone's throat.

Blue nodded. "Right." His gaze wandered to the floor-to-ceiling windows, to the darkness outside. Sweat beaded on his forehead and under his arm.

Eventually, Halo came back. Her eyes were red, the skin around them a little puffy, but her posture seemed erect enough, strong enough. She looked at Blue and, businesslike, emotionless, she said the words he didn't want to hear. She said, "It's time."

In the foyer, the grandfather clock tolled.

FOUR

Out the back door, Halo led Blue into a field of stubbly grass, gray in the moonlight and bordered by corn; Brimstone marched behind them. They headed toward a teepee. Smoke drifted from the vent at the top, smelling of burning wood, and light shined through the A-shaped entryway; it fluttered like a wing across the field.

Except for them and the flickering, the night held completely still. No sound. Even the crunching of grass beneath their feet seemed muted, as if they were underwater. Several times Blue wanted to say he'd decided to leave, he didn't care to meet their leader, but he felt he would drown if he opened his mouth.

"Who is he?" he finally managed.

Halo did not slow or look back. "He's like a shaman," she said. "He's the man who can tell you what you need to hear." She stopped next to the entryway of the lodge and gestured him inside with her hand. "He's waiting for you."

Then she lit up a cigarette.

Blue must have stared, because she paused in mid-puff. "What?" she asked.

He said nothing.

She said, "It's an ultra-light."

Grimacing, Brimstone stepped upwind of the smog. Blue, escaping the stink, peered through the teepee's opening.

In the center, a fire crackled and popped, and off to the left lay a deerskin blanket. On the other side, a black bird roosted on a perch of gnarled manzanita, perhaps the same bird from the scarecrow. Nobody else occupied the space.

As in the alley when he had saved the blonde, Blue's legs took over. Only this time he wasn't a bullet. He was water, flowing into a low spot. He hunched over and crossed the threshold.

The warmth from the fire rippled around him like a bath, massaging the knots from his muscles. His eyelids drooped. He straightened up, fighting the desire to lie down, to turn into a puddle.

The bird had disappeared from the perch. Next to it stood an Indian.

"Jesus," Blue said, meaning to shout but unable to, meaning to retreat but too lazy to react. His body didn't even tense; the air had turned into an opiate.

The Indian chuckled. He had dark skin and long black braids behind each ear. Instead of a headdress and regalia, he wore jeans and a long-sleeve denim shirt. A black feather was tucked in his hair. "I have many names, son, but Jesus is not one of them." He walked around the fire, moving like a breeze through bluegrass, smelling of rich tobacco and pine sap. He held out his hand. "My given name is Horse with Wild Mane," he said, "but I am known as the Crow."

Some part of Blue refused to touch the hand, for some hands harbor snakes. But the Crow smiled, and his brown eyes twinkled with the fire, like a father's, like a friend's. Blue accepted the handshake, finding the Indian's palm callused and firm along the knuckles, soft and inviting at the heart. These hands had chopped trees and gutted deer, they had cupped injured birds and planted seeds in the soil.

The Indian studied Blue's face, and crow's-feet wizened the skin around his left eye, making him appear grandfatherly, curious and wise. Blue wondered what the Indian saw.

In the fire, a teakettle whistled. It sat in the coals.

"Please," the Crow said, motioning toward the deerskin blanket. "Sit."

Blue nodded and drifted to the bed. It was soft and sleepy. He sat cross-legged, though he wanted to recline.

The Indian knelt and lifted the kettle with a potholder. "I was born on a reservation," he said, his voice deep and resonant and alive. "A Crow reservation in Montana. My father taught me to ride horse and herd buffalo. He taught me to fish. He shared everything with me, told me how my mother died giving birth to me, how she gave her life for me. 'Calm Water,' she told him, 'our child must see the sun, he must swim in the river, he must fly,' and she pushed until she could not push anymore.

"My father shared with me, shared the moon and the sun with me, and so I shared with him. I confessed when my friends and I shot the buffalo. I talked to him when I had to cry. But I never told him about my dream."

The Crow paused to pour fluid from the kettle into two tin cups. It burbled and steamed. He held one out to Blue. "Tea?" he asked.

Blue nodded and took the cup. He sipped it. It scalded his lip and throat, but he barely felt it. The tea tasted something like lemon and pepper and mint, but not a mere combination of these flavors. No, those essences combined could only produce a ghost of this.

The Crow sipped his own tea and continued his story. "I was always a bird in the dream. I flew through the Bighorn and across the prairies and over the waters of the Yellowstone. But in the *nightmare*, I became a wolf. I hunted moose and deer. I became addicted to blood. I was a set of teeth, a ravenous stomach, and nothing else. And that was fine. Until I mauled the child.

"The boy's father tracked me to my den—my father's house. He watched me sneak in through an open window, curl up on my bed, and turn back into a boy. He would have shot me, but my father stopped him; he had known for quite some time what I was becoming. It was his secret too, something he never shared with me, something we kept from each other, hidden beneath our beds. But that man wanted to kill me, and my father worried. He did not know what to do.

"The day he died, my father took me fishing. 'Son,' he said, 'in each man there lives a power—a gift from the Creator. He would have us use it for good, but in each man there also lives a beast, selfish and hungry, and it would have us use that power for evil. Part of our test in life is to tame this beast. If we fail, the beast will eat us and the ones around us and the ones we love, and that is bad.' And then my father brought out a knife."

From behind his back, the Crow withdrew a blade. He slid it out of its leather sheath, and it glimmered in the firelight, seven inches long and fixed to a deer-antler hilt. Something twitched in Blue's legs, some flight instinct, but the rest of his body slept. Somewhere in the back of his mind behind all the lazy clouds, he hoped the Crow meant no harm.

With a low, dark voice, the Indian quoted his father: "'If you cannot tame the beast,' he said, 'then you must kill it. Do you understand, my son?'

"I nodded, though I did not understand. My father gave me the knife—but the look he gave me was much heavier."

The Indian sighed, and the older half of his face aged. That part was much older than any man should be.

"That night while I dreamt of the wolf, the boy's father came for me. He had shut my window so I could not get back in the house. He chased me, tried to shoot me—but my father stepped in to take the bullet. He fell dying and told me to fly, told me to see the sun, and I did. I became the bird and I flew. Eventually I landed here.

"The farmers who owned this house let me live on their land, and I farmed for them. They raised me. The wolf wanted to kill them, but I threatened it with the knife and distracted it with deer and rabbit, keeping them out of the gardens. Eventually I tamed the wolf. The farmers passed of old age, and I grew to understand what my father had said. Our powers are meant to help people. If we cannot control the evils we commit, then we must sacrifice ourselves for the sake of our community."

Blue tipped his teacup to his lips but he had already finished. At the bottom, tea leaves formed some kind of beast, maybe canine, maybe reptilian, baring its fangs.

The Indian sighed again. He held up the blade and appraised it with a grave expression. "A very long time ago," he said, "my people asked the Creator to help them defeat a great enemy. The Creator said he would, on one condition: my people had to prove themselves—they had to jump off a cliff into the water, where an archer waited to shoot whoever leapt. Nobody was brave enough. Except one man. The arrow killed him before he hit water. '*Iilak bacheek*,' the Creator said, '*there* is a man.' And then the Creator fashioned my people into warriors.

"I, like that man, do not fear death. Many times have I aimed this knife at my heart. But I persevered. Not out of cowardice, but out of hope. I knew I could conquer my beast." The Crow sheathed the blade and offered it to Blue. "May you persist out of hope and not cowardice."

Firelight and shadow ebbed and flowed so that ravens seemed to flap silently above their heads, feathers falling, wings beating the air. Wood crackled and popped. The Crow waited, patient, like a rock.

After staring at the knife for a long time, Blue finally accepted the gift. It was heavier than it should have been, loaded with grave responsibility and foreknowledge, as if it knew what blood it would spill. Blue held it as if it were a relic, fragile and precious.

The Crow sipped his tea.

Still cradling the knife, Blue asked, "Who am I?"

The Indian smiled. "I do not know. But I *do* know that, before the end, you will discover that for yourself."

Outside, Halo shouted. Blue looked toward the exit.

"Go," the Crow said. "Help them."

A gunshot startled Blue into motion. He glanced back at the Crow, but he wasn't there. There was only the bird, flying out the top of the teepee with the smoke.

FIVE

Around the side of the teepee, holding 9mm Glocks, Halo and Brimstone stood over a body. The man wore overalls and a plaid shirt like a farmer. Gases bloated his corpse and poisoned the air with decay, and his eyes and mouth glistened with reddish-yellow bodily fluids. He looked as if he had been dead for a week. Halo had shot him in the head.

"He came out of the corn," she explained. "He's like the ones from the alley. Some sort of zombie." She took off a glove and knelt. Blue shuddered as she pressed her hand to the dead man's temple, thinking about all the germs and diseases. Had this been summer instead of autumn, the body would have been wriggling with maggots.

Halo closed her eyes.

She's reading it, Blue thought. Absently, watching her work, he undid his belt and hung the knife from it. What did she hope to learn from a cadaver?

Something rustled in the corn.

Then something else.

Multiple somethings.

Hundreds.

"There's more," Blue said, pointing, stepping back.

Brimstone leveled his gun at the corn, waiting, jaws clenching, eyes narrowed; Halo was engrossed and unaware, her hand practically cemented to the farmer's head. Blue glanced at the gun in her hand and wondered if he should grab it—he glanced at the house and wondered if he should run. He had the knife, but if Halo was right, if these were zombies, only severe brain trauma would dispatch them.

He didn't know how he knew that (another memory? something gleaned from films?), but it seemed like common sense. Or instinct. The knife would only be useful once or twice; if he drove it through an eye socket, it would likely stick in the bone.

The zombies staggered out of the corn first, all tattered country dresses, plaid shirts, blue jeans, and suspenders, all festering wounds and marbled skin and milky eyes.

After that came the rats. Waves of them.

Brimstone glared at Blue. He pointed at Halo and waved his hand. *Cover her*, he was saying. He opened fire on the attackers, muzzle flashes licking the dark. His bullets kicked up flesh on cheeks and necks, and more than half blew chunks out the back of rotting heads. He was a good shot. The slide on his 9mm locked back, and he ejected the magazine, dug a fresh one out of his cargo pocket, and jammed it into the gun. He pulled back on the slide and let it shut. By the time he was ready to aim, the rats were on them.

The rodents poured over the corpse on the ground, gnawing at its flesh, gnawing at Halo's hand. They scrabbled over Brimstone's boots and climbed his camouflage pants. They climbed Blue's pants as well, clawing, biting—he shook some off, pulled some off, kicked some off. Brimstone ignored them. Some had gnawed through his shirt and into his skin. Blood began to bloom behind the white fabric.

And the zombies. They were closing in. Too many of them for Brimstone to manage. He stopped to reload, to bat a few rodents off his chest. He put his hand into his cargo pocket—and his fingers stuck out of a hole the vermin had chewed. All his magazines had fallen out, lost in the stream of vectors. He bent to paw through them.

A gun, Blue thought. *Need a gun.*

A buzz built in the air. Very faint but very real, a mere phantom of the energy from the alleyway; the piece of black polymer that formed in Blue's hand looked like a melted toy pistol: useless. He threw it, tried conjuring a better one. Same result. His battery, as Halo had called it, was still charging.

Squishing rats beneath his tennis shoes, Blue yanked Halo's gun out of her free hand. He stood, ready to shoot, and a zombie lurched toward him, this one from around the other side of the teepee. More closed in on that front.

Blue's bullet punched through the corpse's eye. The body fell to its knees, fell to its face, and then lay still. The other dead farmers kept coming. He fired five times and dropped two of them—how many bullets left? Three? Four?

Blue backed up. "We're surrounded!"

Brimstone turned to Halo. He went to grab her, drag her to her feet, but she stood up by herself. She looked at Brimstone, calm and a little dazed, apparently unaware of the corpses converging on them, oblivious to the rats gnashing their teeth on her leathers. "We need to leave," she said.

Brimstone sneered, as if to say *No kidding*, then swung his fist back to smash the skull of a zombie about to jump on his back.

Blue shot a woman in a bloodstained nightgown. And then he heard the panting—in his head, in his bowels, in his dreams.

Something else was in the corn.

Something blacker.

Something hungry.

The ground shook with its approach. The rats scampered away. And that's when the world turned into a nightmare.

The sky darkened: no stars, no moon, just an oil spill smothering the heavens. Beneath their feet, the grass crumbled away, leaving old cracked dirt and dust. The hide covering the teepee wrinkled, cracked, grayed, and aged, and faces began to grow in it, old moaning faces with chapped lips and holes for eyes. They caught fire from the inside out and began to scream. Little devils of flame leapt about them, goring them with fiery pitchforks.

And the panting. It was everywhere, echoing, waxing, thundering with bass, and getting hungrier.

Halo turned her head toward the approaching sound, and all the light went out of her cheeks. "The garage," she said, barely audible. Then much louder, "Go!"

Brimstone went first, plowing through the zombies like a wrecking ball, throwing broken bodies aside: crushed skulls, caved-in ribs, broken arms and legs. Halo and Blue ran in his wake. They both had guns now; Halo had drawn a backup from a shoulder holster under her trench coat. Blue's last bullets hit a neck, a chest, and Halo edited his mistakes, punctuating skulls like a pro.

The garage was appended to the rear of the Greek revival. The house had aged. The white paint had flaked off, leaving dead wood eaten through by carpenter ants and termites. Windows were shattered. Parts of the roof had caved in. The structure looked warped and disjointed, as if sections of its foundation had failed, sinking rooms and hallways into the cellar.

Blue glanced back.

Beyond the zombies and the burning teepee, back in the corn, a massive silhouette approached, ripping the cornstalks aside as it came, throwing them into the air. Only they weren't cornstalks. They were dried human beings with papery skin, all shuddering in the wind.

Blue ran faster.

Nearing the garage, Brimstone retrieved the door opener from his front pocket. He pressed the button but the gadget seemed to be out of batteries: the garage door sat crooked and motionless in its frame. That didn't stop him though. He put his shoulder right through the door, cracking and smashing the wood. He left a ragged hole big enough for Halo and Blue to step through. A hole big enough for the zombies to breach. Which they did.

Halo dispatched a few with her gun, and then all three of them piled into the van, Blue in the back. The vehicle had begun to rust and lose its paint, and cobwebs floated in the corners. Brimstone turned the key. The engine sputtered. The zombies beat at the windows.

Brimstone tried again and this time the van started. He wrenched it into drive and drove through the zombies and right through the door, wood shrieking down the sides, bodies bouncing off the bumper, some of them rolling onto the hood. The van jumped over corpses like speed bumps. It cleared the garage, out onto the driveway, and fishtailed in the gravel, barely missing an undead gas-pump attendant wearing a STIHL cap.

The beast loped toward them across the dirt field. Darkness obscured it, and Blue could only tell that it was black with glowing red eyes. It was huge, and it was panting. In his head, in his ears, on the radio. The different versions overlapped, intensified, a chorus of greedy respiration, like hundreds and thousands of slobbering dogs.

The monster clawed aside the teepee, sending embers into the air. Embers, blood, and strips of flesh.

"Faster!" Blue shouted.

The van skidded as they rounded the house. The monster disappeared around the corner, and soon they were in the corn, the living corn. The desiccated bodies groped for the car, their frail hands disintegrating against it, hundreds and thousands of faces whipping by, every mouth warped into perpetual misery, pleading, begging for harvest, for sweet release.

Blue was surprised to find himself weeping, cringing back from the specters, feeling their desperation eat at his bones like dry rot. "Go away!" he screamed. "*Go away!*"

And just like that, they did. They leaned back, rustled, and became corn. The panting faded and disappeared completely by the time the van reached the main road. The sky cleared, and the moon showed through again. Static on the radio. No beast behind them. Thank God.

Blue looked forward—and suddenly boiled over. Reaching between the door and the seat so Brimstone couldn't get at him, he pressed the gun to Halo's temple.

SIX

"What the hell is going on?" Blue demanded. "Tell me now—tell me everything—or I'll blow your brains out!"

Brimstone went to reach back for Blue, probably to pummel him, but Halo stopped the giant before Blue had a chance to recoil. "Just drive," she said. "Trust me."

Brimstone turned back to the wheel. He punched the ceiling, leaving a big dent, and he scowled at Blue in the rearview mirror. Blue avoided eye contact but kept the giant in his peripheral vision just in case.

Calmly, Halo asked, "What did the Crow tell you?"

"You're psychic—you tell me."

"I can't," she said. "I can't see inside his tent."

"Well maybe that's because he told me jack shit. You know, he almost had me convinced that he was saying something worthwhile. But it was bullshit. And I think he put drugs in my tea. Hell, he practically told me to kill myself!"

Halo paused. "He didn't tell you who you are, what your purpose is?"

"Hey, *I've* got the gun here! *I'm* asking the questions!"

"But you're out of bullets," Halo said. She was right. He had released the slide to make the gun appear loaded. Unfortunately, he still couldn't generate his own ammunition.

"Oh yeah?" Blue pulled out the knife the Crow had given him. He pressed it to her throat, hard enough to indent the skin. "This doesn't need bullets."

Brimstone went to hit him again, but Halo's hand shot up, palm out. The giant stopped, rumbled, a volcano pent-up with magma. Blue didn't understand why Halo seemed so calm. Maybe she knew he wouldn't kill her. But *he* didn't even know that. He certainly felt unpredictable, twitching and sweating and spitting when he talked, his mind flitting about like a startled bird. He didn't even know himself.

"That corpse told me something," Halo said. "I know where we need to go now. But that's all I know. The zombies, the thing in the field: those are as new to us as they are to you—"

"You said you'd help me find out who I am," Blue said. Tears burned at his eyes, and he blinked, bit them back. Some of the dry rot, some of the corn's desperate ache still lingered in his marrow. "You said you'd help me."

"And we are," Halo replied. "Someone as powerful as you, someone as out of control—we have to figure out what you're capable of and how you can tame it. And I know where to dig now. So please..." She laid her hand on his. She was wearing a glove, but her touch was light, soft, and he could feel warmth spread out from her palm and up his arm, dawning in each cell, making new. "Trust me," she said.

The tears burned hotter, salty and brimming. He clenched the knife, clenched his teeth, red in the face and ready to roar, ready to just slit her throat and be done with it, let Brimstone rip his head off so the blue would fade to black and he wouldn't have to worry about it anymore.

He caught motion in the corner of his eye: the Crow, taking flight from a cornfield. The Indian's face shimmered briefly on Blue's window, faint, just a reflection, just a ghost, and then they left the bird behind. "Our powers are meant to help people," the old man had said. Back in the alley, Halo and Brimstone had helped. They had saved his life. They had saved the woman.

Growling, Blue slumped back in his seat, every muscle fatigued, his eyes weary and carrying bags underneath. "I don't care anymore," he said. "I don't give a damn."

Halo said, "But we do. Now get ready. We're almost there. And Stone?"

The giant looked over at her.

"Turn left."

As they drove, Blue slouched in his seat and stared at the floor mat, only half-listening as Halo explained what the dead man had revealed. "Not much," she admitted, healing Brimstone's rat bites as she spoke. "Mostly the blue gloom. But I did see a house and a boarded-up door. I think maybe we're supposed to find something there. Maybe another clue. I'm not sure."

She said something about a man as well, a drunkard, but Blue didn't quite catch it. He didn't quite care. Not until they pulled up to the house.

It was a Gothic Revival, with a steeply pitched roof, cross gables, and windows with pointed arches. Bargeboard ran along the underside of the main gables in a symmetrical tangle of flourishes and vines, and the one-story porch morphed into a gazebo to the right of the house, capped with a finial that resembled a pawn.

The flowerbeds bordering the brick foundation of the porch were matted with dead weeds. The lawn was dead too, bare earth in some spots. The two dogwoods on either side of the flagstone walkway were barren skeletal things that scratched at the darkness.

Blue sat upright and stared out his window. He remembered this house, a glimpse through the blue fog. He had been here before.

"No one's home," Halo said, and Blue knew she meant it was abandoned.

Why was it so familiar?

Halo and Brimstone exited the van with a pair of flashlights and a few guns and ammunition stashed in a box beneath the passenger seat. Blue just stared until the giant yanked open his door. Halo marched down the walkway, and Brimstone pushed Blue along after her.

The house stood in a field, city lights shining like stars beyond it. No neighbors. So if this was a trap, if the giant and the healer were tricking him, Blue's scream would die halfway across the field. It would never reach any ears.

But if it wasn't a trap, if Halo was telling the truth, if the keys to his identity lay within those walls—suddenly Brimstone didn't have to nudge him anymore.

Halo was already up the stairs, across the porch, and to the door. She gripped the knob and paused. Blue and Brimstone stood behind her.

"What's wrong?" Blue asked. He would've opened the door by now.

She shook her head. "Someone is still paying taxes on the property."

"What's your point?"

She shook her head again. "I don't know. I can't see clearly enough. Something's blocking me." She pushed open the door, which was already ajar. Its hinges groaned and the whole house creaked, as if waking to their presence. Halo shined her light inside.

The foyer was completely bare. No furnishing whatsoever. Not even a rug. Just a staircase leading to the second story. That's not how Blue remembered it. He remembered a coat rack. He remembered a houseplant. He remembered sunshine.

They all stepped inside. Brimstone explored with his light.

"What's that smell?" Blue asked, nearly whispering, feeling as if he had to, as if the house might hear him if he didn't. Beneath the dust, dry rot, and mold lingered something musky and fecal, something animal.

Halo walked forward, down the hall along the stairs, toward the back of the house. Brimstone drew his gun and followed.

Hesitating by the door, Blue scratched at the knife's deer-antler hilt. He slid the blade in and out, keeping his hand on it, ready. He glanced out the door, considered leaving, going back to the van, but Brimstone had taken the keys. When he turned back around—at the top of the stairs stood a child. He was shrouded in darkness, yet parts of him glowed, as if something up there were casting a dim light. He was blond, about eight years old, and he was wearing pajamas. He, too, looked familiar.

"Hey," Blue called. He took a step forward and the child ran, disappeared without a sound. Blue took chase. He heard wrenching noises from where Halo and Brimstone had gone, something like nails being pulled out of wood, but he ignored them. He would find his own answers.

At the top of the stairs he saw the boy vanish into a bedroom on the left, the only furnished room: a child's bed, a closet, and one toy box. The boy was gone when Blue came in. A faded blue ball sat in the middle of the room. Blue knelt and picked it up. It had teeth marks in it. Something about it made him shudder.

"That's mine," the little boy said.

Blue gasped and jumped back.

The child stood in front of the window, glowing. Blue could see right through him. "You're not real," he said.

Downstairs, someone clopped through the foyer and something liquid splashed. Blue tuned it out. Whatever was happening, he didn't care.

The child held out his hand. "Give me my ball. It's mine."

Blue threw it underhand, and it passed right through the boy's stomach, as if he were nothing more than smoke. The boy didn't bother picking it up.

"It's hunting you now," he said. "It'll catch you soon."

"What, that thing? What is it?"

"It's what chewed the balls."

Before Blue could say anything, gunfire erupted below. Halo shouted. Then the door to the bedroom clapped shut. Blue tried it. The knob wouldn't turn. The door seemed to be sealed.

"Don't leave me," the child said. "I can tell you secrets. Things you want to know."

Blue let go of the knob. He flinched with every gunshot but tried not to, tried to tune them out. "Who am I?"

The child said, "Look out the window."

"That's not what I asked. I—"

The boy pointed toward the pane. "*Look.*"

Blue marched over, shivering as he walked through the child. He got right up to the window and looked out at the backyard, which was hemmed in by a solid wood panel fence and haunted by two dead Japanese maple trees. Weeds lay lifeless in an old sandbox near the back.

"I don't see—" Blue began, but then he did.

A man with graying hair emerged backward from the door, emptying a red can across the threshold. He threw the can into the house and started digging in his pocket, glancing through the door toward the gunfight. Obviously Halo and Brimstone weren't shooting at him; otherwise he would be dead. The man pulled out a silver Zippo and rolled the striker, producing sparks but no flame.

"Ask me again," the child said. "What you asked before."

"Halo," Blue muttered to himself. And then he bolted across the room. The door was unlocked this time. He jerked it open and dashed for the stairs.

"It's coming for you!" the child shouted, but Blue barely heard him, barely cared, just a bullet now, doing what bullets do best.

He made it to the bottom of the stairs just in time to hear the loud *fwup!* of gasoline igniting. Fire roared down the hall and erupted in the foyer, blocking his path. He was trapped. And Halo was practically screaming. Brimstone, of course, didn't make a sound.

SEVEN

Fire engulfed the foyer, especially the walls, blistering wood and sending up the fumes of burnt gas and burning timber. Only a thin trail of lit fuel ran like a fuse down the hallway.

Something dripped into Blue's hair. More droplets pattered his shoulders, and when he looked up he found a thunderhead swelling directly above him, his own personal cloudburst. The water began to pour, cold, invigorating rain. It soaked his clothes and flowed down the stairs, hissing and steaming as it hit the burning gas, not doing much to put it out, unable to dilute or stifle the petrol. Blue blinked up at the cloud—impossible! he had never seen anything like it, a storm inside a house, defying the laws of meteorology, defying *reason* and confirming miracles, reviving that deep sense of wonder typically lost to adults—and Blue felt that if he peered deep enough, looked hard enough, he would see stars, heavens, a whole universe enveloped in this one little cumulonimbus, and perhaps somewhere in there a god.

"Blue!" Halo called, her voice muffled by wood and insulation, sounding from somewhere beneath him.

She needed help.

He vaulted over the balustrade, down into the hallway, landing next to the flaming fuse of gas. Keeping to the right, leaving puddles and runlets and streams in his path, he ran the way Halo and Brimstone had gone, toward the back of the house.

The kitchen had turned into a furnace. The arsonist had splashed gasoline everywhere: the walls, the cabinets, the L-shaped counter—even the ceiling.

If not for Blue's shield of precipitation, the heat would have been unbearable. Even now it flushed his skin.

To his right, another hall, this one shorter, led to what looked like a dining room, also ablaze, light flickering up the bay window. The hallway featured two doors: one to a bathroom and one that was closed, positioned beneath the second-story staircase. It looked as if it had been boarded shut, but someone—probably Brimstone—had pried off the two-by-fours. It was on fire, frame and all, a portal into Hell. And that's where Halo's cries originated.

Blue grabbed the doorknob. His hand sizzled and he pulled it away, yelping and branded. He kicked the door. The jamb cracked. He kicked again. A third time. Once more. The wood finally gave and the hinges screeched as they warped and pulled out of the jamb, forced the wrong way.

By the light of the fire and the two flashlights below, he could see most of the basement, boxes stacked and casting shadows, old lamps and coat racks and couches crowding the edges, a lay-down freezer pushed against the back.

Halo stood in one corner next to a stack of boxes full of plastic dinosaurs and army men, full of caped heroes and tiny monsters. Some kind of silver thread wrapped the lower half of her body so she couldn't move. Empty magazines lay at her feet and she was shooting at something in the air, something like huge black widows with wings. She hit one and it exploded into yellow blood and innards, mixed with exoskeleton shards. More arachnids just spilled out of the sacs that dangled from the ceiling. On their bellies they sported red hourglasses.

Brimstone had dropped his gun. A blob of pustules and goiters and tumors and sores pulsated beneath the staircase, its long tentacle wrapped around the giant's waist, pinning his arms to his sides. The blob was trying to feed him into its mouth, but he had planted his boots on the incisors of the upper and lower jaw, grunting, red in the face and pushing. The thing had other tentacles and other mouths, but they were busy plucking the spider things from the air and eating them, crunching them between their teeth, slobber mixed with yellow ichor.

"Blue!" Halo yelled, glancing at him between shots. "Get Stone!"

Blue tried to conjure a gun or a weapon, anything other than the knife, but he couldn't. He wiped the hair out of his eyes, splashing water. He turned, spotted the two-by-fours, noticed the nails sticking out like fangs. Blue thrust one into the inferno until the end caught fire, and then he charged down into the cold and clammy. The rain above him stopped.

He didn't make it far before a tentacle tripped him.

He hit the stairs with his knees, elbow, and chest, upside-down. The feeler pulled him between the steps by the ankle, dragging him into the darkness. The blob chortled, its breath stinking of methane.

Blue let go of the two-by-four torch so he could hold onto the steps. The edges of the wood bit into his fingers, into the blister on his palm. His knuckles began to ache, his grip began to slip. The blister popped and drained.

Reloading, Halo cursed and batted off the spider wasp spinning silk over her stomach. Briefly, she played her flashlight over the blob, illuminating its bulk beneath the stairs. A huge eye glanced toward her, quivering like jelly, and then her light was back on the spiders and she was shooting again.

Blue reached for the two-by-four, holding onto the stair with one hand. He grabbed the stud—and then the tentacle pulled him through. He rapped his chin on the step, forced to bite down, and a Milky Way exploded across his vision. He could see enough though. Could see the blob's eye glistening in the firelight.

Blue slammed the burning end of the timber against the eye, driving in the nails. The flames sizzled and hissed in the thing's tears, singing its cornea. The blob squealed. It flung Blue into a pile of ski equipment and reached for the two-by-four. It let go of Brimstone too.

That's when Halo ran out of bullets. She snarled and spit and fought, but the widow wasps swarmed her, completely mummifying her in silk.

Blue stood, and Brimstone picked up a ski pole that had fallen from the pile. He held it out like a lance and ran full force, impaling the blob beneath the stairs. It squealed, farted, and thrashed its tentacles, taking out steps, toppling boxes, knocking Brimstone aside.

Blue grabbed the giant's gun, which he had dropped, and he shot at the spiders still scurrying toward Halo. The sacs hanging from the ceiling kept vomiting more. Blue glared at one—and his body surged with energy. The sac burst, a splatter of yolk and black exoskeleton, and the others burst too, one after the other, the leftover membranes dangling like popped balloons dripping goo.

Swatting at a few spiders, Blue went to Halo's side and brushed the arachnids off her cocoon. Brimstone grabbed the gun from him, pushed him out of the way, and slung the healer over his shoulder.

"I've got her," Blue protested, but the giant didn't listen.

Beneath the stairs, the blob let out one last mewl and then slouched, sighed, and deflated.

Seconds later, new abominations peeked their heads out. Little screaming bat things swooped down and ate the strange moths that suddenly billowed up, their dusty wings flittering like a million tiny voices whispering secrets, and from under the workbench a colony of mutant dwarves no bigger than infants dragged themselves out from behind a stack of crates. Their bodies were a jumble of extra arms, legs, and idiot heads, their eyes rolling, milky, and blind, and each one was bald and wrinkly and liver-spotted, as if ancient. The physically impaired ones lapped at the spider guts, shoveling the ruined meat into their mouths. The others brandished javelins made of chair legs, broomsticks, and curtain rods; they fixed their eyes on the live meat.

Brimstone carried Halo toward the stairs and Blue followed, slipping and sliding in the yellow gore that covered everything, wanting to help, to be the one who saved her. The deformities hurled their javelins and missed as the three climbed toward the kitchen, toward the red glow and the smoke. Blue's rain cloud poured again as the heat began to bake him, parch him, scald him.

Like a lion through a burning hoop, Brimstone ducked through the basement doorway and retreated into the bathroom across from it. As Blue entered the hall, part of the kitchen ceiling collapsed and the child's bed fell through, startling fireflies.

Blue entered the bathroom.

FIGHT

Brimstone had propped Halo against the sink and was tearing the silk away from her face. Her eyes were rolled up in their sockets and a dozen spider bites welted her cheeks and forehead. Many of them were healing, closing up, disappearing. Halo mumbled something and her eyelids fluttered. Brimstone shucked the rest of the webbing and tossed it in the tub. Her gun, still lightly gripped in her hand, had been wrapped up inside with her. The giant tucked it in his waistband. Then he held Halo out to Blue. He wanted him to carry her.

Blue shook his head, took a step back, wiped water out of his eyes. "She's too heavy, I—"

Brimstone thrust a finger at Blue's personal weather system. Then he rubbed sweat off his own forehead, as if to emphasize the heat and its effect on flesh. The giant's skin was red and his shirt was soaked around the pits, reconstituting some of the blood from the rat attack.

Blue kept shaking his head. "I can't—"

Brimstone pushed Halo into his arms. She slumped against him, helpless, vulnerable, and warm—so warm—like an armful of sunshine. Her energy lit his cells as if he were a plant photosynthesizing the light. He had a brief urge to shove her back into the giant's custody—he didn't want to protect her, *couldn't* protect her—but he nodded instead. "Okay. All right."

Brimstone tensed, as if reconsidering, as if he had decided *not* to trust Blue with her life, ready to take her back. But then he sighed and nodded too.

The giant poked his head out of the bathroom, looked both ways, and popped back inside. He pointed through the wall toward the dining room opposite the kitchen. Blue didn't argue; he could think of no other escape. He scooped Halo up in his arms and they exited into the hall.

The dining room wasn't an inferno like the kitchen, but it was bad, a nest of twitching red dragons breathing smoke. Brimstone rushed into it. His cargo pants caught fire, and then he crashed through the bay window, into the back yard. A shatter of glass and he was gone.

Blue readjusted Halo in his arms, hefting her because she had slid down. His shoulders and biceps began to ache. She was heavy. And he would have to run. Waterworks or not, the blaze would melt them. He took a step forward, faltered back. He couldn't do it. He would drop her, he would trip.

She rested in his arms so peacefully, her eyes shut now and blinking against the raindrops, her eyeballs moving back and forth, dreaming, her face without blemish, her hair streaming like liquid gold across her forehead. And then she wasn't blinking as much. The rain had begun to abate—he had almost drained his battery, and soon the clouds would clear up and they would cook.

So he hefted her again and ran into the firestorm. At first it recoiled from his shield with a hiss, but as his personal downpour subsided to a shower, a drizzle, a drop, the red dragons gnawed their way in and bit his hand, grazed his throat, threatened the artery there. Halo's hair, her beautiful, gold-spun hair, began to steam.

Glass crunched beneath his feet.

The window.

He jumped through—and crumpled to the ground, cutting himself on the glass; it glittered everywhere. Halo rolled out of his arms. And then Brimstone was there, dragging them away from the house and the heat and the smoke, into the dead yard. His cargo pants smoldered, but it looked as if he had stopped, dropped, and rolled.

The giant hauled them toward the back of the fence, preparing to break through it when somebody screeched. It was the arsonist, scrabbling at the pickets, trying to climb over them.

"Stay—stay away from me!"

"That's him!" Blue said, pointing. "That's who started the fire!"

Brimstone's brow furrowed. He dropped Blue and Halo, grabbed the arsonist, and slammed him against the fence.

"Please—" the man began, and Brimstone slammed him again.

Blue checked Halo: lying in the dead grass, eyes still closed and ticking. He got up and confronted the arsonist. "What the hell? Why're you trying to kill us?"

"Keep away from me," the firestarter said, reeking of whiskey. He hadn't shaved in weeks, sporting a beard like some salt-and-pepper mold, and his eyes seemed heavy, as if they had taken in so much that the skin beneath them sagged. His irises had probably once been blue but he had long cried out the color, leeching them a dead gray. "Don't touch me—"

Suddenly, the man focused on Blue, really *focused* on him. "You," he said. "I know you. Who the hell are you?"

Blue frowned. "I... what're you—"

"It's *you*," the man interrupted. "Oh Jesus, that's fucking impossible!"

Blue grabbed the man by the shirt, his dirt-stained, puke-stained shirt. "Do you know me? Do you know who I am?"

Brimstone stepped aside but stayed close, a rock, always ready to roll.

The arsonist kept shaking his head, mouth agape as he tried to shrink away; he tried and tried, but Blue had him pinned—so the man pulled out a gun, jammed it in his mouth, and blew the back of his skull all over the fence, a boom, and then a wet slap of blood, brain, and hair. Little red drops misted Blue's face.

The firestarter gained weight, more than his sack-of-kindling corpse was worth. He slipped out of Blue's hands, slouched against the pickets, and drooled blood.

Blue turned, stumbled, and puked, his eyes shut tight. The suicide was burnt into his vision—the man's cheeks inflated from the blast, the back of his head disgorging. Blue had to bite down, clench his stomach, and swallow the thick saliva to stop more vomit. After a moment the gag reflex began to unknot. He wiped the blood off his face.

Boots scuffed dirt, clothes rustled, and nails screeched as they pulled free from wood supports; boards clapped to the ground. Brimstone had made a hole in the fence. Once it was big enough, he slung Halo over his shoulder and walked into the field.

Blue wiped his mouth and gazed at the house. From the window above the kitchen, the ghost boy looked out, flames beating at him like windy Japanese maples. He locked eyes with Blue—was he crying, or smiling?—then he walked back and disappeared into the fire.

Blue spit bile in the dirt. He cleared his throat, straightened up, and wandered through the fence.

NINE

Brimstone was laying Halo in the back seat of the van as Blue arrived. The giant positioned her head carefully and brushed the wet hair out of her face. He wiped a raindrop from her cheek, gently, tenderly, and then he shut her in. When he faced Blue, tears welled in his eyes, water from stone. The water quickly evaporated. His expression set like concrete.

From the sky, a piece of darkness fluttered down and perched on one rail of the luggage rack. It was the black bird. It squawked, hopped along the rail, and with a flap of wings it jumped off behind the van. Seconds later the Crow emerged.

Brimstone stepped in front of Blue and stood face-to-face with the shaman. The giant nodded at Halo through the window of the sliding door.

"I'm not a medicine man," the Crow said. "I cannot make her well."

Brimstone flexed his jaws, but the Crow didn't step back, flinch, or react in any way.

"You must go," he said. "It's coming." He pointed back the way they had come, toward the Greek Revival. Dark clouds rumbled in the distance and red lightning struck. Beneath the crackle of the house fire, Blue could hear the panting.

"It's hunting you now," the Crow told him.

Brimstone glared at Blue and hit the van window with the bottom of his fist. He stomped around to the driver's side, flung himself behind the steering wheel, and slammed the door.

The Crow shook his head. "Tread softly around him," he advised. "He is strong, smart, and loyal, but protective. And jealous."

Blue only half heard him, focused on the approaching storm. "Where are we supposed to go?" he asked. "How the hell are we supposed to outrun that thing?"

"You are not. In the end it will catch you. And you must face it."

"I can't fight something like that. I—"

The Crow laid a hand on Blue's shoulder. "You can and you will. When the time comes you will know exactly who you are and exactly what you have to do."

Blue's muscles relaxed beneath the Crow's palm. He sighed.

The Crow smiled, a grandfather on the wizened side of his face, a father on the other. "I will be watching over you," he said. He pointed to the sky.

Blue nodded and the Crow nodded back. The shaman disappeared behind the van, and with a rustle, with a flap, he flew away, once again a bird.

Brimstone honked, started the engine. Blue climbed into the front seat and they left the house to burn as the storm festered in the distance, as the lightning grew closer and closer.

They traveled in silence down the country road, bearing west, away from the city, away from the beast. The road headed straight to nothing, just fields and, in the distance, woods. Blue had no idea where they were going, and it was pointless to ask Brimstone. Even if the giant could speak, he probably would have answered with a threat.

Blue flicked on the radio. Static.

Brimstone frowned. He turned to check on Halo, as if hoping the noise might rouse her. It didn't.

Blue pressed the radio's seek button: oceans of white noise and dead air; a ghost voice, maybe a preacher; clearer now and definitely a preacher, preaching about how man was made in God's image—and then the panting, loud and clear as if the beast were *right there* in the van.

Halo sat up.

Blue flinched, recoiled, almost cried out.

"I need a cigarette," Halo said, staring straight at him. She took one out and clamped it between her lips, but she didn't light it.

Brimstone shut off the radio and turned to give Halo her gun. He looked relieved, as if a breeze had washed over his face.

Halo put her hand over his. "Thank you," she said, speaking around the filter, and then she took the firearm. "I'm okay now. But… I think we're going the wrong way. I think we need to go to the city."

"Why?" Blue asked as Brimstone pulled off the road and parked on the gravel shoulder. "What's in the city?"

Halo bent to retrieve spare magazines from the ammo box beneath the seat. "I saw something when the spiders bit me," she said. "Some kind of vision. From their venom, I think." She sat upright and slammed one of the magazines into her pistol. She pulled back the slide and loaded the first round.

"It was this endless web cast in space," she said, "like a giant dreamcatcher, strung with planets and stars and galaxies instead of beads. This giant spider was carrying me toward the center of the web, toward some kind of building. I couldn't really see it—there were cobwebs all over it—but then it exploded into this bright, blinding light that burned the web. The spider ran from it. I don't know if the light ever caught up, but I know that's where we have to go. To that building, to the source of the light."

Blue raised an eyebrow. "A giant spider? Doesn't sound like a place I want to go."

Halo shook her head and took the ultra-light out of her mouth. "I don't think there's an actual spider. I think it's just... I think it's a symbol. The spider is the person who spun the web, the one who started all this... I think the spider is you."

Blue frowned, and Brimstone stared at him hard. The van idled, grumbled

"What," Blue said, "you're saying I'm responsible for all this? The zombies, that thing..." He pointed toward the storm and the beast at the eye of it. "You're saying I caused all that?"

Halo said, "I know it's hard to believe. But in that alley, you made a gun appear out of thin air. You moved a Dumpster with your mind and you made it rain—and you made those zombies as well. Your battery isn't drained, Blue; I was wrong about that. Your subconscious has just been busy creating other things."

He stared out the windshield and chewed the inside of his cheek. Then he opened his door and put his foot down, ready to get out.

"Blue," Halo said, grabbing his arm. "Where are you—"

"It's hunting me—it wants *me*—so let it have me." He tried to pull away but Halo held on. She was stronger than he had imagined.

"You think it'll stop after it's killed you?" she asked. "You think it'll just disappear? We have to kill this thing, Blue, and we have to kill it together. But to do that, we have to go to the building. Because the light I saw, *that's* what saves us. I don't know why and I don't know how, but I know. So what makes you think so differently?"

He sighed and looked up at the sky. No black bird watching over him. No North Star, no discernable god. And even if he created one, he would still have no guidance. He was as alone as the moon in the sky.

"The Crow told me I had to face it," he finally said. He let the admission linger awhile. Halo didn't say anything, and he didn't think she would. The Crow's message meant too much to her; she would listen. "He said that when the time came, I would know what I had to do. And what I can't do is lead that thing into the city. I won't."

Halo's grip on his arm softened. He could have pulled away, *should* have pulled away—she was giving him that choice—but Halo had more to tell him and he would respect that.

"Remember how I said my mom wanted me to be a doctor?" she asked. She didn't give him time to interrupt. "Well, I *was* a doctor. For a while, at least. I tried hard to do it with traditional medicine, no miracles. And it worked... until we got the car crash victim. He had a crushed chest and we couldn't do anything for him. So I took off the gloves and I healed him. I did what my mother always wanted me to do and I *saved* him.

"They fired me after that. Said my gift was a liability. Because they couldn't explain it, couldn't guarantee that it wouldn't do any harm. That's when I realized: if you want to work miracles you have to do it on your own. But the sad thing is, Blue, the pure irony of it is I could have saved more lives as a regular old doctor than I do now. I made a rash decision and more people will die because of it.

"And you," she said, "you can't even control your powers. The beast would swallow you whole. And it wouldn't stop there, Blue. It would take out the city, maybe even the world. So your decision would end up killing us in the end. But if you stay, if you come with us, I will do anything and everything to train you. I don't think we can stop you from making the monsters—I think that's too deep in your subconscious—but I think we can control the surface stuff. Because that bright light—maybe it's *you*. Maybe you're supposed to learn to harness your gift. Maybe that's how you stop this thing."

He looked at her then and he didn't care that Brimstone was practically quaking, though he understood why, understood the giant's jealousy over their connection. Something flowed between them despite Halo's glove, a current, an energy, healing them both, his eyes full of ocean, hers full of sky, each reflecting the other.

Blue glanced at the corn. It would be so much easier out there in the dark, alone and detached. It would be so much simpler. No faces out there to haunt him once they were gone. No heat to warm him. Just the numbing cold.

In the south, the lightning faded away, a burn, a blush, an emptiness. Blue thought maybe it was over, maybe the beast had returned to whatever hell had spawned it. But then a bolt struck in the east, as if the storm had teleported, and he realized something: the beast was on the move, tracking their scent. It was at the Gothic Revival now.

Its next stop? This cornfield.

He shivered. Halo's hand helped alleviate some of the tremors. But then she released him, and he realized how cold and unstable he felt without her to anchor him.

"You can stay if you want," she said. "You still have free will. But I want you to know we're going to that building. I believe it's our best chance. I'm not sure it'll work without you, but… I think it's worth trying."

He sighed and gazed into the corn. The stalks moved in the wind, and for the briefest moment they came alive, a sea of lost souls groping for him.

"Okay," he said, and he lifted his leg back into the van.

"Good." Halo laid her gloved hand on his shoulder. "Good." She told Brimstone to drive them back toward town and asked Blue to sit in back with her.

"Lesson number one," she said once he had settled into the bench seat. "Focus…"

TEN

"Concentrate," Halo said, her voice barely audible over the engine; they were almost to the city, traveling the highway, the skyline like a starry heavens in the distance. "See the object," she said, "as if it were real, with texture, consistency—even the taste and smell of it."

Eyes closed, hand held out, Blue pictured a joint, white paper wrapped around sticky buds of marijuana, twisted at both ends. He didn't know whether he'd been a stoner before the alley, but he knew exactly how the pot would smell: herbal and skunky. His cells craved the drug too, cried out for its sweet relief.

Something dropped into his hand.

Halo said, "That's not how you imagined it." She had admitted she could see inside his mind, could see the objects he imagined, and she was right about the joint. In his palm lay a wad of ripped paper and loose weed. As if something had chewed it up and spit it out.

Blue cursed and threw the rubbish onto the floor. Brimstone shot him a dirty look in the rearview and actually reached back, picked up the debris, and discarded it in the ashtray. Before the beast had aged the van, before the dust and cobwebs had settled in, the vehicle had been immaculately clean, and even now it was free of trash; not even an old cup sat in the cup holder. Blue remembered Brimstone's pink apron and realized the giant was the maid. Blue would make sure not to dirty up the place. It might be his death if he did.

"Try again," Halo said.

He did, and this time the joint came out with its end torn off.

Halo furrowed her brow. "It's like in the *Phaedo*."

"Excuse me?"

"It's a dialogue. By Plato. He believed that perfect forms exist outside of time and space and that all material objects are based on them, just flawed copies of them. With you it's like you're picturing the perfect form of a joint, its fundamental jointness, but when it comes out it's imperfect."

Blue considered this. He could remember creating only one functional thing: the gun from the alley. Everything else had been useless, like the lump-of-plastic guns he had made in the Crow's field. But his monsters seemed to work just fine.

He didn't want to think about it anymore. "No," he said, "I meant, 'Excuse me, do you have a lighter?'" He went to put the joint in his mouth, but Brimstone snatched it from him. The giant crushed it in the ashtray along with the first one.

Halo gave Blue a deadpan expression. "No smoking," she said—and then she grinned, her face lighting up like a sunrise.

Blue wasn't laughing. His hands shook and he needed something to calm him down.

Halo's smile faded. "Try making something else," she said. "Something simpler."

Blue grunted and shut his eyes. His mind went blank. He could think of nothing but marijuana smoke, inhaling it, rolling it off his tongue. But then something began to appear in the darkness: a ball, perfectly round and perfectly blue.

"Focus," Halo said, and he imagined the texture of the ball, smooth like a blueberry; he imagined the new rubber smell. He could even imagine how it would bounce.

Blue held out his hand... and like at the Gothic Revival, he was hit with a sense of déjà vu—a memory coming back? Had he done this before?

Suddenly a ball sat in his palm. Except it wasn't blue enough. And it sported teeth marks. The sphere emitted silence, like some strange broadcast of anti-noise filling the van with its pulse, drowning out the rumble of the engine and the hiss of tires on pavement, hushing everything except Blue's breathing, which sounded too much like the panting of the beast.

He dropped the ball and it rolled under Brimstone's seat. Normal sound rushed back in. Blue was sweating and cold. Halo was too.

"Maybe we should stop for now," she suggested.

Blue agreed.

And then Brimstone honked, swerved, and barely missed a SUV reversing toward them.

ELEVEN

In the southbound lanes of the highway, cars raced away from the city, some of them crashing, piling up, blocking traffic. Countless drivers had abandoned their vehicles in the gridlock and were running between the stalled cars, stampeding, trampling each other. One lady ran into oncoming traffic. A truck mowed her over and her body rolled and flopped to a stop, her white, lily-patterned blouse ripped and flapping, bloody skid marks left in her wake.

Not too far back, zombies were chasing down pedestrians, tackling them, gnashing throats, releasing jets of blood. The zombies stretched as far as Blue could see, down the onramp and into the city. And in the distant night, emergency lights flashed and fires blazed, little signals of disaster. Helicopters flew around with spotlights.

In the northbound lane, separated from the southbound lane by a concrete divider, drivers were backing up, using the shoulder of the freeway, veering around each other. Brimstone maneuvered between them, tires screeching with every abrupt turn. He avoided the pedestrians that had spilled over the divider as well.

"I can hear their screams," Halo said, weeping silently.

Blue thought about putting an arm around her or putting his hand over hers, any contact to rekindle their connection, to heal her, to comfort her. Instead, he grabbed the handle above his window as Brimstone dodged a Humvee.

Ahead, the city exit was clogged with a pileup. Brimstone steered toward a small gap between two cars turned sideways to form an accidental roadblock. He was going to bull his way through.

Blue sat forward. "What if it's a trap?" he asked. "What if the spiders *wanted* you to see that building?"

Halo shook her head and Brimstone wasn't listening anyway. He rammed the cars. Blue hit the back of the driver's seat. Metal shrieked against metal, tires skidded, and just as they busted through, Brimstone braked sharply. The way ahead of them was jammed with stalled cars. Zombies were pulling people out of their vehicles, shattering windows and dragging the occupants out through the holes, tipping compact cars onto their sides, onto their backs, rioting.

A mob began to converge on the van.

"Turn around," Blue said. "Back up, get us the hell out!"

"No." Halo pulled him back. "We need to keep going!"

"On foot? They'll eat us alive!"

"Then you'll to have to move these cars," she said.

"What? I can't—"

"Yes, you can. You moved the Dumpster and you can move these. Just *concentrate*."

The first zombie had made it to the van. He wore a black suit and a tie made to look like a keyboard, his eyes milky, his face pale, his scalp peeled back in a flap over his ear. He hammered at the front passenger-side window and groaned.

His friends weren't far away, a mix of suits, Goths, and homeless people, of gas-pump attendants, waiters, and movie-store clerks. They were slower, more decayed, their clothes stained with bodily fluids, their skin runny and their noses slumped. Some bore hideous wounds, gunshots to the chest and arms, legs broken by clubs or bumpers, useless limbs dragging.

The van would be engulfed in less than a minute.

"You have to do this," Halo said, clutching Blue's arm, her glove creaking with the pressure. "You have to."

"All right," he said, "all right," and he closed his eyes. His thoughts ricocheted like a dozen bullets. His body trembled and he felt as if he might crumble, cell by cell, no more stable than a sand castle built by the sea. For a second, his mind formed a clear picture of the bedlam outside, of the cars and the corpses, and he tried to picture the vehicles steering out of the way. A familiar hum began to build in the van, and the windows began to vibrate. He could hear tires bitching against concrete as they slid an inch—and then the passenger window shattered. Blue's eyes snapped open; the energy waned.

The dead businessman reached in, bringing in the stink of rot. Brimstone shot him. More corpses took the man's place. The giant kept firing.

"I can't do it!" Blue said. "I can't concentrate!"

"Then I'll help you!" Halo took off her gloves. Blue's skin suddenly buzzed in anticipation, craving her flesh against his, eager despite the circumstances. She planted her palms against his temples, hot and sweaty, and lights went on inside his mind.

"Focus," she said, repeating it over and over like a mantra. "Focus."

Beneath her words, that river of voices flowed, what Halo suspected to be the collective consciousness, a mix of whispers, screams, growls, and conversations, growing louder and louder until Blue could distinguish individual words—*help*, *fuck*, *hate*—until images surfaced, faces patched together like Picasso paintings, strings of numbers and equations floating like debris; diagrams, schematics, blueprints, essays, novels, paintings—*everything*—individual people even, their thoughts buzzing around their heads like flies. Halo was among them. The zombies too, their thoughts shrouded in the blue fog.

Blue could see the building Halo had dreamt, a multi-story construction swaddled in webs; he could see the route there, clogged with cars and people and ambulances and death—he could see it perfectly, and when he thought about clearing their path, the cars crumpled to either side of the road, metal crunching, shrieking, folding in on itself, parting like the Red Sea before Moses. Blue zoomed in on the zombies next—not all of them, not even most of them (he couldn't reach that far)—but he wrangled all of them within a ten-foot radius of their path; he got inside their heads and—*pop!*—hundreds of headless corpses went down in a shower of pulp.

Halo let go, fell against the sliding door, and Blue slumped like an empty sack. Brimstone stared back at them, pale and sweating. He had stopped shooting, and his zombie targets lay around the van without any heads, their brains and scalps and skulls plastered everywhere.

"What'd we do?" Blue asked, sounding distant.

Halo shook her head. "I... I don't... We'd better go." She pointed, her arm sagging as if full of lead; the zombies beyond the blast radius were already regrouping, climbing over the wall of compacted cars.

Brimstone put the van in gear. It clattered as it moved, the fender pried loose from plowing through the roadblocks, the grille smashed and rattling. The tires bounced over the headless corpses in the road; Blue could barely brace himself, he was so drained of energy.

The path Blue and Halo had cleared continued down the main strip of the city. *To the building*, Blue thought. He shuddered and tried to conjure a spike strip or a piece of jagged metal or broken glass, anything to pop their tires, anything to stall them. He didn't have the energy.

Ahead of them, zombies chased people into the road. Halo told Brimstone to keep going, they were almost there, but he slowed down and shot zombies through the broken passenger window, helping their prey run free.

"There," Halo said, pointing, sitting forward, suddenly energetic again. Twenty blocks away and around a bend, the building loomed above the others, just a solid tower reaching to the night sky, no cobwebs, all its lights burning. "It's a hospital," she said, squinting into the distance as if she could see something that Blue could not. "It's hard for me to see inside. Like at that house. Like something's blocking me, but... there's... I can see the outside and there's zombies surrounding the whole thing." She turned to Brimstone. "Think you can tear us a hole?"

He nodded and flexed his hand on the wheel, eyeing the streets for targets.

"Good," she said, lying a hand on his shoulder. "We can't do this without you." She sat back and looked at Blue. "Ready?"

He fidgeted with the deer-antler knife. No sign of the beast. No storm nor waking nightmares. And no sign of the Crow. He avoided Halo's eyes, ignored her question. He could never admit how he was feeling, could never divulge the tremors in his belly, the emptiness in his heart. Halo didn't pursue the issue.

Ten blocks from the hospital, a construction worker corpse caught a teenager by her purse and pulled her in, tearing at her shirt, trying to get a bite as she thrashed and beat at him and tried to mace him to no effect.

Brimstone slowed, as if planning to pull over, as if planning to help.

"We can't," Halo said. "If we save her, we have to save him"— she pointed to a man standing atop his truck with a tire iron, hitting back zombie hands—"and we have to save them"—she indicated a family stuck in their station wagon on the other side of the divider, completely surrounded by the undead. "And if we save *them*," Halo continued, "hundreds will die. The longer we're away from that building, the more blood we'll have on our hands. We need to keep going."

Brimstone stared at her in the rearview for a few seconds as the girl screamed and gunshots erupted somewhere down the road. Then he stopped the van and got out.

Halo cursed and went after him.

Blue glanced at the steering wheel. The giant had left the engine running. *I could leave*, he thought. Just back up and go. Get the hell out.

He managed to quell his flight instinct, realizing how selfish abandoning them would be.

In the street, Brimstone hurled the construction worker against the nearest building. It didn't kill the zombie, just shattered its bones, leaving it to twitch and crawl. The giant had slung the girl over his shoulder by the time Halo caught up. Other people cried for help as zombies poured out of an alleyway. Halo and Brimstone looked back—and a tentacle burst from the manhole behind them. The lid went flying and crashed through a display window, beheading a mannequin.

"Halo!" Blue yelled.

The tentacle lashed out. It plucked the girl from Brimstone's grasp and twisted around her, twisted until she vomited gore. It dragged her into the sewer, chased by Halo's bullets. It didn't hide for long. It came back. It came for them.

They shot at it and dashed for the van. A few rounds punched holes in its skin; it reared back and writhed.

Blue opened the sliding door and Halo jumped in. Brimstone ran around the van, got behind the wheel, and actually took time to put on his seatbelt, out of instinct, out of habit, out of pure compulsion: who knew? He put it in drive, stomped the gas, they peeled out and—the tentacle whipped the passenger door. The van tilted, rolled on its side, and crashed into the wall of junked cars.

Blue lay on the back passenger window, which had become the floor. He was bleeding. Halo lay on top of him. The moans of the dead closed in.

TWELVE

"You all right?" Halo whispered, her face inches from Blue's. Her breath, minty, smoky, quivered across his skin.

He nodded, then winced and held his head.

"You hit it," Halo noticed, checking the side of his skull. "Can you stand?"

He nodded again.

Halo pushed herself off him, pressing the air out of him until she could support herself on the back of Brimstone's seat. "Stone," she said. "Stone?" She reached down over the edge of the seat, and the giant grasped her hand, held it against his chest and gave it a squeeze.

"We need to get out," she said.

He nodded and let her go. With his bare hands, he snapped his seatbelt in half. He stood up, boots on his window, and nudged Halo back. Then he smashed the passenger-window-turned-skylight above him. Chunks of safety glass rained down like hail.

Grabbing the edges of the window, the giant lifted himself out. He lay on the side of the van and stuck his arms back in for Halo.

"Blue first," she said, helping him to his feet.

Brimstone shook his head and pointed at her. He wouldn't even acknowledge Blue.

"Just *go*," Blue told her. "Cover us."

Halo seemed to contemplate it, studying him for a moment, and then she nodded and let the giant hoist her outside. She stood and pulled out her gun, but before she could start shooting, Brimstone picked her up over his head, one hand under her neck, the other under her buttocks.

"Hey, what're you—"

He threw her. Her scream grew distant as she flew. And then it cut off.

The giant poked his head through the broken window.

"Why'd you do that?" Blue asked.

The giant sneered at him and stood up. He backed up to the edge of the bus as if getting a running start, facing the way he had hurled Halo. He had probably thrown her to safety and was now preparing to join her.

"Hey," Blue called.

Brimstone ran forward—

"Hey!"

—and jumped.

The tentacle caught him midair. It constricted around him for a moment, dangling him there, and then it yanked him out of sight.

Blue cringed, gawking up through the window, waiting. Gunshots erupted from Halo's direction. *It's her*, Blue thought. *She's still out there.*

He glanced around for a gun of his own—he suspected the box of them had come out from under the seat and had scattered everywhere—but he found only the blue ball. He couldn't create a firearm either. Not even a lump of plastic.

The tentacle returned.

Blue held completely still. He didn't even breathe.

The feeler, thicker than a telephone pole, quested along the sliding door. It left a trail of slime on the glass. The tip of it found Brimstone's shattered window and tested the glass teeth still lodged in the seal. Blue tensed, hand on his knife, ready for it to enter, ready to stab, twist, and gore. Zombies groaned closer and closer; Halo's gunshots grew farther away. They suddenly ceased. The feeler stopped, as if considering something, and then it slithered off the van with a heavy dragging sound.

Blue let out his breath.

Something jerked the van.

He stumbled, caught himself on the driver's seat, got his bearings.

"Blue!" Halo called from somewhere in the distance. "Get out!" She started firing her gun again, and the bullets pinged off the back of the vehicle.

He caught a glimpse of the tentacle rearing back, leaking blue blood from bullet holes, and he understood what was happening.

The feeler took hold of the van again—probably by the back axle—and towed it closer to the manhole, metal screeching against concrete.

Knocking his elbows and his knees, clawing at the seats for purchase, trying his best not to flail as the tentacle jerked the van closer and closer, Blue clambered into the front. He stood up, crunching the hailstones of glass beneath his shoes, bracing himself on the steering wheel. He grabbed the edges of the window above him, grimacing as glass bit into his fingers. He did a pull-up. The van jostled, almost knocked him down, but he held on, legs floundering until he found footing on the side of the driver's seat. He climbed out and the movement rolled him off and tossed him to the concrete. It knocked the wind out of him. The tentacle kept pulling the van, metal and concrete generating sparks.

A zombie grabbed Blue's ankle. A fat, putrefying corpse, its face runny and black, reeking of decay. It went to bite him and—*boom!*—a hole opened above its right eye and the back of its skull expelled sickly matter.

"Up here!" Halo yelled. "Come on!" She stood on a fire escape in an alley on the other side of the divider. She shot a few more corpses closing in on him and then had to reload. Fortunately the tentacle was busy rummaging through the van, as if it thought he were still in there.

Struggling to breathe, Blue got to his feet and hobbled. His hip hurt. Must have bruised it. He vaulted over the divider where no cars were piled against it, and he scurried across the street, dodging other pedestrians and zombies as Halo shot down on them from above. She lowered the ladder for him and he scaled it. She raised it before any of the zombies could get to it.

They broke through one of the windows along the escape and barged into the apartment. It was empty; Halo had sensed it. The carpet was cobalt and recently shampooed—the room smelled of the cleaners—and the walls were a disturbingly blank white. People screamed throughout the building and more gunshots rang outside, sirens blaring, coming and going on other blocks.

Halo went to the window facing the street where the tentacle was now plucking up new victims, disinterested in the van. "Brimstone," she said. "That thing ate him."

Blue said, "I'm sorry. I—"

She whirled around, her eyes full of tears, her cheeks flushed, her hair looking frayed. "I can't believe he did that to you. He was going to *leave* you! I can't—I didn't see that coming, I—" She turned back to the window and paused, as if hoping he would surface. "It's hopeless now," she said. "We needed him. We—" She sobbed. "Damn him—goddamn him!"

She buried her face in her hands and slumped against the wall.

Blue shifted from one foot to another, scratched at the knife and glanced around. He could find nothing in the blank room to hold his attention. So he sat by Halo and embraced her, rested her head against his chest so she could hear his heartbeat and know: in a city of corpses, there was still life.

The screams and the ruckus died down outside as people found hiding places, dispersed, or died. Zombies groaned and beat at windows and doors, and sirens went on and on but went nowhere; the emergency vehicles had stalled.

Blue stroked Halo's hair, the warm sunshine of her hair, and for the first time since the Crow's tent, he felt at peace. She looked up at him, the skin around her eyes red and puffy, but her eyes clear and bright. She was about to speak, and he thought she might admit to something, maybe acknowledge the pleasant glow between them, the energy that had already healed his wounds from their fray with the tentacle.

She said, "I think I know why he did that to you."

Blue stared at her a moment. He wished she wouldn't dwell on it, didn't want to feel her sob against him again, those bruising, bone-deep sobs. He wished Brimstone hadn't affected her that profoundly—the traitor—but he didn't have the heart to stop her.

"It's my fault," she continued. "He's always had a thing for me."

Blue frowned. "Did you—"

She shook her head. "He was like a brother to me." She stared off into nothing, her eyes misty as if she were seeing something far away, deep in the past. "You know why he couldn't talk?" she asked.

Blue said nothing. The question was rhetorical and she would tell him no matter what he had to say.

"When he was a kid," she said, "his dad was an alcoholic, a mean drunk, and he liked to knock Stone's mom around. So Stone stood up to him one day. Broke his nose and knocked him out cold. Stone went to help his mom—his dad got her really good that time, bruised the hell out of her face—and when he had his back turned"—she cleared her throat—"his dad came to, jumped on him and started slashing his neck with a steak knife. Cut all the way to the vocal chords, nicked his carotid artery. Stone's lucky his neighbors called the cops, or he would've bled to death."

Blue could think of nothing to say. So he brushed Halo's hair out of her face and hoped the silence would return. But outside came the noises of the zombies, and those were worse. It sounded too much like panting.

Halo nestled deeper in Blue's arms. "I always thought if I had been there, I could've healed him; I could've saved his voice." Tears welled up in her eyes again.

"You can't blame yourself," Blue said; he had to say *something*.

She frowned and pulled away. "No, that's what people say, but it's bullshit. We *have* to blame ourselves. The guilt is the only thing that makes us try harder to save the next person, to save as many people as we possibly can." She stood, crossed her arms, and looked out the window. "And now we've failed." Her voice had a dangerous hollowness to it, a dark lack of hope, as if her sorrow hadn't just bruised her bones but had sucked them clean of marrow.

She lit a cigarette, took a drag, and then let it smolder.

Blue stood too. "We can still do this." The words rang empty, but he found he would say just about anything to assuage her hope-lessness.

"Brimstone's dead, Blue. We needed him: those zombies, they're guarding that building and they're not going anywhere."

"You could help me concentrate again," Blue suggested. "We could use another death pulse."

She was silent for a moment, as if considering it. "No," she finally replied, "that would sap all your energy. And you would *need* your energy. It won't work."

"Then we'll just sit here," Blue said, suddenly hot in the face. "We'll just sit and watch the world die." He stormed over to the other side of the room and sat against the wall, arms crossed, knees drawn up to his chest.

Several minutes passed. While Halo finished her ultra-light, Blue probed the blue fog in his head, tried to fan it away and reveal memories, some clue to what was happening. He had remembered the Gothic, had even recognized the child. But the only true memories were from tonight. Halo glowed brightest among them.

"Hey, Blue?" she said.

"What."

"Did you build the staircase over to the next building?"

He got up and went to her. "No," he said, peeking out over her shoulder, craning his head to see left along the brick. "At least not that I'm aware of."

"Well someone built it," Halo said. "Because it wasn't there before."

From their apartment block to the taller building next to them, a wooden staircase ascended over the alley, supported with a trestle like a railroad bridge.

As with the monsters, Blue could have spawned it subconsciously. The alternative was that someone else had created it.

"Let's go," he said, grabbing Halo's hand and starting toward the fire escape.

"What?"

He took her by the shoulders, locked eyes with her. "You said we couldn't get over there, that it was impossible. Well this is proof that nothing is impossible. This is our chance. *This* is our miracle."

She looked at him for a long moment, her face expressionless, and he feared she would laugh at him or refuse to leave, raise questions about the origin and safety of the stairs. Instead she kissed him. The smoky-sweet taste startled him, aroused him. Her lips were plump, silky, and warm, gliding over his, parting to reveal their hot, moist secret. The sun rose behind his eyes, and the kiss was over.

"Lead the way," Halo said, and she squeezed his hand.

THIRTEEN

The moon had almost set, and the soot of night had covered all the traffic jams and buildings. Fires had spread, filling the air with smoke: burning rubber, burning wood, burning flesh. Bodies littered the street, and in the west the beast's storm raged. Blue listened for the panting, but it was still far away. He wondered for how long.

Halo waited behind him as he stepped onto the parapet that enclosed the rooftop. The staircase rose in front of him.

In the alley below, a mob of zombies pulled apart a woman's corpse. They had gnawed off most of her arm and were now digging into her stomach. More came to dine. As they feasted, the woman sat up; she shoveled some of her own guts into her mouth. Other victims were getting up as well, ravaged, drained of blood, yet animate. Whatever curse or infection his mind had engineered worked fast.

"Jesus," Blue muttered, and he looked away.

The staircase reminded him of the one in the Gothic, old stained oak with a tooled balustrade; if he had created it, perhaps his subconscious had copied the one from the house. He almost expected the ghost child to be at the top, standing next to a blue ball. He wasn't.

Blue stepped on the first stair with his right foot. It seemed stable enough, didn't wobble, sag, or crack.

"Be careful," Halo said as he trusted the step with his full weight.

"I think it's safe," he told her.

Halo stepped up behind him and gave him an expectant look. He took the next step. It creaked but didn't give way.

"I don't think it'll hold both of us," he said. "Let me go first."

She nodded and Blue climbed to the top. The roof was abandoned up there, nothing but cooling units, vents, and pipes.

"Clear!" he called.

Halo jogged up and hopped down from the parapet, breathing a little heavier. "What now?" she asked. It was good to hear the old vigor in her voice, but Blue didn't know what came next, didn't know how to sustain her hope. He glanced around.

"There!" he said, pointing. They both ran over to the front of the building where a catwalk of the same stained oak spanned the canyon of the street; it connected to another building of the same height, and from his vantage Blue could see more oaken catwalks and staircases connecting rooftop after rooftop, and beyond that, towering over them all, the hospital.

"Think they go all the way there?" Halo asked.

"Probab—"

The air quivered behind him. Blue whirled. Dodged. The zombie lunged past him and fell, landing face-first on the sidewalk, rotten flesh splattering, bone shattering, the t-shirt and jeans barely containing the slop.

Halo shot the second corpse that appeared, a flagman in an orange vest. The back of the flagger's head became a pit surrounded by wiry dishwater hair.

Halo slammed in a new magazine. "Last one," she said. "Ten rounds."

Moaning, groaning, and shambling like drunks, a group of walking dead emerged from behind the stairwell housing. They hadn't been there before. Neither had their stench, that reek of gases and liquefying flesh.

Blue said, "Let's go," and they ran across the catwalk, both at the same time. It bowed in the middle, but like the staircase, it held. Rings of light appeared above their heads, actual halos; as with the cloudburst, Blue hadn't meant to conjure them, but there they were, lighting the way. He and Halo ran from roof to roof, avoiding zombies as they appeared from the shadows, shooting them if they got in the way, jumping their bodies, running, running, shoes and boots clopping on the wood—they were almost there. One more stairway, this one leading to a window on the seventh floor of the hospital.

Zombies guarded the first step.

Halo executed two of them and cursed. "Almost out," she said.

More ganged up on them from behind. Hordes of them, guts distended with organs that had fallen loose, clothes stained with blood and blood-tinged bodily fluids, faces melted beyond recognition. Some dragged their feet, shoes scraping on the roofing. They all gurgled or groaned.

Blue and Halo backed up against the parapet facing the street; they had nowhere else to go. Halo trained her gun on the zombies, jumping from target to target as if not sure which to shoot first. "There's too many!"

Blue closed his eyes. He imagined a magazine full of bullets—and lightning struck in the street behind them. They both flinched, whirled, flash-blind.

The panting.

Quiet at first but intensifying, echoing out of every alleyway, reverberating through every building. The zombies weren't groaning, they were panting—everything was panting. Even Blue felt himself panting, panting, panting. Lightning struck again, louder than a gunshot, tinting everything red. It began to rain.

"The beast," Blue said, barely audible beneath the panting and the downpour.

On the street a rip appeared in thin air, as if the world were just a painting, thin, two-dimensional, and much shallower than it appeared; as if it were just a painting and something was tearing through from the other side. "It's coming."

FOURTEEN

Enlarging the rip, a tangle of arms and legs emerged, moving like cilia on the bulk of the beast. Nightmares rippled outward from the tear. Vehicles rusted. Roads and sidewalks fissured and grayed. Buildings grew mildew, mortar disintegrated, and windows became maws filled with fangs of glass. Everything had aged, everything abandoned, years beyond the end of mankind. And the zombies: tentacles sprouted from their skulls, long, black, and lined with suckers. Some corpses grew extra body parts, all black and dripping.

The beast kept pushing through.

"Shoot it!" Blue shouted.

Halo fired three rounds: the first punched through one of the beast's numerous hands, the second struck a kneecap, and the last hit the body. The wounds didn't slow the monster down. The zombies kept closing in.

"I'm out!" Halo shouted. She released the Glock's slide and holstered the weapon.

The closest corpse came at them. Its tentacles reached for her, its two extra heads slobbering and biting the air.

Fffffttt!—an arrow sank into the zombie's eye. It fell back in a spurt of liquid, bowling over one of its brethren.

Blue glanced across the street through the rain. The Crow stood on the building opposite them, a silhouette holding a bow, two feathers sticking out of his hair. He shot three more zombies, all eye shots, and then he was a bird flapping away.

"Come back!" Blue shouted after him. His words were lost beneath the panting.

"We'll have to jump!" Halo yelled. She put a hand on his shoulder to brace herself and went to step up onto the parapet.

"No," Blue said, pulling her back. He glared at the zombies and then shut his eyes. He thought of little time bombs ticking inside each of their heads, could actually *see* inside their skulls, could see the organism that had reanimated them, a black blob attached to the inside of the forehead, its feelers hardwired to the main control centers of the brain, like puppet strings.

Tick-tick-tick—the zombies closest to him turned to fireworks from the neck up, a blast of light, gore, and flopping tentacles.

Blue turned to the corpses guarding the staircase. The air wavered and the zombies crumpled as if crushed in giant fists. Bones cracked, splintered, and crunched inward, poking out of flesh, ripping it, shredding it, reducing the guards to heaps of ruined skin, runny entrails, and meat, all awash in the rain.

Blue's muscles went slack from the exertion; his knees went watery and he almost collapsed. Halo slung his arm over her shoulder to brace him. "Come on," she said. "We can make it." She helped him to the final staircase.

The varnish had worn off the wood, leaving worm-eaten lumber suffering dry rot. Halfway up, a tongue lolled over it, drool diluted with runoff. The hospital had morphed into a goliath of sinew, musculature, ribcages, and spines, and the tongue led into the jaws of a giant glowering skull, something Blue had seen before, something he had dreamed. A nightmare.

He second-guessed their decision to enter it, but the random mass of tissue seemed like a setting, not a creature, brainless and unaware. If it killed, it would be the result of function, not intent.

On the street, the beast roared. The rain shook, the building shook, pieces of staircase went tumbling into the side street. Blue went deaf. The world became a silent film, grainy with rain, saved from black and white only by their luminous crowns. Everything shuddered as the beast moved like an earthquake. He couldn't see it over the edge of the roof but he knew it had fully emerged from the rift. It was coming.

The hospital, despite its hideous growth, was their only refuge.

Halo shouted something, nothing at all, her breath spraying water from her lips, her hair dripping like melting light, each drop illuminated at first, then going dark as it fell. She hauled him up the stairs. He couldn't hear the wood crack but felt it sag, felt it shift underfoot.

The panting filtered back in. Then the rain and Halo shouting: "Keep going, keep going! We're almost—"

One of the steps caved in. Her foot went through and they fell to their chests. The truss split. The structure tilted to the left, Blue's side. He scrabbled for purchase, fingernails gouging wood. Splinters bit to the quick. He slid into the balusters, the whole balustrade gave way, and he felt empty space open beneath him, felt his stomach lurch.

Grabbing the side of the stairs, Halo seized his left arm with her right hand and wrapped her legs around his back, one under his armpit, the other over his shoulder. Her grip was slipping on the wet wood, one knuckle at a time. Blue found a foothold, the stub of a broken baluster, but it slowly pushed loose.

"Shit!" Halo said as a zombie appeared on the tongue above them. It had four arms, a Shiva. It also had tentacles, like snakes for hair. The tentacles reached down.

"Shit, shit, shit," Halo said, trying to lift herself and redouble her hold.

Face fat and red with blood, Blue glanced at her gun. It was in the holster on her left hip. If he could get it, if he could hold it in his hand, he thought he had just enough energy to manufacture bullets. But his right arm, his *free* arm, was pinned between his side and the edge of a step. And the zombie's tentacles were closing around Halo's biceps and neck.

"Hurry," she said.

Blue wiggled his arm. It dislodged, and his elbow thunked wood. He reached around her thigh, found the holster, found the strap that buttoned down the gun—and the staircase cracked and slanted more. His hand flailed, groped.

They weren't falling.

They were rising.

The zombie was reeling them in.

Again Blue reached for the Glock. He unbuttoned the holster, got his hand on the grip. The tentacle hoisted Halo onto the tongue. Her feet pressed into the flesh, water and drool pooling around her boots, and she pulled Blue up by the arm. The zombie pounced, opening its mouth to bite her.

Blue shot it in the face.

The corpse fell, pulling Halo down on top of it. She screamed and beat at the body with her fists, pulled at the suckered pythons around her neck. Blue withdrew his knife. He knelt and cut through the tentacles, through the gristle and meat, gripping the handle so hard the antler indented his palm. He helped her stand. The suckers left red circles around Halo's neck, but they quickly healed. One wound did not: the bite on her cheek.

She touched it gingerly with the fingertip of her glove. The rain washed blood out of it, diluting it, turning it pink in the heavenly light above her head. They had no time to say anything to each other—the tongue retracted and pulled them into the skull. But all they needed was one shared look, her eyes trembling, his shocked wide.

They entered the dark mouth.

And the teeth clamped shut behind them.

FIFTEEN

Inside the skull, the throat lined the hospital's hallway, stinking of bad breath and bile. At the end stood a door with light pouring out all around its seams, a bright, white light.

"That's it," Halo said, and she started forward.

"Wait." Blue caught her by the arm. "Your cheek," he said. "It's not healing."

"We don't have time—"

"You can heal the bites. I've seen you. In the alley. That blonde. Why aren't you healing it?"

"This zombie was different, Blue. Mutated. Maybe it was stronger. Now let's go."

He shook his head. "Those people on the street. They were bitten. They—"

"I know," she said, frowning. She had already paled, and the nimbus above her had dimmed. "I know what happens when a zombie bites you. But in a few minutes, that won't matter, will it?" She pulled away from him and marched down the throat.

"Halo!" Blue chased after her. She went through the door without pausing, letting the light pour out. It was only fluorescent light, nothing divine, nothing that would save the world. And the space beyond the door looked like a normal hospital room. A boy lay in bed, hooked to monitors and an IV. He appeared to be sleeping—or comatose. The same child had haunted the Gothic, the boy with the ball. Only this boy was real.

Blue ran to catch up. As he entered the room, the door slammed behind him. Halo didn't seem alarmed. She stared at the child. "He looks exactly like you," she said, and he did: blond hair and eyes full of the sea. He wore a bandage around his head. Halo took off her glove and approached him.

"Wait," Blue said, but she had already pushed her hand under the bandage, onto the child's temple. Energy rippled out from the connection, making waves in the air. Blue stepped forward—and the waves swept him away.

He tumbled into that stream again, into the voices and thoughts and images, now intermixed with screams, and blood—oceans of blood—corpses rising, eating, gorging, and dripping blood from their chins. The currents whirled him and twirled him and whisked him along. They channeled him into Halo...

(he saw her mom, crushed and dying and trapped in her car; saw her patient, his chest crushed but expanding, *healing* beneath her hands; and saw Brimstone smiling, Brimstone gone)

... then he passed through her and into the boy—silence. Darkness. But not for long.

In the distance, a web of neural lightning flashed, synapses and dendrites forked with luminescence. Black widows scuttled across the web, hourglasses glowing red on their bellies. They spun more webs in the ether, and in their creations little movies flickered to life, composed from a mosaic of stars and galaxies so the screens jumped and jerked, so they darkled and lightened, septillions of screens twinkling into infinity.

In one film, the boy...

(*Gregory*, the voices whispered)

... walked into the living room of the Gothic Revival, where his father was watching zombies on TV. His dad was the same man that had set fire to the house, the man that had shot himself right in front of Blue, only here he didn't have as many wrinkles around his mouth and eyes, not as much grime packed into his pores. He yelled at Gregory to go to his room.

With a fizzle, the psychic movie sped through a montage of Gregory's mother getting her throat torn out by a corpse the boy had accidentally conjured; and then, after a blip, Gregory lay awake in his room, in the dark. His father entered, just a silhouette. He came to Gregory's side—and shot the boy in the head.

The movie skipped to a new scene: the father was crying, yelling, hugging the boy, shaking him, telling him to wake up; then he was dumping his son's body in front of a hospital, drinking, sobbing, and speeding away as galaxies spiraled shut and the stars of his motion picture faded to black.

Not far beyond, another screen flared to life. Here, one version of Gregory lay in the hospital bed while a nurse monitored his vitals; the other version of the boy, the ghostly version, sat Indian-style on the floor, materializing action figures with his mind. Blue was one of those figures. The others were zombies, mutants, and arachnid wasps, things with tentacles and too many eyes. One of them, which had dripped out of the boy's head, out of his *subconscious*—like a poison—was an indistinguishable tangle of arms and legs and shouting heads and fingernails and penises and mouths, like a hundred toys melted together into a charred mass, slobbering, pissing, shitting, and bleeding.

The toys symbolized the boy's creations—*he* had generated all the monsters, had pulled all the ideas and anatomies from the collective consciousness and from the horror movies his dad watched. Like God he had created Blue in his own image; he had spit him out into an alleyway with no memory and no identity and no guidance, yet with free will and a spark of the divine.

On the floor, the boy watched as the Blue figurine and the plastic beasties stood up by themselves and engaged in battle, as the black monster slithered toward them, turning the floor to entrails.

The voices began to pant—all of them, the sounds overlapping, tripling, intensifying. The walls of the hospital room began to respire. The floor turned to gristle and bone.

The beast would be upon them soon.

Blue, Halo said, her voice echoing, full of static and shorting out. He looked across the hospital room. She stood over Gregory, hand on his head, her eyes shut in concentration. Yet she had a second head, this one a sketchy holograph overlaying the other, darker and saturated, twitching and blurring and looking straight at him.

Blue... I—I can't—

She paled and collapsed to the floor. Like a million light bulbs burning out, the vision died, leaving the room dim. Some magic, some amount of life and soul escaped through Blue's pores, and he stooped, feeling like a bag of meat and bones and nothing else.

He was panting.

The building rumbled and instruments rattled and shook. The boy's pulse sensor, clipped to his finger, rapped against the rail of his bed. The heart monitor registered earthquakes in peaks and depths.

Blue knelt at Halo's side. The bite on her cheek had begun to pus. The vessels around it had gone red with infection. Her eyes were sunken, her lips chapped. But she was still breathing, panting like everything else.

"Blue," she said, and he could hear her, despite the beast's greedy respiration and the tremors in the earth. "He made you. He... he made *it*."

"I know," Blue said. He had seen the action figures. He had looked closely and had seen no figures of Brimstone, Halo, or the Crow. Which meant they were real, the world held more than one miracle, more than this boy's ability to create. There were real mortal gods.

Halo coughed. "He's made more," she said. "He's made more people like you... and like him. *Creators.* This isn't—" she coughed again and it spattered her lips with blood.

"Jesus," Blue said.

She wiped it off and ignored it. "It's not only happening here. It's... *everywhere.*" This time when she coughed, the blood could not be ignored. It came out, bright and gleaming, all over her chin and chest.

"Shit," Blue said, glancing at the door. "You have to get up. We need a death pulse. We..."

Halo stared at the ceiling. Her belly had sunken, along with her cheeks. And the sun in her hair had gone out.

"Halo?"

She said nothing.

"Halo!" He shook her, smacked her, vaguely aware that he was crying.

Out in the throat, the beast roared. Creased flesh grew over the room, covered in what looked like tiny worms, and the sprinklers on the ceiling morphed into organic valves. The room had become a stomach. Except certain parts had remained. Like the lights. And the medical equipment. And the window.

The stomach valves opened, spraying acid. It burned Blue's skin, ate holes in his clothes, but the boy: some kind of mucus slicked him, protected him, made him one with the belly.

The beast began to tear at the esophageal sphincter, the pucker that was now the door.

Blue cradled Halo's body and shut his eyes. He rocked and chanted, lips to her ear, "I need you, I need you, I need you."

The lights went out.

And the beast's claws tore through.

SIXTEEN

Some life remained in Halo's cells, some rudimentary energy that lingered even after the spark had faded from her eyes. Blue held her close and focused on it, drew from it, amplified it, ignoring the beast as it shredded the sphincter, ignoring the acids and his rapidly dissolving skin, the big droops and sores.

"Halo," he said, envisioning her, glowing and vibrant. He remembered her crouched in the alleyway healing the blonde like an angel, remembered her holding his hand as he tried to leave the van, sharing her life force, giving him hope with the blue heavens in her eyes. He imagined her warmth, the smell of smoke and herbs in her hair, the vague taste of mint and cigarettes on her lips and tongue. She was almost real, trembling there on the verge of existence.

The beast tore through the last bands of muscle, its heads gnashing and grinding and screaming. Three of them were canine— all hairless, corded, and black—and some were insectile with mandibles and compound eyes. The black widow legs growing on its left side scrabbled at the doorframe beneath the flesh, exoskeleton clinking against metal. The tentacles whipped and wriggled, and the two giant human heads at the behemoth's center stretched out on elongated necks: one head with long hair, a heart-shaped face and plump lips; the other with short hair and whiskers—it was Gregory's mother and father. They bickered, nonsense shouts and spittle, but their focus was on Blue.

A limb shot out. Its talons raked through Blue's side. He flew against the wall, and Halo's body splashed facedown in the acid. Blood and excrement washed into the bile; Blue's side, laid open, spilled loops of intestine, chunks of kidney, and spaghetti-like nerves torn loose from the spine. He tried to hold it all in. It stank of raw meat, minerals, and feces, a horrible, humid stench. He should have been dead or unconscious or too deep in shock to think, but traces of Halo's essence coursed through him; it granted him a few last moments of clarity.

Baring the spider fangs beneath its human necks and the red hourglass on its underbelly, the beast came for him. It reared back—and the window shattered. A bird, phasing into a man, burst into the room. The Crow was only human for a second before he hunkered down on all fours, sprouted fur, a snout, and deadly jaws. The Crow, now wolf, snapped down on the throat of the beast's female head. Blood as red as magma spurted out around his teeth.

Blue tried to stand up, cradling his guts—they were turning creamy in the acid—but his body didn't respond. He slumped. His eyes fell on Halo, flesh pulp floating around her. Light shuddered at the edge of his vision, and then he was overcome by the dark.

Blue found himself in a long tunnel with light at the end. He floated, disembodied, and he fluttered to the light like a moth. The luminescence shined so pure and dazzling it sang, a chorus of angels praising a magnificent dawn. Trumpets and harps joined in, the voices climaxed beyond soprano, and Blue became a sustaining note of bliss.

Halo materialized in the light, draped in robes of particles and waves. "Blue," she said, and she opened her arms to embrace him. He entered her light, absorbed it…

… and awoke in the Crow's teepee.

The Indian sat before him, holding out the deer-antler knife. "A very long time ago," he said, "my people asked the Creator to help them defeat a great enemy. The Creator said he would, on one condition: my people had to prove themselves…"

Into the birds of firelight and shadow, the Crow stood. He held out his hand. "Are you ready to prove yourself? Are you ready to discover who you are?"

Blue blinked, looked down at himself, found that he was really in the hospital, eviscerated and blinking back acid. Halo's glow radiated from his heart, a golden aura casting beams and rays about the room. The beast squinted and clawed at the wolf, who still tore at the monster's throat. The beast's female head hung lifeless, its tongue lolling, its eyes glazed. Its blood discolored the bile.

Threaded with light, Blue's insides began to suck back into their cavity. Membranes mended and sealed organs in their place. Muscle knitted together and skin healed over it all, healing even where the acids had burned through, leaving neither scab nor scar. And the river of voices flooded the banks of his mind. He found he could divert and isolate flows as easily as operating faucets.

He looked up at the Crow, and his mind split between two realities: in the teepee, he took the Indian's hand and followed him outside, where the sun rose behind the mountains; in the hospital, Halo's light lifted him to Gregory's bed.

Wind stirred hair across the Crow's face as he and Blue stepped to the edge of a cliff. At the bottom, an archer waited in the water.

The Crow handed his knife to Blue. "Go," the Indian said, "conquer your beast," and then he flapped away into the dawn.

Blue looked down at the boy asleep on the bed. Gregory: Blue's past, his present, his creator. He pressed his hand to the boy's temple just as Halo had done, teleported again to that black expanse of neural webbing and movie screens composed of solar systems and shooting stars, now displaying city streets clogged with zombies, now showing basements and alleys crawling with tentacles like snakes. A sun dawned in space, and the black widows scurried for darker havens. The sun found them.

Roaring, the beast stabbed the wolf with its scorpion tail and flung him against the wall. The canine morphed back into the Crow, and he lay writhing as the neurotoxin shorted out his nerves and made his muscles flex.

The abomination stormed into the room and reached for Blue.

And Blue focused on every walking corpse and monster, everything he and the boy had created, himself included, hoping he caught everything, hoping he didn't leave any creators out there to wreak havoc; he focused on the beating inside their chests, merged them into one pulse, one organ, exposed and lying on the bed in front of him—and he swung the knife, he jumped off the Crow's cliff. The archer's arrow pierced his chest just as the blade plunged into Gregory's heart.

"*Iilak bacheek*," the Crow spoke inside his head. "*There* is a man."

Blue's light brightened and brightened, and brightened still, burning the stomach lining away from the walls, ceiling, and floor, the flesh bubbling and crisping and snowing embers. Out on the streets, the divine sunrise set fire to the zombies; they burst into fireballs and then into ash. The beast, growling, took a few more steps. Its skin crisped and peeled away, revealing its skeleton, its bones smoldering red before it disintegrated in the light. Blue exploded too, and his white brilliance blasted around the world, so blinding that all the survivors—hiding from the undead in closets and sewers, in vaults and bathroom stalls—shielded their eyes, so intense that from space the earth became a fleeting star; and on the final note before Blue's consciousness flared into the universe, he remembered kissing Halo, her lips soft and warm, and that one memory cleared the fog from his head, pushed and compacted it so that the hospital room filled with bouncing balls, no teeth marks, just new rubber, bouncing, bouncing, perfectly round and perfectly blue.

About the Authors

DAVID DUNWOODY writes from the seat of unholy terror, Utah. His work has appeared in volumes 1-3 of *The Undead*, from Permuted Press; *Fried! Fast Food, Slow Deaths*, from Graveside Tales Press; and *Read by Dawn II* from Bloody Books. His zombie novel *Empire* will be published by Permuted Press in 2008. The online version can be read at EmpireNovel.com.

RYAN C. THOMAS works as an editor in San Diego, California. You can usually find him in the bars on the weekends playing with his band, The Buzzbombs. When he is not writing or rocking out, he is at home with his cat, Elvis, watching really bad B-movies. Visit him online at www.ryancthomas.com.

D.L. SNELL is an Affiliate member of the Horror Writers Association, a graduate of Pacific University's Creative Writing program, and a freelance editor for Permuted Press. Snell's first novel, *Roses of Blood on Barbwire Vines*, pits zombies against vampires. David Moody, author of the *Autumn* series, calls it "violent and visceral...beautiful and erotic," and Bram Stoker Award-winning author Jonathan Maberry says, "[I]t has all the ingredients needed to satisfy even the most jaded fan of horror fiction." For more information, visit www.exit66.net.

JOHN SUNSERI is a horror author from Portland, Oregon who specializes in traditional horror fiction and Lovecraftian horror. John spent two years at Yale University studying a major in English and now manages a restaurant. Writing since 2001, John has published over 50 short stories. In 2007 his first novel, *The Spiraling Worm*, co-written with Australian author David Conyers, was released by Chaosium.

Day by Day Armageddon

by J. L. Bourne

An ongoing journal depicting one man's personal struggle for survival, dealing with the trials of an undead world unfolding around him. An unknown plague sweeps the planet. The dead rise to claim the Earth as the new dominant species. Trapped in the midst of a global tragedy, he must make decisions... choices that that ultimately mean life, or the eternal curse to walk as one of them.

ISBN: 978-0-9789707-7-2

EVERY SIGH, THE END.
(A novel about zombies.)
by Jason S. Hornsby

It's the end of the world: 1999.

Professional nobody Ross Orringer sees flashes of cameras and glances from strangers lurking around every corner.

His paranoia mounts when his friends and family begin acting more and more suspiciously as the New Year approaches.

In the last minutes before the clock strikes midnight, Ross realizes that the end may be more ominous than anyone could have imagined: decisions have been made, the crews have set up their lights and equipment, and the gray makeup has been applied.

In the next millennium, time will lose all meaning, and the dead will walk the earth.

ISBN: 978-0-9789707-8-9

Permuted Press
The formula has been changed...
Shifted... Altered... *Twisted.*™
www.permutedpress.com

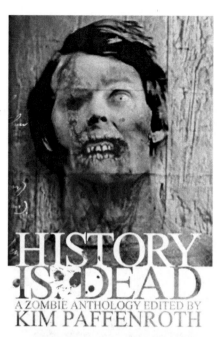

JOHN DIES AT THE END

by David Wong

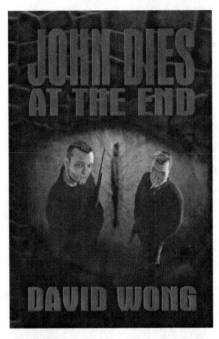

It's a drug that promises an out-of-body experience with each hit. On the street they call it Soy Sauce, and users drift across time and dimensions. But some who come back are no longer human. Suddenly a silent otherworldly invasion is underway, and mankind needs a hero.

What it gets instead is John and David, a pair of college dropouts who can barely hold down jobs. Can these two stop the oncoming horror in time to save humanity?

No. No, they can't.

ISBN: 978-0-9789707-6-5

THE OBLIVION SOCIETY

by Marcus Alexander Hart

Life sucks for Vivian Gray. She hates her dead-end job. She has no friends.

Oh, and a nuclear war has just reduced the world to a smoldering radioactive wasteland.

Armed with nothing but pop-culture memories and a lukewarm will to live, Vivian joins a group of rapidly mutating survivors and takes to the interstate for a madcap cross-country road trip toward a distant sanctuary that may not, in the strictest sense of the word, exist.

ISBN 978-0-9765559-5-7

THE UNDEAD
ZOMBIE ANTHOLOGY

ISBN: 978-0-9765559-4-0

"Dark, disturbing and hilarious."
—Dave Dreher, *Creature-Corner.com*

THE UNDEAD
VOLUME 2
SKIN AND BONES

ISBN: 978-0-9789707-4-1

"Permuted did us all a favor with the first volume of *The Undead*. Now they're back with *The Undead: Skin and Bones*, and gore hounds everywhere can belly up to the corpse canoe for a second helping. Great stories, great illustrations... *Skin and Bones* is fantastic!"
—Joe McKinney, author of *Dead City*

The Undead / volume three
FLESH FEAST

ISBN: 978-0-9789707-5-8

"Fantastic stories! The zombies are fresh... well, er, they're actually moldy, festering wrecks... but these stories are great takes on the zombie genre. You're gonna like *The Undead: Flesh Feast*... just make sure you have a toothpick handy."
—Joe McKinney, author of *Dead City*

Printed in the United States
129816LV00002B/1-99/P